AKIN TO MURDER

Ray Harrison

Constable London

First published in Great Britain 1992
by Constable & Company Ltd
3 The Lanchesters, 162 Fulham Palace Road
London W6 9ER
Copyright © 1992 by Ray Harrison
ISBN 0 09 471130 5
The right of Ray Harrison to be
identified as the author of this work
has been asserted by him in accordance
with the Copyright, Designs and Patents Act 1988
Set in Linotron Palatino
and printed in Great Britain by
Redwood Press, Melksham, Wiltshire

A CIP catalogue record for this book
is available from the British Library

To Tim and Jean Marsh

1

'I suppose before long you will be spending half your time playing cricket,' Bragg said grumpily.

Morton smiled. 'We have been playing for weeks,' he said. 'After the dry spring the pitches are in perfect condition.'

They were strolling down Gracechurch Street, in the warm June sunshine, having lunched in a pub overlooking the river Thames. The fine weather was making Bragg restless. It was well and good, being a sergeant of the City of London police, in mist and gloom. There were always throngs of people around you, rushing about their business; you were a part of the greatest commercial centre the world had ever known. And an important part, make no mistake. Yet he had only to feel the sun on his back and he was itching to be in the Dorset countryside of his boyhood; to be driving a pair of shire horses along a leafy lane again, a load of planks or sacks of coal on the lorry behind.

'Well, at least we shall not have the Australians over this year,' he said gruffly. 'Last summer, you were either playing for England, or else you were buggering about in the records section, because you could not be relied on to finish a proper job!'

'You sound a little jaundiced today, sir,' Morton said with a grin.

'Jaundiced? I should bloody think I am! We haven't had a sniff of a half-decent case for weeks . . . You know what will happen, don't you?'

'What?'

'That sod Cotton will be off to the Commissioner; complaining that his men are overworked, while we waste our time on trivialities.'

'I scarcely think that Inspector Cotton would advance his cause much, in that way,' Morton said lightly. 'After all, these trivia have been largely imposed on us by Sir William himself. He can hardly use us as his personal detective unit at one moment and abandon us to the mercies of Inspector Cotton the next. It is your acuity and flair that give the Commissioner the sense of being a real policeman, instead of a mere figurehead.'

'Well, I wish he would give us something to get our teeth into,' Bragg grumbled.

They waited for a gap in the endless stream of hansom cabs, brewers' drays, omnibuses, then crossed over and turned into Lombard Street.

'I was wondering,' Morton said casually, 'if, with effect from tomorrow, you would agree to the same arrangement that we had last year.'

'What is that?'

'If you remember, I was allowed to cut short my Saturday morning duty to get to the Blackheath Cricket Club's matches . . . I would, of course, make up the time lost by writing up reports, and so on, in the evenings.'

Bragg scowled. 'Why don't we put posters all over the Square Mile,' he suggested, 'asking the cracksmen and assorted villains to please stay at home on a Saturday, because you want to go buggering up and down a cricket pitch in fancy dress?'

Morton laughed. 'I can understand that it is a little frustrating for you, sir. But you know that Sir William is keen that I should keep up my cricket. He has repeatedly said that since I have been playing for England we have had a better class of recruit to the force.'

'Huh! Only in his head, we have . . . Anyway, if there are to be no international matches, I would not have thought it would matter this year.'

Morton smiled. 'In some ways it is even more important. At the end of the season they will be picking the team to tour Australia in the winter. I would very much like to be selected.'

'God Almighty! How long a job would that be?'

'The first match begins, in Sydney, on the fourth of December. The last is due to end on March the sixth.'

'So, you will be leaving England in the middle of November?'

'I presume so.'

'And, it will be the summer of eighteen ninety-five, before you get back!'

'Yes.'

Bragg sighed irritably. 'I cannot fathom you, lad,' he said. 'You pretend your Cambridge degree and your upper-crust background don't matter. You say that you are as committed to police work as anybody else. Yet, if you get the chance to knock a little red ball out of a cricket ground, you'll sail to the other end of the bloody world, and to hell with the job!'

Morton chuckled.

'It is no laughing matter, lad. If you are only going to work six months in a year, you ought to pack it in and make way for somebody with ambition; somebody who is not just playing at policemen . . .'

Bragg checked. There was a disturbance ahead. A knot of people was gathering, a frantic voice shouting: 'Police! Police!'

Morton sprinted towards them, with Bragg trundling behind. The crowd had formed outside the office of an estate agent, and was growing by the second. Bragg pushed his way to the centre, where Morton had cleared a space around a white-faced young man.

'What's all the fuss about?' he shouted.

'It's Mr Witney . . . He's dead!'

Bragg glanced up at the signboard above the window.

London   WITNEYS   Winchester

'Right, lad. Disperse this crowd, then come inside.'

Bragg seized the young man's arm and pushed him into the building. Inside, a woman in her mid-twenties was slumped over a typewriting machine, crying hysterically. There was another desk, covered with a litter of papers. On the walls were framed photographs of grand town houses and country mansions. If they were anything to go by, this was a well-connected and prosperous business.

'Where is the body?' Bragg demanded.

'Through there.' The man gestured to a door in the back wall of the office.

Bragg opened it, and checked on the threshold aghast.

'Christ! He's dead all right!'

The body of a middle-aged man lay prone on the floor, in front of the desk. His head was twisted unnaturally to one side, and there was blood everywhere. A pool was standing on the surface of the cream oriental carpet; blotches were on the chair legs and the skirting board. Bragg crouched down in the doorway and peered around. There was a thin smear of blood on the polished parquet in front of him: an irregular oval, with a clear patch in the middle.

Morton came and stood behind him. 'Good God!' he exclaimed. 'I have never seen anything like this!'

'Right, lad.' Bragg got to his feet. 'I want you to go and get Professor Burney, the pathologist. I reckon this is one he should see before we touch it . . . Oh, and go to the coroner's chambers on the way back. Tell Sir Rufus Stone I want this case.'

'Yes, sir.' Morton strode to the door and was gone.

Bragg turned to the outer office. The young man was sitting at a desk, gazing woodenly at the window. Bragg crossed and took the chair opposite him.

'And who might you be?' he asked.

The man shifted his gaze to Bragg. 'John Syme,' he said dully. 'I am the chief clerk.'

'Then, if you are the chief, where are the Indians?'

'What? Oh . . . I am the only clerk, if that is what you mean.'

'I see. And who is the chief typewriter?'

Syme's eyes flickered over to the sobbing young woman. 'That is Cissie Fox. We are the only assistants here.'

'And the man in the back office?'

Syme swallowed. 'Mr Jethro Witney,' he said unsteadily. 'He is our principal.'

'Who found him?'

'I did.'

'When?'

'Just now. I came back after lunch, started to go in to Mr Witney with the letters for signature . . . and there he was.'

'Did you touch the body?'

'No! I did not go any further than the door.'

'And Miss Fox?'

'She was working her machine when I came back. She made a remark, then went on with her work.'

'What did she say?'

'She asked if I had had a nice lunch.'

'I see . . . Where did you eat?'

'Where I normally do. The Grapes, in Clements Lane.'

'Where did your boss live?'

'In Winchester – Brook Street.'

'Winchester? Why, that is seventy miles away! Did he stay in London, during the week?'

'No. He travelled up every day. He would arrive at half past ten in the morning, and leave soon after five.'

'That is a funny sort of working day . . . What number in Brook Street?'

'Seventeen. I gather it overlooks the cathedral.'

'Have you never been down there?'

'No.'

'I see. Well, I suppose we shall have to get the local police to tell his wife.'

'He has not got a wife. I think she died years ago.'

'Any children?'

'Just the one daughter – Julia.'

'Hmn . . .' Bragg pondered. 'How long have you worked here?' he asked.

'I came straight from school. The business was owned by Shilling-fords then.'

'When did it become Witneys?'

'Seven years ago. They already had an office in Winchester . . . It is an old-established firm.'

'So, they were opening a branch in the big city, eh?'

'Not a branch.'

Bragg looked up sharply. There had been a fractional change of tone, a hint of bitterness. 'What, then?' he asked.

'They were run as separate businesses.'

'Oh? How do you know that?'

'I am entitled to a commission on the profits of this office, so it has to be treated separately.'

'But that would not prevent the branches being treated as one business, would it?'

Syme looked down at his clenched hands. 'I suppose not,' he mumbled.

'What rate of commission did you get?' Bragg asked.

'Two per cent of the net trading profits.'

'That sounds very generous.'

Syme's lip curled. 'He wanted to keep me, didn't he? I reckon at that moment, when old Mr Shillingford died, I could have walked away with half the business.'

'I see . . . You were not over-fond of Mr Witney, then?'

'He was all right, as a man.' It was a flat statement, with no hint of trying to retrieve a false step.

'And yet somebody has thought fit to murder him.'

'Yes.'

'In a particularly gruesome way.'

Syme flinched, and did not reply.

'You have some business books here, I take it,' Bragg said.

The man eased back his chair, opened the centre drawer of his desk and pulled out two ledgers.

'This is the cash book,' he said, 'and this the inventory book.'

'What is an inventory book?'

Syme opened the second ledger. 'In the front we put details of all the properties we handle – the address, the owner's name, type of property, asking price or rental, rate of commission . . . In this section at the back, we enter the commission due to us.'

Bragg turned the ledger round and flipped through the pages. 'I see . . . So, when the commission on a sale is received from the solicitor, you close the entry in this book. I take it that a corresponding entry is made in the cash book.'

Syme nodded absently.

'And, where you are just collecting rents for a client, the figure comes from a copy of the statement you supply him at the end of the year.'

'That is right.'

'Good.' Bragg stood up. 'While we are waiting for the pathologist, I will go and sit with our late-lamented, and browse through these books.'

He went into the rear office, closed the door behind him and, tiptoeing round the body, sat at Witney's desk. He scrutinized the top for anything untoward, any clue as to why he had been murdered. There was an appointments book by the inkstand, but it showed no entries for that day. A surveyor's report lay on the blotter, the pages open at the middle. Did that mean an unexpected visitor? Or was his death somehow connected with the report? Bragg sat down and began to read it, weighing every mention of dry rot,

damp walls, decayed brickwork as a motivation for murder . . . No.
It would not serve. After all, Witney had been merely an agent,
his representations covered by a plethora of disclaimers. Even if
this report reflected badly on Witney – perhaps detailing mis-
descriptions – the deal had not been closed. No one had been hurt
or defrauded . . . Disappointed, perhaps, but that was hardly a
reason for murder. The door opened and Dr Burney, the pathologist, came in. He glanced at the corpse, his round cherubic face
beaming.

'Ah, sergeant. I see that you have something special for me! I
thought as much. It is not often that I am summoned to the scene
of the crime – not often enough, if I may say so. What is the
background to this one?'

Bragg stood up. 'That is the owner of the business, sir. He was
found by Syme, his clerk, when he got back from lunch. We were
passing the door when he yelled out – and that was ten past two.
The inference is that Witney was alive when Syme went to lunch,
an hour earlier.'

'And the young lady?'

Bragg suppressed a flash of irritation. No wonder Burney was not
summoned to a murder scene as a routine measure. He was as bad
as the coroner – amateurs, both of them. Full of bright ideas, but
without the discipline to build a coherent case.

'She will keep,' he said shortly. 'You can see what a state she is
in.'

'Indeed.' Burney put his bag on the desk and bent over the corpse.
'Hmn . . . Very nasty. Very nasty indeed . . . Throat cut with a very
sharp instrument, clearly. The body is still warm . . . Died a little
over an hour ago, I should say. I will take the rectal temperature
when I get the body back to the mortuary.'

He straightened up and looked around the room. 'Interesting,' he
murmured. 'There is very little blood.'

'Very little?' Bragg exclaimed incredulously. 'It is all over the
place!'

Burney gave his slack grin. 'If you look carefully, sergeant, you
will see that we are presented with a situation where that colloqui-
alism is manifestly not applicable.'

'How do you mean, sir?'

'Look at the ceiling . . . there is no blood there. Look at the walls.

13

With the exception of that area on the skirting, near the body, there is no blood on the walls either.'

'What does that signify?'

'Well, if you were standing at the spot where the subject's feet are, and I sprang upon you and cut your throat, I would expect blood to spray out over the walls, the floor, possibly even the ceiling.'

Burney knelt down by the corpse and gently moved the head. Bragg had to look away, to fight off sudden nausea. The throat had been cut to the very backbone.

'But there is enough blood on the floor,' he said gruffly. 'Surely you are not suggesting that he was brought here already dead, and the throat-cutting was a blind?'

There came a thump of boots in the outer office and the door was flung open. The coroner stood in the doorway, his leonine head thrown back theatrically.

'Ah, Burney! You have anticipated me.' Sir Rufus marched into the room, Morton following discreetly. 'What have we, Burney? A stabbing?'

'No, Sir Rufus, a throat-cutting. I was just debating the possibilities with Sergeant Bragg.'

'Possibilities?' the coroner exclaimed. 'I would have thought that we are confronted with a palpable certainty! He did not receive that cut while shaving!'

'No. But you are in the right area – a razor was almost certainly used.'

Sir Rufus swung round truculently. 'Has it been found, Bragg?'

'I have not yet had time to make a thorough search, sir,' he said.

'Then I suggest that you do . . . I take it, Burney, that there is no doubt as to the cause of death?'

Burney looked up absently. 'No. The subject certainly bled to death . . . But I am intrigued by the pattern of the bloodstains.'

'Come, Burney,' the coroner said roughly. 'Surely forensic science has not yet advanced to the stage where homicides are categorized by patterns, like wallpaper?'

Burney was unruffled. 'The distribution of the blood can be illuminating, Sir Rufus. As I was remarking to the sergeant, there are no stains on the upper walls. The majority of the blood is on the carpet; indeed, it is saturated under the head and upper body. Now,

14

had the subject been facing his attacker, I would have expected a very different pattern. After all, both the left and right carotid arteries have been cut. The blood would spurt out.'

'Are you saying that the attacker would be covered in blood?' the coroner demanded.

'Not in this case, I think.'

Burney ran his fingers caressingly over the head of the corpse, ruffling the hair, then moved to the nape of the neck. 'Ah, yes,' he murmured.

'Yes what, man?'

Burney got to his feet. 'I shall be able to give a considered opinion, when I have performed the post-mortem examination,' he said. 'If it is any help to Sergeant Bragg, my preliminary assessment is that the subject was first struck from behind with a blunt instrument, which rendered him unconscious. He was certainly lying on his face when he was murdered. If I am right, his assailant lifted the head, placed the razor under the throat and cut upwards.'

'That would account for the bulk of the blood being under the body, eh?' Sir Rufus mused.

'Indeed!'

Bragg intervened. 'Would the murderer have bloodstains on him, sir?'

Burney thought for a moment. 'He would be very fortunate to escape it completely. But let us consider. This is clearly a pre-meditated killing, the murderer has stunned his victim, and thus has some time in which to carry out his dire purpose. Time enough to take off his coat and roll up his shirt-sleeves . . . I would think it highly likely that he carried no visible bloodstains when he left, particularly if he put on gloves.'

'So it could be anyone?'

Burney smiled. 'That is within your province, sergeant, not mine. Now, if you will arrange to have the cadaver conveyed to the mortuary, I will carry out a full autopsy.'

'When will you have finished, sir?'

'I could certainly give you a firm opinion by the end of the afternoon, if I can have the subject within the next hour.'

'Very good, sir.'

Burney picked up his bag and went out. After a moment's hesitation, Sir Rufus strode after him.

15

'Thank God for that!' Bragg muttered. 'The two of them together is a bit much.'

He went into the front office, where Syme was staring into space. The girl's desk was empty, her paraphernalia tidied away.

'Where is Miss Fox?' he demanded angrily.

'I sent her home,' Syme said dully.

Bragg seemed about to explode, then changed his mind. 'Very wise,' he said quietly. 'If you will give me the office keys, you can go too. Write Miss Fox's home address down for me, will you? And yours as well.'

'I don't know that I should . . .' Syme began.

Bragg stepped across, seized him by the collar of his jacket and lifted him from his chair like a puppet. 'You will do as I bloody tell you!' he snarled, then dropped him. 'The addresses, then bugger off!'

Syme swallowed, his eyes staring. Then he picked up a pencil, scribbled briefly on a sheet of paper, threw a bunch of keys on his blotter and slunk out into the street.

'That is better!' Bragg smiled expansively. 'Now we have the place to ourselves . . . Better lock the door.'

'I alerted the ambulance when I went for Dr Burney,' Morton said. 'I told them to be here at half past three.'

Bragg pulled out his battered gunmetal watch. 'In a quarter of an hour . . . Well, I suppose we have nothing more to learn about the corpse than the pathologist has already told us. All right, you go and have a chat with Miss Cicely Fox, see what she has to say about it. I will wait here for the ambulance, then take the records back to Old Jewry. Who knows, we might have a bit of luck!'

Morton stopped at the entrance to a street in Stepney. The small terraced houses were sooty and dejected, the pavements broken. Along the middle of the roadway was a rutted trench, filled with cinders and broken bricks. That was an indication of how little the authorities cared about this neighbourhood, he thought. They had been compelled by the government to lay sewers, years ago, but they had not bothered to reinstate the road surface. People living in areas like this did not matter. Nowadays, the councillors preferred to spend the ratepayers' money on grandiose town halls that would perpetuate their own names. Morton snorted in disgust and went in search of Cissie Fox's house.

At least number twenty-two showed signs of being inhabited by someone moderately house-proud. The pavement in front of it was swept clean, the paintwork of the windows and door had recently been washed, the brass door-furniture shone. Morton knocked and waited. After a few moments, he heard the turning of a key and the door was opened a crack. He presented his warrant-card at the gap.

'Police,' he said. 'Is this where Miss Cicely Fox lives?'

After a momentary hesitation, the door swung open. A sharp-featured woman in her early fifties stood there, her brow creased in a peevish frown.

'What do you want?' she asked. 'Why can't you leave her alone, after what she's gone through?'

A little girl appeared at the back of the hallway, only to be shooed away by the woman.

'I take it that you are Miss Fox's mother,' Morton said diplomatically.

'And what if I am? There's no call to go chasing innocent girls and upsetting them.'

'I assure you that I would not dream of upsetting your daughter, ma'am. But it is important that I see her immediately. She may have information that could be vital to us.'

Now there was a figure in the dim depths of the passage.

'Who is it, mother?' The voice was drained and lifeless.

'A policeman. He wants to talk to you about what went on. I don't think you should, in your state.'

'It doesn't matter. I will see him.' She disappeared.

The mother looked doubtful, then stood back and beckoned him inside.

Cissie Fox was sitting in a small prim parlour, cluttered with photographs and cheap knick-knacks. She motioned him to a sofa, while the mother took up station by the door, arms folded.

'Mr Syme quite understandably sent you home,' Morton began, 'before we had a chance to speak to you. It is obviously important that we get your account of what happened before it fades from your mind.'

The young woman looked up, her eyes puffy and red-rimmed. 'I don't know anything Mr Syme couldn't have told you,' she said slowly. 'I went out at one o'clock and came back at two. We thought Mr Witney was still out. He usually is, at that time . . . Then Mr Syme got up from his desk, to take in some letters I had done, and . . . and found him.'

'I see. Where did you have lunch?'

'In the Nicholas Lane gardens. I take sandwiches.'

'Did you meet anyone there?'

'No . . . Then I went shopping.'

'Right. Did you know your employer well?'

The eyes stared at him briefly. 'No,' she said.

'So you have no idea who might have killed him?'

'That's enough!' Mrs Fox advanced into the room glowering. 'I won't have you upsetting her with your questions. Can't you see she's worn out?'

'Very well.' Morton got to his feet. 'Just one more thing. When you got back to the office, after your lunch, had Mr Syme already returned?'

'Oh, yes. He was sitting at his desk, I am sure of that.'

'And, did he leave for lunch before you?'

'Yes . . . Yes, he did.'

Carrying a cardboard box of ledgers and files, Bragg went round the corner to Clements Lane. The Grapes was a modern public house, with mahogany doors and large, etched windows. Inside was a big horseshoe bar with two ranks of beer pumps. There were plump banquettes round the walls, and a scattering of small tables with stools. The room was virtually empty; a few solitary drinkers sat contemplating infinity. A waiter was going round the tables, collecting the debris of food and empty glasses. Bragg approached him.

'Police,' he said. 'I wonder if you can help me.'

The man lifted an eyebrow. 'I'll try,' he said guardedly.

'There has been a murder, round the corner. I am told that a man called John Syme usually has his lunch here. I want to know if he was in today.'

'Sorry mate,' the waiter said, with a trace of relief in his voice. 'I have only been working here for a fortnight. I don't know who is a regular and who isn't.'

'Syme is a smallish, rat-faced man with a little moustache, brown hair and greenish eyes.'

The man was shaking his head before Bragg had even finished. 'No. I cannot recall anybody like that. Sorry.'

'Is the owner in? He might know who I am talking about.'

'This is a managed house . . . Mr Brown is out, at the moment. But he has not been here all that long, either.'

'All right. Don't bother!'

Bragg stomped out of the pub in a dudgeon. Barmen were all the same; deaf and blind, the lot of them. One look at a warrant-card, and their memories went blank. But have a bit of a punch-up in the bar and it was: 'Why did the police take so long in getting here?' He waved down a passing hansom, and directed it to Old Jewry.

Twenty minutes later, he was sitting in his room at the police headquarters. He had sorted the papers into piles on his desk and was just pulling out his tobacco pouch when the door opened.

'Ah, Bragg.'

The Commissioner, Sir William Sumner CB, came diffidently into the room. He was a short, stiff man. Before his appointment he had been a lieutenant-colonel in command of an infantry regiment. It had become traditional to appoint a senior military man as head of the force. But after the Trafalgar Square riots, in eighteen eighty-seven, the practice had been heavily criticized; so he would probably be the last. Perhaps, Bragg thought, that knowledge increased his natural indecisiveness.

'I hear you have been appointed coroner's officer for the Witney case,' Sir William said.

'That is right, sir. I was at the scene moments after the body was discovered, and Sir Rufus decided to have a look himself.'

'Yes . . . yes. He was quite a distinguished man, Bragg.'

'Witney, you mean?'

'Yes . . . In City terms, that is. He was a member of the Carpenters' and the Plaisterers' Guilds. Had he lived, he might have become Lord Mayor, in time.'

'But my problem is to find out why he did not live.'

'Quite.'

'The trouble is, sir, that while he had a business in Lombard Street, he also had one in Winchester; and that was where he lived.'

'Yes. I knew him slightly, of course.'

'It could well be that the reason for his death lies at the Winchester end.'

'I suppose that is so.' Sir William sighed. 'Well, Bragg, all I can say is that you must do your duty, and pursue your enquiries wherever they lead. But I do hope you will keep expense to a minimum. The Court of Common Council is becoming very concerned over the cost of policing the City.'

'I will bear that in mind, sir,' Bragg said gravely.

'Yes . . . Well, I hope that you are successful. On the whole, he was a pleasant enough man. I would not like to think that his murderer would cheat the gallows.'

'Have no fear, sir. We will get him.'

'Yes . . . yes.' The Commissioner backed out of the room and closed the door behind him.

Bragg took a length of thick twist from his tobacco pouch, and began to cut thin slices with his juice-stained knife. This was going to be a tricky case, with another police force involved. Mind you, it generally happened that way. There had been precious few murders, in his time, where the victim not only worked in the City but lived there also. Nowadays, the clerks and such came pouring off the trains of a morning. Many of them lived as far as fifteen or twenty miles away. When they went back, in the evening, the City was empty . . . But normally it was the Metropolitan police you were dealing with. The City sat in the middle of the Met's area like a yolk in a fried egg. So, over the years, a code of practice had evolved. You knew where you were with them, what you might be able to get away with. The Winchester police would be different. In his experience they would be defensive, resentful of the wider experience of a London detective, even obstructive. It was strange that, in a murder case, the legal basis for an investigation lay with the coroner in whose area the body was found. The victim might have nothing to do with the locality, be there by pure chance, but the enquiries must be directed from that place. Yet Witney had only been working in London for seven years; lived as far away as Winchester. It was really more likely that the reason for the killing lay there . . . Even allowing for the fact that it was easier to make enemies in the course of trading than socially, Winchester was still the more likely.

Bragg absently rubbed the flakes of tobacco between his palms and teased them into his pipe. There was one thing on the credit side: the Commissioner was taking a personal interest in this one; and he had implicitly accepted that it would take time and money. So Inspector Cotton would not be able to put the screws on him . . . With his pipe drawing well, he set to work on the records from Witney's office. The financial books were straightforward, revealing little about the transactions they represented. On the whole it was a small business, but sound. The bulk of the income was represented by commissions received through acting as agent for the owners of commercial properties. In these cases, the remuneration was two or three per cent of the rental income – unexciting, but presumably safe, as long as you cultivated the right people. So far as sales of property were concerned, they seemed to be limited to small shops and the odd warehouse. The photographs of mansions and town houses, in the office, must be little more than a come-on. Unless, that is, they represented the link with Winchester. Bragg knew virtually nothing about that city. It was one of those places that had been important in bygone days; but progress had left it stranded in the past. He supposed that it must be a county town; for Hampshire, probably. Anyway, it was likely that there were some fine buildings down there . . . Fine buildings and impoverished people. That would make sound commercial sense of a link with London. City money buying substantial country property. It was happening all the time, though he had not realized that it had spread as far as Winchester.

He took down a railway timetable from the bookshelf. After all, Witney had travelled there and back every day. He thumbed through the pages. Hmn . . . So the terminus was Waterloo station. That was not easy to get to, from the City. It would be well enough in a couple of years, when they got the new Waterloo to City underground line running. But, at the moment, the best bet was a cab over London Bridge, then through Southwark. That could well take over half an hour; more if you were unlucky.

It was an odd sort of life that Jethro Witney had lived. Up and down like an automaton. Leave home at half past eightish; after seven when he got back, day in day out . . . Ah, he had forgotten to ask if Witney came in on a Saturday morning – a small point, but it might be relevant.

The door opened, and Morton entered. He hung up the shabby

bowler that he wore for work, and drew up a chair to Bragg's desk.

'Well, lad, how did you get on?'

Morton gave a wry smile. 'I found myself confronted by a dragon of a mother, who was bent on seeing me off. Then our tantalizing typewriter appeared on the scene, and all was well.'

'Stop buggering about, lad,' Bragg exclaimed irritably. 'Tell it straight!'

'Sorry, sir. Miss Fox had regained her composure, and told me what little she knew. It seems that she went out for lunch at one o'clock, eating her sandwiches in the Nicholas Lane gardens. She got back to the office at two o'clock.'

'And Syme?'

'He went for his lunch before Miss Fox, and had already returned when she got back.'

'I see.'

'There is a small point, sir, which may have no significance. Syme did not take the letters into Witney's office until Miss Fox had returned.'

'So?'

'She said that Witney was normally out at that time – no doubt cultivating clients over a convivial City luncheon!'

'Get on with it!'

'Had I been Syme, I imagine I would have taken the letters into Witney's empty office before settling down to my afternoon's work.'

'You think he wanted a witness to the discovery – that he might have killed Witney himself?'

'It must be a possibility.'

'Well, I certainly was not able to confirm Syme's story that he had taken his lunch in The Grapes. You know what these pub people are like. They recognize you when you are holding out a tip and are blind the rest of the time.'

'They have little inclination to love the police, certainly.'

'And what about Witney? Did she see him go out at all?'

'I did not establish that, one way or the other. Just as I got round to the subject of her employer the dragon-mother called a halt. I did not press the matter; it will wait.'

'Hmn . . . What will happen to the business now, do you reckon?'

'In theory it should come to a standstill. As a matter of strict law, the death of the master discharges all servants. However, that is unlikely to be implemented. The value of such an enterprise would lie in continuity of operation.'

'It sounds as if the daughter will inherit. I cannot see her running it, can you?'

'I would think her interest would be best served by a quick sale, as a going concern.'

'To someone like Syme, perhaps?' Bragg said slowly.

'He certainly knows the business.'

'Yes . . . In fact, the backbone of it consists in looking after the properties of two trust estates; rented commercial property mainly. If they went elsewhere, there would no longer be a business.'

'Which perhaps explains why Witney came here every day.'

'To suck up to the trustees, you mean? Maybe, but I think there was more to it than that. According to Sir William, he was deep into City politics, a member of two livery companies, ambitious to become Lord Mayor. I reckon this lot set him a rung or two above his cronies in Winchester.'

'It is, I suppose, regrettable but inevitable,' Morton said lightly, 'that our profession should incline us to think the worst of everyone.'

'What? . . . Shut up, lad. I'm thinking . . . Our friendly reporter Catherine Marsden's family came from Winchester, didn't they?'

'Yes, indeed. Her mother was born there, and lived there for a time after her marriage.'

'Good! This case is going to be a bit tricky in all sorts of ways. A bit of local knowledge could come in handy. Why don't you have a chat with Miss Marsden? See what you can find out about the place. You never know, you might pick up something about the Witneys.'

Morton smiled. 'Nothing could give me greater pleasure, sir. In fact, I am to have the honour of escorting her to the opera tonight. I am sure that I could introduce the subject.'

'Right. And, by the way, there will be no cricket for you tomorrow, lad. We are off to Winchester, before the Commissioner gets worried about money being spent!' He got up from his desk. 'Let us go and see if our friend Burney has finished reducing Witney to cat's-meat, shall we?'

They set off up Basinghall Street, towards Golden Lane. The sun had disappeared behind a layer of thick, grey cloud. As they approached the mortuary it began to rain, and they were glad to dash inside the grim building. Burney's assistant, Noakes, was sluicing down one of the grey stone slabs that were ranged around the walls.

'Will you go in, gentlemen,' he said affably. 'Dr Burney is expecting you.'

They went through a doorway in the corner, and into a small whitewashed room. In the centre was a mortuary slab, on which lay the body of Jethro Witney.

'Ah, there you are!' Burney beamed at them. 'I have not yet begun the examination of the thorax. I am afraid that I was a little delayed, and I felt that you would prefer me to concentrate on the site of the injuries. After all, whatever the general state of the subject's health, there can be little debate about the proximate cause of death, eh?'

'No, sir,' Bragg said stolidly. 'Were you able to establish the time he was murdered?'

'Within the usual limits, yes. It is clear that death occurred between one o'clock and two o'clock this afternoon. I expect that adds but little to your store of knowledge.'

'It adds certainty to our presumption.'

'Very good, sergeant! Almost epigrammatic . . . Yes, well, my examination of the head has not been totally devoid of interest. I have been able to establish my own presumption – that the subject was struck down before the throat was cut. Perhaps Constable Morton would be interested.'

Morton reluctantly moved to the slab.

'Look at the back of the neck. You will see that the spinous process of the third cervical vertebra has been fractured, with attendant subcutaneous extravasation of blood. The area of bruising is approximately three inches long, and one inch wide. You grasp the implications, of course.'

Morton swallowed hard. 'It was a violent blow,' he said. 'Violent enough to produce insensibility – as you suggested this morning.'

'Indeed. A little higher, and death would have supervened immediately. Anything else?'

'Well, that, combined with a width of one inch, suggests that he was hit with a weighted stick, or a cosh.'

'Not exactly a cosh, because there appear to have been two protuberances, as indicated by this area here . . . But a blunt instrument, certainly.'

'Could it have been done by a practised killer, sir?' Bragg asked.

Burney pursed his flaccid lips. 'Practised? In the sense of being a habitual murderer?'

'Yes, sir.'

'That seems a rather extreme hypothesis . . . Effective, certainly; but perhaps merely lucky.'

'I am trying to get a picture in my mind of the kind of man we are looking for.'

'Well, I may be able to offer some pointers.' Burney picked up his probe. 'As you can see, what we might call the axis of the blow is not straight across the neck. Rather, it slants upwards quite markedly, along this line . . . That fact could suggest that the assailant himself was significantly shorter than his victim.'

'Or herself?'

'Ah, that is a question impossible of determination, sergeant. Certainly a female could have struck the blow. After all, it was not in itself fatal. A woman could easily have done it.'

'We did not find any object such as you describe at the scene.'

'I see. Well, speculation on my part is unwise and borders on the unprofessional. I shall merely report, at the inquest, that the subject died from loss of blood, caused by the severance of the carotid arteries.'

'You still think it was a premeditated murder?' Bragg asked.

'It would be most injudicious of me to pre-empt the coroner's findings. Nevertheless, the killer seems to have provided himself with the necessary implements in advance, and either created, or taken advantage of, his opportunity. Above all, the force used was excessive, on any count. There was hate in it, Bragg, hate in it.'

'Thank you so much, James, for taking me to *Don Giovanni*. Everyone has been praising the production sky-high, but I was not prepared for it to be so lavish!'

Catherine's face, in the light from the street lamps, was radiant.

'The costumes were certainly impressive,' he said.

'Yes! . . . and the singing! The Don was quite marvellous. *La ci darem la mano* just entranced me! I would have given way to his blandishments without another thought!'

'I hope not!'

25

'I could not have resisted . . . the music!'

Morton laughed. 'Perhaps the reason I have reservations about the opera is that there is no appealing female character!'

'Spoilsport!'

'To me, it is uncomfortably perched between comedy and tragedy,' he persisted.

'Come James! It could hardly be tragedy. The Don's end was justly deserved – all those hundreds of women deflowered and disgraced!'

They were in a growler, trotting at an easy pace along Piccadilly; a feeling of happy familiarity between them.

'We live in a strange society,' Morton said thoughtfully.

'Why is that?'

'Well, from any objective point of view, *Don Giovanni* is a public celebration of infidelity; the hero a debaucher of virtue, the dominant emotion carnality rather than love. Yet men take their wives and daughters to see it, they applaud wildly and throw flowers.'

'But opera is art, not life!'

'Exactly. And, once away from Covent Garden, they can go back to their conventional lives. Babies will be brought by storks, or found under gooseberry bushes; sex will become again the great unmentionable.'

Catherine laughed. 'It is fortunate for you that my boarding-school education opened my mind, as well as my eyes, or I might think you were making an improper suggestion.'

'I am sorry!' Morton said contritely. 'I was merely making a point. I did not remotely mean to offend you.'

Catherine smiled. 'You did not offend me. I know that you are totally honourable and considerate. Nevertheless, there are proprieties that neither of us should wish to disregard! Now, will you come in for a few moments?'

The cab drew up before the Marsdens' house in Park Lane. Catherine's father was a fashionable painter, able to command a thousand guineas for a portrait. As a result, he could maintain his family in some style. She took a key from her bag and opened the door. They went up to a comfortable sitting-room, overlooking Hyde Park. Mrs Marsden was seated reading a novel.

'Ah, there you are,' she said vaguely. 'Did you enjoy the opera?'

'It was utterly marvellous, Mamma!'

'Good evening, Mr Morton. Would you care for a drink or anything?'

'No thank you, ma'am. I only dropped in to thank you for the loan of your daughter. She brought magic to what otherwise would have been merely a pleasant evening.'

'James!' Catherine cried delightedly. 'I do believe that Mozart has dangerously infected you. If you are not careful, you will turn into a mere courtier!' She settled herself elegantly on one end of the sofa.

Morton smiled and sat beside her. 'I regret that I can stay only a moment,' he said. 'I have a full day ahead of me tomorrow.'

'Half full of work, and half of cricket?' Catherine asked teasingly.

'Alas, all work! Sergeant Bragg and I are bound for the wilds of the West Country; to the very edge of civilization, where savage tribes go about painted with woad.'

'Where on earth is that?'

'A place called Win . . . something . . . I have it! Winchester!'

'How dare you!' Catherine cried. 'Those selfsame early Britons include my own ancestors – as well you know!'

'I thought I must have heard of that barbarous locality some-where . . .'

Catherine rolled up a magazine and threatened him with it. 'Do you retract?' she cried.

'Yes! Indeed I do.'

'Very well . . . I shall think of an appropriate penalty later. In the meantime you shall tell us why you are going to that most delightful of cities.'

'Ah,' Morton's voice became serious. 'That is definitely not a matter for a summer's evening.'

'It is a crime, then, is it not?' Catherine demanded accusingly.

'Yes, it is.'

'Why did you not let me know? I could have got something about it into tomorrow's edition . . . There is no point in my being a reporter on the *City Press* if my own friends are going to keep newsworthy titbits to themselves!'

'I only wish it were a titbit,' Morton said gravely. 'In fact, it was a particularly gruesome murder in Lombard Street.'

'In that case,' Mrs Marsden said severely, 'it is hardly a subject proper for drawing-room conversation, Mr Morton.'

'I entirely agree, ma'am.'

27

'Oh, Mamma! Why have you always to be so unenthusiastic?' Catherine exclaimed. 'Just when I have a good story in my grasp!'

'I thought the whole reason for your unseemly outburst was that you had not!' her mother replied.

Catherine turned back to James. 'I do think it is unfair of you!' she cried. 'You are eager enough to enlist my help, yet you are never willing to reciprocate.'

'I am sorry,' Morton said contritely. 'My only justification is the sure knowledge that your editor would have allowed, at most, the merest mention of it.'

Catherine frowned. 'I know that Mr Tranter sees the paper as being largely concerned with financial and economic matters. But a murder within the City boundary is of the most immediate concern to us all. Was it in a public place?'

'No. A man called Witney was killed in his office, between one and two o'clock this afternoon. He was found by a member of his staff, returning after lunch.'

'Good heavens!' Mrs Marsden murmured. 'No one seems safe nowadays.'

'And how does this matter involve Winchester?' Catherine asked.

'The victim lived in Winchester and travelled up to London daily.'

'I see . . . So, it was not a random killing; and you think the reason behind it might lie in Winchester?'

'It is an aspect we are bound to explore.' Morton turned to Mrs Marsden. 'I wonder, ma'am, if you might have known the family.'

'Goodness! I suppose that I might have done so, though it is twenty years since we lived there.'

'His name is Jethro Witney. He was the principal of an estate-agency business with offices in both Winchester and the City.'

'Witney . . . Yes, I do vaguely recollect the name. Though there is no connection, in my mind, with estate agency. I am sure my sister Phoebe could help you. She married a local solicitor, so she has kept in touch with everyone there.'

'Then that shall be your penance,' Catherine interposed. 'Consultation with my relations shall be done through me, and me alone!'

Morton smiled. 'Tomorrow we shall merely be seeing the close relatives of the victim, and making contact with the local police. But after that, who knows? Perhaps Sergeant Bragg will be glad to take up your offer.'

2

Bragg banged irritably at the bell on the police-station counter. It was criminal for it to be unattended, he thought. What if there were an accident, a disturbance? What were the public supposed to do? He lifted the flap and went behind the counter, then poked his head through a door at the back.

'Shop!' he shouted. There was no response. He came back to the public side again. 'Ring that bell, lad,' he said gruffly. 'And keep at it till somebody does come.'

Morton grinned. 'I shall probably end up being arrested for causing a public nuisance,' he said.

'Huh! I could fart louder than that thing. No wonder Winchester is the back of beyond if this is how they carry on.'

Morton began to strike the bell, each depression of the plunger producing a mere ping. 'I am sure that you are less than generous, sir,' he said. 'So far as I could see from the train, Winchester seems to be a very attractive place. At first glance, I could happily live here.'

'And go to sleep for the rest of your life? . . . Where the hell is everybody?'

At that moment a round face, with a soup-strainer moustache to rival Bragg's own, peered round the door.

'Hello! I was down the bottom of the yard.' The constable came through to the counter. 'What can I do for you, gentlemen?' His smile was genial, his accent broad and welcoming.

With an effort, Bragg controlled his exasperation. 'Sergeant Bragg and Constable Morton, of the City of London police,' he said, producing his warrant-card. 'We have come down about the Witney murder.'

'Ah, yes . . . I expect you ought to talk to the Inspector about that.'

'Is he in?'

'Well I know he was going down to the vet, about his horse. She went lame last week, after she was shod. I reckon the blacksmith put one of the nails in crooked. It seemed all right, at first, but next day she durst hardly put her near-side front hoof on the ground. They took the shoe off, but it didn't seem to get any better.'

'But is he in?'

'He might be. I'll go and see.'

'Christ Almighty!' Bragg exclaimed, as the constable disappeared again. 'Well, if you want to live in Winchester, lad, you are welcome! I reckon nothing has changed here since the sixteen hundreds.'

'Believe it or not, sir, there are some people who would think that eminently desirable.'

The constable reappeared. 'Will you come this way, gentlemen?' he said, and beckoned them through the door behind the counter.

They followed him down a gloomy corridor, to a room overlooking the yard. A burly man, in a black frock-coat, was sitting at a desk. He was leafing through a report and disregarded the interruption. The constable gestured Bragg and Morton to take chairs and withdrew. They sat in silence for some minutes, watching the Inspector glance through page after page, never acknowledging their presence. Bragg was almost bursting with suppressed anger; but it was much as he had expected. The London police forces were always in the newspapers; the nation must seem to disregard what went on down here.

The Inspector reached the last sheet of the report. Even as his eyes were drifting down the page, he began to speak.

'So you are London bobbies,' he said slowly.

Bragg said nothing until the Inspector closed the report, and raised his head.

'Sergeant Bragg and Constable Morton, sir, of the City of London police's detective department.'

'No doubt you have some identification.' The voice was not exactly hostile, rather it held a calculated indifference.

Bragg laid his warrant-card on the desk. The Inspector scrutinized it, then passed it back. 'And what are you doing on my patch?' he asked frostily.

'A resident of Winchester, named Jethro Witney, was murdered yesterday in the City,' Bragg began.

'That is your affair,' the Inspector interrupted. 'The City coroner will be responsible, not ours.'

'I know that. I have been appointed the coroner's officer for the case. We have just popped in as a matter of courtesy.'

The Inspector's lip curled unpleasantly. 'I wish your courtesy had extended to informing the family yourselves, instead of sending me a telegraph,' he said. 'I had to do it myself; it was most unpleasant. The young woman went near out of her mind.'

'I can understand that,' Bragg said guardedly. 'Do you know the family well?'

'More know of them. The father was a bigwig here, as well as in London; and he made sure you knew it.'

'And the daughter?'

'She is not much more than a girl; but nice enough in the ordinary way.'

'It must have been a bad shock.'

'Shock! I have broken bad news often enough, in my time, but this was the worst, by a long chalk.'

'Of course, she had already lost her mother.'

'Yes, some years ago.'

'And how old will she be now?'

The Inspector considered for a moment. 'In her early twenties, I would say. She has one of those strong faces; it is not all that easy to tell.'

Bragg let the conversation die, then: 'I suppose you know of no one down here, who would have wished him dead?' he said.

The Inspector snorted. 'That's a bloody stupid question, sergeant, and you know it!'

'Yes, sir,' Bragg said contritely. 'At least there is nobody here who bore him ill will.'

'Not so that you would expect them to murder him. But he meddled in public affairs; and you cannot do that, at the moment, without making enemies.'

'I see. Was he an unpleasant kind of man?'

'I expect he was all right, if you happened to agree with him.'

Bragg rose to his feet. 'Well, thank you for your time, sir,' he said stolidly. 'It has been most helpful.'

The Inspector looked up sharply. 'And don't go turning over any can of worms here, without you tell me,' he said truculently.

'Of course not, sir. You can rely on me to maintain the courtesies.'

Once outside, Bragg and Morton set course towards the squat tower of the cathedral. Looking around, it was evident that the town had been built in a large hollow, surrounded by low rounded hills.

31

Even on a warm, windless day, smoke from house chimneys hung above the roof-tops. In the winter, Morton thought, the fog would be dreadful. Certainly the fabric of the great West Gate was blackened, and polished like a boot where shoulders had rubbed it.

They paused while a company of infantrymen marched across their path. Clearly Winchester was a garrison town. Morton's father, Lieutenant-General Sir Henry Morton, had served in a series of colonial campaigns with regiments from all over Britain; but he had never mentioned one based in Winchester. Not that it was entirely surprising. Until eighteen eighty-one, the British regiments of the line were merely given numbers – as, say, the Fifty-fourth Foot. So, only in recent years had their title linked them with a particular part of the country.

'Here we are, lad,' Bragg interrupted his reverie. 'That is Brook Street. Cross over.'

They found themselves in a narrow street, lined with tall Georgian terraces. Though they must now be very near to the cathedral close the tower had disappeared from view. It seemed to be a very nobby district, Bragg thought. The houses were well cared-for and there was a constant procession of smart butchers' carts and bakers' vans. There would not be any work-roughened hands among the wives in these houses. The street began to curve to the east and, through an entry, they could see the dark bulk of the cathedral not a hundred yards away.

'That must be the house, sir,' Morton said. 'The blinds are drawn, and there is a wreath on the door.'

'Right, lad. Give the bell a pull.'

They stood for some moments, then heard steps in the hall. The door was opened by a young woman, clad entirely in black. Her dress was trimmed with heavy black crape, round her neck were strands of jet beads, her hair was tied with black ribbon. She clenched a black-bordered handkerchief in her hand.

'Yes?' she asked in a dead voice.

'I am sorry to disturb you,' Bragg said kindly. 'We are police officers. We wish to speak to Miss Witney.'

'I am she.' The girl still stood woodenly in the doorway.

'May we come in?'

'Er . . . yes.' She stepped to one side and the two men went in. She no longer seemed to care about the social niceties.

'Can we sit down to talk, miss?' Bragg said quietly. 'We have come down from London.'

'Yes. Come into the sitting-room; I will ask cook to make us some tea.'

She opened a door at the end of the hall and gestured them into the room. Bragg whistled in surprise as he went in. The window revealed a most magnificent view of the cathedral, over trim lawns. The house was built facing the north-east corner of the choir. On the left was the serene beauty of the lady chapel; to the right the choir, with its elegant flying buttresses, contrasted with the stark austerity of the Norman transept.

'This must be one of the most beautiful sights in England,' Morton murmured.

'It would cost a pretty penny to rent this house, if you could pick it all up, and put it down in London,' Bragg said. 'You can see what the Inspector meant about Witney letting people know he was a bigwig.'

They stood for some minutes, looking around them. The room was furnished with solid mahogany pieces. In the alcoves on either side of the fireplace were bookcases filled with old leather-bound volumes. Morton glanced at the titles; they were obscure treatises and translations from the classics. They must have been acquired purely for their effect. In the centre of the room was a small octagonal table, on which was a bowl of white flowers. Beside it, facing the fireplace, was a long sofa, and comfortable armchairs were set by the window.

The door opened and Julia Witney appeared. Surprisingly she was carrying the tea-tray herself. She put it on the table without speaking, and began to set out the cups.

'I am sorry that we have to trouble you in this way, miss,' Bragg said quietly. 'But it cannot be helped, if we are to find out who killed your father.'

She looked at him from red-rimmed eyes. 'I fear there is very little that I can tell you,' she said.

'I am Sergeant Bragg, and this is Constable Morton. We are from the City of London police, and we were first on the scene.'

The girl flinched as she poured the tea. The local Inspector was right, Morton thought. She had a strong face. Not that she was ill-looking; far from it. But the bone structure dominated. The chin

33

was long and pointed, the cheek-bones high, the nose sharp. Her face was not unlike Catherine's, Morton decided; but each feature was fractionally more emphatic, tending to coarseness instead of beauty.

'I must ask what you may think is a silly question,' Bragg said.

'What is that?'

'Can you think of anyone who might have wished your father dead?'

'No!' The reply was instantaneous, automatic.

'Well, clearly someone did. And, since he died in London, we have the job of finding his killer.'

Julia took a cup of tea and sat on the sofa. 'I do not see how I can help you, sergeant,' she said. 'I knew relatively little about my father's interests and acquaintances.'

'Yes. But you will appreciate that, for us, there are two broad possibilities. He was killed by someone who knew him in Winchester, or by someone who knew him in London.'

In the ensuing silence Morton reached over and took a cup of tea.

'Can you help us on that, miss?' Bragg asked.

'Help you?' She looked dazedly at him.

'Had he any enemies in Winchester?'

'Enemies?'

'Well, ill-wishers.'

She appeared to concentrate her mind briefly. 'I do not think so, sergeant.'

'I suppose he spent very little time here, since he went up to London every day. Did he go up on Saturdays?'

'No. He used to attend the Winchester branch on a Saturday morning.'

'I see. Where is that?'

'In St George's Street.'

'Is it run by a manager?'

'Yes.'

'Who is that?'

'Mr David Branksome.'

'What sort of a person is he?'

She thought for a moment. 'I know very little about him. I am sure that he must be capable or Papa would never have engaged him.'

'Of course . . . How long have you lived in Winchester, miss?'

'Is that important?'

'It may be.'

She sighed wearily. 'I was four years old when we came here. My father was left the business in the will of his Uncle Arthur.'

Bragg smiled. 'That was nice of him.'

'Yes. My father was a qualified chartered surveyor, so it probably seemed appropriate.'

'I see. Where were you living at that time?'

'In a little village in Dorset, called Slocombe Magna. It is near to Wareham. At that time, my father was employed by the town council of Poole; so he was able to make the journey daily.'

'I went to Slocombe Magna once,' Bragg said amiably. 'It struck me as very out-of-the-way.'

'It depends on what you expect from life, sergeant.'

'I suppose that it does . . .' Bragg looked at the remaining cup of tea on the table. His throat was parched, but it wasn't seemly to interrupt the conversation to reach for it. Apart from anything else, it would make the girl feel she was neglecting her duties as hostess. That might raise an antagonism in her. 'Did your father have any worries, that you know of?' he asked.

She considered briefly. 'He had many responsibilities, but no worries that I am aware of.'

'Was he active in the affairs of Winchester?'

'Apart from mere social occasions, you mean?'

'Yes.'

'Only, I think, in church matters. He was invited by Dean Kitchin to become a member of his committee on the cathedral churchyard.'

'When was that, miss?'

'I suppose some nine or ten years ago. At about the same time he was asked to join the committee for the restoration of the Great Screen.'

'What is that?'

'The stone reredos behind the high altar.'

'I see. Your father's opinions would be valuable there, I can understand that . . . So, he did not get involved in local politics?'

'No.'

'And, what about you, miss? How do you pass your time?'

For a moment a sardonic smile touched her lips. 'I, sergeant? . . .

I paint a little, I write letters, I engage in good works . . .'

'So you only saw your father in the evenings, and at weekends?'

'In broad terms, that is so.'

'You never became involved in the business?'

'No. Papa would have considered it inappropriate.'

'Hmn . . . So you lived a lonely life, at best.'

She stuck out her chin determinedly. 'I am twenty-one years old, sergeant. I am able to engage in any activity which is proper for someone of my station. My lot has been neither better nor worse than that of thousands of girls in my position.'

'And, what now? Will you take over the running of the business?'

She smiled deprecatingly. 'I am hardly qualified to do that. And I believe that it is unwise for a woman to put her trust in employees in such a situation . . . I shall consult with my relatives in Slocombe Magna, and with the family solicitor, then make up my own mind.'

'That's the way, miss,' Bragg said admiringly. 'Is the solicitor in Winchester?'

'No. He is Edward Lazenby, of Lazenby Nugent & Co. They practise in St James's Street, London.'

'I see. Society lawyers, are they?'

'I cannot answer that question, sergeant.'

'Hmn . . . As your father's next of kin, would you have any objection if we went to talk to Mr Lazenby?'

'None whatever.'

'Good. Would your father have made a will, do you think?'

Julia pursed her lips. 'I presume so. He was a methodical man.'

'Do you happen to know who his executors are?'

'No, sergeant.'

Bragg brooded for a moment, then looked up. 'When did you last see him, miss?' he asked.

To his surprise, her eyes filled with tears. 'At breakfast, yesterday morning,' she said, and blew her nose on her dainty handkerchief.

'What is so upsetting about that?' Bragg asked gently.

'We . . . we had a difference of opinion. I am sorry to say that I got up from the table and left him there. On any other occasion, it would not have mattered in the slightest. Now I am filled with regret.'

'I am sure he would not want you to be worried about that,' Bragg said in a fatherly voice. 'I bet it was something and nothing.'

'Indeed! Its very triviality makes my action seem all the worse – that we should part with bad blood between us.' The incongruity of the remark seemed to strike her, and she shivered.

'So, how did you spend that day?'

'Immediately after breakfast I took my sketching pad into the country, and stayed there till late afternoon.'

'Where did you go?'

'Up St Catherine's Hill. There is a wonderful view of Winchester from its top.'

'How did you get there?'

'I walked, of course! It is no more than a mile and a quarter.'

'And back again?'

'Yes.'

'Did you see anyone?'

She cocked her head reprovingly. 'I must have seen several people in Bar End Road, but I do not remember them. Nor is there any reason why they should remember me.'

'Do you recall what time you got back here?'

'Not precisely. It would be about half past four. We generally begin preparations for dinner about five o'clock. Papa likes to sit down on the stroke of eight . . .' Her voice trailed away; she put her handkerchief to her eyes and began to sob.

Bragg waited until she had regained control, then cleared his throat to get her attention. 'Is your father to be buried here?' he asked.

'Yes. I gather that it is to be arranged for Wednesday.'

'I see. Well, the inquest will be opened on Monday, so there should be no difficulty in getting a burial order.'

'Oh.' A look of bewilderment crossed her face. 'It is all so complicated; and I feel utterly helpless . . .'

'Don't you worry yourself, miss,' Bragg said solicitously. 'There is no need for you to be at the inquest. Just leave everything to the undertaker . . . Now, where did your father keep his private papers?'

'There is a safe in the corner of Papa's study. They would be either there, or in his desk.'

'Do you have a key to the safe?'

'I know where it is kept.'

'Then I will spend an hour or so browsing through the papers, while Constable Morton has a chat with the manager of the Winchester branch. Where is it, did you say?'

'St George's Street.'

'Right. Off you go, lad!'

Morton got directions to St George's Street from a passer-by. It lay just beyond the High Street and ran parallel to it. The Witney office was thus a mere five minutes' walk from the house. In its window, also, were framed photographs of properties. But here there was only one mansion; the others were small town houses, shops and villas on the outskirts of the city. He pushed open the door. The office was laid out on the same lines as that in Lombard Street. A typewriter was busy at her machine in the far corner. Another desk was by the door. By it a young man was standing, deep in conversation with a prosperous-looking customer. Morton signalled that he would wait and strolled over to examine the photographs of properties hanging on the wall. From what he could hear, Branksome was being put under considerable pressure to conspire against his client by over-stating the seriousness of certain defects found in a property that Witneys were selling. Finally the man departed, uttering something very like a threat. Branksome turned to Morton.

'Can I help you, sir?' he asked in a pleasant voice.

'City Police.' Morton showed his warrant-card. 'I just want a chat. Is it convenient?'

Branksome smiled ruefully. 'I would gladly close the office for a while.' He crossed over and locked the door.

'Do your customers always behave like that?' Morton asked.

'No. It is merely that the man who has just left senses an opportunity.'

'I see. His approach was hardly diplomatic!'

'Oh, people are direct down here, one does not expect finesse. He clearly feels that, with Mr Witney dead, the business will be in some disarray.'

'And, will it?'

Branksome considered for a moment. 'Well, the day-to-day running of this branch was always left to me; and there is no reason why that should be affected. But Mr Witney dealt with the important clients on a Saturday morning. Such people may only wish to deal with a principal, so our connection may suffer there.'

Morton drew up a chair to Branksome's desk. 'What does the Winchester business consist of?' he asked.

Branksome thought for a moment. 'I suppose that eighty per cent of our income is commissions for collecting rent from, and generally managing, small terraced houses and shops. The rest comes from sales of property on behalf of clients.'

'Do you ever speculate, by buying property and selling on?'

'Not in my time. Indeed, I cannot see Mr Witney becoming engaged in anything like that. He was a very upright, strictly professional man.'

'I see. You will understand that we are casting around to find a reason for his murder. Someone, clearly, had a violent hatred for him.'

'It was bad, was it?'

'Yes, it was bad.'

Branksome shook his head sadly. 'Poor Julia.'

'You know her?'

'Yes. She often pops in. She is a very charming person.'

'*De haut en bas?*' Morton asked, with a smile.

'What?'

'No matter . . . Was she involved in the business?'

'No. Interested in it, certainly, but her father would never let her work here. She once suggested that she might learn to keep the books, but he would not hear of it . . . And he was right, of course. Miss Julia is a real lady.'

'I see. How long have you worked here, Mr Branksome?'

'Seven years. I did my training with Millingtons, on the other side of town.'

'And, how old are you now?'

'Thirty next birthday.'

'I take it that you live in Winchester.'

'Yes. At the moment I lodge with Mrs Treadwell, in Monks Road.'

'So, you are unmarried?'

'Yes.'

Morton brooded for a moment, then: 'What is going to happen to the business?' he asked.

Branksome dropped his gaze. 'I cannot say.'

39

'I suppose that his daughter will inherit it,' Morton suggested.

'She certainly ought to!'

'Is there anyone else in the running?'

'I cannot say. I know very little about the family.'

Morton leaned back in his chair, hands clasped behind his head. 'What would you advise her to do about this branch?' he asked. 'Sell it?'

'No!' Branksome looked up defiantly. 'It is a good business. Why should it be sold?'

'But you said that she knows nothing about it.'

'Why need she? It runs perfectly well as it is.'

'So, Mr Witney did very little at this branch?'

'That is the size of it. He would come in for a couple of hours on a Saturday morning, and look through what had happened during the week. He used to sign a few letters, but nothing more.'

'What kind of letters?'

'To his cronies, to keep them sweet.'

'And, will the business be able to maintain that personal connection, now he is gone?'

'I could not do it. But Miss Julia could, if she set her mind to it.'

'I understand. What about the London branch?'

'I have no knowledge of that . . . If it were up to me, I would let it go.'

'You mean sell it?'

'I expect so.'

'Right. Now, can you tell me if anyone in this area had cause to violently dislike your employer?'

Branksome thought for a moment. 'No. Not so far as to want him dead, if that is what you mean. There has been some ill feeling over the cathedral recently, but it could hardly be that.'

'How was your employer involved with the cathedral? In a professional capacity?'

'Well, you might say as much. He was on one of the committees that dealt with the fabric of the building.'

'I see. And how could he incur such vindictive hatred as a mere member of a committee?'

'I am not saying that he could. I know nothing about it. I am a Baptist myself.'

Morton got to his feet. 'Well, we shall clearly have to go through the records, in case something in them rings a bell. Can you pack them up for me?'

'You want to take them away?'

'I would hardly think it would be good for the business, to have policemen sitting here for days on end!'

'How far back do you want to go?'

'Say, the last five years.'

'That is the current books, then. How long will you be keeping them?'

'For a few days only.'

'Very well. I will see if I can find a cardboard box.'

Julia Witney unlocked the safe and left Bragg in the study to examine the papers. This room also overlooked the cathedral. It seemed to have bulked large in Witney's life, Bragg thought; it and the City of London. He had certainly wanted to be in the limelight. But perhaps it was not all that surprising. He was a widower, his life must be empty.

Bragg pulled out his tobacco pouch, and began to fill his pipe . . . Not that it necessarily followed. He was a widower himself, after all; and his life was full enough. But the cases were not the same. His own wife had died when she was twenty-one giving birth to their only child. The baby had died too. Married and doubly bereaved within two years – that was the pattern with him. In Witney's case, he had a fine upstanding daughter and maybe his wife had only died recently. To come in middle age it must hit you hard. All those years of living together, all the things you had bought together, still there to remind you. He snorted. The only thing he still had was a china tea cup with *A Present from Bournemouth* on the side that they had bought on their wedding day. It was all a long time ago . . . And they would not have been happy. Of course, she had had to live in a police quarter, in London. But she'd been a country girl; she was out of her depth in the big city. She had tried, sure enough, but she was homesick and miserable. Perhaps death had been a way out.

But this room showed a woman's hand. Although it was a study, the curtains at the window were elegantly draped, the window-seat cushions were covered in matching fabric. In the corner, by

41

the fireplace, was a display cabinet full of knick-knacks; a vase of flowers stood on its top . . . That must be the daughter's doing, of course. She was familiar with the niceties of middle-class living; she had not just been dragged up by servants.

Bragg lit his pipe, then turned to the pile of documents he had collected from the desk drawers. Many of them related to recreational activities. Witney was obviously a member of the local cricket club – Morton would approve of that! A manila file held the records of proceedings at the cathedral committee meetings; they would wait. Another contained papers relating to meetings of the Plaisterers' Guild and the Carpenters' Guild. Bragg wondered if they could in any way be connected with Witney's death. His own daughter had described him as methodical. And if he had got in with the City fathers so well within seven years, he must have been pushful too. Suppose he had thwarted somebody in the process . . . somebody even more ambitious than he was himself? Well, it could not be dismissed out of hand. Plenty of men would strangle their grandmothers to be Lord Mayor of London – with a baronetcy thrown in for good measure . . . Yet Witney did not have a son to pass the title on to. So why bother?

The safe contained family papers. There was a bundle of life insurance policies, which Bragg set aside. There was Witney's birth certificate, his certificate of marriage to Mary Alice Cranston, the birth certificate of Julia, and the death certificate of his wife – on the second of February eighteen eighty-six. Eight years ago. When both of them were thirty-five and they had been married only fourteen years. What a waste . . . But Julia had had a mother for thirteen years. That was more than a lot of girls managed.

There were a few documents left. One was a list of shareholdings in various companies. There were question marks against most entries, which had been cancelled by a tick as if shares had been bought. Attached to it was a skeleton statement of assets under general headings, as if Witney had been in the process of ascertaining his current wealth. There was also a family tree, showing Jethro Witney, and Julia as his heir. The last document was a typewritten letter addressed to Jethro, from Lazenby Nugent & Co. It was dated in May eighteen ninety-two.

Dear Jethro,

When you signed your new will, last week, I ought to have suggested that you consider advising Thomas Witney, the other executor, of its contents in general terms. I feel it is always better for the family executor to take the leading role in carrying out the last wishes of a client.

My best wishes to Julia,

Yours, as ever,

Edward

Bragg went in search of Julia. He found her in the back sitting-room, staring glumly at a group of people wandering about the cathedral lawns.

'Can I have a word, miss?' he asked.

'Of course.' She got to her feet and followed him to the study.

'It is this letter, miss. Have you, by any chance got your father's will?'

'No.' She took the letter. 'I did not know anything about his making a new will . . . May eighteen ninety-two? I do not understand why he should do so two years ago; but obviously he did.'

'Then, you have never seen it?'

'No.'

'And you are not aware of its terms?'

'No. Have you not found it?'

'It was not in the safe, or the desk, where you would expect it to be.'

'Goodness! If it has been lost, I wonder what will happen.'

When Morton got back to Brook Street, he decided to beg a cup of tea from the cook. It was a ploy that Bragg used to great effect. Most families, particularly from the *nouveau riche* middle class, ignored their servants. They lived alongside them, accepting their service as due, and thereafter treated them like domestic pets. As a result, they did not guard their tongues when the servants were around.

He pushed open the area door, with a twinge of trepidation. It always seemed so easy for Bragg. Because of his intimidating bulk, the friendly confiding manner he adopted came as a relief. People relaxed, talked carelessly, unburdened themselves. He could not remotely simulate that approach himself. When he first joined the police, almost six years ago, he could have played the part of a fresh-faced beginner; but no longer. He would just have to take his chance. He went down the short passage to the kitchen.

'Hello! I wonder if there is any possibility of a cup of tea. As I expect you saw from the teacups,' he said with inward relish, 'I did not get the chance to drink mine earlier on.'

The cook smiled expansively. 'Of course! You are one of the London policemen, I suppose.' Her face clouded. 'This is a terrible business,' she said. 'It's turned the poor love's life upside down.'

'You mean Witney's daughter?'

'Yes.' The cook set some cups on the table, and poured water into a teapot from a kettle simmering on the hob. 'Mind you, I know what I would do, in her shoes.'

'What is that?' Morton asked casually.

'Why, get rid of this house! She's nothing but a slave to it. She has no life of her own, at all . . . If you ask me, he wanted it that way. Wouldn't have a proper housemaid; only a cleaning woman, twice a week. For a house this size! Said there was only the two of them, so it didn't get dirty.'

'Was it different when his wife was alive?'

'I don't go back that far, but from what they say, she was a woman with plenty of go in her . . . Milk and sugar?'

'Please.'

'I think Miss Julia ought to have stood up to him more. He had plenty of money; there was no call for him to treat her like an unpaid skivvy.'

'Surely not!'

'It's true! He wouldn't even let me have a kitchen maid. It was unnecessary, he said; Miss Julia could help me. But he still wanted a full dinner when he got home.' She pushed a steaming cup over to Morton. 'There was no need for it! Sometimes he would tell me about the grand luncheons he'd had in London; ask me if I could do a particular dish. So he didn't stint himself there. But he still wanted everything just so when he came home.'

'So, she helped you to prepare the vegetables for the evening meal?'

'Indeed she did, bless her! Well, I couldn't do that too. The master was always wanting complicated recipes that took hours to make.

I couldn't do everything . . . Anyway, I think she enjoyed the companionship, if you understand me.'

'Do you mean that, in a sense, you took the place of her mother?'

The cook bridled. 'Oh no! I would never think of doing such a wicked thing!'

'No, no! You misunderstand me,' Morton said hastily. 'But you were another woman, part of the household; someone she could ask for advice, confide in . . .'

'She did that, all right . . . It's a funny thing, the master was a nice-seeming man, all full of himself, always pleasant – even to the likes of me. Yet, with Miss Julia, he seemed to want to shut her up. After all, she's over twenty-one; she should be having a bit of fun, if she's ever going to.'

'But how could he prevent her from enjoying herself? He was away in London every day.'

'I know, but she never could go out in the evenings . . . And how many young men of her class are around during the day?'

Morton grinned. 'Ah, now you are matchmaking!'

'No, I never!' she said sharply. 'But I reckon he had his fun in London, so why shouldn't she? . . . Mind you, he didn't know everything!'

'So she had an admirer in Winchester . . . David Branksome, possibly?'

'Him?' She snorted contemptuously. 'He hasn't a look-in, whatever he may think.' She lowered her voice conspiratorially. 'No, it's a young man from London. How she met him, I don't know. But he comes here sometimes. She once told me he's an engineer, and he calls when he has to pass through Winchester for business.'

Morton dropped his voice in turn. 'And do you leave them alone in the house together?' he murmured suggestively.

'Hey! What do you take me for? . . . No, he knocks on the door, about eleven, and waits outside while she gets ready. Then off they go together.'

'When does she return?'

'Usually at half past four; in time to get ready to help me.'

'And she comes back alone?'

'Yes. If you ask me, she goes to the station to see him off.'

'He must have a very accommodating job,' Morton remarked.

'I reckon he works for himself.'

'And Julia has never mentioned the name of this man to you?'

'No; and I wouldn't want to hear it. In this sort of situation the less you know the better.'

Morton got to his feet. 'Well, one thing is sure, the situation has been changed in no uncertain manner. What will happen now?'

The cook pursed her lips. 'I don't know. It will be up to her, won't it? But you mustn't run away with the idea that she's a weak woman, who can't take care of herself. She did what her father wanted because it suited her . . . And I don't think she would have stuck it much longer, if you want my opinion.'

'And, now that she is a wealthy heiress, suitors will come flocking.'

'You don't need to worry about Miss Julia,' the cook interrupted. 'She's got her head screwed on all right. She will come to no harm.'

Bragg usually kept his Sundays sacred. Not that he went to church. He had given up believing in an omniscient, all-powerful god; who, in his goodness, could muck away a young woman and her new-born child as if they were rubbish. He had tried to go along with it. For months, after they had died, he had been at church every Sunday; looking for solace, trying to understand. But it was no good. He could not believe the platitudinous rubbish the parson dished out: that if you put your trust in God, all things would be bright and beautiful. For his money, if there was a higher being controlling man's destiny, then it was capricious and evil; you had to struggle against it as best you knew.

He spent the morning in the tiny back garden of the house where he lodged. Mrs Jenks was a sharp-tongued widow of about his age. He had come here when Tommy Jenks was still alive. Tommy had been a prosperous dustman, with his own horse and cart; so she had no need to take in lodgers. However, she had advertised, and must have liked the look of him – or perhaps it was just that she felt safer with a policeman in the house. Tan House Lane was on the eastern fringe of the City; Jack the Ripper country was just over the border. Not that she and Tommy were of a mind. He plainly resented the arrangement; thought it reflected badly on him as a provider. But it had turned out to be a godsend. Tommy cut his hand on a tin can. He shrugged it off as nothing; there was scarcely a week that he didn't get a nick of one kind or another. But it had taken bad ways, and within the month he was dead. That was nearly twenty years ago. He should have left then. But she had needed him – and perhaps he had wanted somebody to need him. Anyway, he had stayed on, paying his rent on the nail, putting up with her stodgy cooking.

By noon he had forked over the flower beds and weeded between the rows of peas. He had clipped the lawn the previous week, so that did not need doing again. Blast it! Why was he so restless? He had earned his day off. He'd only got back home at ten, the previous night, but he could not shake off the feeling that he ought to be doing something . . . It was the savagery of the Witney killing that was worrying him. Suppose it wasn't just an ordinary murder – hatred flaring between two business associates, for instance. Suppose it was a lunatic, who could strike again. Who might, even now, be bludgeoning some innocent person and slitting their throat . . . And him sitting on his arse in the garden, pretending to relax.

Once lunch was over, and he had flattered Mrs Jenks by asking for a bit more of her Spotted Dick pudding, he took his hat and walked briskly to London Bridge station. John Syme lived in Sutton. That was to the south – way out in Surrey, fifteen miles away. It seemed a bit ambitious for even a City clerk – however chief he was. It was not a part of the country that Bragg knew, so he gazed with interest over the sunlit fields, as the train pottered on from one small station to the next. Compared with the area north of London, this was empty. Once out of the station you were straight into shabby, uninteresting countryside. The farms didn't seem in good heart, to him. Some marshy patches could easily have been drained, if the farmer had a mind to it. And even the June sunshine could not bring this landscape to life. He could remember old men in Dorset who swore that the coming of the railways had ruined farms by the score. Well, they would have to be relying on the memories of their grandfathers' talk; but there could be sense in it. You only had to poke your head out of the window and you got an eyeful of soot and ash.

Bragg was glad when the train finally pulled into Sutton station. He went up the steps from the platform and found himself in a wide courtyard giving on to the main road. He strolled down the street and saw a cab-rank near a crossroads. A couple of hansoms were waiting there, the horses nuzzling into their nosebags. The drivers were leaning against a wall, chatting. Bragg gave them Syme's address. At first they were unsure about it. There were evidently several areas of new housing on the outskirts and the street names were not yet familiar. Eventually a decision was made and the first cabby swung himself up into his high seat. Bragg dig not bother to pull the flaps over his knees; it was a hot day, a little air would be welcome.

From what he could see as they clattered down the hill, Sutton was a pleasant town. The shops looked varied and prosperous. There was even one claiming to supply French *patisserie*! There must be plenty of money in some people's pockets. They turned down a side road. For the first two hundred yards it was lined with mature elm trees; substantial villas lurked behind screens of shrubs. At a sign announcing Chilton Grove, however, there was an abrupt change. The trees became spindly mountain ash, the metalled surface deteriorated into rutted clay, and new semi-detached houses jostled along the road. They were large, with three storeys, and their yellow London-clay brick made them look like brash interlopers. In the distance Bragg could see similar houses in various stages of construction.

He opened the hatch on the roof and told the driver to let him down. Then he walked slowly along the verge. One or two householders had planted hedges, installed gates to keep the world at bay. Some had screwed numbers or name-plates by the front door. Here and there a lawn had been conjured into existence, bordered by delphiniums and lupins. Syme's house stood between two such gardens. The contiguous one was trim and bright, full of flowers and low shrubs. In contrast, the garden of Syme's house still looked like a building site. There were half-bricks and broken slates scattered about its rutted surface. The difference was made more marked by the fact that there was no dividing fence. One assumed that the responsibility for providing it lay with Syme, and he had not discharged it. It was odd, Bragg thought, that a new house could look neglected, yet it did. There were no curtains at the windows of the top storey, broken tea-chests littered the path to the patch of yellow earth at the back of the house. There was no pride in it, no elation at possessing such a home. And yet it was a fine house, for a chief-of-nobody clerk.

Bragg strolled up the path and hammered on the front door. He heard children's voices calling, then footsteps in the hallway. The door was opened hesitantly. Syme stood there, a look of blank surprise on his face.

'What do you want?' he asked irritably.

'I thought we might have a chat,' Bragg said amiably. 'The office, on Friday, was not the best of places to talk, was it?'

For a moment Syme seemed about to close the door in Bragg's face, then he stepped back and beckoned. Bragg followed him into the front sitting-room. The floor was covered in linoleum, and there were no carpets. Apart from that, the room held most of the furniture one would expect. There was a sofa, and a table covered with photographs under the window. The swagged mantelpiece was crammed with knick-knacks, there was a what-not in the corner supporting a thriving aspidistra. And yet it all seemed dowdy; it looked like the handings-on of half a dozen maiden aunts. It was at odds with the confident assertiveness of the house itself.

Syme gestured to the sofa and slumped into a chair. 'What is it, then?' he asked.

Bragg made a business of settling on the sofa, placing his hat beside him, making sure that the skirt of his frock-coat was not rucked under him. Then he looked across, with an encouraging smile.

'I really came to inform you that you will be needed at the coroner's court, tomorrow morning,' he said.

'What for?' Syme's eyes were wide with alarm.

'Well, he will have to hear evidence of identity, and evidence of discovery. You can do both jobs.'

'Oh, God! He will not be . . . there, will he?'

'Mr Witney, you mean? No. He will be scarcely recognizable by now. Our pathologist, Dr Burney, makes a real meal of a case. Particularly where a head injury is involved. You thought it looked bad enough on Friday. I tell you, you would need a lot stronger stomach by now.'

Syme's face was pinky-grey, his jaw clenched tight. 'I just don't want to have to see him again,' he muttered.

'You won't . . . I expect you have seen enough of him. I shall not forget it myself, in a hurry. I've only seen one worse, in my twenty-two years with the force, and that was where the head was . . .'

'For Christ's sake, leave off!' Syme shouted. 'I haven't slept a bloody wink since Friday. Every time I close my eyes, it's there in front of me. I am nearly out of my mind!'

'Yes, it takes a bit of getting used to,' Bragg said amiably. 'An odd sort of chap, our friend Witney, don't you think?'

'Odd? Why?'

'Well, he has a perfectly good business in Winchester but, instead of carrying on like the country gentleman he is, he takes to trailing up to London every day.'

Syme sniffed. 'Well, he wanted to be Lord Mayor, didn't he? He wasn't interested in the business. If you want to know what I think, he was put up to it by his cronies.'

'Whatever makes you think that?' Bragg asked, simulating astonishment.

'Well, we act for two big estates; they form the bulk of our business. The trustees are big men in the City already; I reckon they would use anybody to get richer – and the Corporation has a lot of property.'

'But, how could that benefit individuals, however influential?'

'Why, a great deal of it is on the fringe of the City, near-slum buildings, and the leases are about to expire. If you got in at the right price you could make a fortune.'

'I see. Have you any evidence that Witney was involved in such a scheme?'

'I don't need any. Like you said, why would he neglect a good business in Winchester, to set up here?'

'But he bought a thriving business from Shillingfords – at least, I assume it was thriving.'

Syme looked stonily at the toes of his boots, thrust out in front of him. 'He paid what it was worth, I expect,' he said shortly.

'You did not know much about it in those days?' Bragg asked.

'Mr Shillingford used to keep the books. I just collected the rents.'

'And in recent years you have kept the books and collected the rents!' Bragg said jovially.

'That's about it.'

'And here you are, living in a fine house, in a prosperous neighbourhood. Almost one of the gentry yourself!'

Syme seemed about to explode in anger but controlled himself. 'You can see perfectly well how I am fixed,' he said bitterly.

'You've looked at the books. You have seen how he has cheated me!'

'Would you put it as strongly as that?' Bragg said cautiously.

'How else would I put it? He has never played fair by me. I am supposed to get two per cent of the net profits from Lombard Street. I agreed to it, because I had a good idea of Shillingfords' profits. It seemed a good deal. But Witney charged the cost of entertaining all and sundry against the business income. It was not right! It had nothing to do with the business, really. But when I spoke to him about it, he said I could accept it or leave.'

'So you accepted it?'

'Of course. There aren't any better jobs around, unless you have a qualification. But it was not fair! Last year I got a salary of a hundred and thirty pounds. But because of all the non-business expenses the trading profit was only three thousand seven hundred pounds. So, with the commission, I ended up with a miserable two hundred and four.'

'Hmn . . . That would not go far, with a house like this.'

Syme looked up angrily. 'That's another thing! Early this year, he called me in, said there could be changes in his circumstances; that he might not be able to give as much time to the business. He said he intended to make me a partner. I would be a solid City businessman, that was what he said. So I took him at his word; we left Stepney, and bought this place.'

'You actually bought it?' Bragg could not keep the incredulity out of his voice.

'Yes,' Syme said defiantly. 'For what it is, it was cheap. And the interest is not that much more than it would cost to rent it.'

'But you are sorry now?'

'Wouldn't you be?'

Bragg smiled. 'I live in lodgings. It is no use asking me. I never aspired to being a solid City businessman . . . But, what will happen now?'

Syme sighed despondently. 'I don't know. I shall just live each day as it comes.'

'Well, there is no one in the family that could run the business. Why don't you make a bid for it?'

'And what do I use for money?'

'You could borrow, surely?'

'With this place round my neck?'

'I see. Well, we must hope that the new owner will take the same benevolent view as Mr Witney . . . Now, can we talk for a moment about Friday?'

'I suppose so.' Syme picked nervously at his skimpy moustache.

'Who went out for lunch first, you or Miss Fox?'

'Let me think . . . I did. She said she had a letter to finish. Mr Witney used to sign his correspondence straight after he got back from lunch – which could be any time between two o'clock and half past four.'

'And did you get back before her?'

'Yes.'

'Did Mr Witney go out for lunch?'

'Not that I am aware of.'

'Is the front door of the office locked at lunch-time?'

'We all three have keys. The last out locks it.'

'I see . . . Now, then, when you got back, Miss Fox had finished her bit of typewriting and gone for lunch. Was it your job to check her work before the letters went in to Mr Witney?'

'Yes.'

'So you did that as soon as you got back, I suppose.'

'I cannot really remember, but I expect so.'

'You see, we do not understand why you didn't take the letters in to him as soon as you got back. Why wait for half an hour, before taking them into his office?'

'I don't follow you.'

'Well, for all you knew, he might have been sitting at his desk, waiting for them.'

'But I thought he must be out because the door was locked when I got back.'

'Ah, then that accounts for it . . . By the way, here are the keys you gave me. You might as well open the office again. Oh, and you can get the back office cleaned up now. I expect it is beginning to smell a bit, with all that blood.'

3

Morton arrived at Old Jewry next morning to find Bragg leaning against his desk, staring out of the window.

'Good morning, sir!' he said breezily. 'What is on the menu for today?'

Bragg looked round. 'Well now, why don't you decide? Let me see what you have learned, these last three years.'

'Very well.' Morton strolled to the centre of the room. 'From a procedural point of view, we shall have to attend the inquest. That will take up most of the morning. And we could usefully see if Dr Burney has any additional observations which might help us.'

'Yes, a good idea.' Bragg turned to pick up a box of matches from his desk, but it slipped from his fingers and slid across the floor. Morton stooped to pick it up. Suddenly there came a violent blow between his shoulder-blades, that sent him sprawling.

'What the devil! . . .' he burst out, getting to his knees. A smile was lurking below Bragg's untidy moustache.

'Sorry, lad,' he said, 'it was just a little experiment; a rehearsal, you might say.'

'Then next time you might warn me!'

'Ah, but that would have spoiled it . . . You remember Professor Burney going on about the slanting bruise; suggesting it might be somebody fairly short. Well, I was not all that convinced by it. There was a lot of weight behind that blow. If we had to assume it was done by somebody striking upwards, we would be looking for a short thickset person.'

'Does that really follow?'

'I can see you have not done much carpentry, or you would know. If you are knocking a nail in high up, you cannot get your weight behind it.'

'I will allow that most of your corpulent carcass was behind that blow,' Morton said, easing his shoulders. 'So, what has it proved?'

'Not much. It could have been done by almost anyone. All you need is somebody who will act as a gentleman is supposed to – somebody stupid, like you . . .'

'Or Witney?'

'Or Witney, yes. Once he is bending over, you can put your full weight behind the blow.'

'And, if you were standing behind your victim, he would see nothing . . . But are you serious, when you say that anyone could have done it?'

'Perhaps not quite anyone . . . but remember what Burney said. The blow was not expected to be fatal; the murderer brought along a razor to complete the job.'

'Not expected to be fatal because of the build of the assailant?'

'It's possible. It need not be a man – nor even a brawny woman.'

'So, someone like Julia Witney is not excluded?' Morton murmured.

'While you were making up your mind whether to come in this morning, lad, I was looking at the railway timetable. She could have easily got up to the City by twelve o'clock. And there is a train from Waterloo that gets into Winchester at twenty to four. There was ample time to stroll back home and start helping cook to make the dinner.'

Morton's forehead wrinkled in thought. 'But is she capable of murdering her own father?' he asked. 'I acknowledge that they had a disagreement over breakfast, but that is a far cry from taking a train to London and perpetrating a calculated murder.'

'You have a funny notion of women,' Bragg said sardonically. 'Believe me, women can hate more than any man, when they are put to it.'

Morton smiled. 'Certainly the cook is convinced that Julia has been having a secret liaison,' he said.

'And been treated like a skivvy by her father, don't forget that.'

'But why need that lead to her murdering him? Surely she could have simply walked out of the house, never to return.'

'Real life is not like melodrama, lad. With all your money, you cannot put yourself in her position. She has nothing of her own, I expect her chap has precious little as well. She has not been brought up to earn her own living. Outside a good marriage, she's useless. Then again, she is an only child; been brought up in the expectation that all her father's wealth would be hers, one day. She's not going to let that go easily.'

'I found it interesting that she said no one would be able to vouch for her painting expedition on St Catherine's Hill.'

'Yes. She was almost challenging us, wasn't she? The cook is right, she is a very self-assured young woman.'

'I suppose,' Morton said thoughtfully, 'that her father might have disapproved of the young man who has been calling. If so, she could have decided that, of the two, she could dispense with her father . . . But would she not then have acted in concert with the young man, let him do the dirty work?'

'I'm not excluding him, lad. What I am saying is that we need not include him. And I reckon she would have thought the same. After all, would you fancy being married to a murderer for the rest of your natural?'

'Indeed not! So Julia is a suspect and, for similar reasons, her admirer cannot be excluded either.'

'Right.' Bragg sat at his desk, and knocked out the ashes from his pipe. 'What do you reckon of the Winchester manager as a murderer?' he asked.

'Branksome? I suppose he is a possibility. From what the cook said, he has dreams of marrying Julia and taking over the business.'

'But there did not seem to be any interest on her part . . . Mind you, she could be a lot cleverer than anyone allows. They could just be pretending that there is nothing between them; then, when it has all gone over, they could quietly get married.'

Morton laughed. 'I think you ought to be a playwright, sir! The plot could be fit for the West End with one elaboration.'

'What is that?'

'Why, she should get one admirer to commit the murder, then marry the other!'

Bragg scowled. 'I reckon she might be devious enough to, as well . . . Anyway, while you were wasting your time yesterday, I went down to see our friend Syme.'

'In Sutton?'

'Yes. He is in a deal of trouble. He has gone and bought a big house there, on a promise from Witney that he would make him a partner. Borrowed the money, of course. Now he can see his job vanishing too.'

'Presumably he could not afford to buy the business?'

'No.'

'So his interest must lie in its continuance.'

'On the face of it, yes.'

'And you do not see him as a suspect?'

'I would not go so far, lad. He has been harbouring a grudge for a long time. Witney used to charge the cost of entertaining expensive friends against the business income. As Syme saw it, two per cent of every day's luncheon bill was coming out of his own pocket. That rankled . . . And we don't know what this partnership promise was worth.'

'How do you mean, sir?'

'Well, you would normally expect a partner to get a healthy slice of the profits, wouldn't you? Now, if we are to believe Syme, Witney told him he would make him a substantial City gent. But suppose he found out he was going to be a partner only in name; perhaps entitled to a bit more by way of salary, but no share in the profits?'

'I suppose he would be put in a rage by such news – particularly so if he had over-extended himself financially. But would that not lead to a sudden flare-up of anger, rather than a premeditated killing?'

Bragg pondered. 'You know, I reckon he is in such a state that he could well have done it. And one or two things point in that direction. You yourself said that he didn't take the letters to Witney's office until Miss Fox was back to witness the discovery. Then there is the so-called locked door. According to Syme, neither he nor Miss Fox would have locked it when they went to lunch because Witney was still there. Can we really believe that a murderer would come in from outside, kill Witney, close his room door, then bother to lock the street door before escaping?'

'I suppose it is possible. It would provide an additional barrier against discovery.'

'Maybe . . . But there is another thing. If you remember, Syme swore that he went no further than the doorway of Witney's room: that, as soon as he saw the body, he ran to the street shouting blue murder.'

'That is so.'

'I don't know if you saw the footprint on the polished wood.'

'Yes. It looked as if someone with a huge hole in the sole of his boot had trodden in the blood.'

'Right . . . Well, when Syme was telling me his troubles yesterday, he had his legs stretched out towards me. One of his boots had just such a hole in the sole.'

Bragg and Morton went to the coroner's court, later that morning, for the inquest on Jethro Witney. They sat on a pew-like bench at the back, where they had a good view of the proceedings. After a few minutes, Syme appeared. He nodded briefly at them, then went to speak to the usher. He was placed on a bench at the front, near to the witness-box. Soon the court began to fill up with moneyed men in morning-coats, and rumpled clerks; all there for the excitement. There was a table beneath the dais for the press. Morton was relieved to find that Catherine had decided not to attend the inquest – or had not been allowed to do so by the editor.

A few minutes before eleven o'clock the jury took its place on the right. They seemed cowed, overcome by the weight of the responsibility placed upon them. Perhaps, thought Bragg, Sir Rufus Stone had been instructing them as to the way in which he expected them to conduct themselves!

Precisely on the stroke of the hour the coroner appeared. The clerk's gabble was drowned by the shuffle of boots as they all stood. Sir Rufus bowed to the jury, then to the assembled public, and took his seat under the resplendent City coat of arms. To Morton he was like an aged actor, his grey head thrown back, dominating his audience. There was a murmur of conversation as everyone sat down, immediately quelled by the clerk's gavel.

'The case of Jethro Witney deceased, your Honour.'

'Ah, yes.' Sir Rufus leaned forward to make a note in his book. 'Who is to give evidence of identity?'

'Mr John Syme, of Chilton Grove, Sutton, your Honour.'

'Is he present in court?'

The usher strode over to Syme and hustled him into the witness-box. He thrust a Bible into his hand and coaxed him through the oath.

'Now, Mr Syme,' Sir Rufus said in a business-like tone, 'am I to understand that you knew the deceased well?'

'Yes, your Honour,' Syme mumbled.

'What's that?' Sir Rufus barked. 'Speak up, man! You have to be clearly heard by the jury, over there.'

'Sorry, your Honour . . . Yes, I knew him well.'

'Were you related to him?'

'No, your Honour.'

'In what capacity did you know him?'

'I worked in the same office, for seven years, your Honour.'

'And you have no doubt that the body you have been shown is that of Jethro Witney?'

Syme dropped his head. 'None whatever, your Honour.'

'Very well, you may step down.'

Syme returned to his seat while the coroner made a brief note in his book.

'And, who gives evidence of discovery?' Sir Rufus asked.

'Mr John Syme, your Honour,' the clerk intoned.

Syme had barely sat down, and there was a titter from the back of the court as he got to his feet again.

'Silence!' Sir Rufus glared, scanning the crowded benches. 'If there is any more disturbance, I will have the court cleared!'

Syme took his place in the witness-box, and held out his hand for the Bible. The clerk shook his head reprovingly. 'You have already been sworn,' he muttered.

'Mr Syme, is it correct that you discovered the body?' The coroner's voice held mild irritation and reproof. Perhaps, thought Morton, even he was exasperated at the inflexibility of the ritual.

'Yes, your Honour.'

'Where was the discovery made?'

'In the office, your Honour.'

Sir Rufus leaned forward. 'Will you please restrain yourself from saying "your Honour", every time you open your mouth?' he said sternly. 'I am sensible of the veneration due to my ancient office, but let us keep it within bounds, shall we?' He gave a cold, artificial smile, then recorded the answer in his book.

'Where is the office situated?' he asked.

'At sixty-six Lombard Street, sir.'

'Good!' the coroner said approvingly. 'And, what is the nature of the activities carried on there?'

'The estate agency owned by Mr Witney . . . I worked for him,' he added.

'And how came you to discover the body?'

'I went, after lunch, to take some letters for signature, and found him lying on the floor.'

The coroner held up his hand lest Syme should be tempted to give the grisly details, then recorded the answer. 'And, what was the date and time of this discovery?' he asked.

'About five minutes past two, on Friday the fourth of June.'

The coroner made a note, put down his pen and closed the book. 'This inquest is adjourned *sine die*,' he intoned, 'so that appropriate enquiries can proceed.'

Everyone stood up; there was more bowing and the coroner was escorted out of the court.

'So that is what we are,' Morton murmured. 'Appropriate enquirers!'

'Yes.' Bragg pushed his way through the throng, and grabbed Syme's arm. 'Sorry,' he said genially. 'Did I startle you?'

'No . . . er, no.'

'You remember Constable Morton? I expect you will be seeing a good deal of him.'

'I see.' Syme looked bemused.

'Have you opened up at Lombard Street this morning?'

'Yes.'

'Is Miss Fox in as well?'

'Yes.'

'Good. I forgot to mention . . . we had a word with Witney's daughter, on Saturday. She seems to be taking it well.'

'I see.'

'I expect she would want you to keep on as usual.'

'Yes . . . Then I'll be going.' He backed away and vanished into the crowd.

'No harm in reminding him that we are around,' Bragg remarked. 'Now, what next? It is too early for a pie and a pint.'

'I wonder, your Honour, if we might go to see his Honour the solicitor in this case,' Morton said, with a grin.

'Lazenby? That's not a bad idea. He might be able to clear up a point or two. Where does he hang out?'

'St James's Street.'

'Right. Grab a cab, lad.'

* * *

59

They relinquished their hansom in Trafalgar Square and walked along the Mall in the noonday sun.

'Of course,' Morton said innocently, 'we could spend an hour or two pondering in St James's Park. A relaxed mind is a percipient one, after all.'

'Huh! You bloody would, wouldn't you? Watch the skirt parading up and down! A fat lot of enlightenment that would bring.'

'You do not see a woman at the bottom of this case, then?'

Bragg looked round sharply. 'Why should there be?'

Morton smiled. 'The relationship between the sexes seems to give rise to most murders,' he said.

'But Witney was a widower, he was free to do as he liked.'

'Exactly . . . To be free with other men's wives.'

'All right, whose?'

'Except for his daughter and the typewriter, we have not yet encountered any ladies; but he was in his mid-forties and vigorous. We should not dismiss the possibility.'

'Well, you worry about the women. In my book, this case is going to be about money.'

'How uninteresting!'

Bragg scowled. 'That's fine coming from you,' he said sarcastically. 'You've more money than the Bank of England! You have no idea what ordinary people will do to get their hands on a bit.'

He swung into Marlborough Road, his boots hammering on the pavement. Morton let him go, conscious that he had overstepped some unfathomable boundary of propriety in Bragg's mind. But, by the time they had crossed into St James's Street, Bragg's irritation had evaporated.

'What number was it?' he asked.

'Twenty-one, according to the classified telephone directory.'

They sauntered along, peering at the doorways between the shops of fashionable hatters, bootmakers, tailors. This was the heart of London's clubland; articles on display were directed solely towards the rich, and prices were not even mentioned. Morton could see Bragg's mood darkening again. He was relieved when the sergeant stopped and peered at a board inside a hallway.

'This is it, lad,' he said gruffly. 'Lazenby Nugent & Co. Top floor, of course.'

Morton followed him up four flights of stairs, till he paused on the top landing to get his breath.

'I begin to wonder about Mr Lazenby and his practice, sir,' Morton remarked.

'Why is that?'

'Well, the address is most impressive; I could hardly think of one carrying more prestige in the whole of London. But to be marooned on the top floor hardly indicates an eminent connection.'

Bragg's moustache twitched in a smile. 'Why not, lad?' he said smugly. 'You could hardly get any higher!' He pushed on the door and marched into Lazenby's office.

They found themselves in a large room, with shaded electric lamps dangling from the ceiling. Through the window was an endless vista of rooftops. Two men in their early twenties sat at tables near it. From their stiff collars and morning coats it appeared that they were articled clerks. An older man, in a frock-coat, was standing by a desk.

'What can I do for you, gentlemen?' His tone held a note of obsequiousness that irritated Bragg anew.

'Police,' he said brusquely. 'I want a word with Mr Lazenby.'

'I see.' The clerk looked at them gravely. 'May I know the matter, concerning which you wish to see him?'

'No.'

The man hesitated for a moment, then padded off to a door in the back wall. He knocked, went inside briefly, then beckoned them. As they went into the room, a man turned from the window, hand outstretched.

'Edward Lazenby,' he said in a rich baritone. 'How can I be of service?'

He was in his late forties, Morton decided, well-built and athletic. His shaven cheeks were already betraying his heavy beard.

Bragg shook his hand. 'Sergeant Bragg and Constable Morton, of the City Police,' he said. 'I would like to have a chat about one of your clients.'

Lazenby smiled. 'Insofar as it is proper to do so, I would gladly help you. May I know the name of the person you are concerned with?'

'Jethro Witney.'

'Ah.' The smile faded. 'Yes. That is a dreadful business. Do I take it that you are investigating his murder?'

'That's right, sir.'

Lazenby walked slowly back to his desk. 'Please sit down,' he murmured. 'I only learned of his death this morning. I was away over the weekend. It was not until one of my clerks showed me the newspaper report, an hour ago, that I was aware of it.'

'It was a nasty business,' Bragg said sombrely.

'Yes . . . It is such a tragedy for his daughter. Now she has no one.'

'Well, that is not strictly true, sir. She has got relatives down in Dorset.'

'But not close relatives.'

'That is right enough.'

'And, why have you come to me?' Lazenby asked affably.

'Naturally, we have been down to Winchester,' Bragg said. 'We have had a chat with Julia Witney, and poked about a bit – private papers, and so on. What I really want to know about is his will.'

Lazenby frowned. 'Did you not find it?' he asked. 'We do not hold it here, of that I am confident.'

'No. But we found a letter from you, suggesting that he should give the other executor an idea of its contents.'

'That is the advice I normally give, certainly. But, was the will not there also? Jethro was an orderly man, I am surprised that all the papers relating to his testamentary dispositions were not in the same place.'

'I suppose it might turn up, but we had a good look round.'

'I hope so. It is customary to read the provisions of the will after the funeral is over. When is it to be?'

'I understand they are hoping to have it on Wednesday.'

Lazenby turned the pages of his diary. 'There is nothing that cannot be postponed,' he murmured.

'What happens if there isn't one?' Bragg asked.

'A funeral?'

'No, a will.'

Lazenby smiled. 'I thought, for a moment, that you were about to deny to some worthy funeral undertaker the fruits of his profession! As to the will, I see no difficulty.'

'But, if there is no will, how can anybody know what he wanted?'

'Therein, sergeant, lies the benefit of having consulted a solicitor, if you will forgive an advertising puff for my profession! Had he drawn up his will himself, and it could not be found, then the rules of intestacy would have been applied. As it is, I have my office copy of the document. Since, I take it, there is no evidence that he wished to change the provisions of his will, my copy will be acceptable.'

'I see. That is a comfort, anyway. Can you tell me what is in it?'

Lazenby laughed. 'You will have to wait, like everyone else, sergeant! However, for my part I would not object if you were to attend the reading of the will. Then if you have any questions I can answer them to the best of my ability.'

'Would Miss Julia mind?'

'Not for a moment! I know her well enough to assure you of that.'

'It was more than a mere professional relationship you had with Witney, was it?'

' "Mere"? In that context, sergeant, the word must be anathema to any solicitor! Certainly, in the present case, Lazenbys have acted for Witneys for generations. However, I quibble. Please forgive me. I think one might say that between Jethro and myself there was some element of friendship. And in the coming generation the relationship may yet become even closer.'

'How do you mean, sir?'

Lazenby smiled expansively. 'My son and Julia Witney are, shall we say, very close.'

'That's nice,' Bragg said smiling. 'What is his name?'

'Peter.'

'I see. He is the engineer, then.'

Lazenby's smile became quizzical. 'He is a chemical engineer, yes. He is just starting on the lower rungs of his profession, but I think he will do well.'

'Good! It is nice to see young people getting on,' Bragg said warmly. 'Who does he work for?'

'He has set up in practice on his own account. Stratford is hardly the most propitious of areas, but one must start somewhere.'

'Good luck to him, anyway.' Bragg's face became serious. 'Can you tell us anything about Jethro Witney that could be relevant to his death?' he asked.

Lazenby thought for a moment. 'I must confess that I did not know him so intimately,' he said. 'Outside the making of his will, we had not discussed his personal life.'

'Why do you think he bought Shillingfords' estate agency in Lombard Street?'

Lazenby shrugged. 'I presume he thought it a good business opportunity.'

'But he had a perfectly good business in Winchester.'

'And still has, sergeant!'

'That is true enough . . . Tell me, sir. If Julia Witney asked your advice on what she should do with the businesses, what would you tell her?'

'I think you are trying to manoeuvre me into anticipating the reading of the will, sergeant,' Lazenby said with a mischievous smile. 'If I may answer your question in general terms, I have seldom known a woman who was successful in running a business of any size. And that would apply the more particularly, with a business in two widely separated locations.'

After lunching at a pub in the West End, Bragg and Morton went to the City mortuary.

'Your man is over here,' Noakes greeted them, as they went through the door. He was sewing up the abdominal incision, with large untidy stitches. The chest had already been cobbled together. This was no longer a dead man, but some lay figure to display the art of necroscopy.

'Dr Burney has finished, then?' Bragg asked.

'Yes. Well on with a young woman who drank carbolic acid,' Noakes said cheerfully.

'What a disgusting trade you follow!'

'Ah, but you could not do without us . . . Your man is going down to Winchester tonight. There is to be a service in the cathedral, I gather. The body is being collected by the undertaker at four. So if you want a last look . . .'

'No, thank you! Can we go through?'

'Yes. The coroner is with him, but I don't suppose he will mind.'

Bragg tapped on the door of the examination room, and they went in.

'Ah, Bragg! I was wondering where you had got to. I expected you to report to me after the hearing this morning.' Sir Rufus was standing a-straddle the empty fireplace, his hands clamped on the lapels of his frock-coat.

'We went to find out about the will, sir,' Bragg said deferentially.

'Huh! That betokens something approaching desperation on your part.'

'No, sir. We are just being methodical.'

'Methodical! With a dangerous lunatic on the prowl? I will have you know, Bragg, that I do not enjoy having my chambers besieged by clamorous journalists asking impertinent questions.'

'No, sir.'

'Nor, as a senior Queen's Counsel, do I appreciate being hounded through the courts of the Temple by boorish scribblers incredulous of my assertions.'

'It is their job to ask questions, sir.'

Sir Rufus's eyes gleamed in triumph. 'As it is mine to require answers from you, Bragg! It is now three days since the Witney murder. Are you saying that you have no one under suspicion whatever?'

Bragg suppressed his irritation. 'Oh, there are suspects all right, sir; and plenty more to come, I have no doubt. Witney was a widower; off the leash, as you might say. He seems to have moved in two different circles, here and at home in Winchester. It is important that we do not focus on the wrong lot.'

'But, good God, man! You cannot approach a case of this nature at your leisure! If we did but know it, he may be striking down another helpless victim at this very moment!'

'Not in the City, I hope!'

The coroner's eyes narrowed. 'I find your levity singularly distasteful, Bragg,' he said sternly. 'I appointed you as my officer for this case, not only because of the coincidence of your presence at the scene, but because I have found you effective and reliable in the past. Do not give me cause to revise my good opinion of you!'

'No, sir,' Bragg said, abashed. 'But I do not think you need to worry about other murders. In my book, this was no random killing.'

'Huh! I cannot fend off the press with oracular pronouncements. I need facts, man; for my own satisfaction, at the very least.'

'Yes, sir.' Bragg fumbled in his pocket. As he withdrew his hand, a matchbox popped out and skidded across the floor. Burney watched its progress, then ignored it. Sir Rufus's eyes flickered towards it. 'You have dropped your matches,' he said accusingly.

'Ah, yes.' A crestfallen Bragg stooped to retrieve them, his glare daring Morton to grin.

'Well, man?' the coroner said truculently. 'I take it that you have not been wholly inactive these past three days! Or has the weekend of a policeman suddenly become sacrosanct?'

'As I was saying, sir, this was not an impulse killing. The murderer came prepared with the necessary weapons.'

'Mere chop-logic, Bragg!' the coroner interrupted scornfully. 'A man furnished with the means of murder need not have a particular individual in mind.'

'No, sir. But neither does a random killer go into an empty office and through to the room at the back to find a victim. For my money, Witney was known to his killer. More than that, he or she knew Witney was likely to be alone.'

'Hmn . . .' Sir Rufus glared at Bragg, as if he resented his worst fears being discounted. 'Then, who are the suspects?' he demanded.

'Everyone who was close to him, it seems; from his clerk in London to his own daughter.'

'Good God, Bragg! You cannot be serious!'

'Indeed I am, sir. That is why we have to tread carefully.'

Sir Rufus looked at him suspiciously. 'I wish that I could believe in your integrity as readily as I acknowledge your experience,' he said. 'But mark this: the inquest will be reopened in seven days. By then, I want the identity of the murderer to have been established.'

'I see.' Bragg looked duly solemn. 'Would a verdict of "person or persons unknown" not be enough?' he asked.

'Pah! The refuge of the craven and inept. No, Bragg I will have nothing less than a name!' The coroner picked up his top hat from the bench, and marched out.

'So there you are, sergeant,' Burney observed with a twinkle.

'Yes . . . I suppose you have nothing fresh for me?'

'No, sergeant. The subject was perfectly healthy. There was a certain degeneration of the liver, but no more than I would expect in a person of his age and background.'

'And the injuries that killed him?'

'I really have nothing to add. He was first stunned, then his throat was cut. It was as brutal as that.'

'And as methodical.'

'Yes.'

'Hmn . . . That was a word used by somebody to describe Witney, and look where it got him.'

Bragg leaned back in the corner of the railway compartment next morning, and puffed at his pipe for solace. This was an untidy case, seeming to have no boundaries to it. The trouble was that modern life was too fluid, people were next to rootless. It was not just that somebody could work in London, yet live seventy miles away. As much, it was a question of attitudes. Fifty years ago the top layer of City men would have houses in Finsbury Circus, or Islington – within the City, or just over the boundary. Their clerks would have lived in poorer areas, certainly, but cheek by jowl with their employers. Everything meshed together. Nowadays, bosses and workers converged on the City from every point of the compass. Anybody with aspirations – even as illusory as Syme's – wanted to live out of town; relished travelling for hours every day as a symbol of their success. How could he be expected to see a coherent pattern, in such a situation?

'You seem restless, sir,' Morton said cheerfully.

'Are you surprised?'

'I suppose that we are faced with a superfluity of suspects. However, I am sure that your usual systematic approach will unravel the most tangled of webs.'

Bragg looked at him suspiciously. 'You are not taking the piss, I hope, lad,' he growled.

'By no means!' Morton protested. 'The murderer must be someone with a motive, the means of killing and the opportunity. It ought to be a mere matter of elimination.'

'If it is as easy as all that, I might as well take a couple of weeks' leave, and let you tidy it up.'

Morton laughed. 'I fear you would come back to a greater tangle than you left behind! My remarks, of course, assumed the un-remitting application of your innate talent and unparalleled ex-perience.'

Despite Morton's grin, the words warmed him. Bragg felt a lifting of the spirit. Murder was no light matter; the motive had to be strong. And this killing had not been done on the spur of the moment. No, it had to be someone close; the pattern would emerge.

'Did you look at the Winchester branch books last night?' he asked.

'Indeed I did,' Morton said ruefully. 'They were kept on the same basis as those of the Lombard Street branch, as one would expect. But, not having your appetite for business records, I found them somewhat dull and less than enlightening. I am fairly confident that they contain nothing that would precipitate murder, but you may like to have a quick look yourself.'

'Right.' Bragg got to his feet, as the train slid into Stratford station. 'I suppose our friend Peter Lazenby belongs to the Winchester end, if anywhere. Let's see what he has to say for himself.'

They made their way to a large office building, near the town hall. Bragg studied the list of tenants in the entrance hall.

'The top floor again,' he said irritably. 'And I don't suppose there is a lift.'

They toiled up flight after flight of stairs, leaving the roofs of the houses far below them. At last they reached a narrow landing, lit by a skylight.

'Ah, the summit of Mont Blanc,' Morton said chirpily. 'Here is a list of the occupants . . . Yes. P. Lazenby & Co. are number seven oh three.'

'Why the hell does anyone want to be so high up, anyway?' Bragg said breathlessly.

'The height of success! . . . Perhaps it is an overweening sense of pride that afflicts all Lazenbys.'

Bragg turned, disgruntled, and stomped off down the corridor. He rapped on a door and pushed inside.

'Mr Lazenby?' he asked genially.

A young man was sitting at an architect's drawing-board, by the window.

'Yes.' He stood up, stretching cramped limbs. He had a marked resemblance to his father: dark and well built, with an open, appealing face.

'And where is the company?'

Lazenby was momentarily puzzled, then he smiled. 'Not all my clients come to see me here, and the business name may influence some people. To that extent you have the advantage over both me and them.'

'We are not clients,' Bragg said, showing his warrant-card. 'We thought you might be able to help us concerning the murder of Jethro Witney.'

A wooden look came over his face. 'Ah,' he said.

'Your father told you that we had been to see him?'

'No. I did not learn of his death from my father.'

'Who, then?'

'I prefer not to say.'

Bragg strode across, towering over him like an oak tree over a sapling. 'Fancy a night or two in the cells, do you?' he growled. 'Or is it a short drop and some quicklime we should be looking for?'

Lazenby's face blanched. 'I . . . I had nothing to do with it!' he cried.

Bragg's voice softened. 'I'm sure that is right, sir,' he said. 'But we know you are close to Julia Witney. She is upset, as you might imagine; we thought you might take some of the strain off her, by talking to us.'

Lazenby looked uncertainly at the policemen and remained silent.

'Was it her who let you know about it?'

'Yes.'

'How?'

'I found a telegraph waiting for me when I got home.'

'And where is home?'

'I have rooms in Great Swan Alley.'

'That is in the City, isn't it?'

'Yes, off Moorgate.'

'Not far from her father's office.'

Lazenby dropped his gaze. 'I presume so; I have never been there.'

'But you know where Lombard Street is?' Bragg said harshly.

'Yes, of course.'

'Then, there's not much bloody presuming needed, is there?'

'No.' Lazenby subsided on to the edge of a chair.

'So, why are you here?' Bragg demanded.

Lazenby looked blank. 'I do not understand,' he said.

'Why, your lady-love telegraphs you to say her father's been murdered, she's got no mother – an orphan now – living with a cook, in a house you could quarter a bloody regiment in, and you don't rush to be with her? I should think she'll change her mind about you!'

'It is not at all like that!' Lazenby said, with a flash of spirit. 'I admire Miss Witney greatly, I would hope that some day she might become my wife, but she is not my lady-love in the pejorative sense you imply. And, much as I would wish to be at her side, it would be folly. Were I even to spend an hour alone with her, gossip would start. Winchester is not London; it is really no more than a country town.'

'So, you'd happily shaft her, if she came up here?'

Lazenby visibly took hold of his anger. 'Neither Julia nor I have done anything to reproach ourselves with, sergeant,' he said. 'And I will not allow myself to be provoked by you.'

Bragg towered over him in silence for some moments, then turned away.

'Is it a good business?' he asked casually, perching on the edge of a desk.

'It shows prospects,' Lazenby said curtly.

'Ah, yes . . . Prospects. That was the trouble, I suppose.'

'I do not follow.'

'Well, mere prospects wouldn't impress a man like Jethro Witney. He wanted substance, every time. No wonder you had to slink into the house when his back was turned. If he had caught you with his daughter, there'd have been hell to pay!'

Lazenby looked up angrily. 'I have never been inside that house!' he shouted. 'Never!'

'Ah, no. Of course, you could have it off up St Catherine's Hill; there was no need to, was there?'

'You impugn the honour of a pure and gentle young lady,' Lazenby said tautly. 'But I am glad to note that you accept my assertion.'

'What was that?'

'I have never been inside the Winchester house.'

Bragg's tone became casual. 'We knew that all along.' He stood up and walked over to the drawing-board. 'Looks complicated,' he said. 'What is it?'

Lazenby gazed at him in bewilderment. 'It is a plan for removing sulphur products from crude oil,' he said.

'Hmn. Does that kind of thing pay well?'

'It is an experimental process. Should it be successful, it could be remunerative.'

'Were you waiting for that, before asking Jethro Witney if you could marry his daughter?' Bragg asked brusquely.

'Sergeant, Julia is twenty-one years old, and I am twenty-five. There is plenty of time for both of us.'

Bragg stared at him. 'You sound a bloodless bugger,' he said contemptuously. 'Was Jethro's money so important to you?'

'Important?' Lazenby looked confused.

'How many years were you going to play Jack and Jill? Hand in hand down Brook Street, a quick fumble in an alley, then back again till next month . . . Did her father know you called on her?'

Lazenby dropped his head. 'Probably not.'

'If he had he'd have kicked your arse, wouldn't he? . . . Wouldn't he?!'

'No doubt he would have disapproved.'

'I'm sure he would have disapproved,' Bragg mimicked him savagely. 'But you need not worry now. He's out of the way, isn't he? Everything is plain sailing now. Once the will is proved, and Little Miss Muffet has the money, you will be tickling her tuffet, all right.'

Lazenby gazed at Bragg in stupefaction. He did not reply. Bragg looked at the drawing-board for some moments, then: 'Where were you between one and two o'clock on Friday, sir?' he asked courteously.

'I was lunching in The Bell public house, on the corner.'

'I see. Were you on your own?'

His brow wrinkled in thought. 'I think that only Jacko and I were there on Friday.'

'Jacko?'

'He was introduced to me as such.'

'Sounds like a lot of school kids! Do you not know his proper name?'

'No, sergeant. He is the merest acquaintance.'

'Is he a regular too?'

'Not in the sense of going every day, as I do. He is there once, or sometimes twice, in most weeks.'

'Commercial traveller, is he?'

'Perhaps.'

'If you find him, it would be in your interest to let me know . . . Are you going to the funeral?'

71

'I . . . I do not yet know when it is to be.'

'Oh, I can help you there,' Bragg said amiably. 'It is on Wednesday. I expect when you get back to Great Swan Alley you will find a telegraph waiting for you.'

'Perhaps.'

'Well, I look forward to seeing you on Wednesday.' Bragg put on his bowler and clumped out of the room.

That lunchtime Morton ate at The Bell in Stratford High Street. Although he was there from twelve o'clock until two, Peter Lazenby did not appear. When the customers had dwindled to a handful, he went to see the landlord. He was a paunchy, affable man, who readily acknowleged that Lazenby was a regular. So much so, that he could not say for certain whether he had been in the previous Friday or not. As for Jacko, he did not know anyone of that name; but he could have been there. Lacking a description, Morton was baulked. He wandered down to the Metropolitan police station. The duty-sergeant looked dubiously at his warrant-card.

'What is it about, then?' he asked.

'The murder in Lombard Street.'

A glimmer of interest crossed the stony face. 'I saw something about it in the *Police Gazette*,' he said. 'Nearly cut his head off, didn't they?'

'That is the case.'

'So, what do the Swell Mob want of us?'

'One of the suspects, Peter Lazenby, says he lunched at The Bell. If that is so, it could put him out of the reckoning, particularly as the landlord acknowledges him as a regular customer. Lazenby says that a man called Jacko was there also, and could vouch for him. The problem is that no one at the pub recognizes the name.'

'Jacko, you mean?'

'Yes. We are told that he goes there regularly but intermittently. The assumption is that he might be a commercial traveller.'

'Your assumption?'

'No, Lazenby's. Obviously we cannot put a detective in The Bell every lunchtime until he appears. Could you ask the beat constable to pop in, from time to time, to remind the landlord that we want to see Jacko.'

The desk-sergeant pursed his lips. 'I suppose we could,' he said grudgingly. 'All right, leave it with me.'

Morton took a train back to Liverpool Street station, then walked to the offices of the *City Press* in Aldersgate. After a brief chat with the doorman he made his way to the editor's room.

Tranter was seated at his desk, poring over a pile of galley proofs. On every surface around him were scattered reference books and papers. He looked up.

'Ah, Constable Morton! I trust that you have not come in a professional capacity,' he said lightly. 'Though I have little enough time for socializing at the moment.'

Morton smiled. 'My business will be quickly dealt with, sir . . . You recall the Lombard Street murder last week?'

Tranter gave a grimace. 'Will I ever forget it? You would be surprised, Mr Morton, at the number of our readers who were disappointed at our Saturday edition; who felt that we should have wallowed in the tragedy, as if we were no more than a kind of superior *Reynold's News*. I had to tell them roundly that, as we publish only twice a week, even the most sensational of murders has to give place to the duller, but undoubtedly more important, news of trade and economic matters. But I fear we shall lose some readers over it.'

'I am sure that they will come back,' Morton said encouragingly. 'My present mission is, however, obliquely concerned with the same topic.'

'Obliquely?' Tranter looked at him suspiciously. 'I trust that you will not request the inclusion in tomorrow's edition of some . . . some appeal or other, relating to it. That would present a considerable difficulty for me, as you can imagine.'

'Nothing like that,' Morton assured him. 'Our problem is that the victim lived in Winchester. So it is at least possible that his murder was generated by events in that city. We have been down there, and found the police less than co-operative. Now we must find an indirect way of gleaning information about his life there.'

'I understand.'

'You may not be aware of it, sir, but Miss Marsden's family originated from Winchester. Indeed, I gather that she still has relatives in the area.'

'Ah, so there is a conspiracy against me!' Tranter said accusingly.

'I wondered why Miss Marsden should have suggested, yesterday, that she should do an occasional series on cathedrals within a day's journey of London.'

Morton smiled. 'And were you attracted to the idea, sir?'

'Yes . . . yes I was. Indeed, I authorized her to prepare an initial article, to see how our readers react. You will not be surprised, I imagine, to hear that the subject is to be Winchester cathedral.'

'She will be in no danger,' Morton assured him. 'We merely want her to glean information on local matters from her relatives. It is an area that we could never satisfactorily explore ourselves.'

Tranter frowned. 'Yes, yes. I understand that. But I do not enjoy being manipulated, Mr Morton.'

'I assure you, sir, I regret that implication. Clearly, in future, we shall only need to ask . . .'

'I would not go so far, constable,' Tranter said hastily. 'You have my consent on this occasion only.'

'Very good, sir. May I inform Miss Marsden?'

'Yes . . . And tell her, also, that I must have her copy for tomorrow's edition within the hour.'

4

Bragg and Morton arrived in Winchester at ten o'clock on the morning of the funeral. Bragg decided not to go to Brook Street until after the service. He went himself to the National Provincial Bank, while Morton was sent to return the business books. Despite the impending funeral, Morton's spirits were high. They had travelled down with Catherine Marsden, which would be a delight in any circumstances. Furthermore, Bragg had been glum and withdrawn; so they had been able to indulge in their usual badinage without constraint. No doubt the afternoon's obsequies would overshadow the return journey, but already it was a day to remember. He arrived at the Witney office and pushed open the door. The typewriter was sitting at her desk knitting.

'I have brought back the business books,' he announced. 'Is Mr Branksome in?'

'No.' Her needles clicked their way to the end of a row. 'He was not in yesterday either,' she said reproachfully.

'Where did he go to?'

'I don't know. He has done a moonlight flit, if you ask me!'

'Seriously? You mean that he has gone away?'

'He might just be sick, but I doubt it. When he did not arrive this morning, either, I had a look in his desk. He has taken all his belongings – everything.'

'Everything?'

She jerked her head towards a wooden press in the corner. 'There is a pair of old carpet slippers that he used to put on when he came back with his boots wet through. That is all – and you wouldn't be seen dead in them, I'm sure.' She smiled insinuatingly.

'When did you see him last?'

'On Monday. He seemed all right then – full of life, almost excited.'

'I see.' Morton pulled up a chair to her desk.

'I presume that there was no ill will between Mr Witney and him,' he said lightly.

'No! The previous Saturday they had been laughing and joking together . . . They got on perfectly well.'

'Where was Mr Branksome last Friday?'

Her face clouded. 'The day he . . . Mr Witney was . . . ?'

'Yes.'

'I don't know. He was away all day till just after four o'clock. I remember because I had already washed up my own teacup; then I had to make some for him.'

'Did he say anything about where he had been?'

'No. But he was edgy, I remember that.'

Morton smiled. 'Do you think he was sweet on Witney's daughter?' he asked.

'Miss Julia?' A shocked look spread over her face. 'Why? What have you heard?'

'Nothing. I am merely speculating.'

'Well, don't go putting things like that about!' she exclaimed. 'I have never heard anything such . . . and it's not likely, is it?'

'Probably not.' Morton got to his feet. 'Well, I will leave these valuable records in your hands. Be sure to take care of them . . . Oh, Mr Branksome said that he lodges in Monks Road. What number is it?'

75

'Eleven.'

'Good! I may pop in and see him.'

Once outside, Morton sought directions from a policeman and found that Monks Road was on the northern fringe of the town, with open country beyond it. He found the house, and knocked loudly. He waited for some minutes, then heard footsteps from within. A bar was drawn, a lock turned and the door opened a crack.

'Hello!' Morton called cordially. 'Is Mr Branksome in?'

'No.' The door remained almost closed. Morton put his warrant-card to the gap. 'Police,' he said. 'May I come in?'

'Are you sure?' the voice asked suspiciously.

Morton laughed. 'Come on, Mrs Treadwell! Go and get your spectacles, then you will be able to see for yourself!'

There was a grunt, the rattle of a chain and the door opened hesitantly. Mrs Treadwell was in her early sixties, her back stooped, her face wrinkled. 'What is it you want?' she asked sharply.

'We understand from his office that Mr Branksome did not go there, either yesterday or today. They wonder if some mishap has befallen him.'

'Mishap?' she echoed. 'He up and went, didn't he? I goes to our Mildred's for a cup of tea yesterday, and when I gets back, he's gone!'

'Did he take his belongings with him?'

'Every stitch! And never a word to me. I don't know if he's gone for good, or what. I can't keep his room for ever . . . He left me thirty shillings on the wash-stand. I don't know what to make of it.'

'Has he cheated you of your rent?' Morton asked.

'No. He's beforehand now. He's paid up to the end of the month . . . and he's left his latchkey. What do you think I should do?'

'It certainly seems as if he has gone for good and all. Do you know where he comes from? Where his family lives?'

'No. From the Midlands somewhere, is my guess.'

'Have you ever forwarded letters for him, when he went on holiday and so forth?'

'No! He was never one for getting letters.'

'What about last Friday?'

'He didn't get one then . . . I should think it would be the end of April since he had a letter.'

76

Morton smiled. 'I see . . . It appears that he did not go to the office on that day. Have you any idea where he was?'

'It was just the same as any other day, as far as I can remember. He had his breakfast as usual, then went off.'

'At what time?'

'Half past eight. And he was back again at half past six for his supper.'

'Just as usual?'

'Yes . . . So what should I do?'

Morton considered. 'If you want to be very meticulous, Mrs Treadwell, you could hold the room for him until the end of the month and then re-let it. But I hardly think he is going to return, do you?'

Since there was still time in hand before he was due to meet Bragg, Morton strolled to the cathedral. A florist's trap was drawn up by the west door, filled with sprays of white and mauve flowers. He went inside. Despite the brightness of the day, it struck gloomy and chill; a premonition of the solemn ceremony that would shortly take place within it. As he walked down the long nave, girls bustled by with armfuls of flowers. An altar had been set at the east end of the nave, in front of the choir screen. It was dressed in purple and white. Drifts of mauve and white flowers decorated the steps on either side, and wreaths in the same colours had been wired to the great pillars. Suddenly there was a torrent of sound from the organ, that ceased and was repeated with different stops. Perhaps 'gloomy' was not the right word. There was a purposeful excitement in the air. This was to be a great civic and ecclesiastical occasion, something to look back on with pride. The organist was now practising a Bach fugue, the notes mingling in a transcendent tapestry of sound. Morton began to feel that he was intruding; an interloper in the dressing-room, before the grand performance. He wandered back down the soaring nave and into the sunlight.

He found Bragg already in the bar of the Coach and Horses. He was puffing thoughtfully at his pipe, a half-empty glass in front of him.

'How did you get on, lad?' Bragg greeted him. 'I thought you were never coming.'

'Branksome has vanished. He cleared his things from his lodgings yesterday afternoon, and went.'

'Did he now?'

'It cannot have been done on the spur of the moment because he took away his personal belongings from the office, on Monday evening.'

'Well, well! I wonder what he did on Tuesday morning.'

'Of more import is his whereabouts last Friday. He was not in the office on that day either.'

'The day Witney was murdered? That's interesting.'

'The more so as his landlady says he left in the morning at the usual time, and got back in the evening at the usual time.'

'Hmn . . . Do you reckon, lad, that he is in league with Julia, went up to the City with her, and knocked off her old dad?'

Morton wrinkled his nose. 'It is possible, I suppose; but when I suggested a liaison between them, the typewriter greeted it with scorn.'

'If they did do it together, why would Branksome run?' Bragg mused. 'It would just excite suspicion . . . unless you are right, lad.'

'That would indeed be an event!'

'As you said, she could have got Branksome to kill her father, then told him she was going to marry Lazenby! He would hardly want to hang around then.'

'Perhaps we should ask the Winchester police to pick him up, should he ever return.'

'Yes, do that, will you lad? . . . I cannot say that I have had much of a morning. The National Provincial is where the Winchester business banks. A nice healthy balance on his personal account, too, but no more than to promote confidence. He had a deposit box, but nothing much in it. There was some nice jewellery; diamonds and emeralds, by the look of it. Valuable I expect. No doubt Julia will enjoy wearing it, if she doesn't get a hemp collar instead. There were also the deeds of that block of houses in Brook Street. Not only their own but the other three as well. Queerest of all, there was a bundle of letters – written by his wife to him when they were courting. I never thought of him as a sentimental chap. Not that he had them on his bedside table . . . but most men in his position would have burnt them long ago.'

Catherine's cousin, Elizabeth Knighton, met her at the station, and took her on a tour of the shops. They spent a pleasurable morning discussing fashion, recalling childhood adventures, remembering mutual acquaintances. It was almost one o'clock before they arrived at the family house. Catherine inspected it with a proprietorial air. Her roots were undeniably here. It was this rambling creeper-clad mansion that the young William Marsden had come to sketch for its proud owner. Here he had fallen in love with the elder daughter of the house. Here they had lived briefly after their marriage; here her own life had been conceived. The house was in good hands, she decided; well-kept, the gardens carefully groomed. The marriage of Aunt Phoebe to George Knighton had brought new pride and vigour to the old place.

'Catherine!' Her aunt was extending welcoming arms. 'You look lovely! How is everyone? Have you had a good morning?'

Catherine embraced her. 'It is marvellous to be back again,' she said, 'even if the immediate occasion is somewhat lugubrious.'

'Yes . . . I have had luncheon set in the garden. George will be staying in town, so it will be just the three of us. Come along!'

They settled under the trees, to a meal of poached salmon with salad, followed by a fresh fruit compote.

'Why did you decide to come to this particular funeral?' Phoebe asked, as they waited for the iced coffee to be brought. 'I know Jethro Witney was connected with the City of London but I did not think that he was so important.'

'To tell the truth, aunt, I am here as a police spy,' Catherine said with a smile.

'Goodness! That sounds very French Revolutionary . . . Do you enjoy the work?'

Catherine laughed. 'You sound just like Mamma!' she said.

'She has an admirer who is a constable,' Elizabeth broke in. 'I saw him at the station; he is very handsome.'

'A constable . . . ?' Phoebe echoed, frowning at her daughter.

'Not an ordinary one! Everyone expects that he will inherit the family estates, in Kent, and become Sir James Morton.'

'Ah, I believe Harriet has mentioned the name, though she did not seem particularly pleased with the connection.' She turned to Catherine. 'Do you love him?' she asked.

Catherine cocked her head. 'Perhaps,' she said.

'Will you marry him?'

'Probably not. You must remember, aunt, that I am first and foremost a journalist!'

'But you just said that you were a police spy!'

'Life is a little complicated,' Catherine said with a smile. 'Perhaps a police irregular might have been a better description.'

'I would hardly think that "irregular" could ever be "better",' Phoebe said severely.

Catherine laughed. 'Well, today I shall be able to combine both activities. I hope to gather material for an article on Winchester cathedral. I shall try to persuade Londoners that there are impressive buildings to be seen outside the confines of the capital.'

'Good! It is time that the importance of Winchester was more widely recognized. But what of your spying role?'

'In that regard, I am sure that you can be of help, aunt. I do not know what the belief is down here, as to the manner of Witney's death. But I understand that he was murdered in a singularly brutal way.'

Phoebe leaned forward. 'How?' she asked conspiratorially.

'I do not know. James refused to tell me. However, it is possible that he was killed by someone from Winchester, or because of circumstances arising here. Has he been involved in any public or private scandal to your knowledge?'

Her aunt pursed her lips. 'Well,' she said thoughtfully, 'he was prominent in that business over the churchyard.'

'Which church was that?'

'The cathedral. It is properly a church, you know, so the grounds are its churchyard. And, in centuries past, people were buried there – until very recent times, in fact . . . The trouble goes back ten years, I suppose.'

'What trouble?'

'It was all Dean Kitchin's fault – or Gladstone's for nominating him as Dean. Your uncle says that he should have stayed at Oxford, as a historian; he would have done less damage there.'

'So Uncle George does not approve of the Dean either?'

'Perhaps that is too strong a phrase, but he was involved in advising some people affected by the works.'

'What works?'

'Well, hardly had Dean Kitchin taken up his office than he began to have trenches dug across part of the churchyard. Originally it was a monastic foundation – Benedictine, I think – and he was hoping to discover the remains of the ancient buildings.'

'Was he successful?' Catherine asked.

Phoebe wrinkled her nose. 'All too successful; and therein lay the seed of the trouble. He set up a committee to be responsible for the churchyard. And, without more ado, they proposed to remove a great number of gravestones . . . Not the bodies in the graves, you understand, but the stones marking them.'

'I see . . . That could be distressing to the families concerned. Presumably, in time, they would no longer be able to identify the spot where their ancestors were buried.'

'Indeed. And it was done very insensitively. They placed the onus on anyone with relatives in the churchyard, to find out if they were affected and lodge an objection. Jethro Witney was prominent on the churchyard committee and he attempted to ride roughshod over the protestors. There was a great outcry, with public meetings at the Russian Gun and in the market-place. As I said, George was consulted by several of the families affected; he got the cathedral authorities at least to change their approach.'

'Did they withdraw their proposals?'

'By no means! They consented to inform everyone with graves in the affected area, so that they could have the opportunity of objecting. But the end result was just the same; the gravestones were removed willy-nilly . . . I must confess that the lawns enhance the appearance of the cathedral, but the whole matter was handled deplorably. People are still bitter about it.'

'Bitter enough to want to kill Jethro Witney over it?' Catherine asked.

Phoebe raised her eyebrows. 'I would hardly think so. In very few cases were the graves which were obliterated, of recent date.'

'Does that mean it would be possible to identify likely families from the cathedral records?'

'I suppose so . . . This is a particularly ghoulish topic of conversation for a summer's afternoon! However, it cannot be escaped, I suppose. Soon Elizabeth and I will have to change into something suitably sombre.'

'Are you coming?' Catherine asked delightedly.

'Of course! We shall meet your uncle at the west door. It will be quite an occasion, I assure you.'

Since attendance at the funeral was part of the investigation into Witney's death, Bragg decided that their purpose would be best served by splitting up. He would be going to the gathering at the house, after the interment, so he would sit near the mourners. Catherine Marsden would be with her relations, and would be able to observe another part of the congregation. So Morton was instructed to wait until she had taken her place, then find a suitable vantage point for himself. For a time he stood outside, by the west door, watching the stream of people entering the cathedral. There was an excited air about many; no grief, barely even reverence. For them it was more a public spectacle than a solemn rite. Through the open door Morton could hear the elegiac diapason of the organ, reaching out to the passing masses, proclaiming their ultimate fate. He saw Catherine approaching, with her relatives. The other young woman saw him and nudged her mother, who gazed vacantly at him much as Mrs Marsden would have done. Then they passed within. Catherine refrained from acknowledging him. She had remembered her role.

He followed them inside. Here the tolling of the great bell was muffled, its slow booming at odds with the beat of the organ. He walked down the nave. The crowd assembled was diminished by its vastness; seeming to huddle at the foot of the choir screen, suppliants from the wrath of the eternal. Indeed, the cathedral authorities seemed to have gone out of their way to increase the isolation of the bereaved. On either side of the central aisle, the third and fourth rows of seats had been closed off. In front of the gap would be the mourners; those behind had been turned into mere spectators. Catherine's party took their places on the south of the aisle, so Morton went beyond them to a seat on the north side. He knelt for a moment, unable to find an appropriate prayer, then sat and looked around him. People had put on their solemn faces, certainly, but no one looked really sad. For most, it was a superior kind of peep-show. Which, of all these people, would have hated Witney enough to murder him? Was the conventional wisdom right, that murderers were drawn to their victim's obsequies?

There was a reverential shuffling at the west end of the cathedral. Morton turned and could see the choir assembling, the great silver cross held aloft as an assurance of eternal life. The organ stopped in mid-phrase, the bell ceased to toll. The choir processed in silence to the middle of the nave; then the coffin was borne in by a black-coated phalanx, and a straggle of mourners formed up behind. The organ started to play softly, broken half-phrases, questioning notes on a reed stop. The choir began to sing. *Lacrimosa dies illa*. The procession moved forward, bringing Witney to his final account. The music soared upwards, resonating into the far depths of the cathedral. Tears pricked Morton's eyes, more from Mozart's music than the inevitable fate of all mankind. *Judicandus homo reus*. The full tone proud, confident; demanding access to eternal life. The procession was opposite Morton now, the great black coffin surmounted by a single wreath of flowers. *Pie Jesu Domine*. The mourners sidled into their seats; the coffin was borne alone, after the choir, and reverently lowered on to trestles. *Dona eius requiem. Amen*. The files of the choir divided, and passed beyond the screen to their stalls. The music reverberated through the pillars and died away in the fan vaulting.

The congregation knelt. A cleric in alb and chasuble – presumably the Dean – intoned some prayers, and Morton's thoughts drifted impiously to the reason for his presence there. The presumption was that someone in this magnificent building had caused Witney's death; was even now gloating over his success, revelling in his immunity from detection. He looked around him. Most heads were reverently bowed. Some glanced about them, or gazed fixedly into the distance. No one looked triumphant, no one visibly exulted. Was it ever a reasonable expectation?

They stood, and the choir began to sing the ninetieth psalm. The congregation joined in haltingly. *Teach us to number our days*. Morton looked across at Julia. He could see only the side of her head; it was slightly bowed and motionless. A middle-aged woman next to her was gripping her arm, whispering into her ear. *Comfort us again now, after the time that thou hast plagued us*.

As the Gloria ended, a less exalted cleric read a passage from the Bible. Morton covertly surveyed the congregation. Most of them had become bored and were openly looking about them. On such an occasion it was almost as important to see as to be seen. Perhaps few believed the promise of eternal life held out, not just to Jethro Witney but to anyone who subscribed to the necessary tenets. The

83

lesson ended, the reader returned to his seat. There was a pause, then two men and two women came from behind the choir screen and ranged themselves in front of the altar. There was a murmur of interest from the congregation as the organ began to play. A warm contralto voice flowed through the cathedral; *Benedictus qui venit in nomine Domini.* As the soprano, then the bass and tenor joined in, there was a disturbance at the rear of the congregation. Someone shouted in protest, there was a noisy clattering of feet and some twenty people stamped ostentatiously out. Morton wished that he had been further back. Placed as he was, he had no chance of identifying them. But at least it was an indication that not all of the congregation mourned Witney's passing. No doubt the verger of the cathedral would be able to give the names of some of them, if Bragg thought it worthwhile. Now the choir had joined in, their voices ringing in triumph: *Osanna in excelsis.* Julia seemed to be beyond the comfort even of Mozart. Her shoulders sagged, her head drooped; but never once had Morton seen her dab at her eyes.

As the final exultant chord echoed down the nave, the Dean went up into the pulpit. He preached a sermon of fulsome eulogy and doubtful doctrine; one would almost think that Witney had been a candidate for canonization, not murder. As he finished, the undertaker's men filed slowly to the coffin and lifted it on to their shoulders. The organ began the Dead March from *Saul*, and Witney started his final journey.

The coffin was borne to an ornate black hearse, its top covered with wreaths of flowers. Its pair of jet-black horses were fidgeting, shaking the black plumes on their heads. Behind it were two carriages, their horses similarly caparisoned. The women among the family mourners were handed up, and the cortège set off for the cemetery. The men walked behind, hat in hand, Bragg falling in at the rear. To Morton his ragged moustache looked infinitely lugubrious. He watched as the citizens of Winchester joined the procession – Catherine and her relations among them – then he took up station behind. Everyone preserved a respectful silence. Traffic came to a standstill, passers-by stood heads bowed. As they left the centre of the city there were crowds gathered at street corners; soberly dressed, even though they had not been to the service. The onlookers gazed with awe and apprehension. Death was ever-present; could strike down any one of them without warning.

Memento mori. Morbid as it was, this was certainly a city occasion.

The cortège turned through the gates of the cemetery, down an avenue flanked by effigies of weeping angels and broken columns. When it stopped there was such a press of mourners that Morton could not get near the grave. Instead he strolled back and took up a position by the gate, where he would be able to observe everyone leaving. It seemed only moments before he could see the empty hearse approaching, then the carriages. He caught a glimpse of Julia Witney, drawn but composed; then they were gone. The pedestrians walked after them, their gloom lightening. Snatches of conversation could be heard – a woman complaining that her shoes were too tight. Bragg passed without acknowledging him, on his way to the funeral meats. The crowd thinned. Morton could see Catherine and her relations; they seemed to be hanging back, discussing something. As they passed, she caught a glimpse of him and beckoned. He joined them and was duly introduced.

'There is something which I feel you should know immediately, James,' she said. 'It may be important. We were standing near the foot of the grave and I distinctly heard a man near me say "Good riddance to bad rubbish".'

Morton smiled. 'That sounds very infantile,' he said.

'Perhaps. But he was the instigator of the disturbance in the service, when those people walked out. Uncle George says that he is William Rossiter, an implacable enemy of Jethro Witney.'

'Indeed!' He turned to Knighton. 'Did he hate him enough to kill him?' he asked.

Knighton raised an eyebrow. 'Who can tell?' he said. 'He certainly made no bones about his dislike of the man, and one might say that he had substantial grounds for it.'

'What grounds?'

Knighton considered for a moment. 'I do not think that I shall be breaching professional etiquette, after all this time,' he said. 'Some ten years ago, the cathedral authorities proposed to clear the gravestones from large areas of the churchyard. There was a great uproar, but the measure was pushed through – using Jethro Witney as their instrument. Much of the public feeling was, of course, generated by a natural resistance to change. But William Rossiter, and his brother Frederick, were among a handful of people who had real cause for complaint. They owned a recent grave in the affected area, where an infant only was buried. It was their intention that their remains should lie there also, in the shadow of the cathedral. That is now denied to them; and I am bound to say that they regard Witney as the instigator of the plot which defrauded them of that right.'

'Defrauded them?' Morton asked.

'It is scarcely too strong a word. After all, they had paid a not inconsiderable sum for a plot which would hold three coffins. They received no recompense for the fact that their remaining rights were sequestered.'

'But that is not all,' Catherine prompted.

'No. There is the matter of the cathedral music. We are fortunate to have as our organist and choirmaster a very talented musician called Dr Arnold. It is a strange fact, in the circumstances, but he was a pupil of Charles Wesley.'

'Strange?'

'Arnold's musical taste inclines to the florid, the intricate. When he was at Oxford, he became involved with Newman and the Oxford Movement. Dean Bramson was here when Arnold first came, and he kept Arnold's Anglo-Catholic inclinations in check. But once George Kitchin was appointed to the deanery, he was given full rein. He transformed the musical life of the cathedral, certainly; but nowadays it is scarcely distinguishable from Notre Dame in Paris, or St Peter's in Rome.'

'So it was the Mozart that offended the protesters?'

'Yes – or perhaps more, that it was sung in the original Latin. Most people here would regard that as a studied insult, even a desecration of the cathedral.'

'Was that done because Witney was of the Anglo-Catholic persuasion?' Morton asked.

'I would not so describe him. He was musical, certainly, and – if it is not irreverent to say so – he would have enjoyed his funeral . . . He was the kind of man who constantly seeks the limelight. That is not easily achieved by quietly supporting the status quo . . . But I suppose that, in his turn, he was used by the Dean.'

'Why? Is the Dean Anglo-Catholic?'

Knighton pondered. 'No, not doctrinally. One might almost say that the mainspring of his religious faith is cultural rather than theological. He has a lively sense of the dramatic. When he came here the life of the cathedral was little better than that of a large parish church. He has worked relentlessly to make it different. Almost inevitably, that has meant introducing rituals which many of the congregation consider papistical.'

'That was what Rossiter and the others were shouting,' Catherine said. ' "Papists! Papists!" '

'Do you think, sir, that such a person would kill for his own notion of religious propriety?' Morton asked.

Knighton shrugged. 'That is more in your province than mine,' he said. 'But the Parliamentarians cut off King Charles's head in that very cause.'

'Then, I suppose – with the greatest reluctance – that I must deny myself the company of these charming ladies and go to see the Rossiters. Where do they live?'

'In Parchment Street, in the city centre. I forget the number, but it is the only double-fronted stone house in the street.'

Morton raised his hat to the ladies and strode off. He made his way to the High Street and thence to Parchment Street. He easily identified the Rossiters' house. It stood back from the road, with a small front garden full of roses and irises. His knock was answered by a slight, balding man, in a painter's smock.

'Mr Rossiter?' he said warmly.

'Yes.'

'I understand that you were at the cathedral this afternoon.'

'No. That was my brother William. I am Frederick. William is upstairs.'

'Ah. My name is Morton, I was hoping to have a word with him. May I come in?'

Rossiter stood aside and ushered Morton into a large parlour at the front of the house. The settee had been pushed to one side to make room for an easel in the bay window. Frederick picked up a palette and gazed critically at his painting.

Morton went over. 'It is a magnificent building,' he said.

'Yes . . . I always paint the cathedral. I can get five pounds for one of these, from the visitors.'

'Really? That is a good price.'

Frederick gave a gap-toothed smile. 'It helps to keep the wolf from the door,' he said.

'Why did you not go to the service, with William?' Morton asked.

'What? That man? I am glad I did not go. I could not have endured it!' His anger suddenly flared. 'From what William said, it was a disgrace!'

'You mean the music?'

'Indeed! The harlot of Rome has come to dwell in Winchester, Mr Morton. We must rise up and expel her!'

'Perhaps, with Mr Witney's passing, she will depart.'

Frederick frowned. 'Do you think so?'

'I suppose not.'

'I know not!' a deep voice chimed in from the doorway. 'Witney has already departed to the eternal flames. It was not he who foisted on us a papistical travesty of a service, but that son of Beelzebub, the Dean! We have only just begun. But we shall conquer!'

'William, this is Mr Morton,' Frederick said absently, and turned to examine his painting.

'I trust that you agree with us,' William said challengingly. He was a thick-set choleric man, with greying black hair.

'Almost certainly,' Morton replied. 'I must confess that, as a visitor, I was astonished to hear the Mozart Requiem – and sung in Latin, too!'

'And well you might be! But we made our protest, Mr Morton. And we shall continue! No sacrifice is too great to keep out the Pope of Rome!'

'Then, you do not think that Mr Witney's death will achieve it?'

'No sir!' William's voice was getting ever louder and more emphatic. 'He is one the fewer, but that is all. Do you know, Mr Morton, that for weeks we have had a papist crucifix displayed on our high altar?'

'Good heavens!'

'For generations there has been, on the great screen, the painting of the Raising of Lazarus you saw today. It is by an American artist, named Benjamin West. I am no painter, but I always considered it tasteful and perfectly adequate. But the idolators will not rest until it is replaced by a graven image. And Bishop Thorold encourages the Antichrist! He affects to have discovered, in ancient religious writings, a tradition that Christ reigned in glory, not as our risen saviour but nailed to the cross like a felon. All our protests were of no avail. They insisted on placing a crucifix there – for a trial period, so they said. But they had every

88

intention that it should be permanent. Is that the way to treat God's house?'

'It seems very high-handed,' Morton said diplomatically.

'It is more than that! It is idolatry, Mr Morton! There are no lengths to which these people will not go to desecrate our cathedral. You will not credit this . . . The Dean had the notion that, if Christ was reigning from the cross, he ought to wear a crown. This was seized on by the desecrators. So that the laity might get used to this impious notion, they took from the treasury the crown of King Canute and placed it on the head of the idol. Think of that, Mr Morton! The crown of a heathen Danish king, raised up in a place of Christian worship! But the Antichrist overreached himself. God is not mocked! At the end of the experiment, we had enough support to convince even the Dean that it was detested. But we must be vigilant!'

'Was Jethro Witney involved in this?' Morton asked.

'Involved in it? He was Kitchin's poodle! If the Dean nodded, he would yap! . . . But not any more!'

'What kind of man was he?' Morton asked quietly.

William glared at him. 'Why, he was a hypocrite and a swindler! He acted for us, years ago, in the sale of some property – including houses in Brook Street. When we mentioned to other estate agents what we had got for them, they were amazed that we had received so little. It was not until he moved into his latest residence, however, that we discovered he had personally bought not only that house but the other three in the block also! So much for professional qualifications! When we taxed him with it, he said that he had been unable to sell them at all, and therefore had given us more than a market price . . . But he is presently residing in the flames of hell. We are revenged at last!'

Morton was conscious that this interview had got completely out of hand. William's pent-up anger had poured out so relentlessly that there had been no opportunity to give him the criminal warning. All he had learned would be useless as evidence in a trial. He had truly earned Bragg's contempt.

'I should tell you that I am a police officer,' he said lamely. 'I am making enquiries into Witney's murder. It has been useful to gain, from you, an objective insight into his character.'

William was not deterred by the announcement. 'Then, let me

assure you that whoever killed him did society a service,' he said vindictively.

'Would you mind telling me where you were last Friday, sir?'

'Certainly!' William was in no way abashed. 'Frederick and I went to see the Royal Academy Summer Exhibition in London. We had lunch with my son, David, in Swallow Street, then went back to Burlington House again.'

'I see. Does your son work in town?'

'Yes. At Martin's Bank, in Lombard Street. He is a clerk there.'

'Ah. And at what time were you lunching in Swallow Street?'

'We left the exhibition at a quarter to one, so I imagine we would have arrived at the restaurant by one o'clock. David was waiting for us when we got there.'

'And, you finished your lunch at what time?'

'I could not say, with any exactitude. David had to be back at the bank by two o'clock, I remember, and he was concerned that he might be late. I suppose it must have been about a quarter to two.'

Bragg left the cemetery at the rear of the cortège, then took his chance, and cut off down a side-street. He had had enough of sanctimoniousness for one day. Anyway, he would rather the mourners had a chance to relax, after their ordeal. There would be plenty of time before the will was read. He went to the Coach and Horses, thinking that Morton might gravitate there; though no such arrangement had been made. He drank a pint of the local beer, enjoying its zestful, yeasty flavour. There was no sign of Morton. He ordered a half-pint of the same, and leaned back against the wainscot, watching the customers. From what he could see, Winchester was a prosperous enough place . . . It was strange. Why was Witney not content to be top dog here? Why did he have to chance it in London? The reason would probably never come out. Bragg pulled out his pipe . . . it badly needed cleaning. On the train down it had not been drawing well. He returned it to his pocket, and bought a packet of cigarettes from the bar. He went back to his seat . . . Still no Morton. He lit a cigarette and smoked it without relish. If he were honest, he thought, he was a bit out of his depth on this case. He had not got an instinctive feeling for how the people in it would behave. He had never lived their kind of life. Morton would

90

have a better idea. But he was probably squiring Catherine Marsden around by now; escorting her to the station, on the train to London with her, talking airy-fairy nonsense and looking at her tits. He ground out his cigarette, put on his bowler, and marched out into the street.

His ring on Witney's door was answered by a uniformed maid.

'Hello!' he said. 'You are new, aren't you?'

She smiled. 'We are from the agency, sir; hired for the afternoon.'

'I see. Where are they all?'

'In the back sitting-room. Do you know the way?'

'Yes. You need not announce me!' Bragg surrendered his hat and went down the passage.

In the sitting-room were a good dozen people. They were nibbling delicate sandwiches and sipping wine. In the corner another maid stood, with a tray of half-filled glasses. Bragg crossed and took one, then surveyed the gathering. Almost all of them had thrown off their funereal constraint and were chatting in a lively manner. One woman gave a guffaw of laughter and there was a sudden, self-conscious silence; but the conversation was soon as unrestrained as before. Julia appeared in the doorway. She gave him a startled look, then ostentatiously turned the other way. Bragg noticed that Syme was standing on the fringe of an animated group, but taking no part in the conversation. He had certainly not been among the family mourners in the cathedral. Presumably he had been with the onlookers, behind. In some ways, Syme could have lost more than anyone except Julia – or gained more. Bragg crossed over to him.

'What brings you here?' he asked. 'Grief or duty?'

'What do you think?' Syme said irritably.

'Well, let's say I bet you took the fare out of the office petty cash.'

'You bet I did!'

'You found it, then?'

'Found what?'

'The house. You said you had never been here.'

'Yes, I found it all right.'

'You do not seem to know anybody.'

Syme looked about him. 'I met Julia Witney once; that's about the lot.'

'Never mind,' Bragg said in a fatherly voice, 'it will not have been wasted.'

91

'What won't?'

'The journey. After all, I expect you were at the cathedral.'

'So?'

'So, no doubt you asked forgiveness from the Almighty for lying to me.'

Syme's face went white. 'Lying?'

'You told me that once you had seen Witney's body on the floor you kept out of his room. But now we know you were in there.'

'I . . . I did go in, that's true,' Syme said shakily. 'I saw him on the floor, and I could not take it in. I went over . . . to help him. Then I saw how much blood there was and I realized he must be gone. So I ran outside to the street.'

Bragg stared at him coldly. 'Yes, of course. We all knew that was what you would say. It was hardly worth the effort, was it? A waste of breath, really . . . When you reach the stage of having to make a clean breast of it, you know where to find me.'

Syme tore his eyes away. 'I am not staying here to be threatened,' he hissed and, without taking his leave of Julia, made for the door.

Bragg looked round complacently to see a parson bearing down on him, wineglass in hand. It was the Dean. He held out his hand, a benign smile on his face.

'I really must congratulate you,' he said warmly.

'Oh?'

'It was a quite splendid occasion, was it not?'

'Yes . . . yes, it was.'

The Dean moved closer. 'Tell me,' he said confidingly, 'as between one professional and another, what did you think of the music?'

'It was nice enough. A bit involved, for my taste; and I could not understand the words. That apart, it was all right.'

'I think we got the timing of the *Lacrimosa*, to the second. You did not feel it was at all hurried?'

'It seemed to go all right,' Bragg said diffidently.

'Good! Mr Witney's passing was, to say the least, untimely; so our preparations were inevitably hurried. Perhaps, on the next occasion, we shall have more opportunity for rehearsal . . . I suppose old Canon Fortescue is likely to be the next candidate for such an elaborate ceremony. We must pray that his going is sufficiently predictable for us to make the ceremony faultless.'

'Yes.'

'I suppose,' he mused, 'prerogative would demand that his coffin should rest in the choir, rather than the nave . . . Anyway, please convey to Mr Pennyfeather my sincere congratulations.'

'Mr Pennyfeather? Who is he?'

The Dean wrinkled his eyes and thrust his head closer. 'Oh, my dear fellow!' he exclaimed. 'I thought that you were the undertaker's man! Oh, dear! How very amusing!' He tried to recover his solemn face. 'I am so sorry,' he said. 'Please forgive me . . . But you do have an aura of death about you!'

'So I do,' Bragg said grimly. 'I am a policeman, and I am going to hang the person that murdered him.'

The smile faded from the Dean's face. 'Oh, yes . . . Ah, I see that it has gone half past five. I really must be going. So nice to have met you.' He turned and crossed to Julia to make his farewells.

Bragg, deflated and isolated, went over for another glass of wine. As he turned away, Edward Lazenby came over to him.

'I hear that you twisted my son's tail yesterday,' he said in an amused voice. 'I am sure that it taught him at least one salutary lesson!'

'What is that?'

'Always see that you have a good solicitor at hand!'

Bragg snorted. 'How long is this lot going on?' he asked.

Lazenby looked around the room. 'There are still a few outsiders here,' he said. 'Outside the family, that is. Once they have all gone I shall read the will. It should not be long now.'

'Good.' Bragg saw that Julia was standing alone by the door and moved across to her.

'My condolences, miss,' he murmured.

'I did not expect to see you here,' she said icily. 'I would have thought that we could have been left alone, to mourn, for at least one day.'

'Ah, but things are always changing. It would be a queer way of showing respect for the dead, to let his killer get away.'

She pressed her lips together, and said nothing.

'I see you had Mr Syme down for the funeral,' he remarked.

'Yes. He was my father's closest colleague in the business.'

'Of course . . . What about Mr Branksome?'

She looked at him speculatively. 'As you are no doubt already aware, Mr Branksome has left Winchester.'

'Ah. And what caused that, I wonder.'

'I realize that you have your job to do, sergeant,' Julia said irritably. 'But please do not treat me like a mentally defective child!'

'Very well. So, what happened?'

'Mr Branksome came to see me on Monday night. It was most inopportune, but he insisted. He said that he wished to discuss the future of Witneys. He seemed to have it all worked out – to his own satisfaction, at least. He said that the Winchester business is sound and, properly run, would furnish me with a good income. He suggested that my interests would be best served by selling the London business at an early date.'

'Yes. We knew he felt that.'

'But he then had the effrontery to suggest that I could best secure my future by marrying him!'

'Well, you are an attractive young woman. I expect you will get plenty of offers now.'

She looked at him scornfully. 'As you realize, sergeant, I have spent my life, thus far, under the protection of a kind and dearly loved father. I am just beginning to discover what a strange and cruel world it really is.' She took his elbow. 'Now I must return to my duties as hostess,' she said. 'Let me introduce you to my aunt, Ursula Witney. From your accent, you should have much in common.'

She steered him to the other side of the room, where a woman in her mid-thirties was standing.

'Aunt, this is Sergeant Bragg, of the City of London police,' she said. 'He is conducting enquiries into my father's death.' She turned away.

Ursula looked deep into his eyes. 'You will need more than ordinary insight to succeed,' she said in a low, cultured voice. She was good-looking, Bragg thought, her face unfashionably tanned by the sun – and none the worse for that! Shapely, too; she would make a lovely armful.

'Oh, I would not say that, ma'am,' he replied. 'Most cases are just a matter of routine.'

'Not this one, sergeant. There are more than earthly forces at work here . . . lines of power reaching out from this place.'

'Ah.' Bragg was nonplussed. 'Where are they reaching out to, would you say?'

'Perhaps wherever Witneys are.'

'I see. But Jethro is the first Witney to be murdered, isn't he?'

She stepped closer, seizing his arm. 'I lost my own intended, Walter Green, in precisely the same way,' she whispered.

'Did you now?' Bragg said sceptically. 'So you know how Jethro was killed?'

'Yes. My brother Thomas told me.'

'In every particular?'

'Yes.'

'And when did this happen?'

'He was found on the morning of May Day.'

Bragg was suddenly alert. 'Six weeks ago?'

'Yes.'

'Where was this?'

'In Dorset, where we live.'

'Slocombe Magna?'

'Yes. Do you know it?'

'I was born not far away – in Turners Puddle . . . And, how many Witneys are left?'

'Thomas and Francesca, over there by the fireplace; and Lucy, our mother. She could not bring herself to attend the funeral.'

'And, of course, there is still Julia here. Do you think she is at risk?'

'I think all Witneys, and all their dear ones, are at risk, sergeant,' she said darkly.

'That is quite a list . . . And, what is behind it, do you think?'

She looked at him challengingly. 'Nothing that you can counter with your mundane logic.'

Bragg eased himself out of her grasp. 'Tell me, ma'am, what was the posy you threw on the coffin?' he asked.

Her face became impassive. 'A bunch of herbs,' she said.

'I have never seen that done before . . . and what did it signify?'

'It may bring some mitigation. One cannot control the powers, but one can try to placate them.'

There came a loud knocking. Edward Lazenby was standing by the table, his hand raised.

'With Julia's permission,' he said urbanely, 'I think it appropriate that I should now read the will.'

Julia nodded her consent, and everyone seated themselves.

'I have to say, at the outset, that there is a slight complication. Jethro Witney made his will, in my office, two years ago. He signed it in my presence, and his signature was witnessed by two of my clerks. In that document, he appointed me and Thomas Witney as executors of the will. I later wrote to him, suggesting that he should make Thomas aware of the contents of the will. It is to be assumed that Jethro sent the document to Thomas, for it has not been found amongst the deceased's papers. Unfortunately, from what Thomas tells me, he did not receive any such communication. We must therefore presume that the will has been lost.'

There was a concerned gasp from the gathering, a whisper of conversation.

'However,' Lazenby went on authoritatively, 'that does not, in itself, defeat the intentions of the testator. We have a full copy of the will in our files; it is settled law that where a will has been lost, such a copy can stand in its place.'

'Suppose it was never sent to me?' Thomas Witney asked plaintively. 'Suppose he destroyed it?'

'It is, I suppose, arguable. But I have to say that no later will has been found, nor any indications of any such will. From my own conversations with him over many years, I find it inconceivable that he would have taken the decision to become intestate.'

Lazenby paused and looked around. There was a general murmur of agreement.

'Then, I will proceed on that basis.' He produced a folder from his brief-case and took a document from it.

'As I said, a moment ago,' he began, 'Jethro appointed me and Thomas Witney as his executors, and he was so generous as to allow that I should raise the usual professional charges for any legal work done by my firm in connection with it.' He gave a self-satisfied smirk; someone laughed, most kept silent.

'He also appointed Thomas and me to be trustees of the ensuing trust.'

'Trust?' Julia was on her feet, her eyes angry.

'Have patience, my dear,' Lazenby said soothingly. She subsided into her chair.

'He directs us to stand possessed of all his property, with full discretion and the usual indemnities. He further directs us to pay his debts, funeral and testamentary expenses, and to fulfil the following specific bequests.'

He paused until the hum of anticipation had subsided. 'To Mrs Janet Blake, for her faithful service, the sum of one hundred pounds.'

Bragg heard a whisper: 'That is the cook,' from behind him.

'To John Syme, my clerk, the sum of one hundred pounds. To David Branksome, my assistant, the sum of one hundred pounds.'

Bragg looked across and saw Julia's lip curl.

'The balance of the estate is to be held in trust for Julia Witney – subject to an annuity of two hundred pounds per annum to be paid to Lily Fox. Such annuity to continue until her attaining the age of twenty-one years or prior marriage.'

Julia was on her feet, her hands clenched. 'Who is this Lily Fox?' she demanded angrily.

'She is the daughter of Miss Cicely Fox, who is employed in the Lombard Street office.'

'And how old is she?'

Lazenby referred to his files. 'She was born in March eighteen ninety-two,' he said evenly. 'Just over two years ago.'

'This is ridiculous!' Julia shouted. 'Why should he do such a stupid thing?'

'He was satisfied that Lily is his child.'

'His child? By a little whore like that!' Julia could barely keep control. 'I will not accept this!' she screeched. 'I shall contest the will! . . . After slaving for him all these years, he saddles me with paying off his harlot! I will not have it!'

'I would really counsel against that course,' Lazenby said quietly. 'Two hundred pounds is a small sum, in the context of the whole estate. As his executor, I would feel bound to contest such an action. By the time it was settled, there would be little left for anyone.'

'Why should I care?' Her bony face was ugly with rage. 'I do not believe that he wanted this will to stand! He only made it because you said it was the gentlemanly thing to do! As soon as he got it home, he destroyed it. I know him better than you!'

She turned and ran out of the room.

5

'I would swear that Julia did not know the thrust of the new will, lad.' Bragg was sitting at his desk, scraping the carbon from the bowl of his pipe.

'Are you not in danger of giving hostages to fortune, sir?' Morton chaffed him. 'All women are actresses; and men have a fatal predisposition to believe them.'

'Upper-crust idiots like you, maybe,' Bragg said grumpily. 'No, she was never acting. She could hardly contain herself . . . And it was not just discovering that her father had a chance-child. You must remember that she is poorer by it.'

'Two hundred pounds is hardly a large sum,' Morton remarked.

'Huh! I expect your sort would give that for a night with a dolly-mop,' Bragg grunted. 'But, if it goes on till Lily Fox is twenty-one, it will amount to three thousand eight hundred pounds. A lot of people do not earn that in a lifetime!'

'I stand suitably admonished, sir!'

'No, lad . . . I was thinking about it, last night, on the train home – since you had already buggered off with Miss Marsden. It is all to do with money, as I said . . . And it is not just the amount of the annuity. She must have been thinking, these last few days, that she was free of her family's restrictions; that she could start living her own life. Then she finds herself lumbered with this trust; so she will not be in control of her fortune for another nineteen years. I tell you, she was hopping mad.'

'I still have the temerity to believe that you are wrong, sir.'

Bragg pushed a pipe-cleaner into the mouthpiece. 'Oh? How do you see it?' he asked testily.

Morton smiled. 'We are, of course, postulating Julia Witney as the murderess. Now, in my view, the discovery of an illegitimate half-sister would have been no more than an irritant. Even had she discovered Lily's existence at an earlier stage – say, from some indiscreet remark of Edward Lazenby – I could not see that it would have led her to murder her father.'

'I cannot believe that Edward Lazenby would be indiscreet,' Bragg interrupted. 'Considering there is this connection between his son and Julia, to my mind he has acted with the strictest propriety.'

'Then, let us agree that Lily Fox is a side-issue; a relatively minor issue – if you will forgive the punning.'

Bragg scowled at him, and began to reassemble his pipe.

'Julia must always have assumed that she would inherit her father's wealth,' Morton went on. 'And I cannot see any financial factor which would cause her to kill him at this particular time. It is not, for instance, as if he were embarking on personal or business outlay which might rapidly dissipate his fortune.'

'What about his involvement in the City? Our friend Syme thought there was something shady in the offing.'

'So far, we have seen no evidence of that. Until we do, I suggest we regard that issue as mere supposition. Anyway, Julia could hardly have been aware of it . . . No, I still think that sex was the motivating force. I am convinced the cook is right, in saying that Witney regarded Julia as an unpaid housekeeper. From what we know of the man, he would certainly have resisted a marriage which would have upset his domestic arrangements. So, if Julia and Peter Lazenby are as close as we are led to believe, they had every reason to want Witney dead.'

Bragg snorted. 'The trouble with you young folk,' he said irritably, 'is that you think sex is all that matters. But sex has to be paid for, one way or another . . . So, what do you make of Branksome's doing a bunk?'

'Apart from the fact that it supports at least two of my theories, you mean? Well, it is clear that he could have gone up to London with Julia, assisted in the despatching of her parent to the next world, and come home again for tea.'

'On the other hand, if Julia is the hot-arsed bit you would have me believe, he could have been tupping her on St Catherine's Hill, at the time.'

'What a pity that we did not demand to see the results of her artistic endeavours,' Morton said with a smile.

'Oh, she would have had something for us, never fear. I don't trust artists,' Bragg said darkly. 'It is a something and nothing of a job, and Winchester seems to be full of them . . . What do you reckon of the Rossiters then?'

Morton wrinkled his brow. 'Certainly they did not attempt to conceal their animosity; and they are not subtle enough for it to be a double-bluff.'

'I had a look at Jethro's file on cathedral matters, last night,' Bragg said. 'There certainly seems to have been a real ding-dong about turning the churchyard into lawns. But would anybody really commit murder over that?'

'It cannot be dismissed out of hand,' Morton said thoughtfully. 'Even if one allows that killing for one's own particular creed is no longer fashionable. The Rossiters are a somewhat unbalanced pair. I can accept that they might believe their chances of eternal bliss have been diminished, now that they can no longer be buried in the shadow of the cathedral. Nevertheless, it is something of a dead issue, if I may use that expression.'

Bragg made a grimace. 'What about this business over the music?' he asked.

'I can see someone killing for the privilege of hearing Mozart – not the other way round.'

'And their alibi depends wholly on David Rossiter.'

'Unless, of course, their visit to the Summer Exhibition was designed to give him an alibi. After all, he works only a few doors down the street from Witney's office. It would be much more economical for him to pop in, murder Witney, then go off to lunch in Swallow Street. It is not as if the crime would have taken long.'

'For once you are talking sense, lad. It would be easier all round for him to do the killing. Witney banked at Martin's. David Rossiter was more likely than most to know his office routine. He would only go in to do the job if he could see the outer office was empty. And suppose, when he opened Jethro's door, he had found somebody with him; he could always pretend it was bank business, and go away. Witney would never think twice about it.'

'Perhaps we ought to go and question him.'

'Yes . . . Do you know, I have seen that name somewhere else, and I cannot think where.'

'David?'

'Rossiter, more likely. I expect it will come back to me. Let us go along to Witney's office; see how things are.' He put his pipe in his pocket, and took his bowler from the hat-stand. 'We might as well take back the business books.'

It was eleven o'clock when Bragg pushed open the door of the Lombard Street office. Cissie Fox was sitting at her typewriting machine; everything seemed as normal.

Bragg put his cardboard box on the desk. 'Is Mr Syme in?' he asked.

'No. He is out collecting rents.' Her face was flushed and excited.

Bragg smiled warmly. 'So you have heard?' he said.

'About the annuity, you mean? Yes! Mr Lazenby's clerk came, not half an hour ago. There's a letter for Mr Syme, too!' She nodded towards the desk opposite.

'You did a good job, then,' Bragg said sardonically.

'How do you mean?'

'Convincing Witney that Lily was his child.'

Her head jerked up. 'Well, she is!' she said sharply.

'I do not doubt it for a minute,' Bragg said amiably. 'But not many men would be in a hurry to accept it.'

'But it had to be him! He took advantage of me in the office.'

'What? In full view of the passers-by?'

'In his office!'

'Well, he had a nice soft carpet for the job, I'll say that.'

Cissie cocked her head defiantly. 'He wanted to marry me,' she said. 'But his family were against it . . . Still, he promised he would see me right, and he has!'

'Did he provide money for Lily's upkeep, when he was alive?'

'Not regularly. He would give me something for Christmas, and her birthday.'

'So, you are better off this way.'

'I don't know. I might not keep my job, if the business is sold.'

'Mmn . . . I see. I just want to have another look round Mr Witney's room. Has it been tidied up?'

'Yes . . . They took the carpet away to be cleaned. But I don't expect they will get the stain out.'

Bragg looked at her quizzically. 'You seem very chirpy about it all,' he said. 'A deal different from what you were the other day.'

'Well, you have to get over things, haven't you? I mean, you cannot go on grieving for ever.'

'No . . . I suppose not. Oh, I do not know if you are aware of it, but Julia Witney is going to contest the will.'

Her eyes widened in consternation. Bragg turned and led the way into Witney's room, closing the door behind them.

'It's the same old story, if you ask me,' he said, sitting in the armchair. 'She leads him on, for what she can get out of him; he abandons her when he has had his pennyworth.'

'That sounds more than a little cynical,' Morton remarked.

'Oh? I bet she is a bloody sight happier, now she has got some real money out of him, than she ever was before. She could chuck in her job, and live on the annuity for the next nineteen years.'

'Is that why you told her the will might not be sustained?'

'I suppose so. We cannot have the silly little bitch giving up a good job for nothing, can we?' Bragg looked about him. 'So, how about Cissie Fox for our killer?'

'She certainly had a weapon to hand.'

'What is that?'

'The heavy cylindrical ruler, on her desk.'

'Hmn . . . I suppose it is the right size; even someone as slight as Cissie could have stunned him with that.'

'And she might not have needed your matchbox trick to get him into the right position!'

'You mean, they had a bit of fun and games first?'

Morton grinned. 'She would have needed some pretext to get him within range.'

'I suppose so. I did not notice his clothes particularly. Still, she would not have let it go too far; she could hardly have dressed him again . . . I wonder where she bought the razor. Nowhere round here, I should think.'

The door opened and Syme stood on the threshold, an envelope in his hand.

'I thought you had finished,' he said truculently.

'Finished?' Bragg smiled urbanely. 'No, we never finish . . . not till the murderer has been hanged. Sometimes not even then, if we cannot be sure we got the right man.'

'What do you want?'

Bragg lifted a bushy eyebrow. 'Are you not going to open your letter?' he asked.

'It is private,' Syme said coldly.

'I know. It is to tell you that you have been left a hundred pounds, in Jethro Witney's will.'

'A hundred pounds?' Surprise and disbelief spread over his face. After a moment's indecision he tore open the envelope and pulled out the letter. He read it, then gave a deep sigh. 'This will just about save my bacon,' he said.

'It's not much, though, is it?' Bragg remarked. 'Not enough to make you a solid City businessman.'

'It will do to be going on with!' Syme's voice was almost exuberant. 'And, with any luck, I might keep my job here.'

'Miss Fox did better than you, though.'

'Well, she would, wouldn't she?'

'So, you knew about the will?'

Syme looked as if he had been pole-axed. The blood drained from his face. 'I did not know that he would leave anything to me,' he blurted out. 'But Cissie said he had told her she would be all right.'

'I see. All in all, it has turned out well for both of you.'

Syme had regained some self-possession. 'If this business is allowed to slip away, it will not have turned out well for anyone,' he said.

Bragg smiled. 'You ought to put in a bid for it . . . But wait a week or two. I gather that Julia Witney is going to overturn the will, if she can.'

Bragg pushed his way to the head of the queue in Martin's Bank, and thrust his warrant-card at the startled clerk.

'I want to see the manager,' he said peremptorily.

'I . . . I think he is engaged, sir.'

'Well, bloody unengage him!'

'I . . . er. Just one moment.'

Bragg stood drumming with his fingers on the counter-top till the clerk reappeared and beckoned them. He led them into a solidly furnished office at the back of the building. As they entered a small bald-headed man bounced up from his desk.

'May I know the reason for this boorish conduct, in my bank?' he demanded furiously.

'Boorish? Oh, I would not call it that, sir.' Bragg said blandly. 'A trifle emphatic, perhaps; but then, murder is an emphatic way to treat another human being, isn't it?'

'Murder?'

Bragg motioned Morton to a chair, and sat down himself with great deliberation.

'We have come to see you, sir, about the death of Jethro Witney, last Friday. We understand that he banked here.'

The manager looked at him frostily. 'What is that supposed to mean?' he said curtly.

'Well, if you prefer it that way, we know he banked with you.'

'So?'

'So we have come to look at his account in your books, and so forth.'

'Have you a warrant for this action?'

'You cannot have stronger warrant than a grisly murder, sir.'

'I mean, have you got a legal document, authorizing such an examination?'

'Not exactly.' Bragg pursed his lips. 'In fact, not at all. You see, sir, getting a warrant takes time – a whole day maybe. And, while we were doing it, our man could escape.'

'I would have thought he has already escaped!' the manager said smugly. 'It is virtually a week since Witney was killed!'

'Not quite, sir. It will be six days, at ten past two, since we were called.'

'Not exactly rapid progress! I do not know what we pay our rates for!'

Morton expected an explosion of wrath from Bragg, but he merely smiled. 'As I was saying, sir, we are short of time, and I am sure a public-spirited person like you would want to bend the rules to help us.'

The manager looked at him coldly. 'Rules are not made to be bent,' he said.

'You mean there is a rule which says you must not assist the police?'

'Of course not! But the overriding duty of a bank is to maintain confidentiality as to the transactions of its clients.'

'Yes . . . yes. I can understand that,' Bragg said musingly. 'Of course a warrant would not safeguard that.'

'Why not?' the manager snapped.

'Well, if we have to go for a warrant we would specify Witney's accounts and documents, of course. But since you are not co-operating with us, we couldn't be sure that they would be enough.'

'What do you mean?'

'Well, just consider,' Bragg said amiably, 'Witney might have had transactions with people who are also clients of your bank. So we would have to go for the lot. We would move a squad of detectives in, to look at every file, a locksmith to open every safe deposit box . . . I expect it would be best to close the branch. How long would it take, constable?'

Morton considered. 'A week, at least,' he said. 'Of course, as the coroner is becoming so restless, we could ask for powers to remove everything to the police station. The bank could remain open then.'

'No!' The manager's face was horror-struck. 'I think,' he said haltingly, 'that on further consideration, the directors of the bank would wish me to give you my full co-operation.'

Bragg beamed at him. 'That is very public-spirited of them, sir.' He waited for the manager to regain his composure. 'Can you tell us what kind of a man Jethro Witney was?' he asked.

The manager looked surprised. 'What kind of a man? Well . . . he was clearly successful. As to his personality, he was a gentleman; agreeable, a man of his word, upright in all his dealings . . .'

'Sounds like a paragon, doesn't he? But somebody hated him enough to nearly cut his head off.'

The manager grimaced. 'People are saying that it was a haphazard killing . . . That the murderer might strike again.'

'No.' Bragg smiled confidingly. 'This was not random. Witney was picked for some reason . . . perhaps by a madman, but he had a motive, some pattern in his head. It could be an urge to kill estate agents, or shop-keepers in Lombard Street, or even clients of Martin's Bank . . .'

'God forbid!'

'Before we look at Witney's papers, could you give us a quick sketch of his affairs? It will save time.'

The manager clearly felt that he was being drawn deeper and deeper into a morass. 'They were not complicated,' he said reluctantly. 'You will already have seen the business books, and our files will add little or nothing to what you have gleaned from that source. In addition, he had a small personal current account, and a personal deposit account.'

'What kind of sums are involved?'

'In the current account, a few hundred pounds only.'

'And the deposit account?'

'He maintained a steady balance of fifty thousand pounds.'

'Fifty thousand? Good God! Why would he do that?'

'The interest is good,' the manager said defensively.

'He could have got more, if he had invested it in stock!'

'A little more, perhaps. But Mr Witney was a very wealthy man. And, anyway, he could have instant access to a deposit account, whereas he would have had to realize stock to get his money.'

'Was there much movement on that account?'

The manager stared down at his smooth, white hands. 'Naturally,' he said, 'on hearing of Mr Witney's death, I examined his affairs, to see if there might be any repercussions on the bank. I remember being struck by the fact that there had been no transactions whatever since the initial deposit. It was almost as if he had forgotten the existence of the account.'

'Just the kind of customer to have, eh?'

'Indeed!'

'Well, now, can you find us a room where we can look at all the records and files?'

'Yes. You may use my assistant manager's office.'

'And do not forget the safe-deposit box.'

The manager looked surprised. 'Ah, yes. I will have it sent in,' he said sheepishly.

For half an hour they looked at the bank's ledgers, and the files on Witney. They found nothing untoward, nothing new.

'Somehow, I do not seem able to get a hold on Jethro Witney – a clear picture of the man,' Bragg remarked.

Morton looked up. 'Well, we know he was a paterfamilias in the old tradition, an assiduous High-Church Christian, a gourmet, a lecher . . .'

'No, I don't mean that! I just cannot get inside his mind. This bank deposit; why would he just leave it here? He was losing money for five years.'

'Since he seems to have been a prudent businessman, he must have felt that he might gain, in other ways, more than he lost in interest.'

'Such as?'

'Witney was concerned to elbow his way into the governing hierarchy of the City. To make progress, he would have to be accepted as worthy in their terms. You will have noticed, in the bank manager's encomium, the remark that Witney was so wealthy he could forget the existence of a fifty thousand pound deposit . . . But we know that he was nothing like so well-heeled.'

'Very comfortably-off, is how I would have put it!'

'Yet you may be certain that, when discreet enquiries were made, the ruling clique was made aware of his casual attitude to his wealth.'

'You mean he set it up as a deliberate act of deception?'

'It is certainly one interpretation.'

'Yes,' Bragg mused, 'and I cannot think of another. The man was certainly not a fool . . . So where does this leave us? It does not alter anything, that I can see.'

'Except, perhaps, our perception of Witney. He now appears much more clearly as a calculating, manipulative person.'

'Hmn . . . And the person he was most obviously manipulating was his own daughter . . . Bring over that deposit box, lad. I expect I have a key here that will fit it.'

He took Witney's bunch of keys from his pocket and tried them until he found one that unlocked the box. He pushed back the lid.

'Not a lot here,' he said. 'What seems to be the lease of the Lombard Street premises; the insurance policy on this branch, and a bundle of investment certificates. Here you are, lad; you know more about investments than I do, have a look through them.'

Morton untied the bundle and flipped through the certificates. 'They are all holdings in the consolidated fund,' he said.

'Government bonds? Well, that doesn't sound very exciting. Is this more window-dressing, do you think? Surely the bank manager could never get access to the box?'

'It is unlikely, but hardly necessary. I am sure Witney could so manipulate events, over a period, that passing bank clerks saw him apparently depositing bundle after bundle of investment certificates in his box.'

'Yes . . .' Bragg stared absently out of the window. 'I am missing something here, lad; I know I am. It doesn't add up properly . . . All Consols, you say?'

'Yes. I will take a note of the reference numbers.'

'Do that . . . Ah! I know what it is! Among the papers I took from the safe in Witney's home was a list of investments. I did not look

107

at it all that carefully, but I would swear that there were company shares amongst them.'

'But you did not find the relevant certificates?'

'No, neither in the safe nor in the Winchester bank.'

'Nor here . . . That does seem interesting.'

'Interesting or not, we cannot take it any further, the list is back in Old Jewry. What time is it, lad?'

'Just past twelve o'clock.'

'Right. Go and get David Rossiter, will you? Before he disappears for one of his far-flung lunches.'

David Rossiter proved to have inherited the weedy physique of his Uncle Frederick. His manner was decidedly petulant.

'I was wondering how long it would be before you came pestering me,' he said.

'Ah. Your father wrote to tell you what to say, did he?' Bragg said mildly.

'Not at all. He said that you had invaded the privacy of their house in Winchester and that I could expect the same high-handed treatment.'

'High-handed?' Bragg repeated. 'I would hardly call it that. We have our job to do . . . You are David Rossiter?'

'Yes.'

'And you live where?'

'I have rooms in Wide Gate Street.'

'That is in Spitalfields, isn't it?'

'Yes.'

'I find it interesting,' Bragg said innocently. 'Everybody else in this case seems to come from the top of the pile.'

Rossiter flinched. 'There are reasons why that should be so,' he said harshly.

'No doubt. Do you think it proper, sir, that you should be working in this bank?'

'I do not understand.'

'Your family has a bitter hatred of Jethro Witney; yet here you are, working in a bank of which he is a client.'

Rossiter's face paled. 'You . . . you would not reveal to my employers that . . .' His voice tailed off.

'We have no interest in seeing that you lose your job if that is what you mean,' Bragg said. 'But, all the same, it looks a bit odd.'

'I am in no way responsible for the views of my family members in Winchester,' Rossiter exclaimed. 'I left there when I was sixteen, and have only returned for holidays.'

'I see. Tell me, why did your father and your uncle hate Jethro Witney so much? Surely it cannot have been just the grave-space and the cathedral music?'

'I cannot usefully comment on that.'

'Perhaps you will comment, and leave us to decide if it is useful or not.'

'No.'

'You see, the way it is shaping up is this. Your father is so out of his mind with resentment and hatred that only Witney's death will purge it.'

'I can only speak for myself. I care neither for the cathedral music, nor for the loss of the grave-space. I would not be buried in Winchester for a king's ransom.'

'I see. You have finished with the place, have you sir?'

'Yes.'

'And you are wealthy enough not to care about your roots.'

'I did not say that.'

'What are you saying?'

'That since I have been poor all my adult life, I am free from the hankering after what might have been.'

'You are thinking of the Brook Street terrace, are you, sir?'

Rossiter raised his eyebrows, but did not reply.

'Now then, will you tell us where you were on Friday the fourth of June, between one and two o'clock in the afternoon.'

'Yes. I was lunching with my father and my uncle at Kirkland's restaurant in Swallow Street.'

'I thought that is what you would say. I suppose there were no independent witnesses to vouch for the fact?'

'As to that, I am not concerned. We have no need of them.'

After dinner, Catherine spent some time in her bedroom, fleshing out the skeletal notes she had made with information from a library book on Winchester. Then she went downstairs to the sitting-room. Her mother looked up from her reading.

109

'Are you not changing for the drum at Mrs Warburton's, dear?' she asked.

Catherine smiled. 'I have not changed, Mamma, because I have not yet made up my mind to go.'

Mrs Marsden sighed. 'I do wish that you would take life a little more seriously,' she said. 'We are half-way through the Season already and here you are, lolling at home. Other girls of your age are out every night, meeting new people, enjoying themselves. You just do not seem to try!'

'The other girls you refer to do not have a responsible job of work to do.'

'Why should they? They are wiser than you. They realize that true fulfilment, for a woman, lies in a husband and children; not in grinding away all day in an office, then a lonely old age.'

'Poor Mamma! Confess! You are not concerned about me, but yourself. What you really want is grandchildren to spoil!'

'Is that so very ignoble?'

'Not at all! Had you yourself been a little more assiduous in procreating, you would have multiplied your chances considerably.'

'Catherine! Really, your generation has no respect for its elders.'

'But a great deal of affection.'

'Enough of your flattery,' Mrs Marsden said severely. 'I have been meaning to speak to you for some time now.'

'What about?'

'Why, the way you behaved, the other evening, towards James Morton.'

'The way I behaved?'

'You were very flippant towards him. It was not at all seemly.'

'But, Mamma, he had just taken me to the opera. I was very happy and it was entirely proper that I should show it.'

'I would have described it as immodest exuberance. In my day no young lady would have threatened her suitor with a rolled-up magazine – even in fun.'

'He is not a suitor, he is a very charming and amusing friend. Quite the best thing that I ever did was to refuse his proposal of marriage. Had I accepted him I would have had a nursery full of children, and a husband off playing cricket in the Antipodes.'

'You do exaggerate so!' her mother complained. 'It happened only a year ago. Though I agree that you were right to refuse him. Lady

Lanesborough was saying, only the other afternoon, that she would like to introduce you to Lord Tresilian. He has recently inherited the title; estates in Cornwall and a house in Grosvenor Square. He would be a very good match, and he is anxious to meet you.'

'How old is he?'

'In his early forties, I gather. Just the right age for a man to settle down.'

'No, Mamma! I will not sacrifice myself to the whims of a middle-aged yokel peer to gratify your urge to have grandchildren.'

'Oh, dear, you are so vexing!' Mrs Marsden sighed. 'I do so wish that you would try!'

Catherine laughed. 'Then you should teach me, Mamma! Come, tell me how you captured the affections of Papa. How did you seduce him away from the blandishments of Aunt Phoebe?'

'Really! You are quite incorrigible.'

'Do tell me your secret; it must be very potent. From the photographs I have seen, you were even then quite . . . Junoesque.'

Her mother laughed. 'I suppose I was, though I did not feel it. I was convinced that I was quite sylph-like! Poor man, he was lost to one or other of us from the moment he crossed the threshold – not that he realized it!'

'So, how did you do it?'

'I suppose I stood around a great deal, admiring his work and looking, well, winsome.'

'Winsome! So that is the elusive quality I lack. But why you, rather than Phoebe?'

Her mother cocked her head in thought. 'I suppose he saw me as someone . . . reliable.'

'How unromantic!'

There came a knock on the door, and the maid stepped inside. 'There are two gentlemen asking to see you, ma'am. Are you at home?'

'Who are they, Joan?'

'Mr Morton and that sergeant.'

Mrs Marsden glanced at Catherine. 'Very well,' she said. 'Show them up.'

Catherine leapt to her feet and scrutinized her appearance in the mirror. But she was casually turning the pages of a magazine when they were shown in.

111

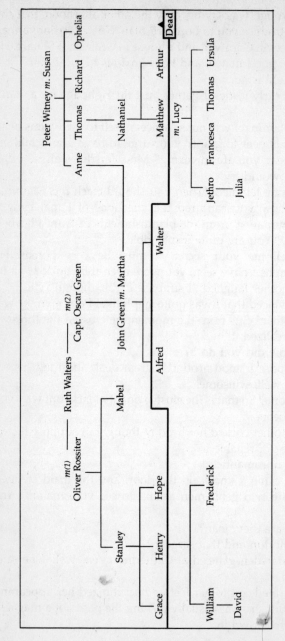

'I am sorry to disturb you at this time of night,' Bragg said. 'But we feel that you may be able to help us.'

'Do sit down, Mr Bragg,' Mrs Marsden said graciously. 'Good evening, James, it is nice to see you again.'

Morton bowed in acknowledgement, then went to sit next to Catherine on the settee.

'What have we been doing, Mamma?' Catherine exclaimed. 'When the police invite you to help them, it presages imminent arrest!'

Bragg smiled. 'No . . . It's that we have a case that is perplexing. I think young Morton came to consult you about it, the other day.'

'Ah, the Witneys from Winchester. Well, sergeant, it is a long time since I lived there. My sister Phoebe would be much more help to you.'

'We do not have that kind of time. Anyway, I think we are dealing with long-ago happenings.'

'I see.'

'As you know, Jethro Witney was murdered. When we came to go through his safe, we found two documents that do not seem to fit. See . . . this is a list of shares, with ticks and cross-ticks. Now, we have gone through Witney's investment certificates and none of them seems to tie up with this list.'

'Strange.'

'Yes, ma'am. The other is a skeleton summary of assets. The headings include leaseholds, houses and land. Now, we know he owned a terrace of four houses – though they ought to be worth a deal more than the figure pencilled in against that heading. But we have not come across anything which suggests that he ever owned any land, as such.'

'How can I possibly help with such a problem?' Mrs Marsden asked.

'I am not saying you can, ma'am. I was just explaining the difficulties we are up against. Now, with them was this family tree . . .' He unfolded the document, and placed it on the table by the window.

'Do you think that this document was connected with the other two?' Catherine asked. 'Or did it merely happen to be with them?'

'That we do not know, miss . . . Now, look at the bottom right-hand corner. You will see there four Witneys – Ursula, Jethro,

113

Thomas and Francesca. The only heir to that lot is Julia. Jethro, of course, was murdered . . . I spoke to Ursula after the funeral. She is barmy, if you ask me; talked about lines of evil power flowing out from Winchester, destroying Witneys and their dear ones.'

'How absurd!' Mrs Marsden exclaimed. 'Who would believe such nonsense in these enlightened days?'

'I am not so sure . . . Look in the middle, there. You see those two Greens – Alfred and Walter?'

'Yes.'

'Well, according to Ursula, Walter Green was her fiancé. He was murdered on the first of May, in precisely the same way as Jethro Witney.'

'Extraordinary!'

Bragg's moustache twitched in a smile. 'I hope not, ma'am. I have not had much experience of the supernatural! But look over to the left.'

'Rossiters!' Catherine exclaimed. 'Are these the Rossiters who walked out of the cathedral? Who called down a plague on Jethro Witney and all his house?'

'The very same, miss. There are William and Frederick, with David on the same level as Julia Witney. It seems that, generations back, the Greens and Rossiters and Witneys were all related to each other.'

'Goodness! I must say that this family tree is a work of art . . . but why would Jethro have gone to all this trouble?'

'Well, miss, we cannot definitely say that he made it . . . He certainly had it in his safe, but it may be nothing more than a stray family paper.'

'But you do not think so, sergeant.'

'Let us say that I think it will bear looking into. There is another interesting thing. With the exception of Jethro and his daughter, all the Witneys live in a little Dorset village called Slocombe Magna. The Greens live, or in Walter's case lived, in the same village. On the other hand, the Rossiters' home is in Winchester – has been for ages, it seems. Now, Jethro Witney moved to Winchester seventeen years ago.'

'From Slocombe Magna?'

'Yes, miss.'

'So, what conclusions do you draw?'

Bragg laughed. 'It is a bit early to start drawing conclusions. We need all the help we can find.' He turned to Mrs Marsden. 'I was hoping that since you are from Winchester, ma'am, you might have some ideas.'

Catherine looked across at her mother. 'Do try, Mamma!' she said pointedly.

'Well, of course I know of the Rossiters. They were the kind of people one was warned against.'

'Were they uncouth?'

'No, dear, much worse. They were unfortunate.'

'Unfortunate?'

'They were held up as an example not to follow . . . a court case, long ago. Quite a *cause célèbre*, I think.'

'What about, Mamma?'

'I cannot remember. It all happened just before I was born.'

'It sounds interesting, ma'am,' Bragg said. 'I wonder how we could find out about it.'

'Leave it to me!' Catherine exclaimed. 'I will go to the Law Courts in the morning. They are sure to have some reference to it in the registry.'

6

Catherine set off for the High Court in good spirits. Once James and Sergeant Bragg had left, the previous evening, her mother had been disposed to talk of her childhood in Winchester, and the people she had known. Gradually the Rossiters had come into clearer focus. They had lived in the house in Parchment Street, now occupied by William and Frederick. Her mother could remember their father, Henry. He had taught art at the local grammar school. There were two unmarried sisters also. She and her mother had laughed rather cruelly about Grace unappreciated and Hope unfulfilled. Catherine had questioned her mother about the ill luck that had come upon them. She had learned little, except that they were cited as a dire example of what happened if you rashly went to law.

Arriving at the imposing Gothic building in the Strand, Catherine followed the signs to the Queen's Bench Division. She went into the room which housed the registry and approached a clerk.

'I am trying to trace a case which was heard around eighteen forty,' she said tentatively.

'Oh, yes, miss?' He was fatherly and genial. 'What sort of a case was it?'

'I am not sure.'

'Well, we have criminal, revenue and personal actions here.'

'I see. It is certainly not criminal, nor is it likely to be revenue.'

'Then, try the personal actions register, over there.'

She went to a counter on which several large bound volumes were stacked. Selecting the one covering the years eighteen thirty-five to eighteen forty-five, she carried it to a table and began her search. It was in alphabetical sections, which reduced the labour considerably. There was a Greene in eighteen thirty-seven; Greens in eighteen thirty-six, eighteen forty-two and eighteen forty-four; and a Greenaway in eighteen forty-one. None of them seemed to chime with her mother's recollection. Somewhat dispirited, she climbed the stairs to the floor above and made her way to the Chancery Division registry. This time, the catalogue of its jurisdiction seemed endless, from *Charges on land* to *Wardship of infants*. She selected *Estates of deceased persons* as being the least esoteric, and was given the relevant register. Once more she began at eighteen thirty-five and plodded through page after page of entries. There were several Greens in every year, so she decided to concentrate on the three years preceding her mother's birth. She began to plough through eighteen forty-two; in no time at all she had a list of twenty cases. That would take her all day to clear! She took her list to the counter and the clerk departed to find the files. It had been foolish, she decided; arrogance compounded by ignorance. She had airily committed herself to research which might take a month of drudgery; and even then might prove inconclusive. She dared not take more than that morning for the task, or Mr Tranter might begin to ask questions.

Thus far he had been tolerant, largely because he had an old-fashioned idea of what was appropriate for a woman to be involved in. He had defined her role as being to write a column on topics which would interest the wives of the *City Press*'s predominantly male readership. The idea had been that City men might buy a copy of the paper to take home to their wives. She had welcomed the arrangement. She was left to choose her own topics; could maintain that her own interests were inevitably those of the women they were trying to cultivate. To forestall criticism, she toyed with the idea of a new series of articles, on City institutions. The objection that the new Law Courts were a few yards outside the City boundary could be overridden. Historically they had been in the City, and people still thought of them as being there. But, could she seriously maintain that a wide spectrum of women – even intelligent well-educated women – were avid for information on how the Law Courts worked? No. She would have to eat humble pie, tell Sergeant Bragg that the task was beyond her, look as stupid as she really had been in attempting it.

'Here you are, miss.' The clerk placed a pile of slim folders on her table. 'These are the registry files, you understand. If you want to follow the full proceedings, we shall have to get the main files from the repository. That might take a day or so.'

'Thank you.'

She turned to the first folder. It was clearly not what she sought, but she flipped through it to get her bearings. She was glad to see that the address of the deceased was prominently displayed on the register sheet stuck inside the front cover. That should ease her burden considerably. From what she could see, the function of the Chancery court was to determine the intention of the testator in cases where the will was unclear. She began to go quickly through the pile, glancing at the addresses. She had almost reached the bottom when she caught her breath. A Winchester address – Parchment Street! The name was Ruth Green, the date of death the eleventh of July, eighteen forty-one. Suppressing her excitement, she took the files back to the counter.

'This is the one I was looking for,' she said casually.

The clerk took the folder from her and glanced at the register sheet.

'Ah, you are out of luck,' he said cheerfully.

'Why?'

'See that note, at the bottom there? Our file went over to the Court of Probate in December eighteen forty-one. That is their reference, if you want to take it down.'

'Thank you.' She noted the number on her pad. 'Where is the Probate Court?'

'Top floor.' He gathered up his folders and disappeared.

Catherine did not know whether to laugh or cry. She glanced at her fob-watch. Already it was half past eleven. She really must be back in the office before one o'clock or the editor would become suspicious. Still, she had the reference number, it ought not to take long.

She had climbed so many stairs that morning, her legs were weary. But she dragged herself up to the top of the building. *Probate, Divorce & Admiralty* the notice proclaimed. Surely this was the end of her quest? She walked over to the Probate counter.

'Yes, miss?' He was a short chirpy cockney.

'I am enquiring into the case of a Mrs Ruth Green, who died on the eleventh of June, eighteen forty-one,' she said. 'This is the reference number.' She turned her pad, so that he could read it.

He sucked in his breath. 'That is a tricky one,' he said.

'Why?'

'Well, you see, when this lady died probate matters were dealt with by the ecclesiastical courts. Then, in eighteen seventy-three, they changed it all around and made this division from scratch like.'

'But, I was told this was your number,' Catherine protested.

'Well, yes . . . It was the church court reference.'

'Have you still got their files?'

'Oh, yes. I can get it up for you. It will have a new number though. Let me see.' He consulted a dog-eared list, his finger travelling down page after page. 'Here we are,' he murmured, 'Gosling . . . Gotobed . . . Green . . . This is it – Green Ruth, eleventh of July, eighteen forty-one. I will give you the new number.' He scribbled on a piece of paper and passed it to her.

'Thank you. When will the file arrive here?'

'First thing Monday morning.'

Catherine turned away irritably. It was too Dickensian for words! Stupid system! Her only consolation was that no one could have done more. Indeed, it was only by her persistence that she had discovered where the file was held and obtained its current reference. Now it was merely a matter of waiting two days. She could not be expected to triumph over the arcane machinery of the legal administration. Sergeant Bragg would just have to wait.

*   *   *

118

Bragg knocked on the Commissioner's door and went inside. 'You sent for me, sir,' he said crisply.

'Yes, Bragg. I was at a function, last evening, which Sir Rufus Stone also attended. I have to say that he is becoming somewhat restive over the Witney case.'

'Well, sir,' Bragg said deferentially, 'that seems a bit unreasonable. It is a bare week since he was murdered; and we have been on the case solidly since then.'

'I do not doubt your assiduity, Bragg, but the coroner understandably wishes to see the matter carried further. He appears to be under a certain amount of pressure from the City authorities – and the press.'

Bragg chuckled. 'It's a change for him to get it, instead of us!'

'It is hardly a matter for levity, Bragg. The public are afraid that the killer will strike again; that any one of them might become his next target.'

'Then, why do you not reassure them, sir? Make an announcement that they need not worry; that this man is not a random killer. It is what we believe, after all.'

'But, suppose that we are wrong? Suppose that, after my giving such an official reassurance, he does lash out again? No, Bragg, that could only undermine the confidence of the public in the police.'

'Well, sir, I am bound to say that, far from narrowing down to one suspect, our enquiries have only resulted in widening the field. In all honesty, we have not yet eliminated a single person.'

'You mean that you still suspect his daughter?' Sir William asked, twisting his lips in distaste.

'Oh, yes, sir. She could have done it – alone, or with either one of her two men friends.'

'Who are they, again?'

'Lazenby, the engineer from the East End, and Branksome from Winchester.'

'Ah, yes. What about those other people from Winchester?'

'The Rossiters? They admit they were up in London; they had lunch with their son, who just happens to work almost next door to Witney's office in Lombard Street.'

'Is there no corroboration of their alibi, Bragg?'

'No, sir. They take the view that they have no need to provide it. And, frankly, I would not know where to start myself.'

'Could you not see the head waiter? They presumably had to book a table.'

'It is not that sort of restaurant,' Bragg said patiently. 'You shove your way in, gobble down your pie and peas and get out again. Nothing so refined as booking. We asked the waiters, of course, but they looked at us as if we were stupid.'

'So, you still have six suspects, Bragg.'

'Eight, at the very least, sir. The clerk and the typewriter at Lombard Street both had the opportunity, and both of them benefited in his will.'

'Enough to murder for?'

'Well, I do not suppose that you or I would think so; but I have known people murder for their granny's copper kettle.'

The Commissioner sighed. 'Do you really see no prospect of narrowing the enquiry?' he asked plaintively.

Bragg tugged at his ragged moustache in thought. 'Only if we decide that we need not get the right man, so long as we get someone,' he said, straight-faced.

'But that would be unconscionable! We could not possibly contemplate it.'

'I agree, sir. Indeed, if we are to be thorough, I do not see how we can avoid widening the field a bit more.'

'Widening it? You mean that there are still more suspects?'

'Let us say that there is a line of enquiry we should quickly follow up, so that we can be easy in our minds.'

'I do not understand you.'

'It was something that was said, just before Witney's will was read. I was talking to his sister. The rest of the family still live in a little Dorset village, out in the wilds. This woman had a fiancé, also living there, called Walter Green. She told me that he had been killed, in precisely the same way as Witney.'

'But this is absurd, Bragg! Did she know what she was saying?'

'Well, she was a bit odd, and we never had the chance to get down to the gory details; but I, for one, would not like to dismiss it out of hand.'

'Really!' Sir William exclaimed petulantly. 'We cannot waste our resources following up every stray remark from half-witted country-folk.'

'Ah, I see that I have given you the wrong impression,' Bragg

120

said contritely. 'These are good-class people, well-educated . . . And the Witneys and Greens were related to one another, long ago.'

'That is the way with villages, Bragg, too much interbreeding! It saps their vitality and mental faculties. I doubt if you would get much further with them.'

Bragg regarded the Commissioner with a level gaze. 'In my view, sir, as a lowly detective-sergeant, we ought to take the matter further, so that it can safely be set on one side. Of course, if you were to give me an order to disregard it, I would loyally carry out your instructions.'

Sir William shifted uneasily in his chair. 'Yes . . . all very proper, Bragg. You really think this factor could be crucial in arresting the killer?'

'I would say no more than that it is possible, sir.'

'Hmn . . . And how would you set about eliminating it?'

'Oh, I think it could well be done informally. I am acquainted with the Chief Constable of Dorset, from that case last autumn.'

'The business of the murders when you were on sick-leave? Do I know him?'

'I believe so, sir. He is Colonel Colegrave – ex-cavalry. He is a great admirer of yours. You met at the Home Office, last year.'

The Commissioner preened himself. 'Did we? Ah, yes. I vaguely remember it.'

'He would be able to give me details of the post-mortem, and so on. I would see no point in taking the matter further, unless this Green man really was killed in the same way.'

'But it might be a total waste of time. For all we can tell, this Green died years ago.'

'Ah, no. Did I not say? It happened on the first of May. Five weeks before Witney got the chop himself.'

'Ah! That makes all the difference.' The Commissioner was suddenly decisive. 'Very well, go and see the Chief Constable, and find out what happened in that case . . . Oh, and give him my regards.'

Bragg got back to his room to find that Morton had finished writing up his notes and was examining the family tree. He looked up.

'Did you get what you wanted?' he asked.

'In the end. He is afraid of his own shadow this morning.'

121

'But, we can look forward to a pleasant weekend in Dorset?'

'I can. You will have other things to do, on Saturday morning.'

'Shame! What are they?'

'That list of shares I found in Jethro's safe; the one with the ticks and cross-ticks.'

'Yes?'

'We cannot be sure that Jethro had not got another cache of securities, hidden away in a box we have not yet found. I want you to go to the Head Office of every one of those companies and examine their list of shareholders. That will tell us whether these are Witney's shares or not.'

'It will take a considerable time.'

'True. But if you get stuck in you might well be able to play pat-ball tomorrow afternoon!'

'Thank you, sir. And, will you be going to Slocombe Magna?'

'I expect so.'

'Slocombe Magna . . .' Morton grinned as he savoured the name. 'It sounds like every woman's heartfelt desire!'

'What? . . . Oh, yes . . . Now, bugger off! I am catching the next train from Waterloo.'

It was two o'clock before Bragg was leaving the train at Wool station. It was a glorious summer's day; the sun was hot on his back but a cooling breeze raised occasional eddies of dust by the path. He took off his coat and carried it, his Gladstone bag in his right hand. There were one or two traps in the station yard; no doubt he could have cadged a lift but he decided to walk. He was lucky. Over the last year he had come down frequently; stayed with his cousin Ted and his wife Emma in Bere Regis. Now they let him leave a set of clothes in their house, so that he could come at a moment's notice.

He stopped for a few minutes on the arched bridge over the river Frome, watching the trout quivering to keep stationary in the current, then struck out in the direction of Bere Regis. This was the best moment of all, he thought, being back home; the sandy dust of the heath on his boots, a kestrel hovering above the gorse. Emma would be surprised to see him on a Friday afternoon. Moreover, it was only a fortnight since his last visit, and he had said that it would have to suffice till July. But she would not mind; she would hug him warmly and put the kettle on for tea. He marched steadily on, loosening his collar and tie in the heat. It was good to feel well and vigorous. At forty-three a lot of men were knackered – from over-work, ill-nourishment, too much drink . . . Well, perhaps he was a bit overweight himself. And these visits to Bere Regis didn't help – particularly now that Fanny's mother had bought the Drax Arms and they were selling Hildred's beer.

He paused at Gallows Hill to catch his breath. He would have an excuse to see a fair bit of Fanny Hildred, this trip. With any luck she would drive him around. His cousin's dogcart was good in its way; right for pottering about. But Fanny's Stanhope gig was a different kettle of fish altogether . . . And it was a delight to see her drive it; urging on the colt, a flush on her cheeks. She was a fine young woman and no mistake; with no side to her at all. In some ways it was a pity that her mother, Amy, was so practical and decisive. When her husband died, she never gave selling the brewery a thought. She stepped into his shoes, going into Dorchester a couple of times a week, to chase the managers and see the orders kept coming in. She was a formidable woman, sure enough.

He picked up his bag and marched off again . . . But Fanny was not made of the same stuff as Amy. She was energetic and athletic for a woman, but she did not have her mother's desire to dominate. As it was, she was missing out all ways. The locals didn't regard her as one of them; how could they, when she was infinitely better educated and her mother owned most of the village? Too good for the farmers and tradesmen; not good enough for the gentry. That was how her predicament had been described. If so, it was a crying shame. In London she would have found a niche; married, maybe, and had children. Now time must be running out for her. She was in her mid-thirties. What a waste! There were times when he fancied there was more than ordinary warmth between them; but you could never tell, with women. And if you presumed too much, that could be the end of everything. Anyway, he was stupid even to think of it! It would be even more of a waste to have her living in London at his level. And it was all well and good him wondering if she was past it; he was forty-three himself. In a few years he would be thinking of retirement; it was no time of life to have fantasies about young women . . . Nevertheless, he didn't feel forty-three; he was just in his prime. A sudden thought struck him; it was June, the eleventh of June! . . . Tomorrow he would turn forty-four. His heart sank. Well, at least he would keep that quiet. It was odd that Mrs Jenks had not dropped a few hints. It had become the custom for him to take her out in celebration – a few port and lemons, then the music-hall. Well, he would have to try to make it up to her some other way. Blast it! It was like being wed, without any of the advantages. It was time he made a change. He looked ahead of him; there was the church tower through the trees, the road beginning to slope away to the village. He lengthened his stride and began to whistle.

He turned into the Old Brewery. Its old brick buildings had been adapted by his cousin for his carrier's business. The large brewhouse had made a fine cart-shed, and there had already been a range of stables. Bragg looked around him approvingly; everything looked trim and well maintained. After the problems of a year ago, the business must now be in good heart.

'Joe!' Emma was running from the kitchen, arms outstretched. 'This is a surprise! I thought you weren't going to come back till next month.'

She hugged him, then held him at arm's length. 'You are not hurt again, I hope,' she said anxiously.

Bragg laughed. 'No! I just found an excuse to play hookey . . . I hope it is convenient for you. If not, I can easily put up at the Drax Arms.'

'You will do no such thing! It's funny, we were only talking about you, over breakfast.'

'Nothing bad, I hope!'

'I was telling Ted that tomorrow is your birthday. We were trying to work out how old you would be.'

'Ah, it was bad, then.'

Emma gave her warm, motherly smile. 'Get away with you! You are only a young lad . . . Ted could not remember if you were a year younger than him, or older.'

'Older, I am sorry to say.'

'Never mind. We will have a little party, and I will make you one of my sherry trifles. How will that do?'

'Since I am not to be allowed to forget my age, it will do very well!'

'How long will you be staying?'

124

'Oh, I shall have to go back on Sunday afternoon.'

'We shall have it at lunch-time tomorrow, then. Ted is out, at the moment, helping one of his drivers to move house.'

'There is no need to worry about me; I have a thing or two to do. Is Miss Hildred at home, do you know?'

Emma smiled knowingly. 'I expect so. I saw her at the butcher's this morning.'

'Then I will have a quick wash and pop round to see her.'

In twenty minutes Bragg had spruced himself up and was strolling round the corner to the Hildreds' house. Its mellow brickwork looked welcoming, reassuring. There was not a touch of flamboyance about it; but, all the same, it was a fine big house . . . a gentleman's house. Too grand for the likes of him.

He beat a tattoo with the door-knocker. After a few moments he heard footsteps within and the door was opened. A short, stocky woman stood in the hall, a pugnacious look on her face. She was in her early sixties. She wore a silk dress, with a sash that only served to emphasize the unattractive squareness of her figure. As if to distract the eye, she had placed string after string of beads around her neck.

'Ah, Mr Bragg.' Her face softened into a welcoming smile. 'I ought to have realized that only you would make such a racket. Come in.'

'I thought that you might be in the garden, ma'am,' Bragg said apologetically.

'Fanny is. I will call her.' She ushered Bragg into the sitting-room. 'Would you like some tea?'

'That would be very welcome. I came straight round from the Sharmans'.'

'I shall make it myself. We have a new maid; flighty little thing she is, but I will lick her into shape. Believe it or not, she has gone to a wedding. On a Friday! Whatever is the world coming to?'

She disappeared, and Bragg looked round him at the things that had become familiar over the last year; the chintz-covered furniture, the light Chinese carpet on the floor . . . not too dissimilar from the one that had been in Witney's office.

'Mr Bragg!' Fanny stood in the doorway, smiling in delight. She was slim and tall, her brown hair upswept. She came across and took his hands unselfconsciously. 'What a pleasant surprise!' she said. 'I did not realize that you would return so soon.'

'Nor did I, miss. But it is not all pleasure, I am afraid.'

'Then perhaps that presages an extended visit. I do hope so.'

She seated herself gracefully on one end of the settee, and Bragg sat down beside her.

'I expect I shall be off again on Sunday,' he said. 'I was wondering if I could ask you to drive me about a bit.'

'Of course! I suppose that this is connected with some dreadful crime.'

'Yes . . . At least, it may or it may not be. I am told that there was a similar one down here, a month or so ago. I wondered if I might learn something by poking around.'

'I see. And where do you wish to be taken to?'

'Tomorrow I want to have a quick look round a village beyond Wareham, called Slocombe Magna . . . Funny name, isn't it? Young Morton said it sounded like every woman's heartfelt desire.'

'Oh, Mr Bragg!' she exclaimed, in a startled voice.

He looked round in consternation. Her face was flushed, her eyes wide.

'My God! What have I said? I am so sorry! . . . I did not realize what I was saying.'

She laid her hand on his arm. 'There is no need to apologize, Mr Bragg,' she said firmly. 'It is I who am acting like someone out of a novelette.'

'There is every need! Such talk is not for your ears.'

'Why not? I was brought up with the village children. I am no different from them. You really must stop regarding me as if I were a precious piece of china.' She leaned towards him. 'I am just as any other woman is, with the same instincts, the same desires.'

He put his hand on her shoulder, could feel her hair brushing his chin. 'That is not so,' he said. 'Not like just any woman; at least, not for me.'

She turned her face upwards, her lips parted. There was a sudden rattle, the door was opened, and Mrs Hildred was pushing the tea-trolley into the room. Bragg pulled back guiltily, hoping that she had not seen.

'Mr Bragg wishes me to drive him to Slocombe Magna tomorrow, Mamma,' Fanny said calmly.

'Then, you will have to allow plenty of time . . . Now, Mr Bragg, try some of this fruit cake.'

126

* * *

After a late birthday lunch next day, Bragg found himself harnessing a sleek, black colt to Fanny's gig while she changed her clothes. When she emerged from the house she was wearing a blue gored skirt, with an open jacket over a frilled white blouse. A small hat was perched on her curls.

'Do you wish to drive, Mr Bragg?' she asked.

'No, not me! It is years since I held the reins – and then it was a two-horse lorry. Anyway, I enjoy watching you drive.'

He handed her up, then hoisted himself beside her. She flicked the reins and the colt moved off.

Until they were well out of Bere Regis Bragg made sure that there was plenty of daylight between them. He did not want any rumours starting. But once they had reached the top of Gallows Hill and turned over the heath towards Wareham, he relaxed. He stopped trying to prevent his knee from touching her thigh. She glanced at him and smiled, then urged the colt into a trot. She looked so healthy and energetic, he thought; a far cry from those pasty-faced clothes-hangers of London women. She was stylish and lively, too; she would be a credit to anyone . . . That was the trouble. What had he to offer her? He was an ignorant country lad, with not even a home of his own.

It was all very well, her saying that she had been brought up in Bere Regis. Her family's way of life was infinitely above most people's; and she had been sent away for her schooling . . . She'd been very forgiving over his gaffe, but she would remember it. Blast Morton, and his buggering about with words.

'You seem very deep in thought,' she said teasingly.

'Me? No . . . I am just enjoying the country air. You do not realize how much smoke and dirt there is in London until you come to somewhere like this.'

'Then, you should come more often . . . What road do we take now?'

With a start Bragg saw that they were already on the outskirts of Wareham.

'Turn right at the main road and over the bridge,' he said. 'I reckon we have under four miles to go.'

Once over the bridge, Fanny urged the horse along the level road.

127

Ahead was the high plateau of the Purbeck Hills. Already the sun was dipping behind them, shadows advancing across the valley. Bragg looked at his watch. It was still hours before sunset, yet the hills were already dark and threatening. As they reached their foot, they saw that the road, pitted and stony, went steeply upwards.

'I think that we ought to walk now,' Bragg said. 'Are you up to it?'

'Of course!'

'I had forgotten about this bit. I have only been up here once before.'

'Please do not apologize. You have no idea how much I am enjoying this. It is a positive adventure, compared to sitting in the garden counting the roses!'

Bragg handed her down, then took the horse's bridle. The trees seemed to engulf them as they laboured up the hill, and a cool darkness enveloped them. Halfway up Fanny stumbled over a stone, and thereafter held on to Bragg's arm.

'This is an eerie place,' she said. 'I can well imagine all kinds of vicious depravity existing in the depths of these woods . . . But you did not tell me the nature of the crime you are investigating.'

'Murder,' Bragg said laconically.

'I thought so. It is a mercy, I suppose, that you can discharge such a task and be so untouched by it, so normal.'

'I would not say that I am untouched, miss; though to some extent, you get hardened to it. What you have to do is think of what the victim might have done with the rest of his life.'

'And, I suppose, of the terrible loss suffered by his family.'

'That too. Though you would be surprised how often they turn out to be the ones you are looking for!'

'You must be mentally a very strong and balanced person to sustain so demanding a task over so many years.'

Bragg smiled. 'Someone has to do it, miss. Ah, we are practically at the top of the hill. I reckon we could get back in the gig.'

The belt of trees ended at the top of the scarp and they were soon trotting through open, rolling country dotted with oak trees and great limestone boulders. Here the afternoon sun was warm on their faces, the birds sang, the green corn rippled in the light breeze.

'This does not seem at all sinister,' Fanny said. 'One can hardly imagine the inhabitants descending to anything as dreadful as murder. Are you intending to make enquiries here? If so, I could well be a hindrance. I would be quite content to stay, with the gig, at the edge of the village.'

'No fear!'

She gave him an amused glance. 'I would be perfectly safe, surely?'

'I have to admit that I spent the last week telling everyone this was not a random murder. But I am not going to chance being wrong.'

'What caused you to link your killing, which presumably took place in London, with one in Slocombe Magna?'

'The way it was done,' Bragg said shortly. 'Look! I do believe this is the edge of the village. What I suggest we do is drive gently round the roads, as if we were out for a breath of fresh air. I do not want to attract attention, so we will not stop. I want to get the layout of the place in my mind, ready for tomorrow.'

'What is to happen tomorrow?'

'Why, I am hoping to persuade you to drive me to Briantspuddle! I want to have an informal chat with Colonel Colegrave, the Chief Constable. I reckon he owes me a favour or two, after last year.'

'As do we all,' Fanny said warmly. 'Life in Bere Regis would have become insupportable, if you had not been there to clear up those dreadful murders.'

'It is nice of you to say so, miss.'

'Do you suppose that the Dorset police might already have caught the perpetrator of the murder here?'

'I would like to think so; but they had not got him a week ago . . . or her.'

'Goodness! Do you mean that you may be looking for a woman?'

'Well, it is not likely, to my way of thinking. They usually go in for subtler methods, like poison. But I am told, by those who should know, that a woman could have done it . . . Now, unless I am much mistaken, that is the village green ahead.'

'Should we go briskly, or dawdle?'

'I suppose that you do not know anyone living here?'

'No.'

'If you had, you could have passed me off as a relative, and we could have taken our time. The trouble is that, at the reading of our victim's will, I saw three people who live here. I only spoke to one,

129

and I doubt if she would remember what I look like, but we had better not take any chances.'

'Briskly, then.'

The village green was roughly triangular, their road dividing to right and left. Opposite them was a row of old thatched cottages. Their outer walls were whitewashed, their roofs in good repair. On the left was a small stone church, while an inn faced the other side of the green to their right. Neither of them was architecturally distinguished; but the inn, at least, seemed cheerful, with tubs of flowers by the door. Fanny pulled the colt to the right and flicked it into a trot. Just beyond the Beaufort Arms was another row of cottages, slightly smaller than the others, but still sound and trim. Beyond them was a large stone house in the Georgian style, surrounded by flower beds and gardens. Almost opposite, on the other side of the road, was a similar house, though this was set in lawns framed with shrubs. The road began to degenerate into a track, and soon they saw farm buildings through the trees ahead.

'I reckon we should turn round, miss,' Bragg said. 'It would look queer if we went any further. There is a handy gate to the right.'

He jumped down and, taking the horse's bridle, manoeuvred the gig round.

'I do not think we could have gone beyond the farm,' he said, hoisting himself up again. 'Perhaps if we had taken the left fork, at the green, we might have struck a proper road. Not that there seems anywhere to go, from here.'

Fanny flicked the colt into a trot. They bowled along with the village green and the church on their left. They could see that slates were missing from its roof; the graveyard was small and neglected. Beyond it was a terrace of moderately substantial houses, four in all, with neat front gardens crammed with flowers. Opposite the church, on the right of the road, was a splendid old house. It had a stone slab roof and mullioned windows; the central door was surmounted by a canopy, its shallow steps flanked by curved iron railings. A freshly raked gravel drive made a gracious arc from one gate to a second, thirty yards further on. From the further corners of the house, mossy walls projected, screening and enclosing the back garden. Fanny caught her breath.

'Who would have expected to find such a wonderful house in a backwater like this?' she asked.

'It is surprising.'

'I would love to pick it up and transplant it to . . . I don't know – anywhere but here!'

Bragg looked back over his shoulder. 'It is in spanking condition, that's for sure. There is a bit of money there, I would say.'

'The road is becoming a cart-track again,' Fanny said. 'I had better pull up . . . There seems to be very little more to this village than we have already seen.'

'Yes.' Bragg jumped down and backed the colt round. 'There is that little lane between the fine house and those cottages, but it would look a bit queer if we went up there. We had better get back.' He climbed to his seat again. 'Funny thing,' he said, as Fanny drove back to the village green, 'all the time we've been here, we have not seen a soul.'

Fanny laughed. 'We can hardly be said to have lingered.'

'I know. But in an isolated place like this, you would think a stray cat would have everybody out for a look.'

'I hope, at any rate, that it has been useful to you.'

'Oh yes, miss. I shall know what Colegrave is talking about tomorrow. I must say that I am grateful to you. I hope it did not inconvenience you too much.'

Fanny smiled. 'No indeed! If we are stray cats, then I am the one who stole the cream!'

After Sunday lunch next day, Bragg took his leave of Ted and Emma. He strolled round the corner to The Retreat, where Fanny already had the horse in the gig. Once out of the village, they turned west, skirting Black Hill and winding down to Turners Puddle, where Bragg had been born. He looked with dismay at the house where he had spent his youth. In those days the yard would have been swept clean; there would be carts and wagons, big shire horses and ponies for the traps. Now it had been taken over by a builder: seasoning timber was stacked along the walls of the outbuildings, untidy piles of bricks and slates cluttered the yard. It was a disgrace! He had been going to point it out to Fanny, but hadn't the heart; it would have given her a wrong impression.

They forded the River Piddle, at this point divided into tiny rivulets, joining and separating again. It was little more than a stream, he thought. Everything down here was overrated. The countryside was soft and rolling, the tempo of life slow. They had no conception of the power of a real river, like the Thames. And if you told them, they would not believe you. Parochial just about summed it up . . . And the better class were no different. They might be aware that they were small fry, but they resented having to admit it.

'You seem very pensive, Mr Bragg.'

Fanny had half-turned towards him, her snug blouse and skirt emphasizing her lissom body.

'I suppose I was thinking about this meeting with the Chief Constable.'

'Surely it will be very cordial! After all, you extricated the local police from a very embarrassing situation last year. I would have thought that they would be eternally grateful.'

Bragg sighed. 'It does not work like that, miss. Nobody enjoys looking like a fool. They will be itching to get their own back.'

'I would hardly think that Colonel Colegrave would be so petty.'

'No, not him. But he is not the one I would be working with, if it came to it. Should it turn out to be Inspector Milward's case, he would rather see the killer go free than help me to catch him.'

'Surely you exaggerate!'

'Not by much, I don't . . . Can you take the left fork here? I would rather avoid my sister's house. They don't know I am here, and I would prefer they didn't on this occasion.'

They drove down a sun-dappled lane, its verges covered with dandelions and willow-herb. After half a mile they rejoined the main road.

'That is his house, on the right,' Bragg said. 'You can go in. There's a good wide drive inside.'

As Fanny pulled the colt to a standstill they heard a voice calling from the garden. The colonel was tall and spare, with a military moustache and a weathered face. He came towards them, secateurs in hand.

'I was just dead-heading the roses,' he said. 'Amazingly early this year, Miss Hildred, are they not? What a pleasure!' He handed her down ceremoniously, then looked at Bragg. 'I know that face,' he said, knitting his brows. 'You are a policeman: but not in my force. Let me think . . . Hah! I have it – City of London! Sergeant Bragg, is it not?'

'That is so, sir.'

'Hmn.' He faced towards the house. 'Baker!' he bellowed. 'Two whiskies, in the garden. At the double!' He turned to Fanny. 'I am afraid that, being an all-male household, we are not well-provided to entertain the fair sex. Would you like a little sherry?'

Fanny smiled. 'I would welcome a cup of tea,' she said. 'May I go and make it? I am sure that you two would prefer to talk alone.'

'Very well. Go through the French windows and you will find your way to the kitchen . . . Get Baker to show you round the house. There are some quite good water-colours, here and there.'

'I would enjoy that.' Fanny walked elegantly across the lawn and into the house.

'Well now, Bragg, is this a formal visit or an off-the-record pow-wow?' Colegrave asked with a smile.

Bragg followed him round to the side of the house, where a table and chairs were set on a terrace. 'I am sure that our Commissioner would prefer it to be the second, sir,' he said.

'I see . . . Do you take water with your whisky?'

'Not when I can avoid it!'

'Good man! So you have given up your weekend and come down to confer with me?'

'That is about the size of it, sir.'

'What about?'

'It could be something and nothing. We had a murder, just over a week ago. Too many suspects for my liking, but shaping up for being a routine case. Then I went to the victim's funeral and the reading of his will. While the mourners were having sandwiches and so forth I got chatting to a woman named Ursula Witney. She is a sister of the deceased and lives in Slocombe Magna, in Purbeck. She said that her fiancé had been killed, in exactly the same way, barely a month before. I did not get a chance to take it any further because they started reading the will and it all degenerated into a family row. But I thought it might be worth popping down, to see if I could find out a bit more.'

'I see. Was the name of this fiancé Walter Green, by any chance?'

'That is the man.'

'And why do you expect to find a connection between the two cases?'

' "Expect" is too strong a word, sir. But, if the woman knew what

133

she was talking about, a link between the two has to be considered.'

Colegrave eyed Bragg warily. 'And how was your man killed?' he asked.

'According to the City pathologist, who is usually right about these things, he was hit on the back of the neck with some sort of cosh. He dropped down unconscious; then his throat was cut with a razor. And not just cut; his head was damned nearly chopped off!'

'Hmn.' A frown settled on Colegrave's brow. 'Well, you have your connection,' he said. 'Miss Witney was perfectly right. Walter Green was killed in precisely that manner.'

'I see . . . How are your enquiries progressing, sir?'

'I begin to wonder if that is the right word, sergeant . . . Just before the killing of Green, a violent criminal escaped from Portland prison. We have been working on the theory that he was responsible for the murder.'

'Is there any particular reason for that?' Bragg asked quietly. 'Did he come from the Isle of Purbeck?'

'No. But there was no apparent motive for Green's death and we calculated that the escaper could have reached that area, from Portland, in the time . . . And there was another factor. Platt would have wanted to get rid of his prison uniform. In view of what you tell me, the coincidence may have been all too convenient – but when Green's body was found he was stark naked.'

'I see. Did you find the prison clothes?'

'No. We made a search of the area but, as you probably know, there are countless places in such rough country to hide a small bundle.'

'Would this man Platt have been likely to make for London, sir?'

Colegrave shrugged. 'Any villain would be likely to try. Once there, he would be safe.'

Bragg pondered. 'I supoose he had plenty of time for it, between the two murders,' he said. 'But I am still uneasy. Why would he kill Witney? He had to go along Lombard Street in the lunch-hour crowds, enter an apparently empty estate agent's office, open the door at the back and go into Witney's room to do the job. And if it were just another random killing, the odds against his murdering two people who were sort of related must be unbelievably high.'

'I agree.'

'What kind of man is this Platt?'

'He comes from the Midlands somewhere. I gather that, at first glance, one would take him for a gentleman. Early on in his career he served a sentence for blackmail; later he gravitated to the more direct method of demanding money with menaces.'

'It could all fit together, then?'

'It could . . . And yet, our conversation has reinforced a doubt that has been niggling away at the back of my mind. With his injuries, Green must have bled worse than a stuck pig. But there was little or no blood in the place that he was found. The inference must be that he was killed elsewhere.'

'Where was he found, sir?'

'Do you know the village at all, Bragg?'

'I had a quick look round, yesterday.'

'Did you? Well, if you turn right at the village green, along the front of the Beaufort Arms, and continue for a couple of hundred yards, there is a big stone house on the left.'

'Ah, yes. Lawns and a lot of shrubs.'

'That is the one. Well, that was his house. He was found on a cart-track behind it, by some farm labourers going to work.'

'Strange,' Bragg murmured. 'Somehow, you cannot see an escaped prisoner carting the naked body of his victim around the place.'

'No. I must confess, that does worry me.' Colegrave's eyes followed a butterfly, as it settled on the table, then flew off again. 'And where does our conversation leave you, sergeant?' he asked.

'I feel pretty certain that we ought to poke about a bit more down here.'

'I was afraid that you might say that. After last year you are not exactly *persona grata* with our people.'

'Could I send down my detective constable? He is a polished young chap, Cambridge degree, good family background.'

'He hardly sounds like a policeman!'

'Exactly.'

Colegrave considered for a time. 'I would not want him to make official enquiries, you understand. And yet I would wish to have access to any material he discovered.'

'I see no difficulty about that, sir.'

Colegrave watched the butterfly as it came to rest on the table again.

135

'What is the name of your constable?'

'James Morton. He is the son of General Morton, the Lord-Lieutenant of Kent.'

'He is an intelligent-looking chap, I presume.'

'Yes, sir.'

'Well, then, I see no difficulty. Let him come down on holiday, or in pursuit of some hobby . . . Let us say that he will be an entomologist. That should give him plenty of scope. There are enough insects on the Isle of Purbeck, goodness knows!'

'Did you have a satisfactory meeting with Colonel Colegrave?' Fanny asked, as they neared Wool station.

'He was very helpful, really.'

'And, what does that mean?'

'He will allow me to send young Morton down here to investigate. He is coming as a scientist – a bug man. It was the Colonel's idea; he does not want his own people to know about it.'

'So, once again, you will be solving a local murder for us.' There was pride in her voice.

'Well, it does seem likely that it was done by the same person as ours.'

'Your use of the word "person" presumably means that you do seriously think the perpetrator might be female.'

Bragg glanced at her non-committally. 'Our pathologist said it could have been done as easily by a woman as a man; but I am not convinced.'

Fanny laughed. 'I hope you will always maintain your sturdy independence of received opinion,' she said.

'There is one thing though, miss.'

'What is that?'

'Morton may want to get in touch with me. If so, he would have to telegraph me; a letter would take too long. But if he sent it from as close as Wareham everybody would know.'

'Indeed! Can I help?'

'Well, would it be too much to ask if he said he was related to you? Everybody knows Hildred's beer in Dorset; and he's a presentable kind of chap. It would make the whole thing more believable.'

136

Fanny laughed. 'To be connected with you, Mr Bragg, is to be involved in the most stimulating events! Why not? He shall be my far-flung cousin.'

'Thank you, miss. And, being related to you, it would be natural that he would come over and see you while he is in Purbeck.'

'Of course! As to the need to telegraph you, I could do it myself from Dorchester. Indeed, should you wish to confer together, it could be done in our house without anyone being the wiser!'

Bragg put out his hand and squeezed her arm. 'You are a grand young woman,' he said warmly. 'There are not many like you round here.'

'You flatter me!'

'Not a bit of it! I know nobody to touch you in the whole of London.'

She allowed the colt's pace to slacken; they went some distance in silence, and Bragg began to feel that he must have offended her. Then she looked round at him, her face serious.

'Of course, you could not have known it, Mr Bragg, but you have indirectly touched on a topic which is currently under debate – somewhat heated debate, I might add.'

'Between you and your mother, do you mean?'

'Yes. As you may be aware, I have no desire to emulate her in sustaining my father's achievements and keeping his name alive.'

'You do not see yourself running the brewery, then?'

'Indeed not! And she is finding it an increasing burden to do so herself. As we have no man who will undertake the task, I have expressed the view that she ought to sell it.'

'I see . . . She would get a good price for it, certainly. But she is still an active woman. What would she do then? Run the Mother's Union and have tea-parties on the lawn?'

Fanny looked determinedly ahead of her. 'I am trying to persuade her that we ought to move away from Bere Regis.'

'Whatever for?' Bragg asked in astonishment.

'Since you left the village in your youth, you cannot realize how dull and stultifying it is to live there.'

'But, where would you go?'

She glanced round. 'For my part, I would prefer to live in London. We have friends in Chelsea; and I find it increasingly irksome to

137

receive letters describing the parties they have been to, the plays they have seen – and to be stuck here in Bere Regis.'

'Hmn . . . London has its advantages, to be sure,' Bragg said thoughtfully. 'But you would miss Dorset more than you think; particularly on a day like this.'

'That may be so. But Dorset is no longer as your childhood memories paint it. Things are changing very quickly. I read in the local newspaper, a few weeks ago, that they are now able to take the impurities out of the oil extracted from the Kimmeridge shale beds. Before long the countryside of Dorset could be changed beyond recognition. I would not wish to stay here then.'

'I see . . . Now, that is interesting.'

'Interesting?' she said sharply. 'It is appalling!'

'Oh, yes. I agree. It just tied up with something else, that is all . . . Well, here is the station. I had better get on to the platform. Thank you for all your help, miss . . . And I shall be looking forward to a telegraph from you!'

7

When Bragg got to Old Jewry the following morning there was no sign of Morton. He spent a couple of hours writing up his notes, then spread the family tree on the desk in front of him. It was all too tempting, to try to link the murder of Jethro Witney with that of Walter Green. Here they were, on the same bit of paper . . . But why? If he were honest he had not got even a sniff of a motive for killing either of them. Well, not real motive, anyway. People like Syme and Julia had got their hand-outs a bit earlier than normal, that was all. And, whatever he had said to the Commissioner, he did not really believe that the Rossiters would kill for their notion of a hereafter . . . Of course, if he were prepared to accept the escaped prisoner theory it would make life a deal simpler – until they caught Platt, that is. But one thing was certain, he would get no thanks from the Dorset police if he proved them wrong.

He fumbled disconsolately for his pipe. He always felt like this after a weekend in Bere Regis. Whatever she said, Fanny would rue changing Dorset for Chelsea, or wherever she fancied in London. It would not be long before she was itching to get back.

The door opened and Morton came in. 'No more hack-work like that!' he exclaimed irritably. 'I have had two days of the most dispiriting drudgery.'

'Only two?' Bragg asked mildly.

'The best part of Friday, the whole of Saturday morning and three hours today! I have pored over registers of shareholders until the writing danced on the page; and with no result whatever!'

'Have you been to all the companies on the list?'

'Yes. I have just come from the registered office of Formby's Cement Works Co Ltd, in deepest Pimlico, since the clerk with the key to the relevant press was away sick on Saturday morning. My weekend of excited anticipation was all to no avail. Jethro Witney did not own shares in that company either.'

'Had he shares in none of them?' Bragg asked, in surprise.

'Not one.'

'Even the ones where the tick had been crossed through?'

'Verily, even so.' Morton sprawled in his chair. 'I trust that you had a more productive weekend,' he said.

'Well, I am in a bloody sight better mood than you, lad.'

'Ah, but you have no doubt been closeted with the comely Miss Hildred.'

'I did see your cousin, yes.'

'My cousin?'

'We will come to that later,' Bragg said briskly. 'Sit down and listen.'

'Do I need to take notes?'

'No. There is not a lot of detail yet . . . I went to the Chief Constable. It seems that Ursula Witney was right. Her fiancé was killed in the same way as Jethro Witney. There was one queer feature though. He was found naked, and the body had been moved.'

'Where was he found?'

'On a cart-track, behind his house. I have drawn a rough plan for you. See . . . he lived more or less across from the Beaufort Arms. We had a little jaunt around.'

'You and the Chief Constable?' Morton asked airily.

'No! Miss Hildred and me. But we did not try to get round the back of the house. As far as I could tell, the only way is up a little lane, between some cottages and a nice-looking stone house.'

'Could you not have promenaded elegantly along? I am sure that you would have made a handsome pair!'

'Shut it!' Bragg growled. 'Anyway, that was before I had seen Colonel Colegrave.'

'I see. Why was it concluded that the body had been moved?'

'Simple. There was no blood where he was found.'

'Killed elsewhere, and dumped naked behind his own house . . . But disrobing was not a feature of the Witney killing.'

'No. But the method was the same.'

'Five weeks apart. I suppose the murderer is not some lunatic, who happened to get his dates wrong?'

'It has nothing to do with the moon. I have already checked it.'

'That, at least, is a relief. And are the honest constabulary of Dorset seized of the fact that their crime ought to have a motive?'

'They think it was an escaped prisoner from Portland – killed him for his clothes.'

'No doubt their chief has other ideas now.'

Bragg looked at him sourly. 'You know, lad, sometimes you are a damned sight too chirpy for your own good.'

'My apologies, sir. Please ascribe it to the exuberance of comparative youth.'

'Or the cheek of sheer ignorance . . . But we are going to put that right. As from tomorrow, you are a Hildred, cousin to Fanny – plenty of money, of use to nobody, only interested in bugs. You can play that part easily enough.'

'It sounds stimulating. Do I stay with the estimable Fanny?'

'Not bloody likely! And remember, they are one of the best families down there.'

'Very well. But where lies the advantage in my adopting their name?'

'Fanny will back you up if people get nosy.'

'Ah, so you are exiling me to the wilds of Dorset, where escaped felons leap from behind bushes demanding one's garments!'

'It took you long enough! You will have to work things out quicker than that in Slocombe Magna.'

'You wish me to stay in the village itself?'

'Yes. Colonel Colegrave says that there are plenty of insects, all over the Isle of Purbeck.'

140

'It is not actually an island, surely?'

'As good as, in olden times. Cut off by marshes from the rest of Dorset.'

'I see. And, are the natives friendly?'

'I would hardly bank on it.'

'Very well. What is my role to be? My operational role, that is.'

'Just poke around. Find out what you can about the people who live there, the people who visit. Try to discover where Walter Green was killed, and why. Posing as an entomologist should mean you can turn up anywhere and find a bug to justify it.'

'And how am I to report to you?'

'If need be you can go to see your Aunt Amy in Bere Regis. Fanny will send the telegraph to me, from Dorchester.'

'Very well. But suppose a telegraph will not suffice?'

'Then I will come down, and we can meet at the Hildreds'. It is all arranged.'

Morton smiled quizzically. 'I have a growing presentiment that I shall certainly need to visit Bere Regis,' he said. 'I could not neglect an opportunity of meeting the enterprising Miss Hildred.'

'You keep away, unless it is necessary,' Bragg said gruffly. 'I do not want them dragged into this without good reason.'

Morton's face became serious. 'Of course, sir. I would not want to involve anyone else in this wretched business.'

'Right . . . Oh, that reminds me. I know where Peter Lazenby was going.'

'When?'

'When he visited Julia Witney, of course! You remember the plan that he had on his drawing-board? Well, it all ties up. They have known for centuries that there is oil in the shale deposits around Kimmeridge. But they could never use it, because it stank to high heaven when it was burned. Yesterday Fanny said that, according to the newspapers, they can now get the sulphur out of it.'

'It was just such a plant that Peter Lazenby was designing.'

'Right. I will bet a pound to a penny he has been going down to Dorset all this time.'

'And where, may I ask, is Kimmeridge?'

Bragg smiled fiercely. 'If you drew a line on the map, from Wareham through Slocombe Magna, it would just about hit Kimmeridge on the coast.'

'So, you think that Peter Lazenby could have murdered both Witney and Green?'

'He could have had the opportunity.'

'But what would have been his motive?'

'That is for you to find out!'

Morton shrugged. 'I have something more pressing to discover,' he said. 'I know very little about insects. Could I not be a geologist? I think I would be much more convincing, knocking chips of rock from boulders with a little hammer!'

'Don't be stupid, lad. One rock is the same as any other. You have to be able to stay there for a couple of weeks, if necessary.'

'I see. Then, I think I should prepare myself with the aid of some expert advice. There is an entomological society in London, I believe.' He picked up the classified directory of subscribers to the telephone system and began to flick through the pages. Then there was a tap on the door, and Catherine Marsden came in.

'May I disturb you?' she asked.

'Of course, miss. Any time.' Bragg set a chair for her at his desk.

'I felt that I had to come immediately, since it could be important.' She seated herself, her face glowing with excitement.

'Is it about the law case?' Morton asked, perching on the edge of the desk.

'Yes! I finally tracked it down, after drawing a blank in the Queen's Bench Division and the Chancery Division. It was exceedingly frustrating!'

'Why was that, miss?'

'It was all concerned with a will. In those days, the administration of the estate of a deceased person lay with the Chancery courts. But the old Ecclesiastical courts still pronounced on the validity of some wills. That is why I have been chasing all over the Law Courts, trying to unearth the file!'

'What days are we talking about, miss?'

'The trouble that impoverished the Rossiters arose over the will of a certain Ruth Green, who died on the eleventh of July, eighteen forty-one. In the papers, the lady was described as "Green, née Walters, formerly Rossiter".'

'That ties up with the family tree, there,' Morton said.

'Indeed! In eighteen hundred and two, Miss Walters married a tea shipper, in India. His name was Oliver Rossiter and he traded from Bombay. Perhaps she was a member of an early fishing fleet of spinsters, seeking rich husbands in the colonies; for she was twenty-nine when they married. They had a son in eighteen hundred and three, and a daughter two years later.'

'Just a minute, miss.' Bragg's thick finger was stabbing at the family tree. 'Here they are – Stanley and Mabel. Go on.'

'Unfortunately, Mr Rossiter died in eighteen hundred and seven. Thereupon his widow married a Captain Oscar Green. Tragically, Captain Green was killed in some minor skirmish in eighteen hundred and eight, within weeks of their wedding. She did, however, bear him a posthumous son in that same year. He was christened John.'

'I have him,' Bragg said. 'He is the father of Alfred Green, and the Walter who has just been murdered!'

Morton came behind Bragg's chair and leaned over. 'So the present-day Rossiters and Greens spring from the fecund womb of this Ruth?'

Catherine wrinkled her nose in distaste. 'If you care to express it that way, yes. Not unnaturally, she returned to England after the death of Oscar; John Green was, in fact, born in Winchester.'

'Where did she live?' Morton asked. 'In Parchment Street?'

Catherine laughed. 'The papers in the court's file did not give a complete family history!' she protested. 'But it is clear that she returned to these shores a wealthy woman.'

'Good for her!'

'Yes indeed. Except for one weakness, she might be held up as an exemplar to our sex. She lived a virtuous life, invested wisely and kept her own counsel.'

'A paragon no less! But wherein lay this moral fragility?'

Catherine twisted her mouth ruefully. 'She had a favourite among her children – John Green. Even worse, she made the fact apparent. As a result there seems always to have been friction between John Green and his Rossiter siblings.'

'It started as far back as that, did it?' Bragg remarked. 'Let me see . . . Why, Stanley Rossiter was the grandfather of Morton's friend William!'

'Indeed, and the ill feeling was exacerbated when, in her declining years, Ruth went to live with John and his family. From a detached point of view, one can hardly be surprised. Apart from being his mother's manifest favourite, John seems to have been the industrious one of the children. He trained as a provision merchant in Winchester, then moved to Wareham and began importing tea from India.'

'His wife was Martha . . . yes,' Bragg grunted.

'As to his sons, Alfred Green was born in eighteen thirty-four, Walter not until eighteen forty.'

'And Walter was murdered on May Day eighteen ninety-four.'

Catherine frowned. 'That event plays no part in my story, sergeant,' she said sharply.

'I'm sorry, miss,' Bragg said contritely. 'I promise I will not interrupt again.'

'As I have indicated,' Catherine continued, 'Ruth went to live in John Green's household in eighteen thirty-eight. She died on the eleventh of July eighteen forty-one.'

'And then the trouble started.'

'Yes, sergeant. At her death she held leases on many desirable properties in Winchester, and considerable investments in government stocks. In her will she left the leases jointly to Stanley and Mabel Rossiter. The investments all went to John Green.'

'I see. That was a bit naughty.'

'Such was my first reaction; but on reflection I can imagine that she thought she was being fair. The Rossiters still lived in Winchester, in houses she had provided for them. Indeed, Stanley had three children by that time. And, who knows, she may have been generous to them in her lifetime. At all events, the will seemed to have been accepted by all members of the family – until the leaseholds were valued.'

'Well, at least Witney cannot have done that!' Bragg chuckled.

Catherine smiled. 'Since my exposition has yet again been interrupted,' she said, 'I will give you one stray piece of information that will interest you.'

'Go on, then.'

'The will submitted for probate was drawn up with the assistance of Lazenby Nugent & Co; the signature being witnessed by John Green and a certain Hector Lazenby. John and Hector were nominated as her executors.'

'The same pattern as for Jethro Witney.'

'Yes . . . As I was saying, when the leaseholds were valued, they

144

were worth nowhere near as much as the investments left to John Green. Immediately the two Rossiters began a lawsuit, alleging that John Green had brought undue influence to bear on his mother when she was making the will. It was at this point that the case was transferred from the Chancery to the Ecclesiastical Court . . . For months there were inconclusive legal manoeuvrings, then, finally, it was set down for hearing in the autumn of eighteen forty-two, before the delightfully named Court of the Arches.'

'So, what happened?'

'Absolutely nothing! The case was suddenly withdrawn by the plaintiffs without any explanation whatever. After months of legal wrangling and, no doubt, enormous solicitors' and barristers' fees, the Rossiters simply gave up and accepted the situation.'

'The will was left to stand?' Bragg asked, incredulous.

'Yes.'

'And it was all done so publicly that the Rossiters got the reputation in Winchester of being losers?'

'So it would appear.'

'Well, one thing is for sure, the Rossiters are still bitter – right down to your generation . . . I wonder what was behind it all.'

Morton escorted Catherine back to her office, and she was gratifyingly concerned when he told her about his undercover mission to Dorset. Then he made a point of thanking the editor of the *City Press* for allowing her to help the police; emphasizing that her contribution had been vital and could well lead to the arrest of the murderer. Tranter had been uncomfortable, to say the least, at this fulsome expression of gratitude. He made it plain that no precedent had been set, but conceded a moral obligation to allow Catherine to continue assisting in the Witney investigation. That done, Morton took a train to Stratford and had his lunch in The Bell public house. He lingered in a corner, watching the steady stream of customers coming and going. It was almost two o'clock when Peter Lazenby entered. He strolled up to the bar, then took his pork pie and beer to a table in an alcove. Morton watched him for a time, wondering if anyone was going to join him, but nothing happened. The landlord left the bar and busied himself in clearing the tables. Morton beckoned him over.

'Police,' he said. 'You were going to let Jacko know that we wanted to see him.'

'Was I?' The landlord scratched his head. 'To be honest, I wouldn't recognize him if I saw him. I told the constable as much.' He moved away, picking up empty glasses as he went.

Morton went over to Lazenby's table. 'Have you found Jacko for us?' he asked curtly.

Lazenby looked up, startled. 'Oh, God!' he exclaimed. 'I thought I had seen the last of you.'

Morton sat down deliberately. 'If you can produce corroboration of your whereabouts when Jethro Witney was murdered,' he said, 'it is possible that you might.'

'I am doing all I can. On the only day that Jacko has been here since we spoke I happened to be away.'

'At Jethro's funeral?'

Lazenby's eyes narrowed. 'Yes,' he said.

'I see . . .' Morton's tone became more casual. 'How is the sulphur extraction project going?' he asked.

'Very well. The client has now accepted the design, and a pilot plant is to be built at the new drilling site.'

'In Dorset?'

Lazenby's brow crinkled in surprise. 'As a matter of fact, yes.'

'At Kimmeridge?'

'No, a little inland – on the edge of Poole Harbour.'

'Good! You must be very gratified.'

Lazenby gave a bewildered smile. 'It should help to establish my reputation,' he said.

'I gather that you did not go to the reception,' Morton said, suddenly incisive.

'Reception? I do not understand.'

'You went to Witney's funeral, but were not there when the will was read. Why was that?'

'I could not spare the time. I was working under considerable pressure.'

'And, of course, you knew the contents of the will already.'

'That is not true!' Lazenby said harshly. 'How could I possibly know?'

'You admitted that you admire Julia Witney – and by no means from afar. I am sure that she has no secrets from you.'

146

Lazenby snorted contemptuously. 'Since your Sergeant Bragg had the effrontery to force himself into the will-reading, you must be well aware that its terms were a total surprise to her.'

'But not to your father, it would appear.'

Lazenby clenched his fists. 'My father would never be so un-professional!' he hissed.

'Not even for his son?'

'And how am I supposed to have benefited from this knowledge?' he demanded.

'Not from the knowledge . . . Do you think she will keep her promise?'

'What promise?'

'Understanding, if you prefer that word. I would have thought that now you are successful, and she has inherited, wedding bells would be ringing.'

'With her father barely cold in his grave? You must know that it would be the height of impropriety.'

'Ah, yes. But you have discussed it?'

'No, I have not! Because of the trust set up under Jethro's will, Julia feels in a way cheated of her inheritance. She, to some extent, blames my father; though how Jethro could have honourably dealt with the situation in any other way escapes me.'

'Do you personally set great store by honour, Mr Lazenby?'

'Of course! How else can a gentleman act?'

'Yes . . .' Morton got to his feet as if to go; then checked. 'By the way, can you tell me where you were on the first of May?'

'Why on earth should that concern you?'

'It is nothing more than a stray point that I want to eliminate.'

'Really!' Lazenby exclaimed petulantly. He pulled a diary from his pocket and turned the pages. 'I had a meeting in Poole, concerning the sulphur extraction project. Since it commenced at nine o'clock I had travelled down the previous afternoon.'

'Calling at Winchester on the way, no doubt.'

'Is that a crime?'

'I would be glad to believe that it did not have the remotest connection to any crime, sir.' Morton turned on his heel and marched portentously out.

He had enjoyed the interview, he decided. It had been rather restrained; Bragg would have been more incisive – savage even. But it had been held in a public place, and there was no call to do more than remind Lazenby that he was under suspicion . . . But he was being unduly modest. He had established that Lazenby had been conveniently to hand when Walter Green was murdered. And there were distinct indications of strain developing between Lazenby and Julia. Was it a falling out of conspirators, once Julia's lethal purpose had been achieved? Would Branksome suddenly appear again? Or was it that Julia's indignation over the will was being, to some extent, transferred from Edward Lazenby to his son? He must write a report for Bragg, that evening.

He went back to the City, then by underground railway to South Kensington. He strolled up Queen Anne's Gate, where he found the offices of the Entomological Society of London. The outer door gave on to a short corridor, with opaque-glazed doors off it. None of them proclaimed that it was an enquiry office. He pushed one open; it was a rather untidy library, with bookshelves along one wall and a rack containing maps on another. There was no one in it. The next was an office, its desks stacked with envelopes and what looked like printed circulars. He skipped a door and knocked at the next one.

'Come in!'

He entered a room that seemed unbelievably untidy. Books were piled on all the chairs, butterfly-nets and wicker baskets obstructed the floor. A plump, balding man sat at the desk; he had green eyes and a puckish smile.

'Can I help you, young man?'

Morton surveyed the room and grinned. 'I am seeking entomological expertise,' he said, 'and clearly I have found it!'

'You flatter me, sir.'

'Neither "flattery" nor "sir" is an accurate description. My name is Morton; I am a detective constable with the City of London Police.'

'Wait a moment!' He half rose from his chair, then plopped back again. 'Of course! Jim Morton the cricketer! I have followed your career, of course, but never seen you – except on the field of play.' He stood up and held out his hand. 'This is a great honour! I am too old to have heroes, but that century of yours against the Australians at Lord's last summer was a display of the most consummate artistry. I shall remember it till the day I die!'

'I am sure you exaggerate, sir,' Morton said with an embarrassed smile.

'Nonsense! Now, how can I help you? Move some books and take a seat.'

Morton lifted the volumes from the nearest chair and looked around him. 'Where shall I put them?'

The man sighed. 'I really must tidy up sometime,' he said. 'The trouble is that when I do so I can no longer find anything! . . . Oh, just drop them on the floor, for the moment.'

'I am hoping to gain an acquaintance with entomology which will be adequate to cloak some investigative activities I am charged with,' Morton said. 'I intended to ask the Secretary to put me in touch with someone sufficiently knowledgeable.'

'I am the Secretary – Edward Poulton. I shall be delighted to be of service.'

Morton smiled. 'Since my ignorance is profound, I must leave you to determine how we can approach the problem.'

'Hmn . . . If you will define your aims, we can certainly attempt to narrow the field. How urgent is the matter?'

'I go to Dorset tomorrow.'

'Goodness! Well, we can but do our best. Dorset, you say?'

'Yes. In the strictest confidence, this is all connected with a particularly repellent murder in the City, ten days ago. We are now aware that there had been a similar murder, in Dorset, on the first of May.'

'And, presumably, the police have not apprehended the perpetrator of the first crime.'

'Exactly. For reasons into which I need not delve, we are unlikely to get co-operation from the Dorset force; so I am going to the area incognito, to see what I can discover.'

'But why as an entomologist?'

'Largely because that is the course suggested by the Chief Constable of Dorset.'

Poulton rubbed his hands. 'This becomes more and more intriguing,' he said, his eyes glinting impishly. 'Why should he wish to conspire with you against his own force?'

'He owes us a favour,' Morton said shortly.

'I see . . . And what is the locality with which you are concerned?'

'The Isle of Purbeck. My object is to be able to search the area clandestinely, for clues which may solve both murders.'

149

'It is a large area, you appreciate that.'

'I know, I am prepared to spend all the time necessary to produce a result – hence my plea for assistance. I anticipate, however, that my efforts will be centred on Slocombe Magna.'

'Slocombe Magna?' Poulton savoured the name. 'I do not know it . . . Can you reach me that roll of maps? The third from the corner of the window . . . Yes, that is it.'

He unrolled the bundle and, extracting an ordnance map, spread it on the desk. 'Would you happen to know where Slocombe Magna is?' he asked.

'Between Wareham and Kimmeridge, I am told.'

'I see . . . Ah, yes. I have it. So, you would be unlikely to go, say, east of Corfe Castle?'

'That might be a reasonable assumption. Is it important that you should know?'

Poulton's eyes gleamed. 'I am becoming perhaps dangerously enthusiastic about this problem of yours; so please tell me if I am talking nonsense. It seems to me that, if you are credibly to spend a considerable time in such an area, in the role of an entomologist, you ought to have a fairly specific project . . . perhaps one authorized by us.'

'That seems an excellent idea. Would it not, however, entail far more knowledge than I can possibly absorb in the time?'

'Not necessarily. Can I assume that you know a little about, say, butterflies?'

'I spent my childhood in the Kent countryside. I once had a butterfly-net, and caught the local species such as the Cabbage White and the Red Admiral. But it was too unrewarding for me; I needed something more active.'

Poulton smiled. 'I am scandalized at such an irreverent attitude,' he said. 'But, since you obviously turned to cricket, I shall forgive you . . . Now, going south from Wareham, you come to a steep chalk ridge, then the limestone plateau . . .'

'There is shale around Kimmeridge, I believe.'

'Perhaps, but that underlies the limestone, and is irrelevant for our purpose. The nature of the soil determines the vegetation, and the vegetation determines the species of butterfly you will find – amongst other factors, of course. Now, there is a butterfly called the Lulworth Skipper, *Thymelicus acteon*, which is found only in an area of a mile or so on either side of Lulworth Cove.' He unhooked a display-case from the wall, and brought it over.

'That's the chap!' He indicated a small tan-coloured butterfly. 'The trouble there is that it is a late species. No one would mount a serious study of it before July. However, this is an early season, so you might encounter the odd one. You ought certainly to be aware of it.'

'There seems to be so little difference between the butterflies in this case,' Morton said. 'I do not see how I shall be able to distinguish one from another when I am down there.'

'There is no need to be downhearted! Most amateurs would need to refer to a book before pronouncing on these little chaps. I will supply you with an illustrated compendium that will show the markings and describe the colours. You will be better placed than anyone you are likely to meet, I'll be bound.'

'Thank you . . . So we have eliminated the Lulworth Skipper. What butterfly should I look for?'

Poulton considered for a moment. 'Perhaps we ought to modify the aim of our project,' he said, 'to cover the possibility, however unlikely, that you might meet a fellow enthusiast. He or she could produce a specimen of your chosen insect, and your need to remain would be gone . . . I have it!' His face shone with delight. 'There are two butterflies which are mainly confined to the south-east corner of Britain – the Chalk-hill Blue, *Lysandra coridon*, and the Adonis Blue, *Lysandra bellargus*. There will, however, be some present in the area you are concerned with, particularly the Adonis, though there may not be many female Chalk-hills at this time of year. Nevertheless, your project shall be to determine the western boundary of their distribution.'

'But, suppose that I found one in Slocombe Magna, would I not thereupon be compelled to move westwards?'

'Not necessarily. One can often find the odd specimen out of its natural habitat. If we define distribution as being where the butterfly can be seen feeding in significant numbers, that should take care of the problem. Now, look carefully at the four specimens on the bottom row.'

'But only one of them is blue!' Morton exclaimed.

'Yes. That is the male Adonis. Handsome chap, eh?'

'The other three are speckled brown – and none of them is much more than an inch across!'

'Indeed.' Poulton rubbed his hands gleefully. 'As I see it, they will be ideal for your purpose. They are not exactly butterflies that the average countryman would take much heed of.'

'I suppose not . . . I wish that I had taken more interest in entomology when I was younger. My knowledge, even now, is exceedingly tenuous.'

Poulton smiled. 'Well, if it will increase your confidence, I will let you have my file of what I call my party pieces. They are snippets that I trot out, at lectures, when the audience is becoming bored. Now, we must provide you with the equipment necessary for your expedition.'

Morton felt somewhat foolish as he carried the awkward wicker basket and the large kite-net through St Botolph's churchyard to his rooms in Alderman's Walk. As he stumbled up the stairs, his manservant appeared. Chambers had been his father's valet, and Mrs Chambers the cook at The Priory. When Morton came down from Cambridge, he had declared in a somewhat self-righteous spasm that he would join the City police, as a way of doing something useful with his life. His elder brother had been gravely wounded, in the Sudan, and brought home paralysed from the waist down. Naturally he was bitter and resentful. Whatever the future held for him, it was James's sons who would inherit the baronetcy and the estates. In an attempt to give Edwin something to live for, his parents had decreed that henceforth he should run the estates. This pretence would have been acceptable had Sir Henry exercised a discreet oversight of affairs himself. But this he resolutely declined to do. It was not merely that his own duties, as Lord Lieutenant of Kent, took up a considerable amount of time. He evidently believed that giving an illusion of usefulness to his first-born was more important than farming efficiently. So Edwin would lie propped up in his room, with plans of the farms and charts of the crops. When his health would allow, the bailiff would go to see him, listen to his orders, then go off and do what he thought best. In such a situation there was no room for a younger brother who could see his own inheritance going to rack and ruin.

Since his bout of pneumonia last winter Edwin seemed to have lost some of the resentful possessiveness over his function. He had become listless, perhaps accepting the inevitability of early death, but not yet reconciled to it. In response, his parents had become even more protective, insisting that his life had not been wasted. It was mainly guilt, Morton thought. His mother had fought against the military tradition of the Mortons; had not wanted her sons to spend their lives in the outposts of an empire that meant nothing to her. As the daughter of the American ambassador to Britain, she had inherited the innate dislike of her nation for the red-coats. Morton suspected that his parents had reached a compromise, for there had never been a suggestion that he should join the army. Now, with Edwin's life shattered by a stray bullet in a minor skirmish, they both felt to blame; he because he had insisted, she because she had not persevered enough.

So, it had been something of a relief to everyone when their younger son had chosen a career that would keep him away from The Priory. Even the quixotry of his joining the police as a constable had not perturbed them. To his father, the ideal of service was paramount. And the decision clearly appealed to his mother's native egalitarianism. But, to some extent, he was a fraud. He did not really live the life of a police constable. He had ample wealth of his own, through trusts set up by his maternal grandfather. And, to make sure that he was properly looked after, Mr and Mrs Chambers had been despatched to run his bachelor household.

'I am going away for some time,' he announced.

'Very well, Master James. Shall I pack for a house party, or a holiday in the country?'

'Ah, there I shall have to rely on you, Chambers. What is the recommended attire for butterfly collecting?'

'Butterfly collecting?' Chambers's smooth brow wrinkled. 'I cannot say that I have given the matter any thought, sir.'

'Then please do so. I am going down to Dorset, for an indefinite period.'

'Dorset? Am I to understand, sir, that this pursuit is to be carried out in the course of your duties?' There was a faintly disapproving note in his voice.

'Yes, Chambers. I have to search a large area of countryside. Butterfly collectors can apparently wander at will, without landowners bothering to challenge them.'

'I see, sir. Country clothes, then.'

153

'Yes. And I must not appear too prosperous.'

'Indeed, sir. I did not assume that such activities would be indulged in by society gentlemen.'

'Enough of this snobbery, Chambers!'

'Yes, sir. Might I suggest your old Norfolk jacket, and your shooting knickerbockers?'

'Will they not be rather warm?'

'I do not believe that it ever gets really warm in Dorset, sir. But I could pack flannel trousers and a blazer to meet that eventuality.'

'Good idea! I could wear them in the evenings, also.'

'As to hats, sir, I would suggest a deer stalker and a straw boater . . . Do I take it that such a person would not concern himself with evening dress?'

Morton laughed. 'I shall be staying at a village inn,' he said. 'Moreover, it is important that I do not antagonize the local people . . . There is another thing that worries me, Chambers. Some of the residents of the village were at the funeral that I went to in Winchester. I do not suppose it is remotely likely that they would recognize me since I sat nowhere near them. The most they could have got is a glimpse as they walked down the aisle, or at the cemetery. But, if you could change my appearance somewhat, it would be an advantage.'

Chambers pursed his lips. 'Then, might I suggest that you wear the spectacles that you adopted in the case of the forged banknotes? They made you look quite studious and reflective.'

'And the springs nearly tore my ears off! I suppose that I could. Where are they?'

'In the centre drawer of the writing table. You might consider something else, also, sir.'

'What is that?'

'It would alter and, if I may say so, considerably improve your appearance, if you were to put back your hair parting to where it was before you met the young lady.'

Morton smiled. 'Miss Marsden, you mean?'

'Yes, sir. It is not quite the thing for a gentleman of your standing to have a side parting. It seems a little . . . well, raffish.'

'But I thought that was precisely the impression I wanted to create!'

'With respect, sir, no. My recollection of amateur scientists is that

154

their preoccupations lead them to neglect their appearance. They would never concern themselves to be stylish.'

'But I have no time to go to the barber,' Morton protested.

'Then, if you will just sit down, sir, I will return the parting to the centre and snip off the long hairs with the kitchen scissors. That will be quite adequate. I am sure that James Morton, the butterfly collector, would not have his hair cut in the Burlington Arcade.'

'Ah. That reminds me. I shall be staying in the Beaufort Arms in Slocombe Magna. I shall register under the name of James Hildred.'

'Hildred . . . I assume that you would only wish to be communicated with under the most exceptional of circumstances.'

'Precisely right, Chambers.'

'Very good, sir. Now, if you will be seated, I will go and get the scissors.'

8

Bragg clumped up the last few steps of the St James's Street building and stood on the landing to get his breath. Without Morton there he need not pretend to be fit. Anyway, that was what young men were for. They hadn't the experience to think straight; all they could do was to chase around like half-broken donkeys . . . All the same, it was a bad sign when your belly stuck out six inches beyond your chest. Perhaps that was why he never got any further with Dora Jenks. Last bank-holiday Monday she had been feeling skittish; badgered him into going to Southend with her. They had walked to the end of the pier, watched the steamers spewing out hoards of East End kids to rampage around the town. They had eaten cockles from a stall on the promenade and listened to the band, like any married couple. On the train back she'd been all excited, singing saucy music-hall songs with the others. But, once back home, she'd shot upstairs like a whippet, and locked her bedroom door. Women! You could never fathom them. But one thing was for sure; a glass of beer was always a glass of beer. He cleared his throat discontentedly, then pushed open the office door.

'Is Mr Lazenby in?' he asked.

The frock-coated clerk raised his head. 'I am afraid that he has a client with him at the moment, sir.'

'Then I'll wait.'

'Very good, sir. If you would like to take a seat over there . . . You will find today's *Pall Mall Gazette* on the table.'

Bragg snorted. 'I'll stand.'

'As you wish, sir.' The clerk went back to his desk and resumed his work.

Bragg stood for five minutes, easing his weight from one foot to the other. The articled clerks by the window were observing him speculatively, as if wagering when he would give in and sit down. He strolled across and examined some pictures; tinted etchings in narrow gold frames. One was a view of Leicester, done sixty years ago. Not that you could see much of the town; some steeples and factory chimneys, with toy-town walls in the middle distance. The foreground was taken up with a herd of cows that seemed to be wading through a tight flock of sheep. Ridiculous! The sheep would have scattered long ago. No wonder the herdsmen had their hands in the air, like puppets. These blasted towny artists came traipsing down to paint the countryside, and when they got there found it wasn't to their liking. They altered it around to suit themselves, and ended up with rubbish like this. Still, the people who bought this kind of thing knew no better.

A door opened. Bragg turned round to see a good-looking woman being ushered out of his room by an attentive Lazenby. At the outer door she turned and held out her hand.

'Thank you so very much,' she said. 'I hardly know what I would do without you.'

Lazenby took the hand, half-bowed over it, then smugly shepherded the woman out of the office.

Bragg stepped forward to intercept him. 'Another satisfied customer, sir?'

'I like to think that all our clients merit that description, sergeant,' Lazenby replied affably. 'Is the fact that you are alone significant?'

Bragg followed him into his room. 'In what way?'

'I was hoping that the reduction in numbers did not imply a diminution of effort.'

'Oh, no sir. We will get Witney's murderer, never fear. I came to ask you how things are going.'

'In what area?'

'Jethro Witney's will.'

'Ah.' Lazenby gestured towards a chair at his desk. 'And may I ask why you have come to me, instead of Julia's solicitors?' he asked with an amused smile.

'For no better reason than that you are on our doorstep.'

'In a murder investigation, I am sure that is an impeccable reason, sergeant! Well now, since we last met I have received a communication from Julia's advisers.'

'Who are?'

'Rawbone & Treblecock, of Winchester.'

'And what do they have to say for themselves?'

Lazenby laughed. 'This is the point at which I would normally dive for cover, behind some such formula as my client's privilege. But here I find myself in the unaccustomed position of being the principal! Well, I can see no reason why the executors of Jethro's will should not share their information with the police.'

'Good.'

'Julia's solicitors have signified their intention to contend that the failure to discover the will derives, not from its loss, but from its deliberate destruction by the testator.'

'So, what will happen now?'

'Clearly something must. The law, like nature, abhors a vacuum. Nevertheless, it is not for the executors to initiate action. We hold a copy of the last will he made, and no one has produced any evidence that he contemplated changing it.'

'So Julia will have to sue you?'

'I very much hope that she will not resort to such a course. It cannot remotely be in her interests to do so. I trust that as her anger subsides she will realize that. After all, she benefits from the bulk of the estate; and the impediment will not last for ever.'

'Nineteen years seems a lifetime when you are twenty-one,' Bragg said. 'But I think what rankles is that the capital is all in trust. She will have to come running to you for every penny that she spends.'

Lazenby shook his head. 'That need not be so. I tell you this, sergeant, in the full awareness that you may for your own purposes feel it expedient to pass the information to the lady in question. I cannot speak for my co-executor, for we have not yet had cause to discuss the matter. But my own attitude to our responsibilities under the will is that we must retain sufficient capital in the estate demonstrably to generate two hundred pounds a year for the specified period. Once that is secure, we can certainly consider making advances of capital to Julia – always provided that it is for a purpose which we, as executors, could approve.'

Bragg snorted. 'Fat chance of my passing that lot on. Anyway, I doubt if she would want to hear it. There is always a catch, with lawyers, isn't there?'

Lazenby looked pained. 'What could any reasonable person take objection to?' he asked.

'Why, you hold every last farthing. You will dole it out like pocket-money, so long as you can tell her what kind of sweets she has to buy.'

Lazenby shook his head. 'I am sorry that you interpret my remarks in that light,' he said. 'Believe me, we would be stretching our duties as trustees, perhaps to a dangerous extent, in so doing.'

'Why?'

'The overriding burden laid on us by the will is to stand possessed of the assets of the deceased. Now, let us take a hypothetical situation. Let us suppose that Julia asks us for a capital advance, which we unwarily consent to. Let us further assume that we advance virtually all the free capital in the estate. Let us then assume that Julia, acting on her own account, invests the money unwisely and it is irretrievably lost. There is nothing to prevent the young lady from suing us, as executors, for an egregious breach of trust. Believe me, sergeant, with a young and headstrong woman involved, there are compelling reasons why we ought to take a prudential attitude to our responsibilities as trustees.'

'Even though your son is, as you say, close to her?'

'All the more so.'

'Hmn . . . And, what will happen if she goes on trying to have the will set aside?'

'I and my co-executor will have to contest the action. There could be a law case of positively Dickensian proportions. The costs could be astronomical since both points of view could be argued endlessly.'

'But you are going a long way to meeting her when you talk about advancing capital.'

'Ah, yes. But that is in the context of a will-trust which is accepted by all parties.'

'So, if it came to court Julia could not win.'

'That is my firm belief. She has no documentary evidence, indeed no evidence at all, to support her contentions. They spring from no more than righteous anger that her future is constrained; and a self-righteous disapprobation of a father whose human frailty is all too apparent.'

'And, on your side, you have the copy will.'

'Yes. But not only that. We would be able to submit to the court Jethro's earlier will, which is consistent with the one we seek to establish.'

'But, if he changed it, that would surely show that he was not happy with it?'

'Rather, that it was no longer appropriate.'

'What is that supposed to mean?'

Lazenby pondered. 'I would not wish you to pass this particular piece of information to Julia – or indeed to anyone.'

'Then you have my word on it.'

'Very well. Jethro Witney changed his previous will because his personal situation had changed.'

'How was that?'

'In it he had left a bequest of a thousand pounds to a young woman who must remain nameless.'

'That is a hell of a lot of money! . . . Why did he have to alter it?'

Lazenby smiled. 'The young lady had been so imprudent as to marry someone else!'

'I see. So her loss was little Lily Fox's little gain?' Bragg said sardonically.

'You could consider it in that light.'

'I can see you would want to keep Julia in the dark about that . . . You know, sir, I find it hard to get Jethro Witney in focus. What kind of man was he?'

'I have no particular knowledge of him as a businessman, sergeant.'

'But as a human being?'

Lazenby wrinkled his brow. 'He was heir to the compulsions of the flesh which affect all men – and women; the corporeal imperatives that clamour to be satisfied. He inclined towards enduring relationships; indeed, it could be said that he behaved with excessive generosity towards the women involved.'

'When my wife died,' Bragg said gruffly, 'I didn't have the wherewithal to choose whether to be generous or not.'

'You too?' Lazenby exclaimed. 'I am sorry to hear it. Both solicitors and policemen share the same fate; the public at large regard them as belonging to a sub-human species of officialdom! At least I was able to profit from Jethro's experience. When my wife died, a few years ago, I ensured that the arrangements I adopted did not entail permanent attachments.'

Bragg suddenly felt gauche and embarrassed. He hurried on, lest Lazenby should ask him about his own experience. 'What can you tell me about this feud between Witney and the Rossiters?' he asked.

'You use the word "feud" advisedly, do you, sergeant?'

'Well, it looks like that to us.'

'Not on Jethro's part, I think.'

'But both William and Frederick Rossiter had a violent hatred of him.'

Lazenby pursed his lips. 'Certainly he did consult me over what he regarded as their slanderous accusations. He took the view that by taking no action he would be admitting the truth of their defamations.'

'And what did you advise?'

'That he should do precisely nothing. My own enquiries – carried out, incidentally, on my behalf by the same Rawbone & Treblecock who now afflict us – revealed that the Rossiters are generally regarded in Winchester as unbalanced religious fanatics.'

'And the property that Witney bought up?'

'You mean the four houses in Brook Street? There was ample evidence that the terrace had been offered to the public, over a protracted period, at a price which latterly declined below the amount that Jethro ultimately paid. The worst that could be urged against him was a trifling disregard of professional ethics – which are not notably strong amongst estate agents, anyway.'

'I see.' Bragg considered for a moment. 'Oh, there is one odd thing that has come up – a side-issue, you might say.'

'What is that?'

'No more than a matter of interest, really. We found out that your firm acted for some people called Green, way back in the forties. The partner involved was Hector Lazenby.'

'I was not aware of that case. I was barely born then!'

'The Greens lived in Dorset – a place called Slocombe Magna.'

'I know it, sergeant. The original Nugent in our practice came from there. Despite all our efforts, the connection persists!'

'Not very profitable, then?'

'An occasional will and the odd conveyance of property.'

'I was talking to Ursula Witney, after Jethro's funeral. She said that Walter Green had died recently; said he was her fiancé.'

'Was killed, would be a more accurate account of events, I understand.'

'Did you act for him?'

Lazenby smiled. 'Since you could establish the fact from the Probate Office, I am happy to admit it.'

'And what did his will say?'

'He was more extreme in his attachment than either I or Jethro! The whole of his estate went to Ursula Witney.'

Morton dismissed the trap that had brought him from Wareham and gazed at the Beaufort Arms. It was a long, low building, of rough irregular limestone blocks. There was moss growing in the thatch, but it looked sound enough. The window-frames were freshly painted, the flagstone in front of the doorway newly scrubbed. He picked up his portmanteau and the butterfly-net in one hand, the wicker basket in the other, then pushed through the door into the inn. A bell on a spring tinkled loudly. He entered a low-beamed room, with settles and long tables along the walls; it smelled of stale tobacco smoke. No one seemed to be about. There was no bar, in the sense of a counter with beer pumps; instead a deal-topped table, with burnished brass jugs, stood by an archway in the back wall. Morton went to the front door and, reaching up, jangled the bell for several minutes. Nothing happened. They ought to rename the pub the Marie Celeste, he thought. Growing impatient, he pushed through the curtain at the archway and found himself in a narrow, flagged passage. It led to a half-open door at the back of the building.

'Hullo!' he called. No reply.

He walked down the passage. Immediately before the back door, it gave onto a boarded area about twelve foot square. This evidently covered the entrance to the cellars, for there was an open trap-door in one corner. Morton went over to it. There was no hint of light from below.

'Hullo!' Still no reply.

He went out into the yard. There was a range of stables opposite, built of the same warm stone, with a loft above for hay. To the right the yard was closed by a dilapidated cart-shed. One door drooped on its hinges, permanently open. Inside, Morton could see a flat lorry and a trap. From the other end of the yard a rutted track curved past the back gardens of a row of cottages, towards the front of the inn. Morton strolled to the corner of the stable block; once there, he could see a path leading to its rear – and hear the squealing of pigs. He eased the spectacle springs from his ears, settled his boater on his head and strode confidently on.

'Ah, there you are, my man!' he exclaimed, in a voice that seemed to come out as an inane gurgle.

A thick-set, swarthy man, with a shock of black hair was standing by a pigsty, his shirt sleeves rolled up his knotted arms. He looked up gloweringly.

'Who might you be?' he asked in a suspicious voice.

'James Hildred. I sent you a telegraph.'

'I have no room,' he said abruptly.

'Of course you have!' Morton said amiably. 'I looked upstairs, when I could not find you.'

'No room that would do for the likes of you. Go to the Red Lion, at Wareham.'

'That would not be at all convenient. I have work to do here and I cannot waste half the day in travelling.'

'Work, have you?'

'Yes. I am carrying out an important survey of certain butterfly species in this area. As an innkeeper, you have an obligation to shelter me. One of the rooms overlooking the green would be perfectly adequate.'

'Butterflies?' he asked, with a mixture of disbelief and contempt.

'Yes. This is one of the richest habitats for thermophilic species in the whole country. And the next few weeks are the critical time for my study. So, you see, I must stay here.'

The landlord hesitated. 'How long, did you say?'

'Until my work is done. Perhaps a fortnight, I cannot tell.'

'There is only plain cooking. I doubt if it would suit you.'

'I have lived on boiled eggs and cheese for weeks, before now,' Morton said airily. 'Now, please be good enough to show me to my room.'

The man spat into the straw at his feet. 'Take whichever you want,' he said grudgingly. 'There will be a dish of stew, at seven o'clock.'

Morton retraced his steps, and selected a room over the front door of the inn. It gave him a view past the church, to the mansion and the farm beyond. To the right were cottages and the house with the lawns and shrubs – behind which Walter Green's body had been found. The room itself was sparsely furnished, with a wardrobe for his clothes, a wash-stand, and a chair by the big iron bedstead. There was a rickety table by the window. Morton placed on it the copy of June's *Entomological Record* that he had read on the journey. He took the letter that Poulton had provided, made a pencil mark on the back and inserted it between the pages of the textbook so that the mark was just visible. Anyone investigating Edward Newman's *British Butterflies* would undoubtedly displace the letter. If they read it, they might be the more persuaded that his visit was innocent. He washed the grime of his journey away, then, taking his butterfly-net, wandered out into the road.

The breeze had dropped and the sky became overcast. It was still very warm, but there was a brooding heaviness in the air. He wondered what to do; there was still an hour and a half to supper. He decided to look round the church, as being the first thing a visitor would be expected to do. Outside it looked dejected, as Bragg had said. As he approached it, a great black crow cawed at him from a pinnacle of the tower. There was a notice in the porch indicating that the parish was served by clergy attached to the Wareham parish. He pushed through the heavy pine door into the back of the nave. The church would, he supposed, have seated a hundred people – perhaps another twenty, at a pinch. But there was little sign that it was used to anything like that extent. Except for the two rows at the front, the pews were thick with dust. The windows were grimy, their sills covered with dead flies. He went up to the chancel. There was an old harmonium behind the pulpit but the choir stalls were as dusty as the pews in the nave. The altar had an elaborately carved front; obviously the gift of some rich patron in the past. On it was a plain white cloth. There was no cross; very little indication that it was a place of Christian worship – or any worship at all.

Considering how prosperous the big houses looked, it was astonishing. He walked slowly back down the nave. Now that his eyes had become accustomed to the gloom he could see that the church was more ancient than he had supposed. The carvings on the capitals of the pillars that marked the north aisle were late medieval grotesques. Was Slocombe Magna one of the communities that were laid waste by the Black Death? At the west end of the nave was the font, unsymmetrically hewn from some ancient boulder of black rock. It seemed to crouch there malevolently, its twisted form inveighing against the Creator. Most of its carvings had been worn by the centuries into unidentifiable bumps. He stooped down to examine the supporting column and almost cried out in astonishment. Beneath the overhang of the font was a sheela-na-gig! There was no doubt about it. She crouched there like a toad, holding open the lips of her genitals with her left hand. A pagan fertility symbol in a Christian church? It was incredible! The carving was crude but bold; and elemental power seeped from the pores of the stone. From this basin were the children of Slocombe Magna baptised; to its power they were dedicated . . . Was Walter Green some kind of sacrifice? Morton hurried out of the building, to still his morbid imaginings.

He crossed the road and looked through the iron gates of the mansion. That was really too grand a description, but it was certainly a substantial house. From its windows the dilapidated church and neglected graveyard would be an eyesore. Yet the owner of such a house must have money enough to restore both, if he wished. No doubt he had grown used to it. Morton walked on, swishing his butterfly-net idly. Perhaps he ought to establish his credentials from the outset. He could at least practise while he was on his own. He swung at a fluttering white butterfly, turning his wrist as Poulton had instructed. He had it! Without doubt, it was a Large White; one of the commonest butterflies in the country. No erudite entomologist would waste his time with such, however enthusiastic he was! Henceforth he must concentrate on small speckled or blue specimens. He wandered on, scrutinizing the grassy verges, appearing oblivious of all else, until he became aware that the road had petered out into a mere cart-track. A hundred yards further on it ran into a yard enclosed with extensive farm buildings. Nearby was another row of cottages, no doubt tied to the farm. Chasing an imaginary insect, he crossed to the other side of the track. There was a well-maintained path leading from the mansion to a small, detached house on the edge of the farmyard. It appeared that this land belonged to the big house, and was farmed by a bailiff. Was it a Witney or a Green, who lurked behind the neatly clipped hedge? He would find out in time.

He turned round and walked slowly back. As he passed the church the crow launched itself from the tower and flapped along his path. He went past the village green. Now, on his left, was Walter Green's house; behind which his body had been discovered. It would be unwise to examine that area, at this early stage. In any case the Dorset police would have trampled all over it. If there had been anything to find, they ought to have it. He walked on, past cottages and a substantial house on his right, until once more the road became a track. There was another farm here, the house and buildings enclosed in a ring of rowan trees. The track was barred by a stout wooden gate; a red ribbon was tied to its top rail. It was a pleasant touch, if somewhat eccentric. In a field nearby was a herd of cows. They, too, had red ribbons tied to their horns. It seemed a rather impractical way of identifying one's animals. He looked more closely. Attached to each ribbon was a small bunch of greenery. Some was fresh, some limp, some almost dried; but each cow had one. Strange . . . He turned and began to amble back to the inn. Strolling towards him were a man and a woman in their early forties. They were dressed in deep mourning, but not even that could conceal the fashionable elegance of their clothes. He must have his wits about him; he had seen those faces in Winchester cathedral!

The man raised his hat, the woman stopped and smiled.

Morton doffed his boater. 'Good evening,' he said. 'I was just taking a stroll around the village before supper.'

'Ah, then you must be the young man who is staying at the Beaufort Arms.'

Her teeth were white and even, her brown eyes friendly. 'My name is Francesca Witney,' she said. 'And this is my brother Thomas.'

The brother nodded, without speaking. So this was Lazenby's co-executor.

'I see, from your attire, that condolences would be appropriate,' Morton murmured earnestly. 'You have clearly lost someone very close to you. Not your mother, I hope. Nothing could be worse than losing one's mother.'

'No.' Francesca's smile became indulgent. 'Mamma is still with us . . . We lost our brother.'

'I am so sorry.'

She waved away his commiseration. 'Have you come here to catch butterflies?'

Morton looked down at his net. 'Not to catch them – or, at least, not to kill them. I have been sent by the Entomological Society of London to determine the limit of the distribution of two butterflies; the Adonis Blue and the Chalk-hill Blue.'

'I cannot say that I have heard of either,' Thomas interjected in a dry, precise voice.

'They are not very striking, but they are pretty little chaps,' he said, borrowing Poulton's phrase.

Francesca turned and began to stroll back, the men keeping pace on either side. 'Are these butterflies important?' she asked.

'Important? Ah, well, there you have me . . . I suppose the world would be just the same, if they had never been made. But they are beautiful, and beauty is beyond price.' He allowed his bespectacled eyes to linger admiringly on Francesca's face.

'So, as other men climb mountains merely because they exist, you catch butterflies?'

'Perhaps. But, at least, I aim to add a little to the store of human knowledge.'

'I am sure that you do,' she said indulgently. 'And we would be delighted to help you in your task.' She paused at their gate. 'Why do you not look at the flowers in our garden? It might be that your butterflies can be found there.'

'You are very kind.'

He followed her along a path that curved across the front of the house, to a flower garden at the side. Thomas mumbled his excuses and went inside.

'I am sure that the gardens in London, such as Kew, have a much more extensive display,' she said. 'But I am really quite proud of my own small contribution to beauty.' The smile was amused, almost challenging.

166

'What a magnificent show!' Morton said warmly. 'Those poppies and foxgloves are quite splendid . . . And what superb delphiniums!'

'What do your particular butterflies require?'

'Well, of course, the butterflies themselves only drink nectar,' Morton said gauchely. 'But to reproduce themselves they need horseshoe-vetch.'

'But that is a weed!'

'Yes . . . yes, it is.'

'How paradoxical, that supreme beauty can only be nourished by the unregarded.'

'Now you are laughing at me.'

She smiled. 'By no means . . . Let me show you the herb garden. That is certainly utilitarian, but it gives me enormous satisfaction.'

A line of apple trees, laden with tiny fruits, divided the two. As they approached them, the black crow flapped heavily away and perched on the ridge of the house.

'I know very little about herbs,' Morton said hesitantly. 'I can see mint and parsley; ah . . . is that rosemary?'

'It is! You see, you are much more knowledgeable than you realize!'

Morton laughed. 'That is the end of it, I'm afraid. What is the one with the chrysanthemum-like leaf?'

'That is a perennial verbena. I keep it here, in the shelter of the house, because it is rather tender.'

'Ah . . . I do not recognize the one with the red stems and green leaves.'

'I am sure that you have tasted it often enough in stuffings – that is marjoram.'

'And the plant that looks like celery?'

'It is, indeed, a wild form of celery.'

'Well, it is most impressive. Do you look after it all yourself?'

She laughed indulgently. 'I have a little help with the digging, and the pruning, and the weeding, and the lawn-mowing! It seems presumptuous to call it my garden, after such a catalogue!'

'I am sure that you are its inspiration, nevertheless.'

'Thank you Mr er . . .'

'Hildred. James Hildred.'

'Well, now, Mr Hildred, I must wean myself of the heady draught of your compliments. It is time that I dressed for dinner.'

'You have been most kind, Miss Witney.' Morton said clumsily. 'I am very grateful.' He squeezed her proffered hand and hurried to the gate.

When he got back to the inn, Morton went up to his room. The textbook was still where he had left it, the letter in it unmoved. So the innkeeper's curmudgeonly reception did not betoken any suspicion about his reasons for coming to the village. He went down to the bar on the stroke of seven o'clock. There were several farm labourers drinking beer and smoking short clay pipes. As he entered, there was a sudden silence. They eyed him with sullen resentment.

'Good evening,' he said cheerfully, as he crossed to a table by the door.

They made no response. After watching him keenly for a while, they took up their conversation again. The local dialect was so broad that he had difficulty in following it. They seemed to be arguing about the merits of certain horses; but they were farm animals, not racehorses. Ploughing and pulling hay-carts were the attributes that mattered. After a few minutes a serving girl brought in a steaming dish and placed it in front of him. A hunk of bread was dropped onto the table by it.

'May I have a glass of beer?' he called, before she could vanish.

She gave him a surly look, then poured ale from a jug into a tankard, and brought it to him.

'Thank you.'

Morton broke off a piece of bread, and poked cautiously about in the dish. He could find precious little meat. There were slices of carrot and cubes of fibrous turnip, even waxy lumps of potato in the greyish water. A few yellow spots of grease floated on the surface, some brown fibres adhered to the vegetables, that was all. He was certainly not popular! He made his meal in an unconcerned fashion, then went upstairs for his kite-net. He might as well make a further demonstration of his mission, before darkness fell.

Some children were playing tag on the green; laughing and screeching, leaping and colliding. They looked uninhibited enough, at least; in fact, totally normal.

'Are you the butterfly man?' A boy of eleven or so had sidled up to him.

'Yes, that's right. What is your name?'

'William Biles . . . I know where to find butterflies.' He had

168

freckled skin and carroty hair. His blue eyes regarded Morton speculatively.

'Do you?'

'Yes. I caught a Painted Lady last week.'

'Did you really? That is a beautiful butterfly! It is strange to think that it has flown a hundred miles over the sea to get here.'

The boy knitted his brows. 'Has it?' he asked.

'Oh, yes. It comes from warm regions near the Sahara desert, and breeds here.'

'I've seen them laying eggs on nettles,' William asserted.

'That's right. Where did you catch it?'

'Do you want to see?'

'Indeed I do!'

'Then, come on!'

He led the way, hands in pockets, down the narrow road by the mansion.

'That is a fine house,' Morton remarked. 'Who lives there?'

'Mr Green.'

'He has a fine walled garden at the back of the house.'

The boy did not reply, but the topic had quelled his exuberance.

'I expect you are too old to be at school,' Morton said.

'I left a year ago,' William said, with a superior sniff.

'I see. And what do you do?'

'I help my father. He is head shepherd at Mr Alfred's place.'

'Is that the man who owns the farm at the other end of the village? The man who ties red ribbon on his gate?'

'No!' The boy's tone was contemptuous. 'He's Josiah Grote. I was talking about Mr Green.'

'I see. Do you have many sheep?'

'Altogether, do you mean?'

'Yes.'

'We must have thousands,' William said expansively. 'They are out in the country at this time of year, not near the village.'

Morton suppressed a smile. 'You must have to walk a long way to get to them.'

'Miles and miles. You never know where they have got to.'

'You are fortunate,' Morton said warmly. 'I live in the middle of London; I never get a chance to see a sheep. They have always struck me as rather difficult to control.'

169

'Nah! Not when you get the knack of it.' The boy's good humour was fully restored. 'You need a good dog, though.'

He turned to the right, along a cart-track that led past the back of the cottages. Beyond them, Morton could see the roof of Walter Green's house. Had his naked body been carried along this track, to be unceremoniously dumped? Its back garden was sheltered by a high thorn hedge. Set in it was a wrought-iron gate, through which Morton could see a woman bending over a flower bed. To the left was a field of young corn. Opposite the gate a wide area had been trampled flat. The Dorset police appeared to have been thorough in their search for prison uniforms, or whatever.

'Good heavens!' Morton exclaimed. 'What on earth has happened here? It looks as if a herd of cows has rolled over it. Was it a whirlwind?'

'Dunno,' William said tersely. He quickened his pace, and came to a clump of nettles just beyond Walter Green's house. 'That's where I caught it,' he said laconically.

'Ah, very interesting.' Morton fumbled through his inadequate store of knowledge for something to say. 'Yes, that is the kind of place you would find a Painted Lady,' he said foolishly. The boy's sudden reticence was affecting him also, causing him to forget the shallow bubbling character he had adopted. 'Now, the species I am searching for lay their eggs on sicklewort and horseshoe-vetch,' he said.

'Plenty of them, all round here.' His tone was almost surly. 'I've got to go now . . . Work in the morning.' William turned on his heel and ran back up the track.

Morton followed him casually, flicking his net at an occasional moth which was braving the hazards of the fading light. When he arrived at the Beaufort Arms the bar was thick with tobacco smoke. A sudden silence fell as he entered, hostile eyes followed his every move. He felt tired and irritable, not a safe frame of mind to engage in light badinage with the locals. He nodded briefly at them, and went up to his room. He lit the candle and turned to the table for his Newman. It had been moved! No longer was the top corner just touching the final letter of the magazine's title. Perhaps the maid had been in . . . He picked up the textbook. The mark on the letter was no longer visible. It was still between the same two pages, but there could be no doubt about it, the letter had been read. Well, that

170

was all to the good, in one sense. It would have reinforced the character he was projecting. But, all the same, someone was abnormally interested in him. He would have to watch his step.

9

Next morning Morton spent an hour after breakfast looking through his butterfly book. As a result, it was ten o'clock before he emerged from the inn. The sky was blue, the air still; it promised to be another hot day. Over his cheese and bread he had been wondering where to start his search for clues. Walter Green's body had been moved to where it was found; that seemed to have been accepted by everyone. And the Dorset police must be assumed to have examined the immediate area thoroughly. If he was to break fresh ground he must begin at the fringe of the village and move outwards. But what was he looking for? The signs of a struggle would have been obliterated by a month's weather, surely? Blood . . . There must have been a great deal of blood, spurting everywhere – unless he had really been killed in exactly the same way as Witney.

'Mr Hildred! Mr Hildred!' William Biles was running across from the cottages, a small ring-net in his hand. 'Can I come with you?'

Morton stopped. 'Why not? Though I do not know where I am going to, yet,' he said, as the boy came racing up. 'I think a little distance from the village would be best; away from the cultivated land.'

William turned and pointed south. 'On them hills, over the valley, is a good spot. There is plenty of vetch there.'

Morton looked round to get his bearings. He realized with some amusement that the area indicated was on Bragg's magical line from Wareham, through Slocombe Magna, to Kimmeridge. Well, he had to start somewhere; that was as good a place as any.

William led the way behind Alfred's Green's house, to the farmyard; then along a hedgerow to the bottom of a sheltered valley. The blackthorn was in full blossom, its scent heavy in the still air. Here and there the purple flowers of deadly nightshade struggled through to the light. At the foot of the hedge were the bloodshot

171

yellow flowers of the henbane. It was summer in all its opulence, Morton thought: a wondrous day, a day for doing almost anything but grub around looking for murderers. They came to a stream; a mere trickle of water in its gravelly bed.

'What is the name of this brook?' Morton asked.

'That's the Corfe River, that is,' William said loftily.

'I see. You have not had much rain recently, it would appear.'

'Not a drop for six weeks. There's hardly any juice in the grass. Unless we get rain soon we shall be in trouble.'

'Ah . . . I thought that you were supposed to be working today, William.'

The boy shrugged his shoulders. 'They gave me time off. I am due some holiday. If you would let me come with you, I'd want nothing better.'

'Excellent! You shall be my Vetch-vinder!'

The boy grinned, then began the gentle ascent to the open grazing land. So, the enthusiast of yesterday had been converted into today's spy. By whom? Alfred Green? But he had a bailiff to run the farm. It would look odd if he interfered in matters as trivial as shepherd-boys' holidays. However that might be, someone was uneasy at his presence. And, from the boy's reaction the previous evening, it was connected to Walter Green's death. He wondered idly who the woman in the garden had been.

'Look! Look!' the boy was shouting excitedly. 'That's a blue butterfly. Shall I catch it?'

'Yes. But be careful not to damage it.'

He watched the butterfly's erratic flight and William's stealthy determination as he stalked it. So, his question was answered as soon as posed. He had only mentioned a blue butterfly to Thomas and Francesca Witney . . . Yet their brother had been one of the victims. Curiouser and curiouser.

The boy came galloping back, his left hand supporting the fold of his net. 'I've got it!' he cried.

Morton peered through the mesh. 'Bad luck!' he said cheerfully. 'I am looking for Chalk-hill Blues and Adonis Blues. This is a male Common Blue. Can you see the brownish tinge on the wings? Now, the male Adonis is rather bigger than this, and there is a row of dark spots near the white border.'

Disappointment showed on his face. 'Shall I let it go?' he asked.

172

'Most certainly! It is not so common that we can spare a single one.'

'All right.' He twisted his net and the butterfly fluttered free.

For the next two hours they systematically covered an arc of grassland about half a mile from the village. There was no point in going further, Morton argued. He had to start from the assumption that Walter Green's body had been carried back to his house, not transported on a cart. He put behind him the possibility that he might have been murdered in his own garden or house. Surely the Dorset police would have covered that possibility? He let the boy chase after butterflies to his heart's content. During that time he caught a brownish speckled insect that Morton was happy to acknowledge as being a female Common Blue; though it could have belonged to any number of species, so far as he knew. At least William Biles was happy. When Morton declared that it was lunch-time he raced back to the village in high excitement, while Morton followed at a more decorous pace.

As he reached the village green, he heard someone calling: 'Mr Hildred! Mr Hildred!' He looked round, and saw a man standing at the gate of the mansion, waving his stick. He turned and strolled over.

'Good morning, sir,' he said cheerfully.

'You are staying in the village, I gather.' He was about sixty years old, balding, and wore a short grey beard. 'We seldom see a new face here . . . Butterflies, I understand.'

'Yes, sir. I am doing a project for the Entomological Society of London.'

'Ah. I do not want to hear about it!' he said hurriedly. 'Have you had lunch?'

'Not yet.'

'Oh. I do not eat between breakfast and sundown, myself; but you would be welcome to a drink.'

'Thank you, sir. That would be most pleasant.'

Morton followed him round the gravelled drive, through a lofty hall and into a well-proportioned sitting-room. It was furnished with heavy, old-fashioned pieces of excellent quality. In the corner, a piece of music was open on a stand. A flute rested on a bookcase nearby. Apart from this, the room looked like a furniture exhibition; all placed precisely, for best effect; nothing out of place.

The man gestured him to an armchair. 'I am Alfred Green, by the way. Will you take whisky?'

'That would be very welcome.'

'Good. I always have a whisky at this hour.' He vanished, and Morton strolled over to the window. For all that it was north-facing, the front garden was a riot of colour. The church certainly looked very neglected beyond it; even mildly sinister, with the crow cawing from its tower. Green returned, carrying a tray.

'I do not trouble my servants at midday,' he said. 'Water?'

'Just a little . . . This is a magnificent house,' Morton said warmly.

'What? Oh, yes.' There was little sign of pleasure on his face. Indeed, its expression hardly seemed to vary.

'Do you own the farm next to it?'

'Own it? No, it is leased from the Beaufort estate.' Green held out a half-filled glass.

Morton took it with a smile. 'If your land extends to the south, sir, I ought belatedly to ask your permission to trespass on it.'

'No need. Everyone goes where they like, here. They are country people, you understand; they know how to use the place.'

'Of course.' Morton sought in his mind for a topic which might prolong the conversation beyond a few seconds. In an alcove by the fireplace was a pile of newspapers – immaculate, symmetrical, untouched. 'Can you tell me how Surrey's match against Yorkshire is progressing, sir?' he asked.

'What? Oh, cricket. I expect it is in *The Times*. I never read it. Anyway, Thomas Witney will only come back from Wareham with today's paper around three o'clock.'

'You buy a paper, but do not read it?' Morton asked in surprise.

'Why not? . . . Every day they are pushing something new at you. If there is nothing to say, they will make it up. Why should you wear out your brain just to please them? All I bother myself with are the financial headlines and prices of company shares.'

Morton feigned puzzlement. 'I had not thought of it in those terms,' he said.

'What is that?'

'The brain – that prolonged use might damage it.'

The grey eyes regarded him with a flicker of interest. 'Everything else wears out with use. So does a brain. My own father wore his brain out. He would keep working and working. He had no need

174

to; he had ample money. That is what happens, if you let the brain get on top. It gets addicted, it wants more and more – then, suddenly, it is worn out.'

'I see,' Morton said earnestly. 'It certainly seems logical. But do you not find your evenings rather empty?'

'Empty? Not at all! In the summer one can walk in the fields; there is never much to worry one there – I pay a bailiff to worry, so I can just go and look.'

'Of course. But the winter evenings . . . ?'

'I play my flute pieces. That does no harm, so long as you do not learn any new ones. And I have my Tennyson. I was named after him, you know. My mother saw herself as imprisoned, like the Lady of Shallot.'

'Is not Tennyson rather taxing intellectually?' Morton asked innocently.

'No! Not the Morte D'Arthur. Not to me, anyway. I have known it for forty years.

> Then with both hands I flung him, wheeling him;
> But when I looked again, behold an arm,
> Clothed in white samite, mystic, wonderful,
> That caught him by the hilt and brandished him
> Three times, and drew him under in the mere.

Magnificent stuff!' He sighed contentedly.

'But, does not the effort of remembering also put a strain on the brain?' Morton asked.

'How can it? It is in there already. It's the constant cramming in of new things that makes it go pop. Take my word for it.'

Morton rose, and crossed to examine a picture over the fireplace. In fact, it was more of an exhibit. On the left was a small oval painting of a somewhat chubby woman; on the right an ink drawing of a young subaltern. Placed incongruously between them was a birth certificate. Morton peered at its faded ink. It had been issued in Winchester and recorded the birth of a John Green on the sixth of June, eighteen hundred and eight.

'This seems an interesting historical document,' he remarked.

'Yes.' Green's eyes remained fixed on his glass. 'The pictures are of my grandparents; the John Green in the certificate is my father

175

. . . My brother Walter got it, for some reason. After he died, Ursula gave it to me – when she moved into his house. That was all I got. It was no use to her.'

'Is that your only family memento?' Morton asked sympathetically.

'Yes.'

'I can see that it must be a matter for regret.'

'Regret?' Green repeated in a slightly more animated tone. 'No, not regret. The more you have, the more you worry . . . Anyway, Walter and Ursula Witney were close, as they say. Why he didn't marry her, I shall never know.' Then a thought seemed to strike him. 'Yes I do . . . Bad lot, the Witneys, interbred more than once. If Walter had not taken up with Ursula his brain would have lasted longer . . . And they say that old Lucy is a chance-child of my own father. Perhaps that was why she wanted to come down here . . . She was married then of course.'

'So, Ursula inherited all your brother's estate,' Morton remarked.

'Yes . . . That is another thing Walter did wrong. He would make a will! Ursula must have talked him into it. Not that I objected. I have enough of my own things to worry about. But it is stupid! It is inviting the worst.'

'Did he die immediately after making it?'

Green's forehead wrinkled with the effort of recollection. 'Within eighteen months of it, anyway. Absolute stupidity . . . Have you made a will, young man?'

'I?' Morton laughed. 'I only have debts to leave.'

'Take my advice,' Green said emphatically. 'Never make a will! You will live longer, that way.'

'But, would you not wish to influence the matter of who inherits your property when you die?'

'No! My brother tried to get me to follow his example, but I refused. There are perfectly good rules to decide it, I understand. I will not wear out my brain deciding who shall have this, and who that; then changing it all, because someone has displeased me . . . There are not many things in this world I am certain of, but the foremost is that I shall never make a will! . . . Now, what about another glass of scotch?'

* * *

176

Bragg was just finishing a resumé of the evidence against each of the suspects in the Witney case, when the door opened and the Commissioner poked his head in.

'Ah, Bragg.' He wandered irresolutely into the room, and peered over Bragg's shoulder. 'I see that you are still working on the Witney case,' he said.

'Yes, sir. It's a real hard one to crack.'

'But you are making progress, I trust.'

Bragg put his pipe in the ashtray, and leaned back in his chair. 'We are working on it full-time, yes, sir.'

'Hmn . . . Have you received any information from Constable Morton yet?'

'Not yet, sir. He has only been gone two days; and I told him not to get in touch unless he had something important to pass on.'

Sir William went over to the window. 'I am not at all sure that, in retrospect, I approve of his deployment in Dorset, Bragg. At a stroke, we seem to have halved the resources available to us at this end.'

'I assure you, sir, I am doing all that can be done here. In my opinion the key to both murders could well be in Dorset. By solving their murder, we could well solve our own.'

'There seems to be very little evidence to support your assertion,' the Commissioner said gloomily.

'I don't know, sir. Since we spoke last, the case against one of Julia Witney's boy-friends has become stronger.'

'In what way?'

'You remember Peter Lazenby, the engineer?'

'The young man who goes to Dorset, by way of Winchester?'

'Yes. You will recall that he had no alibi for the time of Jethro's murder. Well, Morton left me a note, before he went. It seems Lazenby was in Dorset at the time of Walter Green's murder.'

The Commissioner turned to face Bragg. 'That may well be, but these unsupported suppositions of yours are not evidence. I know that I am something of an amateur; and I have scrupulously sought not to meddle in the work of my professionals. Nevertheless, it is to me that the press and the City authorities come, when there seems to be no progress. I am under extreme pressure from the police committee to get results, Bragg.'

'Ah! I was wondering when it would start.'

'What?'

'The pressure to get an arrest – any old arrest.'

Sir William frowned. 'I do not follow you,' he said.

'It was Syme, Witney's clerk, who raised it, sir. But I am sure you were circumspect . . .'

'Stop talking in riddles,' Sir William said irritably. 'If you have some observation to make then please express it clearly.'

'Very well, sir.' Bragg paused as if marshalling his thoughts. 'Of course, you will understand there is nothing that you would call evidence, at the moment; but it could explain a lot of things.'

The Commissioner glowered at Bragg, but would not be goaded into an outburst.

'It seems,' Bragg went on, 'that there are some leaseholds on the fringe of the City – covered with slums, it seems. These leases are about to run out. Now, if the past is anything to go by, the Corporation will not demolish the properties and re-build themselves. Instead, they will just re-lease the area at a higher ground-rent. There was some suggestion that Witney was involved with this, in some way.'

'I do not follow you, Bragg. Even if all this were true, how could it possibly have a bearing on this murder?'

'Well, sir, there is big money to be made in this kind of situation. A lot depends on which proposals reach the committee, and which fall by the wayside. And if greasing palms means you will get preference, then palms will be greased a-plenty.'

'You mean corruption . . . in the City?' the Commissioner asked aghast.

'That was the implication of what I was told. Now, an investigation on those lines would have to delve very deep; might unearth all kinds of fat, white maggots. Much better, they might think, to pressurize the police into arresting a clerk or two, whose motives are obvious.'

Sir William dabbed his forehead with his handkerchief. 'But you told me that you do suspect Syme and the girl,' he said plaintively.

'Of course I do, sir. After all, Syme might have invented this story about the property, to divert attention from himself; and as for Cissie Fox, I am convinced she knew her child would get an annuity if Witney died. No, sir, I haven't taken them off my list, not by a long chalk.'

There was a commotion outside, boots clumping on the landing. The door crashed open, to reveal a white-faced young constable.

'It's happened again, sergeant,' he gasped.

'What has?'

'Lombard Street . . . the estate agent . . . A young woman this time!'

Bragg sprang to his feet. 'Right. You get the pathologist down there, as soon as you can. Any of our people there?'

'Constable Willis, sir.'

'Good. Off you go!' Bragg turned to the Commissioner. 'You will excuse me, sir,' he said, and strode out of the room.

When he got to Lombard Street, he found that a small crowd had gathered outside Witney's office. As he elbowed his way through it, a man seized his arm.

'Potts, from the *Chronicle*,' he cried. 'Can you give me a statement?'

Bragg shook him off. 'Go and ask the coroner,' he said. 'I know no more than you, at the moment.'

He pushed through the door and closed it after him. The uniformed constable sprang to attention.

'Nothing has been touched, sir,' he said, in a parade-ground voice.

'Right, lad. Well done. Go outside now, and keep the crowd a bit further away. We do not want reporters peering through the windows at us.'

Bragg turned to examine the outer office. Syme sat in his chair, staring fixedly in front of him. His face was the colour of dough. There was nobody by Cissie Fox's desk. A half-printed letter was in her typewriting machine. She had stopped in the middle of a word, as if someone had come in unexpectedly. The door to the inner office was ajar; he pushed it open . . . There had been no carpet to soften her fall; she was sprawled on her face in front of the desk, her blood a dark pool round her head and shoulders.

Bragg went back and shook Syme from his daze. 'Who found her?' he demanded.

Dull eyes regarded him. 'I . . . I did.'

'Was it you who sent for the police?'

'Yes.'

'When was this? What time, man?'

179

'I . . . I . . .' His jaw was moving like an automaton's. No sound coming out.

Bragg slapped him hard across the face. 'Pull your bloody self together!' he shouted. 'When did you find her?'

Syme's vacant eyes fastened on Bragg's face. 'After lunch . . . I came back . . . after lunch.'

'What time was this?'

'Af . . . after lunch . . .' He swallowed painfully.

'Was it two o'clock?'

'Yes . . . two o' . . .'

The door opened and Dr Burney came in, a beatific smile on his chubby face. 'I gather that history has repeated itself, sergeant,' he said cheerfully.

'It's not history, not yet anyway,' Bragg said grimly. 'She is in the back office.'

Burney opened the door, and stood on the threshold examining the walls and ceiling. 'I have a distinct feeling of *déjà vu*,' he said. 'The body is in much the same place, also.'

'There seems to be a lot more blood,' Bragg said.

'No more than I would expect. You must remember that on the previous occasion the carpet soaked up a good deal.' He lifted the head by the hair. It swung up as if on a hinge.

'A razor again, sir?' Bragg asked.

'I would think almost certainly so.' He ran his fingers through the hair at the nape of her neck. 'Hmn . . . It would appear, Bragg, to be an exact replication of the first murder.'

'Christ! That's three in all!'

'Three?'

'One down in Dorset, five weeks ago.'

'I can see why you are concerned, sergeant . . . When was the body found?'

'I cannot get much sense out of Syme, at the moment. He says he found her when he got back from lunch, which is normally around two o'clock.'

Burney glanced at his watch. 'An hour and a half ago . . . Yes. It would appear to hang together. I would provisionally put her time of death at, say, half past one. I got your constable to alert the ambulance people; I expect that they will collect the body for me, within the half hour.'

180

'Fine.'

'No doubt I shall see you later, sergeant.' The pathologist picked up his bag and went out whistling under his breath.

Bragg found a little kitchen off the outer office. He half filled a cup with cold water, then came back and flung the contents in Syme's face. He jerked back, arm up defensively. Bragg set a chair opposite him, and watched. After a few moments Syme began to wipe the dribbles from his face and neck. He took a handkerchief from his pocket and dabbed his hair.

'Feeling better now, Mr Syme?' Bragg asked genially. 'Nasty turn you had; particularly after the other one. You found her around two o'clock, you say.'

Syme licked his lips. 'Yes,' he said in a low voice.

'Did you still go out at the same time as each other?' Bragg asked.

'I suppose so. But she seemed to want me to go out before her, today.'

'Why would that be, I wonder.'

Syme took a deep breath. 'I am not being very clear,' he said.

'Take your time, sir. You have had a big shock.'

'Yes . . .' He dabbed at his forehead with his handkerchief, staring at Cissie Fox's vacant desk. 'You see . . . I always go to an organ recital, on Thursdays.' His voice died again.

'What time is this?'

'From a quarter past one to two o'clock.'

'Where?'

'Allhallows church – just round the corner.' He seemed to be slipping into a daze again.

'What has that to do with anything?' Bragg asked roughly.

Syme blinked, as if to bring the incident into focus. 'I wanted to finish adding up some rents, so I was rather late . . . She seemed anxious, as if she wanted to be rid of me.'

'Was she expecting a client, do you know?'

Syme looked up. 'Typewriters do not have clients,' he said flatly.

'But she did not go out to lunch herself. She was waiting for you to go first.'

'Yes.'

'You have no idea why?'

'No.'

'What time did you find her?'

181

'When I got back from the organ recital.'

'Say, quarter past two?'

'Yes, I suppose so.'

'Why was it that you found her straight away? The door of the back office was closed, wasn't it?'

'No, it was ajar. It should have been closed.'

'Did you go straight in?'

'Yes.'

'Why?'

'Because she was not here, and she had been behaving oddly.'

'In what way?'

'In trying to get rid of me.'

'But only today?'

'Yes.'

'Had she acted strangely in any other way?'

Syme looked down at his clenched hands. 'Yes, there was something . . . Yesterday she asked for time off, to see her doctor. She was away for two hours in the afternoon. I thought it was some woman's problem.'

'And, now you are not sure.'

'Well, living in Stepney, it seems odd that she bothered to come back at all.'

'You think it was not her doctor she went to see?'

'I don't know. It might have been.'

Bragg paused for a moment, then: 'Did you see someone at the recital who would recognize you?' he asked.

'I . . . Being late, I just slipped in at the back . . . No, I cannot remember anyone.'

'Put your mind to it. Oh, the ambulance men will be coming soon, to take her away. After that, you had better lock up and go home. And, don't say anything to the newspaper people! Understand?'

'Yes.'

Bragg hurried to the railway station and took a train to Stepney. As he approached Cissie Fox's house he could see children playing in the street, laughing and shouting. Women in aprons stood in doorways, watching them and chatting. Was Lily Fox one of the children, he wondered. No, she would be a bit too young . . . It would hit her hardest of all; only a shrewish old grandmother to bring her up. She would either be ignored or spoilt rotten. Still, she had her two hundred quid a year, if the old woman didn't drink it all. He found the house and knocked on the door. After a few moments it was opened.

'Mrs Fox?' he asked.

'Yes,' she said peevishly. 'What do you want?'

'Police.'

'Oh, you lot again. I thought all that was finished. Why can't you leave the poor girl alone? Anyway, she's at work.'

'I am aware of that, ma'am,' Bragg said gravely. 'May I come in?'

Reluctantly she turned and led him into the parlour.

'What is it this time?' she asked.

'Has your daughter been unwell recently?' Bragg asked sympathetically.

'Unwell? No. She's never had a day's illness in her life.'

'There was no reason, that you know of, for her to go and see her doctor?'

'She never said anything to me,' the woman said sharply. 'What is all this about?'

'Who is her doctor?'

She frowned resentfully. 'When we have to, we go to Dr Turner, in the High Street.'

'I see . . . I am afraid I have some bad news for you, Mrs Fox. Your daughter died this afternoon, in the office.'

Her face went white. Eyes staring, she felt her way to a chair. 'It's not true!' she cried. 'It can't be. She was as right as rain when she left here this morning!'

'I am afraid that it is true,' Bragg said quietly.

'No! It can't be!' she screeched. 'She was all full of herself, this morning, talking about moving to a classier area than this . . . We were going to go to Southend on Saturday. Lily has never been to the seaside before. She'd love playing in the sand . . .' Her voice tailed away, and she began to sob.

Bragg put a comforting hand on her shoulder. 'She has been taken to the City mortuary, ma'am,' he said. 'I will send a constable round tomorrow, in case you want any help with the arrangements.' He placed a little column of sovereigns on the mantelpiece. 'That should see you over the next couple of weeks, until you find your feet,' he said, and went quietly out.

He found Dr Turner's premises easily enough. The waiting-room was shabby, with peeling paint and holes in the linoleum; the air was rank with the odours of poverty and despair. An officious, middle-aged woman challenged him from a desk in the corner.

'Is the doctor in?' he asked meekly.

'Not at this hour! You will have to come back this evening.'

'I am afraid that I cannot wait for that.'

'Then, go home and take a dessert-spoon of castor oil. That is what the doctor usually prescribes – and no alcohol!'

'I don't want . . .' Bragg began.

'It is not a question of what you want; it is a question of what is good for you! If the castor oil has not got rid of the pain, then come back tomorrow morning and see the doctor.'

Bragg took out his warrant-card and placed it on the desk in front of her. 'It is information I need, not medication.'

She peered at it through her pince-nez. 'Oh, police,' she said sharply. 'Why did you not say as much in the first place? Police . . . I do not think we can give information to people like you. I cannot remember ever having done it before. I am sure Dr Turner would think that it was prohibited by his Hippocratic oath.'

'I doubt it, ma'am,' Bragg said drily. 'They did not have policemen in his day. Anyway, you have not taken any Hippocratic oath, and all I want to know is whether a Miss Cicely Fox came to see him, yesterday afternoon.'

'Well, you can see that for yourself! He does not see patients in the afternoons. He is up at the orphanage or the workhouse every afternoon.'

'So, it was not here she came,' Bragg murmured. 'But she is a patient of his?'

'Is she the Cissie Fox with a baby and no husband? Turned-up nose and blue eyes. About twenty.'

'That is her all right.'

'No. She has not been here since just after her baby was born. She had trouble feeding it – pure ignorance, if you ask me. Some people have no common sense!'

'So, she did not come here yesterday afternoon?'

'I have already told you so, constable! Now, please be off. I have work to do.'

Bragg retreated with as much dignity as he could muster. As he strolled to the railway station, he wondered what to make of it all.

184

Of course, Cissie could have gone to another doctor. But if it took two hours it could not have been one near the office. And Mrs Fox had said her daughter was perfectly healthy. All full of herself, and talking about getting away from Stepney. Perhaps she had found somebody else to stuff her. Another child, another annuity, and she could retire for life! But how could she be tied in to the Dorset business? Always assuming that it had been done by the same person . . . At least, one thing was clear; Cissie Fox was not Witney's killer. But she still might have been involved. Her accomplice could have decided she was untrustworthy and knocked her off. That would make Syme the number one candidate. But what evidence was there against him? He had been conveniently to hand for two of them; discovered the bodies. He might have seen advantages in killing both Witney and Cissie; his dazed state could chime equally well with having murdered her. Yet, to make a case, he had to tie him in with the Dorset killing . . . But, perhaps, his first priority should be to tie his other suspects in with the death of Cissie. When he reached the station, on an impulse he took a train to Stratford, instead of going back to Old Jewry.

In half an hour, he was labouring up the stairs leading to Peter Lazenby's office. He paused on the top landing to recover his breath, then went in. Lazenby was at his drawing-board, by the window. He put down his pencil with a theatrical sigh.

'Not you again, sergeant,' he said. 'I begin to feel that either you or your constable will be haunting me for the rest of my days.'

'Ah, Morton popped in, did he?'

'He accosted me in The Bell on Monday – a mere four days ago. Do you mean to tell me that you were unaware of it?'

'Accosted you, did he? That's an odd expression for a grown man to use. Perhaps we should warn Julia Witney off you. She might not get what she expects.'

Lazenby gave him a level stare. 'I thought you had already made up your mind that we were lovers,' he said.

'Oh, no. We never make up our mind; we let the evidence make it up for us . . . How is everything going?' he asked, nodding towards the drawing-board.

'Very well. The detailed design work is a very painstaking task, but fascinating. From a professional point of view, this is my first offspring!'

185

'Then let us hope it is not stillborn . . . Where did you go at lunch-time?'

Lazenby's head jerked round. 'Why?'

Bragg sighed. 'If I had to explain to everybody why I asked a particular question, I would never get any work done,' he said good-humouredly.

'No, I suppose not . . . Well, it is straightforward enough. I bought a sandwich at the stall by the station and ate it in Hackney Park.'

'But, that is the best part of a mile away!'

'One must have exercise, sergeant.'

'You could have got that walking along the High Street.'

'Possibly. However, I wanted to watch a cricket match.'

'A cricket match? In your lunch-hour?'

Lazenby smiled. 'It is one of the compensations for taking the risk of having one's own practice. I watched cricket from half past twelve to three o'clock, then came back and am intending to work till eight.'

'There were other people watching the cricket, no doubt.'

'There was a scattering of onlookers, yes.'

'Did you know any of them?'

'Recognized rather than knew them.'

'I see. And you could hope for nothing better on their side, I suppose.'

'Mere recognition, you mean?'

'Yes. If I were you, I would spend the next week looking for substantial citizens – judges and archbishops might just do – who will swear that you were in Hackney, between one and two o'clock today.'

Lazenby frowned. 'What on earth are you talking about?' he exclaimed.

'You remember Cicely Fox, and the annuity to the bastard child that Julia Witney was so upset about?'

Lazenby's lip curled in distaste. 'I have obviously heard about it.'

'Yes . . . Well, Cissie Fox was murdered, this lunchtime. Carved up just like Jethro Witney. Strange, isn't it? An old groper and a minx on the make; both getting the same treatment . . . I doubt if she will rate a cathedral service, though.'

Morton woke early to the sound of heavy rain. He got up and looked through the window. A farmhand plodded by with a sack over his head and shoulders; otherwise the village was deserted. He decided to go back to bed and refresh his mind from the material on butterflies that Poulton had provided. So it was nine o'clock before he went down to breakfast. This morning there was a little cold ham with the cheese and bread. Did this mean that he was no longer the object of suspicion? If so, it was a small advance; but he badly needed to reinforce it. Unless he could be reported as having caught at least one of the butterflies he claimed to be pursuing, in the vicinity of the village, logic would demand that he should move away eastwards. He decided that this morning he would take the wicker basket with him. It would look more purposeful. By the time he left the inn the rain had stopped and the sun was shining fitfully as the storm drew away eastwards. Nevertheless, he was grateful for the stout boots that Chambers had packed for him. The lush grass in the valley bottom would be saturated. No sooner had he crossed the road than William Biles came racing up, net in hand.

'Still on holiday?' Morton greeted him.

'Yes. I was due two weeks.'

The patent absurdity of the statement almost made Morton smile. At least, it was clear that he would be under observation for the whole of his stay.

'I think,' he said, 'that since everywhere is so wet, I will explore the area well beyond the valley. The sun will warm that first, so the butterflies will soon be out. Are you coming?'

'Yes, I am!'

Within half an hour they were on a level area which was out of sight of the village. Here the turf was fine and springy, cropped close by generations of sheep. Here and there boulders protruded, their contours smoothed by millenia of storms sweeping in from the sea. Stunted trees had been left in the outcrops, with furze and heather.

'There is some!' William exclaimed.

'What?'

'Horseshoe-vetch! I told you there was plenty.'

'Ah, yes. Excellent! Now, if we find some of the butterflies we seek, I think we shall be justified in taking one of each species and sex back to London. That will be proof positive. Do you agree?'

'I thought you said we couldn't spare even one of the common ones,' the boy said doubtfully.

'Ah, yes. It would be quite wrong to kill them wantonly; but in the name of science, it is quite legitimate to take specimens.'

William looked at him uncomprehendingly. 'Shall I go and see?' he asked.

'Yes.' Morton opened his wicker basket, and re-arranged the contents. This masquerade was all very well, he thought, but he had no practical experience in the matter at all. For his part he would much prefer not to encounter any of the wretched insects. His interest lay in quartering the area, in seeking but not finding – or only finding when his real task was done.

'Mr Hildred! Mr Hildred! I've got one!' William was rushing from an outcrop, his folded net held outstretched. He rested it on Morton's arm. 'There, see! It's the one you said I should look for, when I caught the Common Blue!'

It was true. Without a shadow of doubt, this was a male Adonis Blue. It was exquisite in its perfection. It lay still, within the confines of the gauze, almost trustingly.

'Excellent, William! Well done! Now we must kill it . . . You need not be concerned, it will be quite painless.'

The boy's excited grin showed that the butterfly's death-throes would be the least of his concerns. Morton poured a little cyanide onto cotton wool and dropped it into the killing-jar.

'Keep your face away,' he warned. 'This is very dangerous. Now, can you turn the frame of the net, so that I can get the mouth of the jar under the butterfly? . . . Good . . . Now shake the gauze a little . . . Splendid!'

The insect dropped into the jar, fluttered briefly and was still. Morton groped in his memory for the correct procedure. The butterfly had come to rest on the bottom of the jar, with its wings fully extended. According to the book, butterflies rested with their wings together; that was how you could differentiate them from moths. But, of course, this was not a natural posture; this was the sleep of death. So far as he was concerned, it was all to the good. He would not need to go through the procedure of relaxing it, prior to mounting. He took the stopper off the killing-jar and, waving the boy to a distance, he carefully teased the butterfly into a cork-lined box. It rested there in all its perfection; beauty preserved for ever, with a pin through its middle. William came close and inspected it with satisfaction.

'Will you say that I caught it?' he asked.

'Indeed I will! When I get back to London, it will be put in a glass-fronted case, for everyone to admire. And under it will be a brass plate, saying that it was caught at Slocombe Magna on the seventeenth of June, eighteen ninety-four, by William Biles. Your grandchildren will be able to see it in years to come.'

That concept clearly had little appeal for the boy. He jumped to his feet. 'Shall we try over there?' he asked.

'Very well. You explore cautiously, while I repack my basket.'

William worked his way towards a clump of tall trees. As Morton followed him, he saw that it was almost perfectly circular, with a diameter of about a hundred yards. The trees were old, with spreading crowns of young green leaves. Drooping branches screened their trunks. They looked like grey poplars to Morton. In this place they seemed strange, alien. As he pushed through the branches, he could see that they enclosed a space resembling an arena. In the centre was a huge flat slab of stone, its surface powdered grey. Around it were the dead embers of many fires. A path encircled it, the earth beaten hard by many generations of feet. It was an eerie place.

'Mr Hildred!' William was beckoning. He was almost lost in the branches hanging from a tree on the opposite side of the circle. A depression had formed among the surface roots, in which water had collected. On the edge of the pool was a large butterfly; it was probing delicately with its tongue into the brownish water. Occasionally it opened its wings of iridescent violet-blue . . . Morton compared it mentally with the illustrations in his Newman, the description of the colours he should find . . . It could only be a Purple Emperor. Magnificent! The delicate veins of the wings were clearly visible; and there was the ribbon of white over the purple, the mock eye near the lower edge to deter predators. What transcendent beauty! And how strange that, instead of feeding on nectar, it should be sipping murky water . . . Morton was suddenly alert. That was important, significant . . .

'Shall I catch it?' the boy asked.

'No. Let it go' . . . It was not in Newman, it was in the file that Poulton called his party pieces . . . what could it be? Morton cleared his mind, looked up at the trees to distract himself, in the hope that the information would leap into his mind unbidden. The butterfly had sated itself and was fluttering amongst the branches, head-high. William was keeping pace with it, entirely engrossed. It was strange, Morton thought, that someone so young should have so mature an interest in butterflies. And a farm-boy at that. Country children usually had no concern . . . He had it! Purple Emperors drinking from pools in a farmyard . . . feeding on carrion, attracted by blood! He went over to the little pool. Its brown tinge could hardly come from mud in this place. In an area around, under the sheltering branches, the short grass was speckled brown, stones were unnaturally rusty. Morton looked up at the canopy. Most of the morning's rain would have been kept off this spot by the vast green umbrella; the drippings from the outer leaves would have collected to form the pool. Unless Poulton was wrong, it could only be blood. Animal blood, possibly. But what if it were human? What if he had stumbled on the spot where Walter Green had been murdered? It seemed absurd. It was the best part of a mile from his house. And yet . . . He took a jar from his basket, and began to scrape the top layer of soil together, with his hands.

'What are you doing?' the boy asked.

'Why, now that you have found an Adonis Blue, I am wondering if there are any signs of pupation. The caterpillar burrows into the soil, when it is going to change into a chrysalis.'

'But why are you putting the soil into a jar?'

'Ah, that is for an entirely different purpose. By testing the alkalinity of the soil, one can tell how suitable a habitat is for a particular species of butterfly.'

William's face clouded at the pretentious words. 'Well,' he said determinedly, 'I am going to try to catch a female Adonis Blue, then I can have two brass plates in London!'

'Then I will go back to the village,' Morton said, with a smile. 'I shall have to report your success to London!'

The boy's face was suffused with pride and self-importance. It was shameful, Morton thought, to abuse his trust in this way. He sauntered, with his impedimenta, slowly down the hillside in the direction of the village. If Walter Green had been murdered in the grove he would surely have been taken back by the shortest route. That led across the grazing-land to the ford over the stream they called a river, then along the hedgerow to the little lane. He had traversed it once already and seen nothing untoward. He tried to reconstruct the scene in his mind. The body drained of blood, in a great spurt lasting only moments; a few dribbles falling to the ground as it was carried; the residue clotting before they had gone far . . . He could see nothing. The springy turf would hold no trace of their passing; the rain would have washed away any blood that had fallen. Indeed, there would have been no wheel marks, even if it had been brought back by cart. By the time he had reached the outskirts of the village, he had begun to doubt the validity of his conclusions. He was relying far too much on his own interpretation of a passing remark in Poulton's lecture notes. A real expert might ridicule the inferences he had drawn. If Sergeant Bragg had been here, they would have argued it out together, got it into perspective . . . His indecisiveness was an infallible sign of his own inexperience. Well, so be it. Far better that he recognize it and act accordingly. He must summon Bragg for a conference.

'You must be Mr Hildred.' In his daydream he had almost reached the cart-track running past the back of Walter Green's house. A good-looking woman was standing in the gateway, smiling at him. She was wearing a thin cotton blouse and a print skirt; on her finger was a cornelian ring.

'That is so, ma'am.' He strolled over to her.

'And what is your first name?' she asked, with a trace of archness.

'James.'

'Ah! That means "One who supplants". I wonder who you will supplant in Slocombe Magna!'

'No one, I should think.'

'But it is your destiny! Now, I am Ursula Witney. Ursula is a she-bear, strong and resourceful . . . And, what is your birth date?'

'The eighth of December.'

'Saggitarius! I can well believe it. And I am a Virgo. We should have a mutual attraction . . . You met my brother and sister, the other evening.'

'Ah, yes. They were most charming.'

She laughed. 'That is the first time I have ever heard Thomas described in that way,' she said. 'Discreet, reliable perhaps, but he has never thought the social graces worth cultivating!'

191

'Well . . . his sisters more than make up for him,' Morton blurted out awkwardly.

Now she moved closer, her eyes on him. 'Have you been up on the hills?' she asked, her voice low and seductive.

'Yes . . . Actually, William Biles caught one of the very butterflies I am looking for.'

'Did he? That was clever of him.' She was looking up into his face, her bosom brushing his arm. 'Does this mean that you will be leaving us?'

'No . . . not yet. It could be an aberration . . . a single insect out of its normal habitat . . . I shall need corroboration.' She was younger than Francesca, he decided, plumper, more opulent. No wonder Walter Green had been taken with her.

'You must be tired and hot,' she was saying. 'Why not come in, and I will make you something a little special? The inn is scarcely hospitable enough for someone like you.'

'I . . . er. Yes, that would be much appreciated, ma'am.'

'Call me Ursula, please! We are not stiff and starchy in the country.'

She took his arm and drew him towards the garden. As they passed through the narrow gate, she contrived to press the back of his hand against her breast. Morton began to feel the stirrings of a wholly unwelcome concupiscence. Regulations about conduct towards the public – possible suspects – were all very well; but they did not embrace a hot-blooded woman and a policeman passing himself off as a gauche unsophisticate. As they walked down the path towards the French windows, she gaily lengthened her stride to keep pace with his. This meant that she needed to cling onto his arm . . . she was only in her late thirties; not so very much older than he. And everyone acknowledged that she had been Walter Green's mistress . . . It was not as if she was an artless maiden.

'What a beautiful house!' he exclaimed inanely.

'Yes.' Her voice was warm and caressing, her eyes fixed on his face.

'Do you need many servants?'

'I do not have any, at present . . . It has just been left to me, by my special friend.' She dwelt on the last phrase meaningfully. 'Would you like to try some of my restorative cordial?'

Morton wondered from her inflection, if she intended a *double entendre.* If so, James Hildred would never recognize it. 'Yes . . . yes. That would be very nice,' he said.

'It will only take a few minutes.' She squeezed his arm and, with an equivocal backward look, swept out of the room.

Morton walked over to the bookcase, to quell his burgeoning lust. He made his mind concentrate on the individual volumes . . . Thackeray, Scott, Stevenson . . . No Dickens – but a woman like Ursula would have had no time for his mawkish sentimentality . . . He jerked alert. What on earth was this? Scott's *Letters on Demonology and Witchcraft.* How extraordinary! And, not far from it, *Magus: The Celestial Intelligence* by Francis Barrett. Good God! Did they practise witchcraft here? Was he right in thinking of Walter Green's death as some kind of ritual sacrifice? He rapidly scanned the shelves but saw nothing comparable. At the foot of the bookcase was a cupboard, the key in the lock. He opened it. Inside were several leather-bound tomes, of great age. He pulled one out and looked at the title-page. More magic! Quickly he took out his notebook, and jotted down the titles of them all. He closed the cupboard door just as her step could be heard in the passage. There was a distinct smell of old leather bindings in the air. He waved his hands about to disperse it, then tiptoed over to the window before she entered.

'There,' she said, smiling brightly. 'That did not take long.' She was carrying a tray with two steaming cups on it. She placed it on a small mahogany table and held out a cup to Morton. In it was a clear greenish liquid, strongly aromatic. He took the cup from her. At least the scent had disguised the smell of old books. She was watching him intently, a half-smile on her lips. He took a cautious sip. It was disgusting! It tasted like hay boiled with herbs. On the surface floated a delicate creamy blossom.

'Mmm . . . This is interesting.' He took another sip, and she sipped also; a gulp, and she too. It was as if they were taking part in a ritual . . . Ritual! A shiver went down his spine. Had this been the prelude to Walter Green's grisly end?

'I quite like this,' he said tentatively. 'What is it made from?'

'It is a tisane.' She came closer to him. 'It is made from camomile, mint, rosemary and sage . . . and also a little special something.'

It must be very special, Morton thought. He had no feeling of intoxication and yet a strong sensation of well-being was sweeping over him.

'What is the flower?' His voice sounded hollow to him, a little remote.

'Lime blossom . . . Do you like my tisane?' He could feel her thigh against his, her breast seemed to seek him out; he wanted to cry out, laugh aloud, dance . . . She was watching him intently, lips parted. She put down her cup.

'Take a little more,' she said softly.

Yes, a little more, a sip . . . the elixir of paradise. He could hardly taste it now. It was as if his senses had diminished – no, rather focused themselves into an overwhelming carnal desire. She took the cup from him and set it down, then she gravely raised his hands and pressed them against her breasts. His heart was thumping; he could hardly get his breath. All his being was in his clamorous loins – his whole existence lay within her soft body; tearing into her, exploding into nothingness . . . infinity . . . paradise . . . He began to fumble with the cameo at the neck of her blouse. She was pressing hard against him, her breath a soft moan. The catch kept slipping out of his fingers. He nipped it in a frenzy, it twisted open, and the pin went deep into his finger. He jumped back in pain, sucking at the wound. The woman stood there in a trance, her face empty; a voluptuary, a devotee of immemorial arts . . . Morton backed away, suddenly afraid, and ran.

He was barely aware of stumbling up the steps of the inn, and dropping his basket in the corner. When he fully came to his senses, he was pounding down the steep hill, in the cool shadow of the woods, halfway to Wareham. He stopped and wiped his brow. What a weird experience! He smiled to himself, at his abject terror. This was England, Queen Victoria was on the throne, one could sail to Australia in twenty-six days! It was absurd to be afraid of country mumbo-jumbo . . . But he had been afraid. He remembered his decision to summon Bragg to Dorset. There was all the more reason now.

He walked on, to the bottom of the hill and across the marshy levels to Wareham. There he persuaded the driver of a trap to overcome his preference for train passengers and drive him to Bere Regis. Within twenty minutes he was being dropped at the crossroads. He looked about him with interest. He had not imagined that it would be so small. From what Bragg had said, it seemed to be at the centre of a cluster of smaller villages. The others must be tiny indeed. There was a beautiful old church, which indicated a more

194

glorious past, but the present seemed decidedly dull. No wonder that Bragg preferred the bustle of London. Morton asked the way to the Hildreds' house. It was a few yards from the crossroads. It seemed to be a substantial villa; fairly new, and mercifully free of the medieval fantasies that had recently afflicted builders in the suburbs of London. He knocked on the heavy oak door. After a few moments it swung open. A stocky woman stood there, her neck festooned with beads.

'Good afternoon, ma'am,' he said deferentially. 'I believe I have the honour to be your nephew.'

'I wondered when we might see you,' she said in a deep contralto voice. 'My daughter had a letter from Mr Bragg about it, yesterday. I suppose you had better come in.'

She led him into a spacious sitting-room, overlooking the garden. A young woman got to her feet as he entered. She was slim and tall. Although she could not be described as a beauty, she had fine regular features and a clear complexion.

'So soon?' she exclaimed. 'We scarcely knew whether we should take Mr Bragg's request seriously. It sounded like one of the Rider Haggard novels that he likes so much!'

'I am afraid it is all too serious, miss.'

'Please call me Fanny . . . Joseph said that you would only come here in an emergency, or if there was something that we could do to assist you.'

'It is all ridiculous nonsense,' Mrs Hildred interjected. 'Grown policemen squabbling about nothing, trying to frustrate one another. He would be a great deal more use to mankind if he were doing a sensible job like running my brewery, instead of being at everybody's beck and call in London.'

'Mamma!' Fanny was crimson with embarrassment.

'It is true,' Amy asserted. 'He is worth more than that.'

'I agree,' Morton said warmly. 'Yet I fear that he would not. And, were you to lure him down to Bere Regis, the City police would suffer grievously.'

'Rubbish!'

'Not so, ma'am. He is head and shoulders above any other officer. The hierarchy of Inspectors and Chief Inspectors are almost irrelevant. It is men like Sergeant Bragg who maintain a decent way of life for us all.'

195

'You sound like a parson,' Amy said disagreeably. 'But, from what little Mr Bragg has said, you are a bit of an oddity yourself.'

Morton grinned. 'I have that privilege,' he said.

'Privilege! And you skulking up in Slocombe Magna, pretending to catch butterflies. Why cannot the Dorset police work with you? That is what would happen in any other walk of life.'

'I wonder . . . It is a simple matter of rivalry. I am sure that if someone else passed off their beer as yours, you would object strongly.'

Amy smiled triumphantly. 'True. But that does not fit the situation, does it? Now, if someone asked me to make beer for them, to market under their own label, we would both be happy!'

Morton held up his hands in surrender. 'I am clearly out of my depth in the commercial world,' he said.

Amy got up briskly. 'I will get you some tea,' she said. 'Would you like anything special? Darjeeling, rose-petal, jasmine-flower tea?'

'No thank you,' Morton said firmly. 'The more ordinary the better!'

'I am afraid that my mother can be rather direct,' Fanny said, when they were alone. 'She sees maintaining the family involvement in the brewery as a sacred trust.'

'But you do not?'

'Indeed no! Mr Bragg feels that I would quickly become disenchanted were we to go and live in London, but I would dearly like to put it to the test! However, I take it that you have not come on a purely social visit, cousin!'

Morton smiled. 'That is true. I need to send two telegraphs urgently. One to Sergeant Bragg and another to a newspaper reporter called Catherine Marsden.'

'I have heard of her, of course,' Fanny said happily. 'Must you return to Slocombe Magna today?'

Morton pulled a rueful face. 'I fear that I must. Though, for reasons that I would prefer not to discuss, I would gladly stay away as long as possible.'

Fanny smiled. 'You intrigue me,' she said, and glanced at the clock. 'It is still early. If we were to set out in half an hour, you could send the telegraphs yourself, from Dorchester. Then, cousin, I could take you back to Wareham, if that would be convenient.'

196

'I can think of nothing that I would enjoy more,' Morton said feelingly.

'Then that is settled. And, as we drive, you can tell me exactly what you have been up to.'

10

When Bragg got to Old Jewry next morning, he found two telegraphs on his desk. The first was from Morton; the second informed him that the Winchester police were holding David Branksome and required his urgent attendance. Well, it was all very convenient. He could go down to Winchester, then travel on to Dorset. It was Friday, after all; he could make a very pleasant weekend of it. He smiled grimly as he realized that he would be virtually duplicating Peter Lazenby's periodic journey. He went along to the Commissioner's office, but he was not in. Bragg scribbled a note for him, then went home to Tan House Lane to pack a bag.

It was almost twelve o'clock before he arrived at the Winchester police station. The Inspector seemed undecided whether to be truculent or genial.

'You took your time, Bragg,' he said.

'I came as soon as I could, sir. What charge are you holding him on?'

'He has not been charged. We picked him up for you, on suspicion of murder.'

'Right. Can I see him?'

'You can bloody strangle him if you want – moaning bugger! He has not stopped shouting for a solicitor; saying he's done nothing. You had better be able to make this one stick, Bragg. I don't want any shit on my face!'

He crossed to the door and bellowed for Branksome to be brought from the cells. Soon there was a clumping of feet in the corridor and a dishevelled figure was pushed into the room. His coat and trousers were crumpled, his shirt torn. He had not shaved for a couple of days and there was a raw weal across his cheek.

'Branksome, this is Sergeant Bragg, from the City of London police,' the Inspector said curtly.

Bragg studied the man in silence for a few moments, then motioned him to sit. 'You were seen by my constable, over the Jethro Witney murder,' he said quietly.

'Yes.'

'Will you tell me why you did a runner?'

'Left Winchester, you mean?' His manner was uncertain, as if taken aback by this courteous treatment.

'What else?'

'I felt no longer able to continue with my employment.'

'That was a queer thing to do, when Julia Witney needed all the support she could get,' Bragg said reasonably.

Branksome did not reply.

Bragg leaned back in his chair, a contented look on his face. 'Of course, we have looked through the Winchester books. Is there anything you want to tell me about them?'

A wooden look came over the man's features. 'No,' he said.

'I am sure that Jethro Witney was a busy man, and did not have much time to spare on a Saturday morning; particularly as he trusted you.'

Branksome's eyes were staring at the wall over Bragg's head. He said nothing.

'You see,' Bragg went on, 'there are things that do not add up – expenses you have charged that were never incurred . . . You were not very clever, were you? According to the books, on the second of February, you were in two places at the same time – miles apart.' Bragg leaned forward, suddenly brisk. 'You had been lining your pockets ever since you came to Witneys, hadn't you? But now you had bigger fish to fry. Somehow, you had got the notion that you could persuade Julia Witney to marry you . . . You did propose to her, didn't you?'

Branksome said nothing.

'Well, she will give evidence that you did . . . But she turned you down! That must have been a shaker. You were in big trouble then. You had at least enough sense to realize that she would not be able to keep you on as manager. And, with someone new, your little fiddles were going to be found out . . . I expect you would have destroyed the books – had a fire at the office. The trouble was that we had already taken them. So there was nothing for it but to do a bunk – and sharpish, before we cottoned on to what had been happening.'

Branksome's eyes shifted to Bragg's face. 'It is not true!' he said angrily.

Bragg disregarded him. 'Now I have to ask myself why you would risk coming back,' he said urbanely. 'It would have to be a powerful reason, something urgent. And, what more important in your mind than money?'

He gazed at Branksome in silence, for some moments, then: 'Do you know what I think?' he asked. 'I think that, if we went round the banks of Winchester we would find the account where you kept your loot; money you did not have time to withdraw, when you scarpered . . . Am I right? Are you going to let me go round the banks here, till I find it? Or are you going to make things better for yourself by telling me about it?'

Branksome looked down at his boots. 'The District Bank,' he muttered.

Bragg smiled. 'That's better, son,' he said genially. 'It always pays to co-operate with the police . . . And, where were you yesterday lunch-time?'

'I can answer that one,' the Inspector interrupted. 'He was banged up in the nick, here.'

Bragg got to his feet. 'In that case, sir, you can have him. The thefts from the business are clearly your concern. The books have already been returned. I will send you down our papers as soon as I can.'

'You mean, he did not kill Witney, after all?' There was a mixture of irritation and puzzlement on the Inspector's face.

'I mean that I have not got the evidence to persuade a magistrate to remand him in custody. But you will be keeping him tucked up nice and warm, won't you, sir?' He turned to Branksome. 'By the way,' he said, 'Jethro Witney left you a hundred pounds in his will . . . It's a queer world we live in, isn't it?'

Bragg left the police station in high good humour. He had Branksome where he wanted him and, in the process, he had evened the score with the Inspector. It had been an auspicious start. He decided to go and see the Rossiters. He strolled to Parchment Street through streets crowded with shoppers and tourists enjoying the warm sun. As he walked up the path to the front door he saw the curtains move in the window to the right. He banged a tattoo on the knocker. No one came. He put his ear to the letter-box; he could hear raised voices within, though he could not distinguish what was being said. He knocked again. After some moments a key was turned and the door opened a crack. He could see that there was a strong chain securing it; he could not hope to push his way inside.

'City police!' he called.

'What do you want?' The voice was light and peevish; probably that of the painter of cathedrals.

'Just a chat!'

'No! We have been told to say nothing.'

'I just wanted to check that I have the facts right in my notes,' Bragg said cheerfully.

'No!' The door was banged shut and the key turned again.

Bragg mentally damned them to hell. He had no sort of a case to put to a magistrate. If they would not talk to him, he would have to get his evidence from other sources. On the face of it all the Rossiters had motive, means and opportunity, so far as the murder of Jethro Witney was concerned. But what about the others? True, there was a family link with the Greens and the Witneys, but it was all long ago. And, why on earth should they want to murder Cissie Fox? No, he would have to swallow his pride and leave the Rossiter thread, for the moment.

Somewhat disgruntled, he walked briskly to Brook Street and knocked on the door of Julia's house. There was no answer. He knocked again, then could hear her steps in the hall. He stood back, as the door was opened.

'Good morning, miss,' he said affably. 'Or is it afternoon?'

She looked at him coldly. 'I did not expect to see you,' she said.

'I apologize if I brought you down from the top of the house, miss. Somehow, I expected the cook to answer.'

'I no longer have a cook, sergeant. Having challenged my father's so-called will, I find myself with barely enough money for my own necessities.'

'I am sorry about that,' Bragg said sympathetically. 'Is there nothing your lawyers can do about it?'

'As you can imagine, I instructed them to take action. But they say that they cannot compel the executors to be more generous, short of a full hearing of the action.'

Bragg sucked in his breath. 'That sounds bad, miss. There will be precious little left when the lawyers are done. Are you sure you cannot bend a bit? Accept the will under protest?'

'Never!' she said angrily. 'I do not believe that the Lily girl is my father's child!'

'I see. Then there is no way out of it, is there? May I come in?'

'Why?'

'I just wanted a chat.'

'No! My solicitor advised me that I should not speak to the police unless he was present also. That is one piece of advice I intend to follow.'

'Very well. They are Rawbone & Treblecock, aren't they?'

She looked surprised. 'Yes,' she said. 'Mr Fellowes is the partner representing me.'

Bragg pulled out his watch. 'Right, miss. I will meet you at their offices at two o'clock.'

'But, suppose Mr Fellowes finds that inconvenient?' she protested.

'Look miss,' Bragg said roughly, 'this is your father's murder we are investigating. You may hate his guts, but you are not going to get in my way. If Fellowes is not there, somebody else will look after you.'

'And, if I refuse?' she said angrily.

'If you refuse?' Bragg echoed. 'Why, I expect you will find your education being broadened for you . . . I don't suppose you have been in a police cell, have you? Very cramped and uncomfortable they are. Smelly too – unwashed bodies and stale urine. Drunks and petty thieves mostly – and the odd whore. Of course, in a place like Winchester they won't have separate cells for women.'

'Stop!' she cried. 'I am sure that you would enjoy heaping degradation on me – merely because I refuse to be bullied and cheated by men.'

'No, miss,' Bragg said firmly. 'You have it wrong. There is a perfectly reasonable way to do everything. It only gets hard going when you try to flout the conventions. It is nothing to do with me but, for my money, you are behaving like a spoiled child over this will. Keep on the way you are, and you will regret it in the long run. Have you never heard what happened to the Rossiters?'

201

'I told you, I will not answer questions without my solicitor.'

'Right, then be there; two o'clock.' Bragg spun on his heel and marched off.

He had his lunch in the Coach and Horses again. He had been looking forward to it; a big piece of stand-pie and a pint of yeasty beer. But his altercation with Julia had soured the prospect. Bloody woman! And what were her lawyers thinking of, letting her go on with it? Perhaps Lazenby was being too reasonable, giving them the impression he could be screwed for a bit more, then a bit more still. Damn them all to hell! He stuffed the pie down and gulped the beer. He could feel it lying as heavy as lead inside him. A fine start, this was, to his pleasant weekend. Thank God all women were not like Julia . . . True, Fanny was a good bit older than her, but she would never have carried on like this. She was sensible, thoughtful; she would never go off at half-cock like this . . . But Julia had no doubt gone through a lot, these past days, with no one to rely on . . . Except Peter Lazenby, maybe; who might have plotted these murders with her – sat hand-in-hand on the settee, planning how to knock off her father. Dear God! He was becoming confused himself. He should follow his own advice; stick by the rules. He dropped some coins on the table, and went out in search of the office of Rawbone & Treblecock.

He found them in an old house, up an alley off the High Street. He was shown up creaking wooden stairs to a poky garret. There was a desk close to the window, to catch as much light as possible. Julia was sitting there, her face made coarse and masculine by the shadows.

A man rose from behind the desk as Bragg entered. He held out his hand. 'I am Fellowes,' he said. 'I am representing Miss Witney's interests.'

He was in his mid-thirties, balding at the temples and with a protruding Adam's apple. He wore heavy horn-rimmed spectacles. Bragg took an instant dislike to him. He looked a spineless, ineffective booby; all right if you were buying a property or making a will, but not one to stray far from his book of precedents. So far as Julia was concerned, he would be a broken reed. Well, that was her look-out. He wondered briefly whether to give her the criminal warning; that would shake them! But Fellowes was already intent on her saying nothing; it would hardly help matters along. Bragg moved a chair so that he could see both Fellowes and Julia.

'There were one or two areas I wanted to explore with your client,' he said, then turned to Julia. 'Would you mind telling me where you were yesterday?'

Julia glanced towards Fellowes for guidance. He swallowed and his Adam's apple bobbed up and down. 'I shall advise my client not to answer any questions,' he said, 'until their purpose has been made clear.'

He was more nervous than Julia, Bragg thought; as well he might be – way out of his depth. In a curious way, Bragg felt a compulsion to compensate, to be fair. 'Are you going to accept that advice?' he asked gruffly.

Julia looked at him haughtily. 'I would be foolish not to.'

'Very well . . . You are intelligent enough to realize that you are suspected of murdering your father. You have also made it plain that you hate Miss Cicely Fox, and the child your father got on her . . . Yesterday there was another murder; carried out in precisely the same way as your father's; at almost the same time as his; in exactly the same spot. This time the victim was Cissie Fox . . . I have to repeat the question. Where were you between the hours of one and two o'clock yesterday?'

Julia's jaw was clamped tight, her eyes staring. She looked almost ugly. Fellowes was clearly floundering. 'You are implying that my client might have committed the murder of this woman?' he ventured.

Bragg disregarded him, staring stonily at Julia.

She glared back at him. 'I refuse to answer that question,' she said.

There was a pause, their eyes locked, then: 'If you ask me, miss, that is very wise of you.'

Now Fellowes had something within his competence. 'That is a most improper remark, sergeant, as you well know!' He was wagging his finger like a school ma'am whose favourite pupil has been caught with his hand up a girl's skirt.

Bragg turned to him. 'Why is that?' he asked mildly. 'Surely that was precisely the advice you gave her?' He turned back to Julia. 'Well, now we have that out of the way, miss, there are a couple of things I imagine you will want to help me over. I found this list of

203

investments in your father's papers . . . I am sure you would want to be aware of it, as it may have a bearing on the estate.'

Julia took the list and glanced through it. 'I know nothing of my father's affairs,' she said.

'The trouble is that we cannot find any trace of these investments; there are no certificates in his strong-boxes; when we examine the registers of the companies concerned, his name does not appear there.'

Fellowes held out his hand for the list. 'Have you considered the possibility that it might have been superseded?' he asked.

'In what way?'

'That these may be shares that Jethro Witney owned at one time, but subsequently sold.' He handed back the list in triumph.

'We did consider that,' Bragg said gravely. 'But, in that event, there would have been an original entry in the share register, which was deleted when they were sold.'

'May I see the list again?' Julia asked.

'Of course . . . As you see, they are all companies with registered offices in London. Not that it means very much; anyone could invest in them, through a stockbroker. But it seemed possible that your father bought them as a result of his working up in the City; perhaps because he got privileged information. Have you heard him mention any of these names?'

'No. They mean nothing to me.' She returned the list.

'Very well. Now, here is something that ought to mean something to you. It is a family tree, that was found with the investment list. Have you seen it before?'

She looked at it perfunctorily. 'I believe that I saw him working on it, when I took up his bedtime cocoa,' she said.

'When was that, miss?'

'Oh . . . last autumn, I think.'

'Is it accurate?'

Julia raised her eyebrows. 'I would imagine so. My father was nothing if not meticulous.'

'You realize that it shows you were related to the Rossiters, way back.'

'Well, yes . . . I believe that to be the case.'

Bragg frowned. 'Why did you not say so, in view of all the bad feeling between you?'

Julia gave him a haughty stare. 'I was not personally affected by the ill-feeling you mention. I have no interest in ancient history.'

'Well, perhaps you ought to start being interested,' Bragg said. 'The Rossiters were ruined by a lawsuit.'

When Catherine arrived at the office that morning she found a telegraph lying on her desk. It was addressed to her personally! What on earth could it be? She tore open the envelope and pulled out the message. It was from James! She scanned the lines with growing disappointment; sometimes it was interesting – even exciting – to be involved in the cases he and Sergeant Bragg were investigating, but this seemed decidedly dull. And she was a little nettled to find that he had gone down to Dorchester without informing her. Well, she had more important things to do than dash off just because he asked her to. It would have to wait until lunch-time. Indeed, she deliberately dallied over her potted shrimps and toast; so it was two o'clock before she got to the Guildhall and was ushered into the librarian's sanctum. He got to his feet courteously.

'How can I be of service to you, young lady?' he asked.

'I am a reporter on the *City Press*,' she said, passing over her card. 'I have been asked to do some research by the police, but I cannot find any of the books on your shelves.'

'I see. What are the volumes in question?'

She handed him James's telegraph. 'Some of them seem very obscure,' she said.

The librarian looked at the list in growing perplexity. 'Well, for a start, we do not keep books on witchcraft – even one written by Sir Walter Scott. Indeed, I frankly could not suggest where you might find them.'

'Oh dear! You can see that it is regarded as of the utmost importance.'

'Yes.' He pondered, muttering to himself. 'I am sorry,' he said at length. 'I have to admit that I am not equipped even to begin to help you.'

'Is there no one else whom I might approach?' Catherine asked plaintively.

He pursed his lips. 'My only suggestion is that you try the

anthropology department of King's College. If they do not deal with such matters, they plainly ought to . . . Yes, I should try them. They are in the Strand.'

Catherine looked at her fob-watch. She was already a little late. But she had submitted her article for the Saturday edition, and received a grudging commendation from the editor. There was nothing awaiting her urgent attention in the office. She took a cab and was soon picking her way through knots of students to the porter's lodge of King's College.

'Witchcraft, is it?' The head porter was as matter-of-fact as if she had enquired about theology. 'That will be Professor Spooner – though I think I just saw him go out. If not him, then Mr Walford, he is the lecturer in anthropology . . . Tom, will you show the young lady the way?'

The head porter's recollection was proved right, but Catherine had no reason to regret it. Walford was a handsome man in his late thirties, with blue eyes and an easy smile.

'I am told that you will be able to help me,' she began. 'I am a reporter on the *City Press*, and I am researching the subject of witchcraft.'

He looked at her speculatively, then reached over to a bookcase and pulled out a slim volume. 'I will lend you this book. It is a kind of child's guide to the subject. Bring it back any time.'

'Actually, I am trying to identify a number of books on witchcraft for the police. The Guildhall librarian said that you might help me.'

'I would be happy to try.' The smile was a trifle indulgent. 'Do you have titles?'

'Yes.' Catherine referred to her telegraph. 'The first is *Letters on Demonology and Witchcraft* by Sir Walter Scott.'

'Ah, yes. Hardly a work of scholarship. Published by Morley's Universal Library, which gives you an idea of its worth. Indeed, in one sense it is positively mischievous. He transforms serious anthropology into fairy stories. He converts, for instance, legendary figures such as Puck, Robin à Hood and Robin Goodfellow, into an insipid sugar-plum personage he calls Robin Hood. I fear his book is an example of the worst kind of popularism.'

'I see.' Deflated, Catherine jotted down some notes in her book. 'The next is a book by Francis Barrett, called *Magus: The Celestial Intelligence*.'

206

Walford frowned. 'Yes, well, this purports to be a serious study of magical practices. It has enjoyed wide circulation among the literate classes. As a result it has become a kind of handbook for those who wish to relieve their boredom by dabbling with the occult.'

'Is it dangerous?' Catherine asked.

Walford pursed his lips. 'I would say that, of itself, it is no more dangerous than table-tapping, or psychic seances. However, for someone of our cultural background it can scarcely be said to be healthy.'

'The next one on the list is apparently in Latin, and was published in seventeen hundred and sixty.'

'Then you must be talking about the *Grimoire of Honorius the Great!*'

'Yes, indeed.'

'Now we are getting deeper into the world of magic. Pope Honorius the Third, who was pontiff from twelve sixteen to twelve twenty-seven, was a witch. The book you refer to is a compendium of what one might call serious magic. Its introduction is in the form of a Papal Bull, instructing that the *Grimoire* should be used for the purpose of invoking spirits. Essentially, he was adding to the historic function of a priest that of controlling demons under his Apostolic authority. If ever a work can be referred to as diabolic, this is it.'

'Goodness!' Catherine exclaimed. 'It all sounds rather unpleasant.'

'Not only unpleasant, but dangerous. This is where people like Scott do society a profound disservice. They lead us to believe that the demonic forces in creation have been banished by scientific advance; as darkness is banished by putting a candle in a child's bedroom. But there are still shadows.'

'You seem to be taking this very seriously.' Catherine said.

'I do,' he said tersely. 'Are there more?'

'Yes. The *Clavicules de Salomon,* apparently in French.'

'Hmn . . . Now we are in dangerous waters. Are you saying that copies of these works have been found?'

'That is my assumption.'

'I would like to get my hands on them, if it were at all possible . . . This *Key of Solomon* has existed from remote antiquity. There is every reason to believe that Solomon, king of Israel, was a magician. Certainly the Inquisition believed so when they banned this book as dangerous, in fifteen fifty-nine. I have only examined a copy briefly, in Paris, some years ago. But its reputation is clear. It has long been regarded as the most celebrated and feared work of ceremonial magic. If its rites are scrupulously carried out all created things must obey you.'

Catherine smiled. 'You surely do not believe that?' she said.

Walford's face remained sombre. 'I would not commit the folly of treating such lore lightly. I can only hope that these books – if, indeed, they exist – are in an academic library, where they will be used with due caution, and for scholarly purposes only.'

'I have no idea where they might be, except that it must be in the depths of Dorset.'

'That brings me no comfort,' Walford said. 'Until the coming of the railways, Dorset was as remote from civilization as the moon! I can well believe that witchcraft and magic are still taken seriously down there.'

'But, from your strictures on Sir Walter Scott I would have thought that you would applaud the fact.'

'Not if they are being actually practised, young lady. One may smile at children cavorting around on a broomstick hobby-horse, because the symbolism is unconscious. But, if someone seriously set about enacting one of the rituals in the *Key*, to conjure demons and compel their service, the result could be quite literally unimaginable.'

Catherine shivered. 'The man who sent this telegraph to me is a very special friend,' she said. 'Are you suggesting that he might be in danger?'

'So long as he is unknown to the magician; or, at the very least, has not in any way thwarted the magician, he should be safe. But there can be no certainty in these matters. Of their very nature, occult powers are resistant to control.'

'You sound as if you really believe in black magic,' Catherine said. 'It seems totally absurd, at the end of the nineteenth century!'

'Then, let me say that I have spent many years studying witchcraft and magic. I came to the subject with a scientific detachment buttressed by materialistic scepticism. If I do not yet believe in demonic powers, I would not presume to say that they do not exist . . . Is the *Key* the last of them?'

'No, there is one more book – an eighteen eighty edition of *Grimorium Verum*.'

Walford said nothing. He was perfectly still, staring into the distance. The silence was prolonged for minutes; Catherine wondered if he had gone into a trance. Then he began to speak softly from the depths of his abstraction. 'Dear God, no! It cannot be . . . yet there is no *Honorius* in Britain, that I know of . . . and no *Clavicules* outside a library . . .'

'What is it?' Catherine broke in. 'You seem distressed.'

He looked round, alarm on his face. 'I very much fear that your friend has stumbled on an active group of sorcerers,' he said. 'The *Grimorium Verum* has been the manual of conjuration since it was published – by a French Jesuit – in fifteen seventeen. It is not more diabolic than the *Clavicules*, but its ritual is more accessible. It demands no prior knowledge from the practitioner. With this book, anyone could conjure up a demon . . . You say that your friend sent you this list?'

'Yes. He wants me to identify them and pass on what information I can . . . What should I do?'

Walford sprang to his feet. 'Get him away from there!' he cried. 'He is in great danger! Get him out!'

In a panic, Catherine took a cab to Old Jewry and ran up the stairs to Bragg's room. No one was there. She hurried back down to the entrance hall. The desk-sergeant looked at her with amused tolerance.

'You are in a tearing hurry today, miss,' he said. 'Is something up?'

'I need to speak to Sergeant Bragg urgently,' she said.

'Well, he was in, first thing this morning. Then he went off, saying he would see me Monday.'

'You have no idea where he is?'

'No, miss.'

With a sinking heart, Catherine took a cab to Bragg's lodgings in Tan House Lane. She hammered on the front door. After what seemed an age, she heard the rattle of the lock and it was opened.

'Oh, it's you,' Mrs Jenks said crossly. 'There was no need to drag me up all this way. You could have come down to the area door; I am busy in the kitchen.'

'I am sorry,' Catherine said contritely. 'I was not thinking . . . Could I possibly have a word with Sergeant Bragg?'

209

'No, you cannot,' she said sourly. 'He's not here . . . He goes off to work as usual, then back he comes at half past nine. Says he is going off to Dorset for the weekend . . . I don't know what the world's coming to. A man of his age, and all!'

'Where shall I find him, Mrs Jenks? It is extremely important!'

Mrs Jenks looked at her distrustfully. 'He says he stays at Bere Regis, with his cousin. But I think some woman has got her claws into him – wanting clean shirts and collars . . . And we were supposed to be going to Clacton, tomorrow.'

Catherine turned away, her mind in turmoil. She had to warn Bragg of the peril James was in. She could not withhold her discoveries for a second longer than was necessary. She must go and find him herself; there was no alternative . . . She gave a licensed messenger five shillings to scamp his duties in the City and go to Park Lane with a note for her mother. Then she took a cab to Waterloo station, trying vainly to remember the name of the young woman whom James had said Bragg admired.

11

Morton spent the Friday after his encounter with Ursula wandering the uplands. With William Biles at his heels, he explored an area well away from the grove where they had seen the Purple Emperor. He stayed there till long after lunch-time, and the boy was finally successful in catching a female Adonis Blue. William was plainly disappointed at the undistinguished speckled insect, but was cheered at the thought of his two brass plates. When they were finally forced back to the village by hunger they came face to face with Ursula Witney in the lane. She smiled dreamily at Morton and passed on. He was nonplussed. She was acting as if she had forgotten the previous afternoon. Could she possibly be unaware of what had happened? Or, more to the point, what had not happened? He hurried back to the inn and persuaded a reluctant kitchen-maid to part with some bread and cheese. As he ate it in the bar, he reviewed his progress so far. He had caught, through William's unwelcome vigilance and enthusiasm, half the butterflies he was allegedly seeking. And what had he achieved? Precious little. If his notion regarding the Purple Emperor proved to be justified, he would have found the place where Walter Green in all probability was murdered. Beyond that, he had nothing to show for his presence in Slocombe Magna. As to the theory which had brought him to the village – the similarity of murder method – he had made virtually no progress. The Witneys must be the prime suspects, from this aspect. There were three of them living here – four, if one included old Lucy. He had spent a mere five minutes, in the garden, with one of the daughters; a half hour with the other that he neither could nor wished to remember clearly. As to the brother, who on any normal assessment would be thought most likely to be the murderer, he had exchanged no more than two painful sentences in the lane. He ought to be wandering through the village, chatting to the locals, finding out about the bigwigs. He ought to . . . but, in plain truth, he was afraid to. The episode with Ursula had somehow unmanned him. Perhaps she had conjured all the virility out of him, in one drug-induced frenzy of lust. However it might be, he was loath to meet any of the Witneys, for the moment. Yet what else could he do? He could not mope about in the Beaufort Arms. Reluctantly, he went out with his net again. This time William did not join him. He ought to have been relieved; determined to make the most of this opportunity to explore unobserved. Instead, he wandered in-effectively over some of the ground he had already traversed. When dusk began to fall, he went back to the inn and to his bed.

Next morning he felt his old self again. He rose early and by nine o'clock he was walking into Wareham station in search of a cab. Being Saturday, however, it was deserted. He had to kick his heels for half an hour, before he could get a trap to take him to Bere Regis.

This time, the allegedly flighty maid answered the door. She had a bright, lively look, certainly; but surely Amy Hildred had ex-aggerated? . . . Perhaps Amy was the kind of person who had to dominate and diminish everyone around her. As he was being led down the hallway, Fanny emerged from the sitting-room.

'I thought it must be you,' she said with an amused smile. 'I will bring Mr Bragg from the Old Brewery. I shall not be long . . . Oh, and there is someone staying with us whom you may know!'

As the door banged behind her, Morton went into the sitting-room.

'Catherine!' he exclaimed, taken aback.

'I should surprise you more often,' she said teasingly. 'You have never called me by my first name before.'

He grinned. 'I think of you as Catherine,' he said, 'but translate it into Miss Marsden, to conform with the proprieties.'

She raised her eyebrows. 'Are the proprieties so very important?' she asked.

'Oh, yes! Most definitely!'

'You say that with some feeling.'

'I have good reason to – Miss Marsden.'

'But, what on earth has happened to your hair?' she cried.

'My hair?'

'You have gone back to your centre parting! It looks so old-fashioned.'

'Ah, that is part of my disguise! That and my spectacles. You must blame Chambers; he clearly regards a side parting as effete. It was the centre parting that carved out the empire, after all.'

'Wait till I see Chambers!'

'But why on earth are you here?' he asked.

'I received your telegraph about the books and obtained the information you wanted. But when I went to see Sergeant Bragg he had already left. I decided to follow him. As a result, I have made the acquaintance of Miss Hildred. She is quite delightful and, I fear, devoted to that great bear of a man.'

'Sergeant Bragg?'

She laid her finger to her lips, as the front door opened. Fanny appeared, followed by Bragg.

'Can I make you some coffee, cousin?' she asked slyly.

'No, thank you.'

'Then, I will leave you.'

'No,' Bragg interrupted. 'Please stay, miss. You know this area better than anyone.'

Fanny gave a gratified smile and sat beside Bragg on the settee.

'Well, lad,' Bragg began. 'What have you found out?'

Morton paused in thought, for a moment. 'I suppose that it will seem incredible to you, in this wholesome atmosphere; but I think that Slocombe Magna is the centre of a witches' coven, or whatever one calls them.'

'Witchcraft?' Bragg exclaimed. 'You are leg-pulling, surely?'

'No. There are one or two superficial signs; the church is virtually unused, crows fly about unmolested . . . I went into the house that Walter Green used to live in. There was a collection of books apparently related to witchcraft.'

Bragg looked across at Catherine. 'Is that what has brought you down, miss?' he asked.

'Yes, sergeant. I too received a centre-parting telegraph and was compelled to hurry to the extremes of the empire!'

'And, what may that mean?'

The smile vanished from Catherine's face. 'I went to an expert, in the anthropology department of London University. He recognized all the books that James had listed in his telegraph. Some of them are handbooks of magical rites, that he said are very powerful and dangerous. He said that James was in peril, particularly if he had crossed or thwarted the sorcerer or sorceress.'

'Well, he is hardly likely to have done that, with a butterfly net,' Bragg said sceptically.

Morton did not smile.

'My expert lent me a book on witchcraft,' Catherine said with forced brightness. 'Not a dangerous one, I am sure. But I became quite an expert in witchcraft, on the journey down – on rowan trees, and how to make flying-ointment from plants . . .'

'What plants?' Morton asked soberly.

'I shall have to look it up.' Catherine reached for a book on the table. 'Here we are . . . You take some lard – if you cannot get the fat of an unbaptised baby – and mix it with henbane, deadly nightshade, wild celery, thornapple! This has to be done according to a strict ritual – which fortunately is not in the book! Having prepared the ointment, the witch applies it to her forehead, armpits and places which modesty forbids me to mention – and she can fly!' Catherine gave a brittle laugh. 'How absurd!' she said.

'Possibly,' Morton said slowly, 'yet these plants are all found in Slocombe Magna. Francesca Witney even grows wild celery in her kitchen garden; because it is tender – or so she says . . . What does your book say about rowan trees?'

'Ah, I need not look that up; I remember it exactly. The rowan is a defence against hostile magic. A rowan twig tied to the horns of a cow will prevent witches drying up her milk.'

'What about red ribbon?'

213

'In conjunction with rowan, or indeed alone, it can defeat a spell on cattle. Stupid, is it not?'

Morton looked across at Bragg. 'It appears that not all the village is given over to witchcraft,' he said. 'The farm at the western end has been surrounded with rowan trees. The cows have some herbs or leaves tied to their horns with red ribbon; there is red ribbon on the farm gate.'

'Oh, James, please do not go back to that dreadful place!' Catherine cried, her pretence gone. 'You cannot risk your life, over something that is no concern of ours.'

Bragg disregarded her. 'Does this mean,' he asked, 'that the rest of the village is given over to Satan?'

'Certainly, there is nothing similar anywhere else.'

'Including the other farm?'

'That belongs to Alfred Green, the brother of the murdered man. There is no protection against witchcraft there.'

'So, he could be in this witchcraft business?'

'Either that, or he is not superstitious . . . However, I have to say that he walks around the village with a knob-stick whose protuberances are decidedly phallic.'

Fanny blushed, and spoke to cover her confusion. 'We have a long tradition of fairies, in Dorset; black, white and green. I think that the green were the worst. And there used to be a mask in the Dorchester museum, which had been worn at witches' sabbats. It was stolen, some years ago.'

'Ah, yes. The Dorset Ooser,' Bragg said. 'A man's face with bull's horns. I remember seeing it, when I was a lad . . . This is the right part of the country for witchcraft, all right.'

'On the other hand,' Morton said, 'the death of Walter Green might have nothing whatever to do with the witchcraft. He may have been engaged in nefarious practices, but the reason for it may have been mundane enough.'

'Hmn . . . I begin to wonder if any theory will cover all these murders,' Bragg said sombrely. 'Now we have a third.'

'A third?'

'Cissie Fox was murdered on Thursday, at lunch-time. The same time as Jethro Witney, the same spot, the same way.'

'Good God! But why?'

Bragg sighed. 'You tell me.'

'There is no doubt, I suppose?'

'Not according to Professor Burney. Anyway, you should be able to eliminate some suspects, lad. Who did you see on Thursday in Slocombe Magna.'

'Only Ursula Witney.' Morton strove to keep the embarrassment out of his voice.

'What about the others? Alfred Green, Thomas Witney and Francesca Witney?'

'I saw none of them.' Morton could see Catherine looking at him intently. 'But why kill Cissie?' he went on hurriedly. 'The child will still continue to get Witney's annuity, whether her mother is alive or not.'

'You mean, Julia or Peter Lazenby might have done it? Certainly neither of them will give me an alibi.'

'I mean that there seems little point in either of them doing it.'

Bragg mused. 'People do not always think straight,' he said. 'Anyway, they might have thought that the grandmother would cave in, once Cissie was out of the way . . . By the way, Branksome is out of the running for this one; he was in Winchester nick.'

'What about Syme?'

'He was too far gone to question. He will keep.'

'Have you seen Julia again?' Morton asked.

'Yes. Her new solicitor has told her not to answer questions; but she did say that she saw her father constructing the family tree.'

'Did you show her the list of investments?'

'I did,' Bragg said sourly. 'She did not recognize any of them – said she knew nothing of her father's affairs. I reckon I shall be lumbered with the job of looking through company registers, to see what names pop up.'

Morton laughed. 'Then I will gladly remain in Slocombe Magna for a month!'

Bragg brooded for a time, then: 'What kind of man was this Walter Green?' he asked.

'Obviously, I have been unable to converse with people on the matter,' Morton said. 'So I have had to proceed by inference. I have spoken to Alfred, who is his elder brother by some years. Alfred is somewhat dotty. He regarded Walter as being mad for making a will. *Ergo* Walter was sane!'

'What has Alfred against wills?'

'He thinks that to make one is to invite disaster – a view which has, of course, been reinforced by Walter's death. Alfred was adamant that he would never make a will.'

'Had Walter anything much to leave?'

'He certainly lived in a fine house, with some good pieces of furniture – and possibly some interesting books of occult ritual. Everything was left to Ursula Witney, who seems to have been his mistress.'

'Do you think that Walter Green was the leader of the witches?' Catherine asked.

'You mean, on the basis that he held the magical books? It is possible; though, equally, Ursula might have brought them with her from the family home.'

'I saw the Witneys at the reading of the will,' Bragg said musingly. 'Spoke to Ursula. She's barmy, if you ask me. Talked rubbish about lines of power reaching out from Winchester, to knock off people in Slocombe Magna.'

'Was she suggesting that Jethro Witney was a witch?' Catherine asked.

Bragg laughed. 'Having seen the body, I think we can accept that he was a man, all right!'

'That is a common misapprehension,' Catherine said sharply. 'Traditionally the leader of a witches' coven was a man, personating the devil. Indeed, he seems to have been referred to as such, in some parts of Britain.'

'I see . . . Ursula did throw some herbs into Jethro's grave; to ease his passing, she said.'

'Surely that suggests she wanted to ward off hostile magic,' Fanny said.

The discussion languished, as if it had reached a dead end. Then Morton spoke, almost to himself.

'I wonder if we are not placing more weight on the method of killing than the facts will bear,' he said.

'Why is that?' Bragg asked brusquely.

'Well, we know how Jethro, and now Cissie Fox, were killed. We can rely upon Dr Burney's assertion that the *modus operandi* was the same in each case. And, indeed, they have a natural connection, in that they occurred in a particular place. Beyond that, one can see logical motives for both murders. It is only when we try to bring the killing of Walter Green into the same picture that matters become complicated. Might it not be that we are creating difficulties for ourselves? After all, Dr Burney did not see the corpse of Walter Green; and we are precluded from approaching the pathologist who did. We are relying on a description of the injuries given by the Chief Constable of Dorset, who may or may not have seen the body.'

'All right,' Bragg said testily, 'to some extent we are making an assumption. But, by God, we are going to push it to the limit! When you come back and tell me that all the Witneys and Alfred Green were in Slocombe Magna, at the time Cissie Fox was murdered, I'll admit I was wrong. Not until!'

'I wonder if there is something else you might consider,' Fanny broke in. 'I have just been making a will – I inherited certain assets from my father – so I have had to familiarize myself with the process. As you talked, I wondered whether the picture might make more sense if it were turned upside down.'

'How do you mean, miss?' Bragg asked.

'First of all, can you tell me, cousin, if Alfred Green is wealthy?'

Morton smiled. 'Well, cousin, I know that he has a leasehold farm; probably his house is leasehold also. The whole village seems to be part of the Beaufort estate, which presumably has nothing to do with the Greens. As to investments, he certainly must have some. The City news is the only part of *The Times* he will read. Indeed, they must be substantial for him to take the dire risk of wearing out his brain in that regard!'

'And he is older than was Walter?' Fanny asked.

'By some six or seven years only.'

'I see. That is hardly material, but my theory can still be sustained, I think . . . How certain are you that Alfred has not, and never would, make a will?'

'Utterly certain. He argues that the rules for an intestacy are perfectly satisfactory, and he need not strain his brain in worrying about the matter.'

'And this attitude would be well known in the area?'

'Almost certainly. After all, he confided the matter to me, a total stranger, within five minutes of our meeting.'

Fanny considered for a moment, her eyes bright with excitement. 'It seems clear, then, that in the normal course Walter would have inherited Alfred's estate.'

'On the basis that the elder dies first, yes.'

'And Ursula would have got it after Walter,' Bragg interposed. 'That seems to rule her out as the killer.'

'Ah, but you miss my point!' Fanny said. 'What if Walter were murdered to prevent him from inheriting Alfred's wealth?'

There was a silence, then Bragg spoke with a trace of admiration in his voice. 'That's an interesting one,' he said. He took the family tree from his pocket and spread it on the table. 'Who will inherit from Alfred Green, now? Come on, lad, you are the only one here who has any need to bother about stuff like this.'

'The only knowledge I have, is that these things are better left to the experts. I am sure the lawyers fatten themselves on our bovine acquiescence in the doctrine; but, so far, I have followed the herd.' He pored over the family tree. 'So far as I can see, the Greens have a clear connection with the Rossiters, and a rather more tenuous one with the Witneys.'

'I am sure that the Rossiters' withdrawal of the undue influence suit has something to do with it all,' Catherine said buoyantly.

'What, all those years ago?' Bragg leaned again over the document.

'Why not? The hatred is still as intense as ever.'

'There is one odd thing,' Morton broke in. 'Alfred inherited a picture from Walter – not a picture exactly. It consisted of the birth certificate of their father, John Green, flanked by pictures of their grandparents – the dashing Captain Oscar Green and his Ruthless consort.'

'What's odd about that?' Bragg demanded.

'I do not know. It just struck me as odd.'

'Don't complicate things, lad.' He turned to Fanny. 'It seems to follow from what you say, miss, that now Walter is out of the way Alfred will be next for the chop.'

'I suppose that is the case.'

'Then, it looks as if you will have to stay in Slocombe Magna, lad.' There was satisfaction in Bragg's voice.

Morton sighed. 'I suppose so . . . By the way, I have something for you.' He produced the jar of soil from his pocket.

'What the devil is that? . . . . Sorry, miss. I was carried away.'

Fanny smiled warmly. 'You have more weighty matters to concern you than social proprieties, Joseph.'

'It is a sample of soil,' Morton said, 'from the place where I think Walter Green may have been killed. If I am right, the pathologists will find traces of his blood in it.'

'What place is that?'

'A clump of mature trees; about a mile from the village, on the uplands. It is an eerie place. The trees are growing in a wide circle, so it is a deliberate planting. In the middle of the grove is a great slab of stone, which has clearly been the site of generations of fires. Around the slab is a well-trodden path.'

'It sounds precisely like the kind of place where the witches held their sabbats and esbats!' Catherine exclaimed.

'We seem to be getting in above our heads,' Bragg said grimly. 'What is the difference between them?'

'The esbat was the ordinary meeting of the coven; the sabbat took place only four times a year; it was a great feast.'

'When were the sabbats?'

'Candlemas Day, Walpurgis Night, Lammas and Hallowe'en.'

'Walpurgis is May Eve!' Morton broke in. 'April the thirtieth! We have been thinking in terms of May Day, because that was when he was found. It all fits! He was murdered at a Walpurgis night sabbat, up in the grove!'

Bragg looked at the jar of soil. 'Well, whether that be so or not, there's no way you can leave Slocombe Magna now, lad . . . And if you see any sign of one of these esbats, let me know. We are going to be there!'

12

For once, Bragg was glad to get back to London, on the Sunday night. Although Morton had gone back to Slocombe Magna the previous afternoon, Bragg had felt obliged to accept Amy's invitation to stay to tea. During the meal Fanny and Catherine had passed on to her details of the case that he would have preferred to have remained confidential. Amy had been sworn to secrecy by them, but when could a woman resist the temptation to gossip? To them it would give a titillating sense of moral outrage; but Morton's life could be at stake. To give her credit, Miss Marsden understood this. But her obvious anxiety only made it more difficult to consider the situation rationally. When he finally went back to the Old Brewery, he found himself too restless to join in his cousins' conversation. He excused himself early and went to bed.

He slept badly. As soon as Sunday morning dawned, he washed and shaved in cold water. Then, taking some bread and cheese from the kitchen, he walked out of the village and up to Gallows Hill. This was a better place to think; wild and desolate. Here he could start afresh; follow the case through from every angle, examine the validity of each assumption, the value of every piece of evidence. He sat in the sun at the foot of an oak tree, and ate his breakfast. He deliberately tried to clear his mind, still his irritation. He watched a lark whirring into the air – higher, ever higher; listened to its warbling song as it rose out of sight. When he had finished his meal he took off his coat and, folding it, lay down with it as his pillow. Now he could relax, be objective; remember he was a policeman, not the chairman of a debating society. Where should he start? . . . With the murders, of course; they were indubitable fact. No need for conjecture there . . . Except that, as Morton kept mentioning, they were taking the Walter Green murder on trust. All right. Allowing that one assumption, there were three murders, done by the same person. Two in the same place – in the very same room; one a hundred miles away, in a different world . . . What linked them? Was it even sensible to look for a link? . . . Well, at least a pattern; there should be a pattern . . . It was not random killing, with two in the same office . . . But Dorset . . . Where did Dorset fit? . . .

He was awakened by a bumble bee entangling itself momentarily in his moustache. The sun was high in the sky . . . Dear God! It was past twelve; he would only just get back in time for lunch. He had achieved absolutely nothing; and it meant that he had missed the early train back to London. Well, that was a plus; he would not have to listen to Miss Marsden's worries about Morton. If the blasted girl did not want him dented, why the devil didn't she marry him? They could go off and play lords and ladies then, and be useless to anybody. He got to his feet and, with his coat over his arm, set off back to Bere Regis.

Lunch was on the table when he arrived. After it, he and Ted

220

retreated to the parlour while the womenfolk washed the dishes. Some months before his cousin's carter's business had got into difficulties. To help get him back on his feet, Bragg had invested some money in it; become a sleeping partner. That was precisely what Bragg wanted to be. Ted was perfectly capable of running it now. But, whenever he went to Bere Regis, Ted insisted on telling him everything that had happened since his last visit; even asking for his opinion. It was absurd. He was in no position to give him advice. He had driven carts for his father in his early teens, sure enough. But he had rapidly got bored with it and gone into a shipping office as a clerk. As soon as the City police would have him he had joined the force. He was in no position to make business decisions . . . and he had his own problems.

As soon as he decently could, he packed his bag, said goodbye to Ted and Emma and walked round the corner to The Retreat. Over tea, Fanny and Amy treated him to blinding flashes of inspiration, which shed no fresh light on the murders but gave him less confidence in their assurances of discretion. While driving him to Wool station Fanny developed and reinforced her theory that Alfred Green was the key to the puzzle – an Alfred Green who was still unscathed . . . There might be some firm ground to it, but to jump in with both feet would be folly. For once, he was glad to be raising his hat to her retreating back.

During the long train journey, he tried to empty his mind of everything to do with police work, to watch the hamlets flashing by, the shadows dappling the countryside. When at last he got back to his lodgings he had to face a querulous Mrs Jenks: chiding him for not taking her to Clacton, worried because of Miss Marsden's anxiety. All in all, he was glad to draw the curtains on his weekend and climb into bed.

By ten o'clock next morning he was in the office of the Linoleum Manufacturing Co. Ltd in Queen Victoria Street, their share register open in front of him. He turned to see if there were any Witneys. There was one, with an address in Birmingham. None of the Witneys on the family tree was there. There were no Rossiters at all. He turned back to the Greens . . .

Alfred Green, Slocombe Magna, Dorset. 10,000

Good God! That could amount to a fair bit of money. Was Fanny right after all? He picked the three companies on Jethro's list, whose offices were in the same part of the City and went to examine their records. Alfred Green had substantial shareholdings in The Glamorgan Coal Co. Ltd, The London Dry Docks Co. Ltd and The River Plate Telephone & Electric Light Co. Ltd. Four out of four! There was no point in going round the rest; the hypothesis seemed to be proved. But where did that leave him? The list had been prepared by Jethro; that was now a reasonable assumption. The reason for his doing so remained obscure; but it looked as if it had been compiled without Alfred Green's knowledge. It was possible that Jethro had heard gossip about Alfred's investments from his relatives in the village. That would explain the question marks by some of the entries. He would have struck them through once he had confirmed the holding by consulting the company's register.

Bragg left the company's office and went to Golden Lane, where he left the jar of earth and a note for Professor Burney. Then he hurried back to Old Jewry. He got out the outline statement of wealth that he had taken from Witney's safe. If the shareholdings belonged not to Jethro himself, but to Alfred Green, then he had been trying to estimate Alfred's wealth. Why? Bragg took out his tobacco pouch and cut a fill of dark twist. He must beware of jumping into a too-ready acceptance of Fanny's theory. It had to be tested all the way. He rubbed the tobacco to fragments between his palms and fed it into the bowl of his pipe. Of course, it was not possible to know when Jethro had produced this. The family tree was being prepared the previous autumn; was he assembling information about Alfred's investments at the same time? The only way to tackle that problem would be to find out the dates on which the various holdings had been bought. The most recent would give the earliest date at which the list could have been compiled. But the job could have been done at any time after that – right up to the day before Jethro was murdered. To complete the information would be a monumental task if it were to be done without the knowledge of Alfred Green. He could never justify the use of that kind of manpower. Interviewing all the stockbrokers in the City could take weeks. He struck a match and laid it across the bowl of his pipe. When there was a haze of tobacco smoke around his head he settled down to study the document again.

222

Shares	£25,238-17-8
Property	
Leaseholds	20,000
Houses	1,000
Land	? ? ?
Furniture & effects	3,000

The shares had been given a precise figure because, presumably, Witney could get the prices from the *Financial News*. The others were obvious estimates. Being an estate agent, Jethro would know about rental values. And he would be able to estimate the value of the unexpired terms of the leases because his relatives occupied similar property in the village. He would have a fair idea of the value of antiques too; in the Winchester business they probably did a fair bit of auctioneering. As to the entry about land, Jethro was either wondering if Alfred had any land or was unable to decide what it was worth. But anyway, from what Morton had said the whole village was leasehold.

Bragg puffed at his pipe, musing. It would be a help to know what had prompted Jethro to prepare it. In the normal course, Walter would survive Alfred; and the liaison between Walter and Ursula Witney was common knowledge. Julia must have seemed to be in line for all the Greens' wealth, as well as the Witneys'. On that line of argument, Jethro's interest lay in Walter's survival; which would put him in the clear as regards Walter's murder . . . But he was anyway, on the presumption that they were both killed by the same person. Bragg shook his head. His brain was getting in a muddle; going round and round, without ever reaching a conclusion. He pushed back his chair, put on his bowler hat and walked down to The Temple. He climbed the stairs to Sir Rufus Stone's chambers and went to the clerk's room.

'Is the coroner in?' he asked.

'He is,' the clerk said frostily, 'but he has a conference in ten minutes. Some of the clients have already arrived.'

'I promise not to keep him longer than that.'

'Very well,' the clerk said reluctantly. 'But keep your word on that. He is appearing in court first thing this afternoon.'

Bragg went down the corridor and tapped on Sir Rufus's door.

'Come!'

223

Bragg decided that the clients he was expecting must be very important for, as he walked in, Sir Rufus went into a prepared charade of studying an impressive-looking bundle of documents. When he saw that it was Bragg he pushed them aside with a scowl.

'I wondered where you had got to, Bragg,' he said aggressively. 'I suppose you are aware that I appointed you my officer for the Cicely Fox murder; though you have shown no evidence of the fact!'

'Ah, yes, sir,' Bragg said meekly. 'I am aware of it, thank you.'

'Well? What the devil are you doing to catch this man? It is already five days since she was killed!'

'It will be four days at two o'clock this afternoon,' Bragg said quietly.

Sir Rufus sprang to his feet. 'Do not bandy words with me, Bragg!' he cried. 'Have you, or have you not made progress in finding this killer . . . this mass murderer?'

'We have every reason to believe that Miss Fox knew her murderer . . .'

'A child of seven could have deduced that, Bragg,' the coroner interrupted. 'Her body was found in the rear office, as before. They both must have known the killer.'

'Yes, sir.'

'What else?'

'Cicely Fox went to meet someone, the afternoon before she was killed. We think that was her murderer.'

'So, why did he not dispose of her then?' Sir Rufus demanded. 'Instead of leaving it to the next day.'

'We have not yet discovered that, sir. We do know, however, that Peter Lazenby has no alibi for the time of the crime, nor has Syme, the clerk.'

'Good God, man! Is that all you have discovered? Here am I, being constantly harried by newspaper reporters, my own reputation at stake, my competence under question; and you are treating the matter as if it were the theft of a child's pocket-money!'

'I have spent two of those days in Winchester and Dorset, sir,' Bragg said quietly.

The coroner's eyes narrowed. 'Winchester I can, with some difficulty, accept,' he exclaimed. 'But what the devil were you doing in Dorset? Were you, perchance, taking your annual vacation? Or looking for a haven, against a retirement that may not long be delayed?'

Bragg ignored the outburst. 'Have you had any experience of witchcraft, sir?' he asked.

'Witchcraft?' Sir Rufus became watchful. 'You are surely not advancing the proposition that these murders are connected with witchcraft?'

'It is a possibility I would gladly eliminate, if I had the knowledge.'

'Well, I am happy to say that my practice does not extend into that area, Bragg. And I am confident that the same applies to every barrister in these chambers! Witchcraft has not been a specific offence since the repeal of the Witchcraft Acts in seventeen thirty-six. Why do you ask? Or are you merely trying to divert my wrath?'

'There is evidence of a coven of witches in Dorset, sir.'

'What of it? Why should we concern ourselves with half-witted yokels tripping round a maypole? Have they been trampling corn, or poisoning worthy citizens with their love-potions?'

'There was a murder on the thirtieth of April – Walpurgis Night. That is one of their festivals. It was in a remote Dorset village. The method used was identical to that in the case of Jethro Witney and, now, Cicely Fox.'

'Huh! Are you telling me that we have a corresponding coven of witches in the City? That all these murders were carried out as part of some demonological rite? You are off your head, Bragg!'

'I don't think so, sir. You see, there seems to be a great deal of money at stake . . . Perhaps it is just that I have not got the expertise to see the problem clearly. Do you know about the rules of inheritance, sir?'

There was a rap on the door and the clerk poked his head in. 'Your people are all here now, sir.'

Sir Rufus waved him away. 'Inheritance, Bragg? Indeed I do. What is your problem?'

Bragg laid the family tree on the table in front of the coroner. 'This is the man who was murdered, sir. His brother, Alfred is the one with the money.'

'If money is at the bottom of it,' Sir Rufus interrupted, 'why kill the man with none?'

'It is a bit complicated, sir, and I know you have got people waiting. What we really need to know is who inherits Alfred Green's belongings, assuming that he has not made a will?'

'I am reluctant to waste my time advising you on such an unlikely premise, Bragg! In order to confer on the City the benefit of my acting as Her Majesty's coroner, I must earn my modest competence from clients such as those who even now await me.'

'It is not at all unlikely, sir. We know for a fact that he has set his mind against making a will – ever.'

'Very well, Bragg,' the coroner said impatiently. 'What does the estate consist of?'

'Investments, leaseholds, furniture, probably some cash.'

'Personality, then . . . Well, it is perfectly simple. There are no descendants; so you go back up the chart, until you find an ancestor with a descendant living.'

'Walter Green's grandmother was Anne Witney,' Bragg said, pointing at the document. 'Does that mean the Witneys would get it all?'

'Not so, Bragg! It appears that Ruth Green had already two children, by a previous marriage, when Alfred Green's father was born. The law provides that, for this purpose, half-siblings count as full siblings. So the Rossiters are not excluded from consideration.'

'That hardly seems fair.'

'Fair?' Sir Rufus exclaimed. 'Since when has the law sought to be fair? The courts dispense justice, they do not seek to be fair!'

'Yes, sir. So, who gets the money?'

'You have to establish the degree of kinship to the deceased of all living relatives. Those individuals in the nearest degree of kinship share equally in the estate.'

'So how does that work?'

'Well, on the Witney side, Anne, Alfred's grandmother, is in the second degree. But, as she had only the one child, we have to go back a further generation, to find a line with a living descendant. So, we go back to the great-grandparents, Peter and Susan Witney. They are in the third degree of kinship. Now we can trace their descendants, by way of Thomas, Nathaniel and Matthew, to the present generation. Thus, Ursula, Thomas and Francesca Witney are in the seventh degree of kinship to Alfred Green, and Julia is in the eighth.'

'It seems very complicated, sir.'

'Naturally. How would lawyers earn a living, otherwise?'

'And, what about the Rossiters?'

'Well, Ruth, as Alfred's grandmother, is also in the second degree. Since Stanley and Mabel are to be treated as full siblings, they are in the third. Thus William and Frederick are in the fifth degree, and David in the sixth.'

'Does that mean that William and Frederick would get it all?'

'You are an apt pupil, Bragg. Now, will you tell my clerk that I am free, on your way out?'

Bragg wandered back to Old Jewry totally deflated. There would never be any point in a Witney killing a Green; it would only put money into the pockets of the Rossiters. But why had Jethro been interested? He clearly was – to the extent of listing Alfred's assets and preparing a family tree. Did he stop the exercise when he realized the likely outcome? . . . But it was Greens and Witneys who were being killed . . . Killed by the Rossiters? On that basis, one could argue a case for Fanny's theory. Once Walter was out of the way, Alfred's money would go to them in the natural course. And, if they got a taste for killing, they might have had a go at Jethro – they certainly hated him enough. But why Cissie Fox? Where did she fit in? Disgruntled, Bragg decided that he would have to go through every bit of evidence again, to see where he had gone wrong.

Once Catherine had got back to London, away from the over-wrought atmosphere of Dorset, her fears began to lessen. Bere Regis had been a sleepy village, normal to the point of boredom. Surely Slocombe Magna, a few miles away, must be similar? Perhaps the inhabitants were a little more eccentric, but that would be all. As she reasoned away her fears, she became determined to untangle the strand that seemed to have been left to her. No one else appeared to be interested in the Rossiters. Her research into the lawsuit seemed to have dropped into the pool of information without raising a ripple. Yet she would dearly like to know more about it. Why did the Rossiters withdraw the case, after spending so much money and effort on it? It would have cost precious little more to push it to trial. Most people would have considered it worthwhile; and the Rossiters were not lacking in resolution. She got out her notes on the case and read through them. Ruth Rossiter came across as a very level-headed, determined woman. James's 'Ruthless' jibe was almost justified. Yet she obviously had a romantic streak. What a pity that she had been denied happiness by her second husband's death. Oscar Green . . . a Captain in the Thirty-seventh Foot. On an impulse, she put her notebook in her handbag and, making an excuse to the editor, set off for Bunhill Row. She made her way to the headquarters of the London Rifle Brigade. A sentry in a smart green and black uniform was standing to attention at the entrance, his rifle grounded.

'Excuse me,' she said.

'Go away,' he hissed from the corner of his mouth.

'I am sorry. I just wanted to ask you . . .'

'Go away! Can't you see I'm on duty?' His face was staring woodenly forwards, his lips barely moved. 'I'll see you in The Swan, tonight . . . How much?'

Catherine felt like slapping his stupid face. How dare he take her for a street-woman! If he had moved his head a fraction, he would have seen that she was no such thing! Outraged, she turned on her heel and flounced into the building. She found herself in a lofty stone-flagged corridor. At the far end, a flight of steps ran up to the next floor. A man was just beginning to ascend them; he was wearing a frock-coat and looked like a clerk. She might get more sense out of him.

'Hullo!' Her voice echoed down the passage.

'Excuse me,' she called.

He stopped, turned and came to meet her.

'I am a reporter on the *City Press*,' she said. 'I am wondering if our readers would be interested in an article on the Rifle Brigade.'

The man's face lit up. 'What a good idea!' he exclaimed. 'We are, of course, a reserve regiment; anything which might increase recruitment would be welcome. Why not come to my room, and you can tell me what kind of things you want to know . . . for instance, we have a strong connection with Lloyds – the insurance market . . .'

'That is precisely the kind of information I am seeking.' She followed him into a room that was sparsely furnished and oppressively tidy. 'But, before we begin,' she said, 'I wonder if you can help me on another small matter. I am trying to trace the present whereabouts of the Thirty-seventh Foot.'

228

The clerk laughed. 'You must be delving into ancient history!' he said. 'All the regiments of the line were reorganized over ten years ago.' He pulled a slim volume from a shelf behind him and flipped over the pages. 'Here we are, Thirty-seventh Foot . . . They are now the First Battalion of the Hampshire Regiment.'

Catherine caught her breath with excitement. 'I see,' she said. 'Would you happen to know where they are stationed?'

'Well, that battalion might be on duty overseas; but the regimental headquarters would be in Winchester, I should think . . . In Hampshire, there would be nowhere else, would there?'

When Morton went out of the inn that Monday morning he was surprised to hear a bleating noise from the village green. He looked round and saw that a kid was tethered to a stout stake in the centre of the triangle. It had obviously walked round and round the stake, shortening the rope until its nose was against the wood. Morton glanced around but there was no one in sight. He sauntered over. As he approached he saw that there was a green wreath round the animal's throat. He spoke soothingly to the kid and pulled it round the stake anti-clockwise, to unwind the tether. Anti-clockwise . . . Widdershins. Had Catherine not said something about garlands round kids? Read something from her book . . . ? He looked closely at the wreath. Sprigs of verbena bound with green ribbon. Good God! The wretched animal had been prepared for ritual sacrifice! Obviously there was to be another witches' festival . . . But when? Affecting unconcern, he picked up his butterfly-net and strolled down the lane to the farm with the rowan trees. Josiah Grote had become aware of it also. The red ribbon on the gate had been reinforced by placing a large block of rock salt under it. According to the lore in Catherine's book, no witch would dare pass that way. His suspicions confirmed, he determined to find out, if he could, when the esbat was to take place. He drew the line at approaching Ursula; that was well beyond the call of duty! But Thomas or Francesca might let the information slip. He wandered slowly back, peering in the verges as if seeking his quarry. When he got to Francesca's house he pushed open the gate and went towards the kitchen garden. As he rounded the corner of the house he checked in astonishment. Old Lucy was squatting on a low stool; not a foot from her hand was a great black crow. She was feeding it from a basket on her lap.

'Come, Lucifer!' She held out a piece of crust, daubed with fat. 'There's a fine Lucifer!'

The crow hopped forward, seized the crust and retreated. It dropped the bread, placed one foot on it and tore it apart with its grey beak. In a moment the crust was gone, and the bird was cocking its head for more. Suddenly it was aware of him. It jumped clumsily sideways and regarded him with its hard black eye. Lucy looked round.

'Ah! You are Mr er . . . You came the other day.'

'Yes, ma'am,' Morton said deferentially. 'Do you think it might be possible for me to see your daughter for a moment?'

'Oh . . . Ursula, you mean? I heard her speak of you. She is up at the other house now.'

'I was referring to Francesca. She said that I might come to this garden, in search of butterflies; but I wish to know if it is convenient.'

Lucy glanced towards the house. 'Robin!' she called. 'Robin!'

There was no answer.

'Go through the kitchen door,' Lucy said. 'She will be inside somewhere.'

Morton moved forward and the great crow flapped into a tree.

Francesca was not in the kitchen, but had been recently. A great ham was on the table, a vessel close by to cook it in. Through an open pantry door Morton could see enormous pieces of raw beef. Clearly a feast was in preparation – the cold meats for a witches' esbat? On one corner of the table was a basin; it contained a disgusting mixture of fat and herbs. Morton lifted the spoon and sniffed. Ugh! What had Catherine called it? Flying-ointment? He went outside again, to see Francesca coming down the path, a posy in her hand.

'Mr Hildred,' she said. 'How nice to see you!' Her voice was inviting, provocative . . . Inviting to what? he wondered.

'I came to ask if I might search your borders.' Morton felt stupid, he was virtually tongue-tied. It had come out like an obscene suggestion.

Her eyes lingered on him. 'Why not come in for coffee first?' she said. 'I have just made it.'

'Yes . . . thank you.' At least his blurted remarks sounded in character.

He followed her inside and took the Delft mug of coffee from her. She was lithe and graceful; there was sensuality in her every move.

'I did not know that your name was Robin,' he said awkwardly.

She smiled. 'It is Mamma's nickname for me . . . But you may use it, if you wish.'

Morton could well believe it. Old Nick . . . The name bestowed by the devil. Poor robin, to be so maligned.

'How is your quest proceeding?' she asked.

'Oh, very well. I have captured both sexes of the Adonis Blue. Now I must concern myself with the Chalk-hill Blue.'

'Both sexes?' Her voice lingered on the second word.

'Indeed.' He gulped at his coffee.

'Perhaps I should volunteer to help you, now that the Biles boy has gone back to work!'

'That would be very pleasant,' he said self-consciously.

She smiled. 'I shall be busy for a day or so, but after that . . .'

'Yes. Thank you for the coffee.' He put down the mug, and squeezed past her to the garden. As he scuttled away, he could hear her laughing.

He made a cursory inspection of the flower borders, then went out into the lane. He walked vigorously, to regain his poise. These blasted Witney women were the very incarnation of sensuality . . . but at least the coffee had not been laced with aphrodisiac. He glanced over his shoulder as he hurried past Ursula's house, but she was nowhere to be seen. Perhaps she, too, was cooking great joints of meat. He kept walking, over the ford, up the hill to the pasture-land. There was no one in sight. He wandered as erratically as one of his butterflies. Occasionally he flicked his net and mimed the examination of a capture. Slowly he worked his way to the grove. There was no one about. He went behind the trees. Still no one. He pushed through them into the arena. A large pile of logs was stacked by the stone slab in the middle, a mound of kindling wood beside it. There could no longer be any doubt. But when would the esbat be? Unlike the sabbat, it could be held at any time . . . During the next day or so, from what Francesca had said. Perhaps he ought to summon Bragg back forthwith.

He worked his way back to the village, with enough diversions

231

to convince an onlooker that he was still chasing butterflies. As he was strolling back to the inn he met Alfred Green, phallic stick in hand.

'Good morning, Mr Hildred,' he said cheerfully. 'The weather seems to have settled down again.'

'Yes, indeed, sir.'

'Care for a whisky?'

'I would enjoy one very much.'

'Come on, then.' Alfred led the way through the garden, and into his sitting-room. Everything seemed exactly as before; nothing had been moved by as much as a hair's breadth. Alfred disappeared, and Morton strolled over to the fireplace. He gazed at Alfred's grandparents, staring starchily at each other across the fading parchment of their son's birth certificate. He could not rid himself of the feeling that it was profoundly significant. Why should anyone create such a montage otherwise? What was it proclaiming to the world?

'Sorry I was so long. I had to get a fresh bottle.' Alfred set his tray down and poured two fingers of whisky into the glasses. 'A little water, was it not?'

'Please.' Morton wondered how much damage that effort of recollection had done to his brain. Silly old fool! He had as much inkling of what was facing him as the kid on the green.

'I must warn you! You are in great danger!' he blurted out, on an impulse.

'What?' Alfred held out the glass, incomprehension on his face.

'Your brother was murdered. You are next.'

'I . . . I do not follow you.'

'I am a policeman, investigating your brother's death.'

'Why?'

'Because he was murdered.'

'Yes . . . Well, I thought he must have been.'

Morton wondered whether to reveal that he knew about the esbat and decided against it. He took the glass of whisky. 'The person who killed your brother also killed Jethro Witney, and one of his staff,' he said.

'So, you are not hunting butterflies?'

'No.'

'I see. Very well, I have got that straight now.'

232

'We believe that it is all concerned with your wealth, and who will inherit it after your death.'

'I told you last time; it is not something I worry my brain about.'

'Nor am I seeking to burden you with it. But I am concerned to arrest the person responsible for these murders.'

'Hmn . . . I should have known you were too big to be a butterfly collector,' Alfred murmured.

'Will you help me?'

He looked into the distance, cogitating. 'I suppose I shall have to,' he said. 'I would not want to die before my time . . . You say that I am next?'

'That is my belief.'

Alfred held up his hand. 'I don't want to hear the details,' he said. 'I will accept that you know what you are about.'

'I want you to let it be known that you are going to make a will.'

'A will?' He took a gulp of his whisky. 'No! I will never do that!'

Morton smiled. 'You misunderstand me. I want the world to think that you are about to make one. We believe that it will force the murderer to move – flush him out of cover.'

Alfred frowned. 'Well, you have thought it all through; why should I wear out my brains doing the same? What is it I have to do?'

'Just act normally.'

'It would not be normal for me to make a will. Everybody knows that.'

'But we are utilizing that very fact.'

'Well, I suppose you know what you are doing . . . Do you want me to go around telling everyone I am going to make a will? They would think I had gone off my head!'

'No. We must be more subtle than that. I suggest that you should write to a local solicitor, asking him to attend on you for the purpose of making a will. If I know solicitors' clerks, the news will percolate out quickly enough.'

'I don't like it,' Alfred said mournfully. 'I have always been convinced that making a will was courting disaster. Now you tell me that unless I make one, I shall be killed . . . How do you work that out?'

'We are convinced that Walter, your brother, was murdered to prevent his inheriting your money.'

233

'But he was always welcome to it; though he had enough of his own. Why did he want mine?'

'No . . . I appreciate that it is very confusing. Our chief aim is to prevent your being murdered. We are approaching it in this way to give us the opportunity of catching the murderer.'

'Yes, yes. I know that. But I will not make a will for you!'

'Very well. Let us say that you will instruct a solicitor to draw one up but, in the event, you will never sign it.'

'I suppose I could . . . But who would I leave everything to? I have no one close to me now.'

'Our purpose would be perfectly well served, if you proposed to leave it to some charitable institution.'

'Hmn . . . You say you want me to act normally. It would not be normal for me to use a local solicitor. Edward Lazenby drew up Walter's will; his firm have always acted for our family.'

'Very well. In that case, could you drop a hint to someone in the village? It is important that the news leaks out.'

'If I mention it to my bailiff, it will get round.'

'Excellent!'

'But I will not sign it. You understand that!'

'Yes . . . When would be convenient?'

'It is hard to say . . .'

Morton gritted his teeth. 'Until the world thinks you have made your will, your life is in danger.'

'I do not comprehend . . .' He raised his hand. 'No. Don't explain it to me. I am prepared to accept what you say . . . Well, then, I shall have to do it . . . But it cannot be before Thursday.'

'Good. If you will write the letter to Lazenby, I will go into Wareham and post it for you.'

Alfred regarded him owlishly. 'You can trust me, you know.'

'Of course. But I shall need to know precisely what you have said.'

He sighed, then crossed to a bureau and brought some writing paper to the table. 'What shall I put?' he asked.

'Merely ask Edward Lazenby to attend on you at, say, two o'clock on Thursday, for the purpose of drawing up your will.'

'Do we let him in on the secret?'

Morton smiled. 'I am sure he would enjoy the joke, but we must postpone that pleasure for a little time. The important thing is that he should draw it up, in good faith, and that people should know he is doing it.'

'Very well.' Alfred wrote the letter in careful copperplate script and passed it over for Morton's approval. 'I am dashed if I know Lazenby's address,' he said. 'Walter was the man of business. He used to deal with this kind of thing.'

'It is forty-eight, St James's Street, London SW.'

Alfred addressed the envelope, inserted the letter, sealed it and passed it to Morton. 'I hope you know what you are doing,' he said.

'You have not the slightest need to concern yourself, sir. There is, however, one further matter that you might like to consider. It would be very helpful to us if you would prepare a detailed list of your assets.'

Alfred looked up in alarm. 'What, everything? Surely you do not want me to count every silver spoon? Worry my brain about things like snuff-boxes?'

Morton smiled. 'I am sure that a round sum would suffice for such items. But, if you could give us your considered estimate of the value of your property and investments, it would be most helpful.'

'At this rate I shall be finished, whether you save me from the murderer or not,' Alfred said gloomily.

Morton laughed, drank his whisky and took his leave. Before he set off for Wareham he would have to write a letter of his own, telling Sergeant Bragg exactly what he had done.

13

Next day Catherine went back to Winchester. She told Mr Tranter that she needed to get additional material for her article on the cathedral. Indeed, she did return to it. She went round as a tourist would, marvelling at the old font of black Tournai marble, the twelfth-century wall paintings. With a crowd of sightseers, she stood solemnly at the shrine of St Swithin and gazed in wonder at the chantry chapels. Then they trooped into the choir and were shown the squat, defiant tomb of William Rufus, the second Norman king of England. With relish, the guide confided that William Rufus had been a witch; that the sacrilege of interring him in a Christian cathedral had brought the central tower crashing down. It was absurd, Catherine thought. In that event, why had they left his remains there? Did they not fear that he would cause the replacement to collapse also? But, perhaps that was why the existing tower was so short and squat. And witches did exist; magic was still practised . . . She shivered, and walked quickly out into the light of day.

She dallied briefly in the medieval Castle Hall, noting wryly that the columns were of Purbeck marble. It seemed impossible to get away from her anxieties . . . Then she enquired the way to the barracks of the Hampshire Regiment. This time, she did not accost the sentry but went through the gateway and asked a stray soldier to direct her to the regimental office. It was a large room, with several desks manned by a mixture of uniformed soldiers and civilian clerks. An officer stood by a large notice-board, his boots gleaming, a swagger-stick under his arm. He turned as she entered.

'Good morning, miss,' he said genially. 'How may I be of service?'

'I am a reporter on the *City Press*, a London newspaper. I am doing a series of articles on county regiments, their past and their present. I hope that you will help me.'

'I see.' His smile broadened. 'We would gladly be of assistance. Any information you need, we can provide.'

'Thank you. But it is not to be a mere recital of historical facts. We want to give our readers an idea of the life of individual soldiers, past and present. To show the army as a collection of real people, rather than an awesome military machine.'

His face clouded. 'But that is what we are, miss – a machine. We cannot have people thinking for themselves. Discipline is what matters in an army.'

Catherine smiled sweetly. 'I am sure that is so; and we would not seek to suggest otherwise. But, by concentrating on individuals, high and low, we would be reassuring wives and sweethearts, parents of potential recruits, that the army has a human dimension.'

'Hmn . . . yes. I can see what you are getting at. Then, how can we help?'

'The subjects of the articles have already been selected. In your case, we want to concentrate on a certain Captain Oscar Green, who was killed in action in eighteen hundred and eight.'

His eyebrows lifted in surprise. 'Good heavens! What is the point of going back so far?'

'We want to emphasize the evolutionary aspect of the army's organization. So, there will be articles concerning individuals at the time of the Crimean War, and then after the subsequent reorganization. They will deal with other regiments, of course.'

'I can see what you are driving at,' he said doubtfully. 'Well, it is no use coming here for information as far back as eighteen hundred and eight – not concerning individual soldiers, anyway. Colonel Vernon is your man.'

'Colonel Vernon?'

'Yes. He settled in Winchester when he retired; and he is writing a history of the regiment. He has all the old records.'

'I see,' Catherine said, deflated. 'I suppose that I shall have to make an appointment to see him.'

'Not a bit of it! He is a very approachable man; lives just round the corner. I will take you there, if you like.'

Catherine was glad it was not far. He marched off at regulation pace and she was half-running to keep up with him. He stopped at a low brick house, with dormer windows and a red-tiled roof. The flagged path was swept clean, the brass knocker gleamed. The door was opened by a smart maid, who ushered Catherine up the stairs to a room overlooking the back garden.

Colonel Vernon was spare and erect. He listened to her explanation, his grey head nodding in approval.

'An excellent scheme, if I may say so,' he remarked in clipped tones. 'Eighteen oh eight, eh? As a matter of fact, I have just reached eighteen twelve – a significant year for any military man, as I am sure you know.'

'Napoleon's retreat from Moscow; the beginning of the campaign which culminated in the battle of Waterloo.'

Vernon smiled in approval. 'It is refreshing to meet a young lady with a sense of history. Now, then, who are you interested in?'

'A young officer in the Thirty-seventh Foot – Captain Oscar Green. He was killed in action during that year.'

'Yes . . .' He looked at her uneasily. 'I take it that any material I give you will be treated . . . er, sympathetically.'

'Of course. We already know something about him, naturally. I want to flesh out the bare bones.'

237

'Yes. It is just that I would not wish anything you wrote to reflect badly on the regiment.'

'That would certainly not be our intention, or our wish. If you like, I will submit my draft article to you. Should it not meet with your approval, we will not publish it.'

'Hmn . . . Cannot say fairer than that. Very well.'

He crossed to a cupboard whose shelves were filled with orderly rows of files and ledgers. He selected a file and brought it to his desk.

'Thirty-seventh Foot has now become our First Battalion, as you are no doubt aware.'

'Yes.'

'As part of the preparation for my work, I have listed all the personal details of the officers, so he will be here somewhere.' He turned over sheet after sheet of paper. 'Ah! Here we are. Green, Oscar. Born twentieth of August, seventeen seventy-eight. Commissioned into the regiment, seventeen ninety-nine.'

'When he was twenty-one,' Catherine remarked. 'Do you know anything of his background?'

'No. But he must have been a gentleman.' He glanced at her, then looked away.

'But not a gentleman of substance, or he would have joined a more fashionable regiment.'

'You might say that. Though he would have had to buy his commission, in those days.'

'When was he promoted to Captain?'

Vernon consulted his file. 'March, eighteen oh seven.'

Catherine jotted the date down in her notebook. 'Where was the regiment stationed, at that time?' she asked.

'Bombay . . . in India.'

Catherine smiled tolerantly. 'Was that a good posting?' she asked. 'One gathers that some parts of India are very trying for our troops.'

'I was there myself for some years. It is pleasant enough, as things go. Hot in the summer, of course. But there is a hill-station at Poonah. An occasional break up there makes life tolerable. The memsahibs and children spend all the hot season there, of course.'

'So, Captain Green would visit Poonah on leave?'

'That is so.' He was staring fixedly over her shoulder. She glanced round, but there was no one there.

238

'Was there fighting around Bombay at that time?' Catherine asked.

'Not in the sense of a sustained campaign. The odd skirmish with brigands, that is all.'

'Of course! It was a big commercial centre. Wealthy merchants, like Oliver Rossiter, operated from Bombay.'

Vernon's face was stony.

'Then, where was Captain Green killed?' she asked.

He ostentatiously consulted another paper. 'On the North-West Frontier.'

'But that is hundreds of miles away!'

'Yes.'

'Why was he fighting there?'

'He was on detached duty.'

'Is not that strange?' Catherine asked.

Vernon hesitated. 'Let us say that the circumstances were exceptional,' he said.

'I see.' Catherine paused in thought. 'I suppose that the British community mixed very freely – soldiers and civilians.'

'Oh, yes. The Club was the only real social centre.'

'So people like the Rossiters would have been intimate with at least the officers of the regiment.'

Vernon took a deep breath. 'I see that you know all about it,' he said tersely.

Catherine tried to control the sudden spurt of excitement inside her. 'No doubt you would like to put it into perspective,' she said.

'Yes . . . Well.' He cleared his throat. 'It is all a long time ago; but there was no excuse for it. It was thoroughly bad form. Rossiter was well known to the senior ranks, of course. And the army is there to protect the civilians, in every way.'

'So, what happened when Rossiter died? His widow, Ruth, stayed on for a time . . .'

'Yes. I expect she was selling the business, and so forth. She would spend most of the time at Poonah, naturally . . . From all accounts, she was a fine woman.'

Catherine quelled her rising exultation. 'She had two children with her, of course,' she said.

'Yes. In a way, that must have made it seem all the worse . . .

But, give the man his due, there is no suggestion that he was after her money.'

'And she?'

Vernon considered. 'Well, I expect he was a young, attractive man,' he said, with a note of exasperation in his voice. 'No doubt her head was turned easily enough.'

'So they had an affair?'

'Yes . . . Most discreditable, with her husband scarcely cold in his grave. Caused quite a scandal, it seems. There was no other way of dealing with it. Serving officers have to be able to feel that their loved ones are safe and secure. Cannot have philandering.'

Catherine frowned. 'But, I thought she was a widow, at the time.'

'It is the principle of the thing; bad example for the natives.'

'Caesar's wife?'

'Yes . . . And, it appears, Oliver Rossiter had been very well liked. The senior officers were not prepared to condone it.'

'So they took appropriate action.'

'Yes. I got my information from the record of a kind of informal court martial. They packed him off to the North-West Frontier, and he did the decent thing. Saved the regimental honour.'

'And his own?'

'I expect so. The only thing to do.'

'So, the child that Ruth bore, when she got back to England, was Oscar Green's bastard?'

Vernon cleared his throat deprecatingly. 'That is about the size of it . . . Yes.'

On Wednesday morning, Catherine was at Old Jewry by nine o'clock. She found Bragg staring glumly at a letter.

'Why, that is from James,' she cried. 'I recognize the writing.'

'Yes, miss. Everything is happening sooner than I would like. Young Morton wrote this yesterday. He thinks another of the witches' jollifications is coming off, in the next few days. I am going down tomorrow; I shall meet him at Bere Regis, and we will decide how to tackle it.'

'May I come with you?' Catherine asked excitedly.

'No, you may not! I am not having women anywhere near that lot!'

'Really! You men are quite insupportable! You think you have a God-given right to decide women's lives for them! I can understand how Ruth Green felt, and why some of her conduct seems reprehensive to people who are ignorant of the facts.'

Bragg looked at her cautiously. 'I am not going to bargain with you, miss,' he said. 'I don't want your pretty head hanging by a thread. Morton would never forgive me, and he's the best copper we have.'

'Ingrate!' Catherine said rebelliously. 'I spent yesterday in Winchester, for your sake; and this is the thanks I get.'

Bragg tugged at his moustache. 'All right,' he said. 'You can come as far as Bere Regis, if you promise to stay there.'

'Splendid! I will even give some thought to what you might wear. You cannot turn up at an esbat in a frock-coat!'

'That's a point, miss . . . Now, what have you found out?'

'That John Green was illegitimate.'

'What?'

'Ruth Rossiter and Oscar Green were never married. He got her with child, while they were having an affair. The senior officers of the regiment had been friends of her late husband; they saw it as a gross reflection on the honour of the regiment. Oscar Green was packed off to Afghanistan, with instructions to get himself killed.'

'Was he, now? . . . And Ruth came back here?'

'Yes. She must have loved Oscar a great deal, for she adopted his surname and pretended that they had been married.'

'Hmn . . . I do not suppose that she could have done much else, miss, if the child was fathered after Rossiter had been dead some time.'

Catherine frowned. 'Men do not have an ounce of romance in their gross bodies!' she exclaimed.

'Maybe . . . At least, it helps to explain why she favoured John Green over the Rossiter side of her family. I wonder if they ever found out.'

'It seems clear that they did – after she was dead. It can only be this fact that caused them to drop the undue influence suit.'

Bragg considered for a moment. 'You think that was the reason, do you?'

'Yes, sergeant. They might have succeeded in winning for themselves a greater portion of the estate; but it would have been at the

241

cost of proclaiming to the world that their mother was a loose woman.'

'Hmn . . . If you are right, that would make them hate the Greens even more.'

'Indeed! I begin to wonder if John Green might have prepared that picture expressly to rile them.'

'Picture? What picture?' Bragg exclaimed.

'The one James saw in Alfred Green's house. John Green's birth certificate, flanked by pictures of Ruth and Oscar. It is almost as if he were flaunting the fact.'

'At least he wasn't ashamed of it – within the family at any rate . . . So, where does that leave us? I thought I had my mind clear on Miss Hildred's theory about inheritance. Now I am not so sure.'

'Can we not go to Sir Rufus, and see if he has any ideas?'

'We? Why is it "we" all of a sudden?' Bragg said grumpily. 'No. You go back and keep your editor sweet. The coroner and I know how to get on with one another. I do not want it upset by some pushy bit of skirt! . . . Nine o'clock train, tomorrow; Waterloo station!'

Bragg popped into the Commissioner's office to bring him up to date, then hurried down to the chambers of Sir Rufus Stone. He found the coroner shrugging himself into his gown.

'What is it now, Bragg?' he said irritably. 'I am due in court within five minutes.'

'You remember the family tree I showed you?'

'Yes, yes! What is it?'

Bragg pulled it out of his pocket, and spread it on the coroner's desk. 'This is John Green, the father of Alfred Green . . .'

'Yes.'

'It seems Oscar and Ruth were never married. John was their bastard child.'

'Ah.' Sir Rufus glanced at the chart. 'Then, in that case John is regarded in law as a *filius nullius*; he is the son of nobody – not even of his mother.'

'But that's absurd!'

'I am sure you are not the first to have come to that conclusion, Bragg. But it is the law.'

'So, how does that affect what you said to me on Monday?'

'About the inheritance of personality?'

242

'Yes, sir.'

'Oh, there is no difficulty. You ignore the ancestors of John Green, and trace back through his wife's family.' Sir Rufus strode out of the room.

Bragg studied the family tree again. Now Alfred Green's money would go to the Witneys – all of it. There was no point in Rossiters killing Witneys; the Rossiters were out of it. And, from what Miss Marsden said, they knew it. So who the bloody hell was doing the killing?

On the Thursday morning Morton pottered innocuously around the village. After lunch he stayed in his room at the inn. He sat in the window, confident that the overhanging eaves would conceal him. The kid had been taken from the village green. Had it already met its fate? Was the sacrifice part of the esbat, or a prelude to it? Could it be that the esbat had taken place the previous night and they had missed it? He thought through the events of the evening. He had wandered around the village, in the dusk. Lights were lit in all the houses. He had heard the tentative sound of Alfred's flute. In Lucy's house someone had been playing a piano. It had all seemed perfectly normal . . . Could he be wrong about the esbat? Was the kid displayed as part of a harmless folk tradition – perhaps with roots in ancient rituals, but their power attenuated by time? Then he remembered the books on magic in Ursula's cupboard, the potency of the draught she had given him. No, they had to assume the worst.

Just before two o'clock he heard the sound of a horse's hooves. A trap drove into the village and drew up in front of Alfred Green's house. Edward Lazenby got down and went inside. Excellent! So far everything was going smoothly. He went downstairs and sought out the landlord.

'I shall not be back tonight,' he said. 'I am going to stay with my aunt, at Bere Regis.'

The man seemed relieved. 'Right,' he grunted.

'I see we have a stranger in the village.'

'Oh?'

'A well-dressed man has just gone into Alfred Green's house.'

'Has he? . . . I would never have believed it.' His expression was almost animated.

243

'Believed what?'

'They do say he's a-making his will!'

'Oh?' Morton feigned lack of interest. 'I will be back sometime tomorrow,' he said.

He went outside, wondering whether to wait for Lazenby and beg a lift to Wareham. But it was a fine, warm day, the birds were singing, all was going smoothly. He suppressed a niggling anxiety that Bragg might not approve of his initiative, and marched off towards Wareham. When he got to the station he found a trap that would drive him to Bere Regis.

The door of the Hildreds' house was opened by Catherine.

'I saw you from the window,' she said excitedly. 'Sergeant Bragg is in the sitting-room, with Fanny.'

Morton followed her into the room and burst into helpless laughter. Bragg was standing on a low stool. On his head was an old straw hat, with flowers and shining red cherries round the brim. Over the upper part of his body, imprisoning his arms, was a garment that could only be a woman's skirt. Fanny was kneeling on the floor, pinning up the hem to knee height.

'What are you laughing about?' Bragg growled fiercely.

Morton held his sides. 'I had never thought to see anything so grotesque, in the whole of my life!' he spluttered.

'Wait till you see what they have got for you!' Bragg said truculently.

'But why?' Morton sat down, aching with laughter.

Fanny got to her feet. 'You must be disguised, of course,' she said with a smile. 'Catherine is of the opinion that the men will attend the esbat in country clothes; so we are making smocks for you.'

'Smocks! Is that a smock?' Morton cried.

'Well, not exactly. In fact, it is one of my mother's old skirts. But it will suffice. It has only to be seen in moonlight.'

'But . . . but he has no arms!'

'We will cut holes for them. His shirt sleeves will not look out of place.' Fanny suppressed a mischievous smile.

'I hope the birds do not come down for the cherries!'

'You need not crow, James,' Catherine said. 'Your smock will be covered with minute pink roses, and your hat has a snake in it!'

Morton walked round the fuming Bragg, his head cocked on one side, his face as solemn as he could make it. 'Yes . . . yes,' he said.

244

'But that colour does nothing for him, my dear. He has such a dull complexion . . . Now, a stronger shade, say, cerise would give him a lift, transform his whole personality . . . Still, I suppose he could pinch his cheeks, before he makes his entrance!'

Bragg got down from the stool. 'You watch your step, lad,' he said wrathfully.

Catherine interposed. 'Come along, James, off with your coat. It is your turn!'

By the time tea was served, the smocks had been pinned together. They sat in the garden while Fanny and Catherine sewed them. By then Bragg had recovered his equanimity, was even beginning to see the funny side of it.

'I trust that you approve of my initiative with Alfred Green's will,' Morton ventured.

'Well, it is done now. I am not sure that I would have wanted to push that side of it; we seem to have our hands full with this comic caper. Anyway, we are no further with Miss Hildred's theory.'

'Why not?'

'Well, it is sound enough, in its way. But the only thing it has proved, is that the Rossiters had no need to kill Walter Green. They could not inherit, because John Green was illegitimate.'

'Ah . . . So that was it!'

'We are almost back to Rossiters killing for pure spite.'

'And inherited spite, at that. But, what about Cicely Fox?'

Bragg sighed. 'I have no idea, lad. I think the Commissioner inclines to the notion that Syme killed both Witney and Cissie.'

'With the inference that we were wrong in trying to link Walter Green with them?'

'That is about the measure of it. He's a simple soul.'

'Come along, James!' Catherine said. 'It is time to try on the finished garment.'

Morton slipped off his coat and pulled the smock over his head. He twirled round on his toes, his arms extended like a ballerina. 'Will I do?' he asked coyly.

Bragg inspected him. 'What about the hat, miss?' he asked.

'Ah, yes.' Catherine snipped off the decoration, and placed the bare straw panama on his head.

'That is very good,' Bragg said gravely. 'We had a scarecrow like that when I was a lad. No damned use, but classy-looking.'

As the sun dropped to the horizon Bragg took the reins of Fanny's gig and he and Morton drove briskly to Wareham. By then the dusk had closed in and their pace dropped to little more than a walk. The sky was clear, with a crescent moon giving a glimmer of light. They crossed the levels and walked up the scarp to rest the colt. When they had almost traversed the belt of trees, Bragg guided the horse up a cart-track and into a glade. He tied him to a sapling and hung the nosebag round his neck. With Morton leading, they made a detour round the village, across the river and up on to the pasture-land. The clump of trees appeared, black on the horizon. Stooping close to the ground, they worked their way towards it.

'Look at that!' Morton whispered.

Through the overhanging branches the flicker of firelight was visible. Immediately in front of them was a flat cart, a barrel of beer wedged on it. The kid, still wreathed with verbena, was tied to one of its wheels. The horse had been taken out of the cart and tethered to a tree close by.

'We had better get round the other side,' Bragg whispered. 'If the horse scents us, we might as well go home.'

They drew back, then made a wide loop and came up to the grove from the seaward side. They crawled up a hummock between two of the trees. Through the fringe of grass they could look down on the enclosed space. A great fire of logs was burning on the central slab. To their left were trestle tables loaded with joints of meat, loaves and cheeses. A mere fifteen feet below them a crowd of people had gathered. They were dressed in loose robes and smocks; many had demonic masks on their faces. Evidently some kind of ritual was being enacted. A figure with his back to them was officiating. He must be the leader, Morton thought. His legs and feet were naked, he was clad in animal skins. From his head sprouted bull's horns. Ursula was standing in front of him. From the look on her face, she was already halfway to a trance. She was holding a young girl by the hand. Morton had seen her many times in the village: a bright, bouncing girl of fifteen or so. There was a murmur from the assembly as Ursula led the girl around, introducing her to them. Then she brought her back to face the horned figure. In a muffled voice he began to utter what sounded like an incantation; the girl repeating each phrase. Then a man came forward from the front rank and held out a crucifix. The girl glanced at Ursula, as if for support. Then, with great deliberation, she stepped forward and spat on the cross. A hum of excitement arose, faces were twisted into evil grins of satisfaction. It was obscene, Morton thought. It was like the Goya painting of a sabbat that he had seen in the Prado. God! That this could be happening in England, at the end of the nineteenth century! He felt Bragg's hand on his shoulder, pushing him down.

There came the hollow notes of a flute. Morton slowly raised his head. Alfred Green had stepped on to the circular path, was pacing round it widdershins. The assembly was forming up, breast clasped to haunch, snaking after him. Morton heard Bragg's whisper: 'Keep an eye on him!' Now a tambourine had joined in. Kicking and braying, the dancers stamped to its beat. The flute played on, endlessly repeating the same snatch of melody. Surely the devil deserved better tunes?

Now the young initiate had turned from beneath them. She was skipping lightly after the dancers, the horned devil-figure capering after her. He caught and downed her, twisting her on to her back. She lay spreadeagled as he flung up her petticoats and, parting her thighs, lowered himself on her.

'Christ!' Bragg muttered. 'That bugger needs gelding.'

But she was not resisting. Her arm was round his neck, her body straining to meet his thrusts. Then it was over. The devil drew back on his haunches, the girl jumped lightly to her feet and ran after the dancers. The horned figure rose slowly, the firelight on his mask. He seemed to stare straight at them. The face was of human shape, with grossly exaggerated eyes and nose. Brown curls were at forehead and chin, plumes of white hair hung down over the ears. From each side of the mask jutted sharp steer's horns. It was lewd, brutish, evil.

'That's the Dorset Ooser's mask!' Bragg muttered. 'It must be them who stole it. If I could get my hands on that, I would pitch it into the fire!'

The snake dance seemed to be over. The participants were crowding round the devil, their words a meaningless babble. He nodded his head, the horns cutting a menacing arc in the air. He took the tambourine and began to strike it insistently with a metal

247

object. It gleamed golden in the light, testicular protuberances pounding the drum. Palpable excitement spread through the witches. Ursula tore off her clothes and began to gyrate, stark naked. Others formed pairs and began to caper back-to-back. Alfred's flute joined in; short, jerky phrases. Now more tambourines were beginning, the dancers spinning and stamping in ecstasy. Alfred was skipping clumsily on the far side of the circle, as if drawn along by the whirl of dancers. Francesca whisked past them, arm-in-arm with her brother, her face flushed with carnality.

Now Alfred was shambling towards them, into the shadows that hid them. His pathetic attempts at playing the flute were of no consequence now. It was the hypnotic beat of the drums that dominated all. Suddenly, as he passed them, the horned figure launched itself from the twirling dancers. Alfred was knocked sprawling, the brazen phallus raised above his head. Morton sprang as the blow came down; parried it, twisted the devil's arm behind him and threw him on the ground.

'Police!' Bragg shouted, jumping down the hillock and waving his arms. 'Police! Go home, all of you! Go away immediately, and never come here again!'

The drums stopped. There were some screams, bursts of wild laughter; then the dancers began to melt away in the darkness. Only Ursula was left, dancing slowly round the fire, its light orange on her naked skin.

Bragg came over to Morton, squatting on the devil's back. 'Right, lad, let us see what we have caught.'

The devil lay still, though Morton had not injured him. He allowed Bragg to roll him over onto his back, his arms flopping nervelessly on the turf. Bragg took hold of the animal horns and tore off the mask . . . The face that stared up at them, dazed and bewildered, was that of Edward Lazenby.

14

Some days later Bragg and Morton went back to Wareham police station and were shown down to the cells. Edward Lazenby bounced up from his bunk as he saw them. He had been provided with ill-fitting cast-off clothes on his arrival; the devil outfit having been taken as evidence. There was heavy stubble on his face, his eyes seemed sunken. But his spirit was anything but cowed.

'About time, too!' he exclaimed, as the uniformed constable beckoned him.

They followed him to the room that had been put at their disposal for the interview. There were bars at the window. The constable put his back to the door as he closed it. Bragg motioned Lazenby to sit.

'I am sorry it has taken so long, sir,' he said in a neutral voice. 'The weekend always mucks things up, doesn't it?'

'So long as you are now satisfied as to my innocence, sergeant, it is of no moment.' Lazenby was sitting with his legs carelessly crossed, but there was tension in his body.

'Innocence? You could hardly call it that, going around raping young girls; having unlawful carnal knowledge of them.'

Lazenby tried to raise a tolerant smile. 'Perhaps not unreasonably, you have come to entirely the wrong conclusion about that, sergeant.'

'How is that, sir?'

'What you witnessed, from the trees, was part of an ancient ritual; the defloration of a female initiate to the hidden mysteries.'

'I saw that all right – only we call it rape.'

'No. You are in error. There is no human intervention. The officiating priest parts the hymen with a consecrated brazen phallus.'

'Are you saying that you went nowhere near her?'

'I am saying precisely that.'

'She was examined straight away, by a doctor, you know.'

'Then I am content.'

He seemed it too, Bragg thought. From the moment they had started on about the girl, he had relaxed. Well, time would tell . . .

He placed a razor on the table between them. 'We found that, in the grass, just at the place where you were arrested,' he said.

'Good!' Lazenby smiled confidently. 'As you can see, I have need of it.'

'You acknowledge that it is yours?'

'Indeed I do. As you are aware, it has my initials on it.'

'Yes . . . You could hardly deny it, could you?'

'I have no wish to do so, sergeant.'

'Hmn . . . Would you like to tell us why you had it with you, that night?'

'Certainly! Part of the ritual celebration involves the sacrifice of a kid. The animal is rendered unconscious by a blow from the phallic wand, then it is slaughtered by cutting the throat.' He looked at Bragg in mild surprise. 'It is no less humane than the procedure which produces your breakfast bacon, and your Sunday roast beef.'

'The whole thing looked bloody obscene to me,' Bragg said irritably.

'To the outsider, possibly so. But let me remind you, sergeant, there is nothing unlawful about such a gathering.'

'I realize that, sir, in itself.'

'Then you clearly accept that you had no power to arrest me; nor have any justification in detaining me longer.' He got to his feet confidently.

'There are one or two things I want to chat about first, sir,' Bragg said mildly. 'Just sit down again . . . Right! You see, we think we are justified in keeping you here, because we witnessed a felony being committed.'

'What was that?'

'Your unprovoked assault on Alfred Green.'

Lazenby laughed. 'An assault! No, sergeant, you have hold of the wrong end of the stick! It is part of the function of the officiating priest to stimulate the faithful and chastise the laggards. It is a ritual going back thousands of years before Christ.'

'It looked to us as if Alfred Green was going to get the wrong end of the stick!'

'No, sergeant, mere play-acting, a ritual tap on the shoulder.'

'Hmn . . . Walter Green did not just get a tap on the shoulder, did he? He was slaughtered like a sacrificial goat.'

250

Lazenby looked up coolly. 'I knew he had died, of course. But I was not aware of the cause.'

Bragg narrowed his eyes. 'Then, let me tell you. He was found by his house, naked. He had been hit on the back of the neck and his throat had been cut.'

'I know nothing about that.'

'The way we see it, sir, is that they had to take his clothes off because, when he was murdered, he was wearing the same get-up you lot were prancing around in the other night.'

'That is mere supposition.'

'Maybe . . . But he wasn't killed where he was found. We know that, because we have discovered the place where it happened. Constable Morton took a soil sample. Green was killed under the trees of your witches' grove – more or less where the cart was the other night.'

'You seem to have a very lively imagination, sergeant,' Lazenby said.

'Oh, no. We took the sample to Professor Burney, of Bart's Hospital. As you may know, he is the pathologist for the City of London. He said that the soil in the sample was drenched with human blood.'

Lazenby raised his eyebrows. 'Perhaps some unfortunate farmhand had an accident there,' he suggested.

'We do not think so,' Bragg went on. 'We think you murdered Walter Green there, in the same way as you murdered Jethro Witney and Cicely Fox . . . In the same way as you would have murdered Alfred Green, if we had not stopped you.'

Lazenby laughed, his hands raised in protest. 'Your invention is running away with you!' he exclaimed. 'Why on earth should I wish to murder any of these people?'

'Why?' Bragg paused, considering. 'Well, let us take Cissie Fox. We think she was blackmailing you. We think that she saw you coming out of Witney's office, the day you murdered Jethro. Why she did not tell us, I cannot say. Perhaps she was too frightened. Then, I think, she got greedy. Maybe it was the annuity Jethro left her daughter. Perhaps she could see a lifetime of luxury in front of her – of not having to go out to work every day. Who knows?'

'You clearly do not, at any rate. This is all pure conjecture.'

'Not quite all, sir. You see, Cissie asked for time off, the afternoon

251

before her death. She said that she wanted to go to the doctor . . . But she didn't go to the doctor, she went to your office instead. Your managing clerk remembers it quite clearly.'

'Is that so? Then, I am sure that he is right. Remind me of what she looked like.'

'Mid-twenties, dark hair, slim – and pretty in a common sort of way.'

'Ah, yes. I think that I remember. She came to ask me about the annuity – whether she could rely on it, once Julia had decided to challenge the will. I had another appointment arranged, so I could not spend much time with her.'

'Oh, that was it, eh? So, what did you tell her?'

'Why, that there might be short-term difficulties but in the long term I felt the annuity was secure.'

'I see. We think that you promised to bring the money she asked for, to Witney's office the next day . . . It was a nasty way for her to die,' Bragg said musingly. 'I suppose it was the method of killing that put us off at the start. It was vicious; obscenely so. It looked as if no sane human being could have done it . . . it had to be a madman. Yet everybody connected with the case – except for poor old Alfred Green – seemed perfectly normal. The coroner was convinced it was a random killer, to start with. It seemed the best you could say of him, was that his victims felt no more than would a sacrificial goat – a moment of fear, of panic; perhaps a frenzied attempt to get away; then bang! Unconscious; all over for them.'

Lazenby gazed at him unruffled.

'As I say,' Bragg went on, 'the means were obvious enough, but that did not take us very far. Not until we heard about Walter Green's death. I admit we had to take it on trust, because he was long buried by then. But it sounded as if the same person was at work who had knocked off Jethro. Then Cissie Fox . . . a pattern you see. But what linked them? Who would want to kill those three people?'

'Who indeed?' Lazenby leaned back in his chair and crossed his legs.

'One thing we could not understand,' Bragg went on, 'is why there was so little commotion in Slocombe Magna, over Walter Green's murder. But I can see now that they would not have wanted their little capers to be known about. And, I suppose, with that mask on, they would not have recognized you.'

Lazenby's lip curled. 'I am perfectly prepared to answer your questions, sergeant. There is no need for this oblique recital of conjectures.'

'Very good, sir. Did the members of the witches' coven know who you were?'

'No. The identity of the devil . . . er, the officiating priest, is never revealed. I stay at the Stonecutters' Arms, in Corfe Castle, and go to the gatherings by trap.'

'I see. Very convenient . . . And a good way of satisfying your sexual urges, too. If not the little girl, then somebody like Ursula or Francesca Witney, I expect.'

Lazenby did not reply.

'But it was not only the opportunity aspect that foxed us. We had no idea what the motive might be. The coroner is an eminent lawyer, as you know. But even he could not sort it out. After a long time we cottoned on to the fact that Cissie Fox might have been killed for other reasons; but, even then, we could not find a motive for Jethro and Walter.'

Bragg placed the family tree on the table. Lazenby suddenly became tense, watchful.

'Now, we know Jethro prepared this; Julia saw him at it. As you probably know, it shows that the Witneys are distantly related to the Greens.'

He looked enquiringly at Lazenby, but got no response.

'Anyway,' he went on, 'here we had the Greens; two bachelors, no close relatives. It seemed quite legitimate for Jethro to wonder who would get their money, when they died. Now, Walter had left all his money to Ursula, his paramour. Everybody knew that. If she had not killed him for his money – and why should she? – nobody had. Then we heard that Alfred had an obsession about not making a will. And we began to wonder if Walter had been killed merely so that Alfred's money should not go to Ursula.'

'If I may say so,' Lazenby interrupted, 'I begin to lose the thread of your argument.'

'I suppose you do. It was more of a feeling, really . . . But we found a statement of assets in Jethro's safe, with this family tree. When we investigated, we found that it was a list of Alfred Green's assets.'

'But you have just admitted it was a legitimate interest, on Witney's part.'

'Yes. But we think he took the family tree to you, for your advice. After all, you acted both for the Witneys and Walter Green. He might have thought that he would get some fresh insight from you . . . And I expect he did. You saw, from his statement, the investments, property and land that Alfred had. But, when you looked at the family tree you had to tell him that the Rossiters were nearer in kinship than the Witneys. So the Rossiters would get all Alfred's money. That must have been a shaker for Jethro, don't you think?'

Lazenby maintained his silence, looking coldly at Bragg.

'But, of course, you were able to see beyond the question he had put to you. Your firm had acted for the Greens, in the undue influence suit brought by the Rossiters. All the papers were still on your files . . . And, maybe you had been intrigued by the picture on Walter's wall – the one John Green had made to give himself some sort of ancestry. At all events, you knew John Green was illegitimate. That meant the Rossiters were out of the running. For Jethro, that must have been good news. One way or another, his daughter Julia would get all the Greens' money – and there was a lot.'

Lazenby gave a weary sigh. 'We can agree on that last statement, at least,' he said.

'Yes. But what Jethro did not know, or didn't think about, was that John Green's wife was a Lazenby – Martha Lazenby. It took us a long time to find that one out, I can tell you!'

'I totally fail to see the significance of that fact,' Lazenby said evenly.

'Well, I doubt that . . . You see, your son had, by then, got this contract to design an oil-treatment plant, in Dorset. The company was negotiating to buy the land it was to be built on. There was even oil under the surface. They only needed to drill down, and it would come spurting up! I expect your son had talked to you about it, told you where it was. Perhaps Walter Green may have mentioned it to you. He looked after the business affairs of the brothers, after all. Anyway, you got to know it was Alfred Green's land the oil company wanted to buy – for a king's ransom.'

'I begin to tire of all this supposition,' Lazenby said in a bored voice.

'Ah, but it is not all supposition. We went round all the solicitors in the Poole area. In April of this year, you asked Potter & Phipps of Poole to do a legal search on that land. They confirmed to you that the owner of the land is Alfred Green.'

'I fail to see how that fact serves your case.' The voice was still casual.

'As did we, for a start. It was Sir Rufus Stone who spotted it . . . The land the oil company wanted to buy happens to be freehold land.'

'So?'

'It is what they call realty – a real chunk of England, not just a right of use. Realty is treated differently from leased land. The inheritance laws go right back to feudal Norman times. When you are working out who inherits you have got to find the person they refer to as the heir. In those days women didn't count for much, and the stability of the country depended on keeping the large estates intact. So, everything used to go to the eldest son – all the freehold land, that is. And, if somebody died without a son, you had to go back through the eldest male ancestor, and down through his eldest son.'

'I fail to see what relevance this has,' Lazenby said irritably.

'Well, John Green was illegitimate, so the Rossiters are out.'

'If you say so.'

'According to the rules, we have to trace Alfred Green's ancestors through Martha Lazenby. But this time we are not looking for degrees of kinship, we are looking for the eldest male in her line. Now, Alfred Green's grandmother was an Anne Witney; but we have to go through her husband's line – the Lazenbys . . . And you are the only Lazenby of your generation.'

Bragg paused for effect, but Lazenby did not react.

'You got a little breathing space by murdering Walter Green,' Bragg went on. 'The big problem was that Jethro became suspicious; so he had to be got rid of. Then there was poor little Cissie Fox. That must have been irritating to you; but you easily got rid of her. By now, you had no time to spare. Once Alfred had sold the land, you would have lost a fortune. So you had to move. Not that you were worried. All you had to wait for was the next esbat of the coven . . . It was just luck that we stopped you murdering Alfred. Bad luck, for you.'

Lazenby was staring out of the window, his face grim. He looked round. 'You will never be able to prove this farrago of nonsense in a court,' he said.

Bragg smiled. 'Oh, we will, sir,' he said. 'Have no fear, we will!'